METEOR

ROBERT AUSTIN

Title: Meteor.
Cover Art: Seerendip Publishing
Author: Robert Austin
Publisher: Seerendip Publishing
Edition: First printing, 2026
ISBN: 978-1-965273-23-4 (Paperback)
Library of Congress Control Number: 2026904165
Printed in the United States of America

For my wife, Felicia—
your love and faith carried this dream farther than I ever could alone.

ACKNOWLEDGMENTS

I would like to thank my publisher, Adam Mellor, and Seerendip Publishing for helping bring the world of Meteor to life.

CONTENTS

PROLOGUE

It started as a worldwide catastrophe on a day that seemed as normal as any other.

The year was 2056, when a meteor cloud suddenly appeared in space, becoming visible only as it approached Earth. It was traveling at an astonishing velocity.

All of Earth's astrophysicists marveled. They had never seen an astronomical event like it. Their amazement quickly turned into alarm, which spread through the scientific community nearly as fast as the meteor cloud approached the Earth's atmosphere.

Scientists attempted to assess the cloud, but they were unable to see into it. Space shuttles and satellites were launched toward the approaching cloud to determine its chemical composition and measure the size of the meteors.

But the speed of its approach was much faster than had been calculated by the world's finest scientists. Before any satellite could approach it, the satellites failed, losing all power—some even exploding as the cloud engulfed them.

Before shuttles could be launched, the world's space station exploded.

Everyone watched with growing fear and horror as total darkness spread quickly across the sky.

With no way to stop the cloud, all the world's governments targeted the biggest meteors they could with their missiles. Citizens watched in shock as millions of rockets filled the sky.

But there were millions of tiny meteors, none of which seemed bigger than twenty to fifty feet across. Nonetheless, missiles were launched, hoping they would help destroy the biggest before they hit Earth.

To everyone's dismay, as soon as the missiles left Earth's atmosphere and neared the meteor cloud, they too seemed to fail. Occasionally, one would burst into flame as if its fuel had exploded. None of the missiles reached their targets.

The world's leading scientists all confirmed this while government officials sought bomb shelters. The scientists quickly assured their governments that there should be no significant impact damage, as most of the meteors they could see would likely burn up upon entering Earth's atmosphere.

But even they were worried, for the chemical components in the meteor cloud were unknown, and they were asking the same questions as their governments:

Why had their satellites stopped working before the cloud had enveloped them? Why—and what—had caused all the fuel to explode and destroy the space station before the cloud had enveloped it? And why had not one missile reached its target?

Those questions went unanswered as the meteor cloud quickly surrounded Earth and entered its atmosphere.

CHAPTER ONE

Day One: Impact, July 1st

National Park, Wyoming Border

Derek looked up, his eyes flashing with confusion as the once-blue sky above him suddenly darkened. A second later, he felt a sudden chill cross his skin, giving him goosebumps. Surprised, he rubbed his arms and felt frustration build in his mind.

The weather report he had watched yesterday on TV had said there was not supposed to be a cloud in sight for the rest of the week. That was one reason his parents decided to drive to the park last night so they could camp for the entire week.

I hope it doesn't rain, he thought.

After eight hours of riding in the RV to get there, he was glad to be roaming through the forest. The last thing he needed was for it to rain—because then he would have to take shelter in the RV with his parents, which he wanted to avoid after the long drive.

Looking up at the sky with frustration, he was met with a sight that mystified and bewildered him. There was not a cloud in sight. Yet, while he watched, the light-blue sky slowly darkened, and a cold, cruel wind began to buffet him. The wind picked up, whistling through the trees, blowing hard enough to rip leaves from their branches.

A little unsure of what was happening, Derek turned around and began racing through the forest toward his family's RV. A second later, he could see his dad through the RV's windshield. He was waving frantically for Derek to get in, calling him back.

Before Derek could run faster, the wind blew hard against his back. It hit him like a wall—so hard he was pushed forward, his feet tripping over a root. His racing through the forest was brought to a sudden halt as he slammed face-first into a tree, leaving his head ringing.

He grabbed his forehead in pain and looked up just in time to see the same wind that had hit him race along through the forest, disturbing leaves, weeds, and trees until it hit and rocked the RV, which then, to his vast horror, exploded into a ball of fire.

The rushing wind around him suddenly turned into a heavy pressure that squeezed him tightly, emptying his lungs of all air. He felt as if he were deep underwater. His eyes bulged out at the pressure, watering from the horror of seeing the RV explode with his parents still in it.

The pressure in his lungs kept growing until he felt he might cough them up. He struggled for a breath, staggering against the tree as his head began ringing even worse than when he had hit it.

A second later, he was on his back, clenching his throat with both hands as he frantically tried to draw a breath of air. His eyes began seeing silver spots, and he knew he was going to pass out.

His last thought was of his parents. On his hands and knees, he crawled toward the burning RV. The last thing he saw was shooting stars piercing the completely dark sky. A second later, he passed out.

* * *

He awoke sometime later, choking on thick, sandy dust. He sat up coughing and flinched in fear as something fell with a whistle of air and slammed into the ground only a few feet from where he was sitting on the forest floor.

A little terrified, he shot to his feet. Leaning against a tree dizzily, his eyes were wide open, but he could only see darkness. He could hear the sound of air screaming, though, and looked up to see bright traces of light falling out of the pitch-black sky, slamming with thunderous force upon the ground.

Gasping for breath, his chest heaving from the effort, he pushed away from the tree and looked around for shelter. The only thing he could see through the thick black dust was the still-burning remains of his family's RV.

The sight gripped him with fear, stopping him dead in his tracks. Traumatized, he began shaking, unable to move or take his eyes off the RV. Its doors were still closed, which told him the worst was true. His parents had never made it out.

Unable to believe that, he stumbled forward.

"Mom! Dad!" he choked out, looking frantically around for them.

A flash of light blinded him, leaving a flare in his eyes, as something fell from the ash-black sky and crashed into the ground right at his feet.

The force of it tossed him off the ground and through the air until he slammed hard into a tree. He slid to the ground, holding his side in pain while trying to catch his breath through the lungfuls of soot and ash he was breathing in. The air felt thick and weird in his lungs, making him struggle even to get a breath.

When he tried to open his eyes again, all he could see was a dark blur. He had to rub and blink his eyes to get them clear enough to see again. Then he could only see the light of fire. The air was filled with soot and ash, making it impossible to see anything.

By the time he got to his feet again, using the tree to haul himself up, his eyes were able to focus a little more. In front of him, upon the forest floor, was an enormous crater, and in the center of it lay a glowing red chunk of what looked like dirty ice, with burning pieces of metal in it.

It took a while to get his feet under him again this time. With his whole body shaking, he pushed himself away from the tree. He could feel the ground trembling under his feet from each jarring impact, and he looked up to see the sky full of angry red streaks that fell from the black sky like fiery rain.

What was happening? He wondered with growing fright. Had the moon blown up? He thought wildly, close to becoming hysterical.

He shook his head, trying to clear it of the ringing he could still hear, and again his eyes caught sight of his family's R.V. He felt tears quickly well in his eyes and stubbornly rubbed them away, leaving black streaks across the backs of his hands. Touching his eyes made them burn and water even worse than before. But it did not distract him from the fact that he now knew both of his parents were dead. The R.V. was no longer standing upon its wheels; it had been hit and thrown by a meteorite and was now lying half crushed upon its side.

Smoke from the R.V. filled the already thick black air. There was also smoke coming from the ground, though he could no longer see any fires burning, just smoldering embers. Not even the R.V. was on fire anymore.

He looked around, wondering where he should try to hide, but he could see nothing to hide under besides the trees. While he looked, he noticed that all of the meteorites were falling at a slant and that if he could make it closer to the mountain, he could use the mountain's lee to hopefully protect him from most of the onslaught. The mountains he saw were protecting certain areas from the meteors. And if he could make it to one of those areas, he would likely be safe. At least safer than standing in the forest with only trees to protect him.

He hesitated, though, suddenly afraid to leave the trees. The meteorites were falling fast and hitting hard. Leaving the trees, he would be out in the open without even trees to stop a meteor. Not that even the tree he was up against was any better cover than open air, he thought bitterly. The meteors were just bursting through anything they hit, but not the mountain.

A loud, piercing scream filled the air. Then the ground trembled beneath his feet, shaking the tree beside him and making it lose the last of its leaves. It was so close to him that he immediately began to run.

That one was too close, he thought in sheer panic, as he ran with all of his might, gasping for breath and choking on each breath he took. He left the tree behind, lurching in a stumbling run as the ground beneath him shook again from an even larger impact. He held his shirt over his nose, trying not to breathe in the soot filling the air as he ran towards the mountainside.

Within steps, he was hunched over, coughing and spitting out soot. He began coughing so badly that he collapsed to the ground, retching up his stomach as he tried to breathe. He knew he could not stay like this. The meteors were falling everywhere, and the odds were that he would be hit long before he would ever catch his breath. He forced himself up again and ran blindly towards the mountainside and its protective lee.

It wasn't long before he stumbled and slid head-first into a large crater. His skin on his arms burned where it touched the hot ground. He could feel a fierce heat in front of his face and looked up to see a red-hot meteor inches in front of his face.

The smell of his hair burning as he landed in front of the hot meteor jerked him onto his feet yet again, this time with a cry of pain. Then he ran out of the crater, patting his hair to ensure it wasn't on fire.

He had to stop again to get a breath and calm his coughing—dry-heaving when he couldn't.

When he finally made it up into the lee of the mountain, he collapsed upon the ground, gagging on all the dust in his throat and lungs, and shivering in the cold air blowing around him, which seemed to be getting colder by the second.

What am I going to do? He asked himself worriedly as his initial panic began to subside a little.

Above him, the sky was filled with streaking meteorites as far as he could see. Red streaks filled the sky. He could feel the thumping and rumbling beneath him as they impacted the ground. The sight terrified him.

He curled himself in a ball, trying not to cough, as he wedged himself under a rock shelf, trying to stay warm as he watched more and more meteors appear in the dark sky.

* * *

He was unsure how long he had slept, but he was jerked awake again as a meteor fell close to where he was hiding under a rock. When he lifted his head, he saw it had hit right in front of the mountain. The crater it left was at least a hundred yards across. Its impact threw up so much dust and ash that he began choking immediately, feeling the small, stinging bits of hot pebbles slicing into his skin and causing him to come instantly awake—only to pass out again when he could not breathe through the cloud of ash that enveloped him.

* * *

This time, it was a slow process when he came to awareness. He felt so tired and weak, yet he couldn't stop coughing. His shivering from the absolute cold was what stirred him awake. He knew almost immediately that if he did not move, he would freeze to death. Yet he was too terrified to leave the rock he was under. He felt a meteorite would hit him if he left the mountain's shelter.

So, he lay curled up and shivering for a long time until it dawned on him that he no longer felt the Earth trembling beneath him as violently as it had. And hesitantly, as if afraid of what he might see, he opened his inflamed, burning eyes and looked around.

The bite of the cold air sent his body shivering uncontrollably, and he almost regretted lifting his head to look around. It was so dark that he could not see anything but pitch-black night. As if that were a comfort, he slowly sat up, looking around harder, trying to pierce the surrounding darkness, until he could see that somewhere in front of him, seen only dimly through the black haze filling the air, there was a soft glowing light—and with it came the feeling of heat.

Almost instinctively, he found himself moving toward it. The feel of its heat made the air around him seem so cold that it was hard for him to start moving. Breathing the cold air itself made his sore and swollen lungs hurt painfully. Getting to his feet made him instantly lightheaded and dizzy. He had to use the rock to pull himself up, one of his arms holding his side, trying to keep it from hurting even worse.

Once on his feet, he put his shirt over his mouth and nose. Doing so exposed his skin to the cold air, causing him to feel as if he were freezing where he stood. As soon as he started moving, though, he did not allow himself to stop. The dark haze obscured the air between him and the glowing object, keeping him from seeing what was causing the glow and heat.

It was not long before he realized that he had stumbled into the large crater that had been made right in front of where he had taken shelter. His first thought was to get out of it, but he knew that whatever had caused the crater was making the glow and heat, and he was reluctant to leave the warmth he could feel just up ahead of him.

Clenching his side, he stumbled through the crater until he could finally make out the red glowing meteor through the black haze in the air. The closer he got, the warmer he felt. But the smell of the air in the crater was so nauseous that it caused him to dry heave, then choke as he took in lungfuls of soot and ash from off his shirt.

The heat from the meteor was intense, warming him to the core as he approached it. The air blowing at his back was ice-cold compared to it.

The meteor itself seemed to be melting slowly while he watched. It appeared he watched it for hours. When he first saw it, it was over four feet around, but as it melted, it shrank in size until all that was left was a glowing red piece of rounded metal.

He wondered if it was radioactive, but he quickly pushed that thought out of his mind. If it were, then he would have to worry about that later. Right now, his survival was all that mattered. He knew he would freeze to death without the warmth this meteor was bringing him. It was the only source of heat he had. He crouched down six feet away from it, soaking up its heat. It felt like a giant campfire. While it melted, the glow it gave off subsided a little, but it remained bright enough to give him enough light to look around through the haze and see the devastation the falling meteorites had caused. Not that he could see much. The darkness pushed in around him as much as the thick air did.

The pressure in his lungs had not lessened at all. It was as if the whole composition of the air had changed with the falling of the meteorites. And he wondered why no one had known there would be such a meteor shower, and why there had been no warning.

That made him think about his parents again, and he held back his tears as he searched with one hand for his phone. Once he found it, he turned it so he could see it, but the display was blank, and it remained blank as he tried to turn it on. And no matter what he tried, he could not get any light, sound, or anything. It was useless.

His hand got cold quickly, so he put the phone away and huddled closer to the meteor—or what remained. It was now only a foot around, nestled into the ground like a top, tilted on its side. It was still glowing red, but he could see that it was a red and silver combination. It looked like some red metal with silver streaks twirling around it.

Just then, another chill spread through his body, making him shiver, and a second later, all of his vision was obscured as a fierce cold wind came howling through the mountains, swirling ash and soot up from everywhere, making him move closer to the meteor for its heat. He crouched protectively over it as he heard a piercing whistle screech through the air. The sound caused him to freeze in fear.

Meteors! he thought frantically. *What was he going to do?* If he left the heat of the meteor, he knew he would freeze to death within an hour. But he also knew there was no way he could stay here with meteorites falling all around him.

Without thinking, he took off his shirt and threw it over the meteor, hoping it would not burn. He heard it fizzle and quickly pulled it off to see if it had burned. He saw no burn marks through the dust covering his shirt, so he tossed it back on the meteor again. Then, bunching the excess shirt in his hands to hopefully shield them from the meteor's heat, he bent and touched it. He hissed in pain as it burned him, but the pain was not bad—not as bad as dying, he thought. He picked it up with a little struggle, then began making his way out of the crater, laughing and wheezing all the way.

He began to move just in time. Streaks of red light began to fill the dark sky, and the Earth again began to tremble under each impact.

The meteor was a lot heavier than a rock should be. Its weight pushed heavily upon his hands. He could feel its heat easily through his shirt as he tripped, stumbled, and coughed all the way back to the little shelter he had found. Once there, he wedged himself in, putting the glowing meteor between him and the frigid air.

That done, he surveyed his shirt. Much to his great relief, there was not a burn mark upon it, just tons of soot and ash. He quickly put it back on, then, coughing, he began to nurse his burnt hands, rubbing them tenderly.

Outside his shelter, the meteorites continued to fall at an alarming rate, but none of them even came close to where he was. After watching for a minute, he uncurled his hands to see how burnt they were. His fingertips and palms were in pain, but he could not see any blisters forming under all the soot covering them. He flexed his hands a few times and winced in pain, bringing on a spasm of coughing.

When his coughing stopped, he put his shirt back over his nose, then crouched close to the meteor, absorbing its warmth and wondering, as he did, how long its heat would last—and why it was still glowing.

Unable to ascertain an answer, he put his mind to other things and sat down to study the meteor. He could not even imagine what it was made of, but it was beautiful and shiny. No soot seemed to be able to cling to it. It looked like a metal device of some sort. The streaks twirling around it were giving off the glow he saw. Its light bounced off the metallic red of it and gave it a reddish glow. From its almost rounded, cone-like shape, it looked like it had formed as it fell and spun into the atmosphere. But he knew that was not right, because all this part of the meteorite had been covered by the part that had melted off and dissolved.

He sat staring at it for what seemed like hours. The meteors slowly stopped falling again, and it wasn't long after that when sleep found him again.

Day Two: July 2nd

Derek woke to a deep thirst. His throat was swollen and dry, and his tongue felt like sandpaper. He licked his lips and felt them crack open as he lifted his head from his shirt. He was more than a little surprised to still feel the warmth of the meteor next to him, keeping him warm.

He looked around, knowing that it must be daytime again, but it was still pitch-black outside, and he could only see a little area around him, thanks to the meteor's glow. He studied it again curiously. Its glow was still the same, and it wasn't noticeable if the warmth it had been giving off had dimmed. And that freaked him out a bit, as he knew it was not normal; there was no way it should still be glowing and giving off heat—not with how cold it was now in the open.

Feeling a little panicky, he pulled out his cellphone again and tried to turn it on or get it to work, but just by looking at it, he knew it was dead, as was his digital watch. Not even the compass on it seemed to be working right. It was pointing right at the meteorite in front of him, and followed it when he moved the watch around.

He frowned at the meteor and wondered, not for the first time, just how massive this meteor shower was and how much damage it was causing.

His dry lips made him keep licking them, and he knew as he continued staring at the strange meteor that he could not stay in the shelter. He needed food and water—mainly water. Yet he could not leave the shelter without the warmth and light of the meteor.

Thinking of picking it up again made him look down at his hands. They were both sore and tender to the touch, but he could not see a single blister through the grime covering them. He held one of his hands out to the meteor, testing its warmth, feeling it was still too hot to hold without something protecting his hands.

He hacked and coughed, spitting out clotty blood and ash. Then, shivering, he took off one of his shoes, pulling off a sock he tied it around his face over his nose so he could block out some of the dust and not breathe it all in. That done, he put his shoe back on.

He then took off his shirt again, bunching it around his hands so he could pick up the meteor. This time, holding it did not seem as bad. He could feel the heat through his shirt, but the pain was minor compared to last time.

With it firmly in his hands, he looked around, trying to pierce the darkness and see if he could spot any meteorites falling. Failing to see the telltale signs of red streaks of light shooting across the black sky, he hesitantly left the shelter of rocks in search of much-needed water. He walked slowly, using the meteor's light to see the ash-covered ground so he didn't trip or fall into a hole.

The problem he noticed immediately was that at least two feet of ash had covered the ground in most places. That fine ash seemed to float magically in the air like a giant black smog, blocking his vision. Just looking through it made him want to cough.

He stood still, ignoring the coughing spasm, then squinted his blurry, inflamed eyes so he could try to retrace his way back to his family's RV. Each movement stirred the ash, making it harder for him not to cough on it.

He dreaded what he would see inside the RV, but it was the only place he could hope to find water and supplies—that is, if they were not all ruined beyond use.

He held the meteor close to his chest to stave off the frigid cold air surrounding him, making his whole body shiver uncontrollably. He cried out in pain and shock as the shiver caused his arms to pull the meteor all the way to his bare chest.

Two things happened at once. Pain ripped through his chest over his heart, making him almost drop the meteor, which had left a big, wicked-looking purple and bleeding welt upon his chest—so purple he could see it through the dark soot covering his skin.

The second thing was even more surprising and distracted him from the pain. After the meteor touched his chest, it vibrated softly in his hands. It stopped when he pulled it up to look at it curiously. He stared at it, trying to decide if he had just imagined its vibration. Then, thinking he had, he continued toward the RV, careful not to let the meteor touch his skin again.

It took him a long time to reach the ruined RV; it was totally destroyed. By the time he got there, he was wheezing for breath, and it took him a minute to gather enough nerve to walk closer to it. From the meteor's light, he could see how the fire had warped it and where the meteorite had slammed into its side. What had not been burned by the explosion had to have been smashed by the meteorite.

Seeing it made him feel sick to his stomach. He stared at it hopelessly, feeling his eyes water. He did not want to look inside. It felt wrong to do so. He knew he had no choice if he wanted to live, though. He was in the middle of the park with nowhere nearby on foot. He had to find something to drink, or he would die of dehydration.

The RV was tipped onto its side. The meteor had hit the cab and engine full on, and while the back compartment was smashed in and warped by the fire, it looked like there might still be a chance to find something inside. The smell coming from it was so horrible that he began gagging as soon as he got close.

He choked down his tears and walked around the RV, finding a space big enough for him to crawl through. It was the smashed sunroof. Through it, he could get into the living area of the RV. Shivering, he put the meteor gently on the ground, and for some reason he could not understand, he found it hard even to let go. It was like his hands were glued to it with a mind of their own. He did not want to leave its warmth; without it, he would freeze. Yet he knew there was no way he could crawl through the broken sunroof with it in his hands. It was still too hot, and he did not want to touch it accidentally again. His chest still stung like fire from the meteor's touch, and he did not want to feel that pain again.

He placed the meteor down by the opening in the sunroof where its light could still be seen when he entered the dark RV. Then he closed his eyes, put on his shirt, and tried to gather the strength to enter it—knowing what he would see when he did and not wanting to see it.

He rooted through the ash until he found a good fist-sized rock. Then, getting cold, he smashed the rest of the glass out of the sunroof so he would not cut himself crawling in and out. Once that was done, he bent over, wheezing and shivering, and looked inside the camper.

Everything within it was burnt to a crisp, and he could not stop himself from throwing up when he saw his mother's nearly unrecognizable, crumpled body lying against one of the warped metal cabinets.

It took him a long time to calm himself so he would not throw up again. Then, gritting his teeth, tears running down his face, he took a deep breath and squeezed through the hole in the roof. The effort brought about a fierce bout of coughing and dry heaving as the smoke and smell tried to overwhelm him. It almost took him two minutes to get in.

He looked around and saw that all the cabinets had been made of metal. They were warped, but only a couple were open. Inside the camper, everything was black and melted. Hardly anything was recognizable.

He tried a few closed cabinets, but none would open for him. They were warped shut. So, he looked around until he found a metal piece from one of the windows, then he set about wedging them open one by one. The effort kept his shivers away, and when he was done, he surveyed what he had found: some canned food that wasn't too damaged, bulging out as if it had been overcooked; some dry foods—noodles, cereals, and melted oatmeal bars.

All in all, he searched the camper for two hours, trying to salvage anything he could. He could only remain in the camper for ten minutes at a time before he had to return to the glowing meteor to get warm again. But he noticed it took him longer and longer to get cold, even though the temperature had not changed.

Everything he found, he set outside beside the meteor so it would not get lost in the ash.

He had found water in the RV's water tank, but it had been so hot that he had to wait for it to cool off after pouring it into a warped cup for him to drink. Then he filled up three metal canteens with some before he drank some more. He used a pair of melted can openers to open a can of peaches, then a can of green beans, forcing himself to eat the foul-tasting, overcooked food. Those were the only two salvageable cans that had not exploded in the fire. He had not dared to save either one, for he had known they would spoil quickly.

Once back by the meteor, he looked around at everything he had been able to salvage from the RV: two halves of burnt blankets; a pair of his dad's boots, which were a size too big for him but still in surprisingly good shape; a bunch of ruined electronics—a radio, phone, a half-melted flashlight, and a shakelite, which blew up in his hand when he shook it, giving him a nasty cut upon his palm. Not one of the electronics worked. He had heard of EMP bombs that could knock out electricity and keep all electronics from working, and he wondered if maybe that was what this meteor storm did. But how could it do the same thing?

He had found one of his father's hunting and skinning knives in a partially burnt leather sheath. The gun safe had been melted too tightly to wedge open, and all the other knives he had found had melted hilts.

All his stuff had been ruined except for a leather jacket and one pair of jeans that had gotten slightly singed.

He had found the emergency supply box, and it seemed to be intact enough to bandage his palm and chest after he swabbed both with a semi-dry alcohol pad to clean them first.

He then used one of the burnt blankets to fashion a backpack, using his dad's knife to cut strips for shoulder straps, then smaller strips to tie the blanket in a way so that it would be able to hold all of the things he would need to take with him.

When he was finished, he could distract himself no longer. He was filled with curiosity about the meteor. He sat staring at it, watching its steady glow. He could feel its heat in the pleasant warmth that seemed to wrap around him when he was near it, and over the last couple of hours, it appeared its heat could stay around him longer and longer. He knew it must have cooled enough by now for him to touch it. But then, it was not normal. No other meteorite he could see was glowing or giving off heat, nor did they even look like this one. He had looked around, picking up a couple of the smaller meteorites— all black, hard rock. Though some did seem to have little crystal-like structures in them, and some had melted metal, none had come close to this one in glow or heat.

Curious, he reached over, putting his hand near the red and silver meteor. Feeling its heat, it still felt as hot as it was when he found it, and he knew that could not be true. Before he could stop himself, he closed the distance and touched it with his hand.

He expected stinging hot pain, but a surprise came to him. A rush of warmth filled his body, and at his touch, the meteor began to vibrate warmly beneath his hand, shaking softly upon the ground it was lying on.

The warmth traveled up his arm and down inside of him, making his skin break out in an instant sweat. Beneath his palm, the meteor was hot but not unbearably so. He removed his hand to check it, and the second that his skin left the meteor, it stopped vibrating. And the warmth that had filled his body faded away, leaving him wanting to pick it up and hold it.

He hesitated to do so, though. As he studied it and tried to understand it, why had the meteor vibrated at his touch? Was it some kind of machine? Or, more disturbingly, was it alive? If not, was the vibration and warmth just some kind of chemical reaction to his touch?

Studying his hand beneath the soot and ash, it seemed okay, though his fingertips were still a little tender from the last time he had held it. Gathering his nerve, he reached out and touched it again.

This time, the meteor did not vibrate, but that instant warmth again pleasantly filled his body, fighting off all of his chills until he no longer felt the cold air anywhere on his body. It was as if the cold could no longer touch him. He looked down at the meteor with wonder, not understanding how it made him warm like he was—and not caring that it did. It was an incredible feeling after being so cold ever since the meteor storm began.

He curiously traced his finger lightly over one of the glowing silver spirals. He could feel it was no hotter than the rest, but it felt like smooth, slick metal. He traced it all the way to the top of the meteor, which was slightly rounded, and it felt like soft velvet. Touching it, he suddenly knew that, for some reason, this part of the meteor was softer than the rest—more fragile. The meteor vibrated as he touched that part, and suddenly grew too hot to touch.

Surprised, he removed his finger from the top and touched the silver spiral. He instinctively knew he had just been given some kind of warning, making him more curious than scared. The warning had been simple: *Be careful with this part.* He stared down at it almost in awe. He did not want to believe it, but he felt it was alive. He picked it up carefully in his hands and studied the top of it curiously. The top was pure red and seemed a shadeless, shiny metallic color compared to the bottom, but there was no seam to it; the meteor seemed whole.

Holding it, its warmth seemed to fill him until he could no longer distinguish between hot and cold. To him, it was just warm—like he was now the perfect temperature—and no amount of cold could change that.

The meteor kept his attention for a long time before he realized he was getting thirsty again and turned his attention back to the task at hand. He now had a little bit of food in his makeshift backpack: some jerky, nuts, and dried prunes that his mother had seemed to love, as well as some dry foods—noodles, cereal, and oatmeal (some of which had burned). He had already eaten the melted oatmeal bars. He had three full canteens of water and still a little left in the tank. He also had a bottle of water pills to clean any river water he might need to drink.

In his backpack, he had a skillet to cook with, a hunting knife, a couple of hiltless knives, a small pocket knife with all kinds of things in it, some burnt but salvageable clothes, a small blanket, a medical emergency box, and a flint fire kit with a box of matches.

He drank some more water from the tank and sat holding the meteor in his lap, wondering what he was going to do now that he was on his own—stranded in the national park without the slightest notion of where to go to get help, if there was anyone else alive he could find.

And looking up, he wondered how long it would be until he saw the sun again.

CHAPTER TWO

Location: Presidential Shelter, Unknown Location in Colorado

"Sir, we have lost all power. The backup generators will not start, and the one that did start exploded. We have lost contact with everyone. We don't know if it is just because the meteor cloud is obscuring everything or if, as Jean believes, some kind of element from the meteor cloud has rendered all electronics useless," the tall, skinny, balding man facing the president told him before frowning in displeasure and continuing. "Sir, what's more is that we cannot open the doors. They are all controlled electronically. There are manual overrides, but they're hard to get to without power tools. For now, the doors are stuck. I've got men trying to take them apart now, because if we cannot get the power back on, we will have to leave this shelter. We have too many people here. The air will last close to 78 hours—then we will all be dead."

The president, Markus Allumin, frowned at his secretary of state, his face showing worry. He ran his hands back through his greying black hair, and his blue eyes seemed to pierce Edwards as he studied the man who had helped him gain the office he held today. Then he motioned for everyone but his secretary to leave the office.

When they had all left, the president turned his back on Edwards to study the map behind his desk. In his hand, he held a couple of pieces of paper.

"We have both read this," he told Edwards, "and I am willing to bet it is right on the money. If that is the case, then we both know no amount of tinkering you're doing with the electronics of this place will get our power back on. Not now, and probably not fifty to a hundred years from now. Jean Perry is one of the most respected scientists in his field of study. He now believes that some kind of chemical in this meteor cloud has interacted with and neutralized all of the electrons on our planet. If that is the case, we have a severe problem getting our country through. No cars, planes, phones, or electronic gadgets will work anymore. Anything with gas explodes—just like our generator did—which was one of the things Jean speculated about in his report. And you heard the Secretary of Defense. No gun works. No bullet will fire, though some have exploded, rendering the gun useless."

Frustrated, he turned back to Edwards, studying him critically. "We are going to go through the Dark Ages all over again. Those who survive this are going to need strong direction and protection. Jean estimates there will be nearly two feet of ash worldwide when all is said and done. We will be without sunlight for months. The temperature is going to plummet drastically. No crops are going to grow. People are going to starve. Some are going to turn to savagery. And our government system is going to collapse. So, from this second on, we start planning how to save our country."

After Edwards left, Markus sat in his chair and slowly began to draft a plan that might save the country and help restore peace to the places where it would revert to savagery.

Day Four: July Fourth

Location: National Park, Wyoming

Derek was walking down the same road he and his family had driven up just four days before the big meteor storm. Around him was nothing but darkness. Ash swirled in eddies as he walked through the haze in the air. Now and then, he would walk off the road and had to crawl on his hands and knees, sifting through the ash to find it again. Following it was the only hope he had of ever reaching anyone again.

He wore his makeshift backpack on his back, and in his arms, he held the still-glowing meteorite. He hugged it close, feeling its warmth keeping him alive, so warm that his leather jacket was stuffed in the backpack. With just jeans and a T-shirt on, he felt hot. It was a feeling that he would rather have than be as cold as the frozen ash that crunched under his feet. At his waist, strapped to his belt, hung the hunting knife, and on his feet, tied tight, were his dad's hiking boots.

Through the meteor's light, he could see the frozen branches of trees by the road. Everything was dark, and the meteor's light had trouble piercing too far into the ashy haze that filled the air. Now and then, Derek would have to climb a fallen tree to continue following the road. The meteor storm had been bad. He could not believe just how many trees had been knocked over. Once, he lost the road for hours, trying to go around a section where all the trees had been knocked over like bowling pins.

Around Derek's face was a makeshift wrap that he had cut from one of his burnt shirts. His eyes burned from all the ash, his chest burned where the meteor had touched him, and his skin was dry and irritated. To top it off, he was starving for meat. He had eaten the last of his jerky yesterday while thinking about his fourteenth birthday, which was today if he had the day correct. He still had one and a half water canteens and a little burnt oatmeal. He was tempted to drink and eat the rest to fill his growling stomach.

Either way, he would have to find and boil some water tonight if he could get a fire started. The matches did not work right, and with the flint? It was almost impossible, though he got it to work with much effort.

He came through a group of trees, and to his surprise, he saw light up ahead. It turned out to be coming from the first building he had seen since the storm. At the same time he saw the building, he saw the first human in days.

The man looked up when he saw the light coming from Derek, and he stared in shock at seeing him. Then he collapsed onto the ground.

Surprised, Derek hurried forward. He rushed to the man and put the meteor on the ground next to him, bending over the man to see if he was still alive. As he did, he got hit from behind, hard.

Derek heard a weird ringing in his ears and thought he might pass out as he fell to his knees, holding his head, seeing stars as pain crashed in around him. He saw movement and instinctively rolled out of the way to see a baseball bat swish through the air above where his head had been. Anger and fear overrode his pain, and he pulled his knife, slashing the air at his side.

He felt his knife snag briefly, cutting through clothing, then he heard a scream rip through the darkness as he got unsteadily on his feet.

"Get the light he was carrying, and I will take care of him," a loud, commanding voice demanded. He was the one Derek knew had the bat.

The voice came from a shadow on Derek's right.

"My face! Son of a bitch cut my face!" the man without the bat growled as he stumbled into the light the meteor gave off.

Derek caught a glimpse of the man's face as he tried to duck the baseball bat again. This time, the bat caught him on the back of the head as he moved away, sending him sprawling into the ash-filled street. He rolled, forcing himself to move through the pain, and heard the bat slam into the road. Then he was on his feet again.

By then, the bleeding man—who had faked his fall to lure Derek to him—had reached the glowing meteor. Derek saw him bend over and try to pick it up. A second later, a horrified, pain-filled scream tore through the night as the man's hands blistered and burned from touching the meteor. He dropped it and stared at his hands in agony.

The man with the bat turned at the unexpected cry from his partner. Seeing his chance, Derek lunged and slashed at the hand holding the bat.

The man grunted in pain and dropped the weapon, grabbing at his wrist, where Derek had just sliced through the tendons.

Full of anger, Derek stepped forward, lifting the knife toward the man. Seeing him coming, the man's eyes went wide with fear, and he turned and ran. The man with the cut face and burned hands followed, ignoring the glowing meteor.

Suddenly shaking, Derek walked slowly to the meteor, coughing from all the dust he'd breathed in. He adjusted the makeshift scarf over his face and studied the meteor. It seemed unharmed. He bent down, picked it up, and as soon as his fingers touched it, it vibrated in his hands. Then, just as quickly, it settled, sending warmth through his body.

He sheathed his knife and began looking around for the things that had fallen from his backpack, coughing the whole time. Once he was sure he'd found everything, he turned to the building. In its window, he saw the flicker of a candle—and on the porch, two elderly people stood, each holding a shotgun.

When Derek looked toward them, the one closest to him gestured with his weapon, signaling for him to keep walking.

"I'll be telling you like I told them: strangers aren't welcome here. Beat it," the old man said in a harsh voice.

"Herb! He has light, and you saw those men attack him," the old woman beside him said in a kind, worried tone.

"Em—shut up," the old man growled, again motioning for Derek to move on. "Leave, or I'll shoot!" he threatened.

Angry, the old lady threw down her gun. "No, Herb!" she said, turning to Derek with urgency. "That boy needs help. I understand turning away those men, but this? Can't you see—he's only a boy. A wounded one at that. And he has light!" She whispered the last part in an astonished tone.

Derek watched them both nervously. The back of his head felt mushy as he touched it gently, and he could feel blood running down his scalp. He held the meteor closer to his chest and made a silent vow: next time he approached anyone, he would hide it—before someone else tried to kill him for it.

"Boy? What's your name?" the old lady asked.

It took Derek a moment to realize she was speaking to him. He coughed to clear his throat, then winced—both from how raw it felt and from the pain that echoed through his skull.

When his voice finally came, it was cracked and hoarse. It didn't sound like his voice at all.

"Derek," he told her. "I was just looking for someplace to stay—and maybe some food. I don't want any trouble. I've been walking since the meteors fell. This is the first place I've seen." He paused, then added, "I can keep going if you want me to," speaking with more strength than he actually felt.

The old man coughed, spat, and motioned for the woman to pick up her shotgun.

"You're lying," he growled. "Ain't nothing could survive in the open these last four days. You'd've frozen to death or been hit by one of their asteroids. Now get on—we don't need anyone taking what little we've got."

Tired and frustrated, Derek turned to walk away.

"Derek," the old lady called out, worriedly. She leaned her shotgun against the door. "Derek, my dear, stop right there. Let me take a look at you. You don't look in any shape to go walking off alone," she said quickly, pushing the old man aside before he could stop her.

"Emma! Damn it, Emma!" the old man barked. "Get back here! It's not safe out there. Those men could still be lurking—this could be one of their tricks." He hesitated, then followed after her, raising his shotgun and training it on Derek.

Derek turned toward them as they approached. He cradled the meteor protectively against his chest, almost as if to comfort it. As the old lady neared, the meteor suddenly vibrated—almost as if warning them to stay back. But it stopped after a second, as Derek gently ran his fingers over it, trying to calm it down.

As Emma approached, she stared at the light coming from the object the boy was holding. She was genuinely surprised when, as she got closer, she began to feel warmer. Once she was close to him, she stopped, looking at him curiously.

"What do you have there?" she asked, her voice full of wonder.

Derek wasn't sure how to answer, but a lie came quickly to him. "It's a new kind of heater my dad was working on," he said.

"How does it work?" she asked in amazement. "Nothing in our house works anymore—no electricity, no batteries. It was even hard to get the candles to light."

Noticing how muffled she sounded, Derek studied her carefully. It was like her nose was stuffed up. He gestured to the meteor in his arms.

"I'm not sure how it works. My dad never explained it to me. I'm sorry, ma'am. I didn't mean to cause any trouble. I wasn't lying, though. My family and I were vacationing in the park when the meteors hit."

He quickly wiped his eyes with his forearm as tears threatened to fall at the memory of his parents' deaths.

"Shh. It's okay," she said softly, her voice kind and comforting. "You're not causing any trouble. Don't you mind, Herb. Now, let me see your head. You're bleeding pretty badly. I saw those men hit you, and I fired my gun to scare them off—but for some reason, it wouldn't fire. Herb even tried his, and it didn't work either."

"Emma, dear," the old man said in a low, angry voice. "If those men hear that our guns don't work, they'll be back to take everything we have by force."

He turned a sharp look on Derek, sizing him up. Derek suddenly felt wary. Something told him that Herb wasn't as worried about violence as he claimed.

"But what's done is done," Herb continued. "Now, both of you get inside. It's not safe out here. I'll keep watch."

Derek turned to him. "I'm okay. I can help you keep watch, in case they—"

"No, no, dear," Emma said gently, wrapping an arm around his shoulder and steering him toward the house. "You can't see it, but your head's bashed up something awful. Now you come with me, and I'll patch it up the best I can. Then, if you're feeling better, you can help Herb watch the place. But I don't think you should sleep—not with a knock to the head like that. You might not wake up. I can tell by your eyes—you've got yourself a concussion."

Emma led the strange boy into her home and shop, then paused to watch as he looked around. The object in his arms lit the room more brightly than all her candles combined.

But what truly struck her as strange was his eyes.

When she'd looked into them to check for signs of a concussion, they had flashed silver.

At first, she thought it might be a trick of the light from whatever he was carrying—but then she saw the same flash in the glow of her candles.

His eyes had flashed silver.

Derek was led to the kitchen table, and Emma pulled out a chair for him. He carefully—though reluctantly—placed the meteor in the center of the table. When he tried to take his hands off it, he struggled. It was as if the meteor didn't want him to let go. Surprised, he ran his hands lightly over its surface to reassure it.

Then he turned to Emma as she stepped closer to examine it.

"Be careful not to touch it. It can be very hot," he warned her as he carefully took off his makeshift scarf; it was, to his dismay, soaked in blood.

Emma nodded politely. "Yes, I saw what it did to that man when he tried to take it from you," she said, trying to reassure him, even as her mind reeled with questions. Why could this boy handle the object with his bare hands, while it had severely burned the other man?

She studied the object with fascination. Already, much to her relief, she could feel it warming the kitchen. She had never seen anything like this "heating device." It looked exotic—but then again, with so many new gadgets coming out each year, she wasn't surprised she didn't recognize it.

"Take a seat right there," she told Derek. "Let me see if I can clean you up a bit."

Derek shrugged off his backpack and hooked it onto one of the chairs before sitting down at the table, right next to the meteor. He leaned forward slightly, allowing her to inspect the back of his head. That's when he noticed the back of his shirt was also soaked with blood.

"You said you were visiting the park with your family when the meteors came?" she asked gently, hoping to distract him. At the same time, she cleaned the wound—a task made difficult by the ash caked onto his skin and tangled in his hair. Just by looking at him, she could tell he had been out in the storm a long time.

Sitting in the chair, Derek felt himself beginning to doze. Exhaustion was creeping up, making it harder and harder to stay upright. But her question snapped him awake, and he rubbed his eyes to keep them open.

"When the meteors came, my mom and dad were in the RV. I was rushing back and saw them trying to call me into it... Then it exploded. They never made it out," he said, trying to keep the tears from falling.

Emma handed him a bottle of water while she finished cleaning both head wounds, listening as he told her how he had hidden on the side of the mountain and made it as far as he had.

When she finished tending to him, she used a candle to light a fire in the fireplace and began heating a large can of soup. While he ate, she shared her and Herb's story—how they owned the store, the gas station, and the house; how they'd sealed it up tight to keep out the ash and hold in what little warmth they could make; and how they used nose filters that fit inside their nostrils to help them breathe better.

Once he was done eating, Derek couldn't resist picking up the meteor again. Instantly, its warmth and comfort flooded through him. He realized just how attached he had grown to it over the past few days. He didn't know what it was, but he knew, without a doubt, that it had kept him alive. Without its miraculous heat, he would've frozen to death.

He snapped back to attention when he realized Emma was watching him curiously as he ran his fingers along one of the swirling silver stripes, tracing it from the bottom of the meteor back up.

Emma smiled. "I'd treat that heater with reverence, too, after all you've been through. It's been getting mighty cold without sunlight, and it'll likely get colder still. The last three nights have been horrible. It's nice to feel some warmth again." She paused, then added, "You can stay as long as you want—as long as you help Herb watch the house. I feel like those two men might come back. Things could get bad now. This weather's gonna make people desperate, and we could use extra hands in case trouble comes our way."

She smiled again, looking hopeful. "That ain't likely though. We're far from everybody. Not many folks would even try walking through this weather, not without light. I think those two men you ran off'll be the last ones we see around here."

"I'm thinking she's right," Herb said as he entered the kitchen, rubbing his arms for warmth. "Them men'll be back, though. You hurt one pretty bad, slicing his wrist like that. There's plenty of blood out there. If it weren't so dark, we'd see it plain as day. They couldn't have gone far—and when they do come back, we ain't got no guns to fight with."

He gave Derek a long, appraising look.

"I'm old. Even hurt like they are, they're still good enough to take Em and me. But with your help—and the heat you brought—we might have a shot. Don't get me wrong, boy, I fought in my time. I know how to knife fight, sword fight, and even fence. But guns? That's always been my strong point. Without 'em… Well, stay as long as you want, so long as you're helping me keep Emma safe."

Grateful to be able to stay, Derek nodded.

"I can help keep watch. I'm not hurt too bad—just a little tired," he said with a big yawn. "I don't know how much help I can be if those men come back. That was my first real fight. I've been taking Jeet Kune Do since I was eight, but I didn't remember any of it when they attacked me," he admitted honestly.

The old man smiled—his first smile since Derek had arrived.

"You handled yourself pretty well, considering how dark it was and how young you are. Most kids wouldn't have gotten back up after taking a hit like that from a baseball bat. But you took two and still fought them off. So your training must've taught you something. Most other kids would've gotten themselves killed.-"

Just then, a noise sounded from the roof—like someone trying to walk across it.

Derek saw Emma's eyes widen. Herb took off at a run, grabbing something from near the doorway. Derek glimpsed a sword—the kind he'd seen army recruiters carry in commercials. As Herb dashed upstairs, Derek sprang to his feet, but Emma stopped him with a gentle touch on the shoulder.

"It could be a diversion," she said quickly. "Go watch the front window and see if you spot anything. I'll check the ones in the back."

Derek nodded and moved toward the front of the house, pulling his knife from its sheath. He passed from the warm kitchen light into the semi-darkness of the living room, where only a single candle flickered.

The room had two large windows and a front door. Inside, it was clean but cluttered. A big-screen TV hung on one wall with a large couch in front of it, a loveseat to the side, dressers along the walls, an entertainment system, a table, and a few other pieces of furniture.

He moved quickly to one of the windows and crouched down, careful not to be seen. Peeking out, he caught sight of a shadowed figure swinging a bat—right at his head.

Reflexively, Derek tucked into a roll, the bat crashing into the glass behind him, missing his face by inches. He came up on his feet just as the man smashed through the rest of the window and jumped into the room.

"Son of a bitch! How did I miss you?" the man growled.

It was the one Derek had cut across the face. In the candlelight, Derek could see a deep, ragged gash that ran from the man's forehead down his cheek and even through his coat to his chest. Though it wasn't bleeding heavily, the entire front of the man's coat was soaked with blood, as were the hands holding the bat.

"You think that knife scares me, boy?" the man sneered, then charged, swinging the bat with all his might.

Derek almost froze, his heart pounding at the man's sudden attack. He didn't think he had ever been so scared. But beneath the fear, a calm part of his mind—shaped by years of dojo training—watched the man's every move. The attacker telegraphed each action, making it easy for Derek to predict his intent. Derek waited until the man committed to his swing, then dove forward, rolling to the side just as the bat whooshed over his head. As he passed, he slashed his knife toward the man.

But before the blade could hamstring the bat-wielder, Derek cried out in pain—another man had appeared, slamming a metal pipe into his wrist.

The blow nearly knocked the knife from his hand. Only a flash of instinct saved him: he had glimpsed the pipe a second before it connected and managed to shift his arm downward. Instead of a direct hit, the pipe only grazed his wrist. Still, it hurt like hell.

The man with the pipe landed awkwardly after jumping through the same window. Derek reacted instantly—kicking at the man's knee. The strike hit the side instead of the front, but it was enough to knock the man off balance. He crashed into the wall, crying out in pain as his injured wrist slammed against it to break his fall. Derek saw blood spray into the air as the man's bandage came loose.

Derek tried to regain his footing, but the man with the bat was already swinging again, trying to take Derek's head off. Derek dove backward. The bat grazed his nose, and pain exploded in his face as blood streamed down. He cried out as the back of his head collided with the couch, stunned.

The man stood over him, grinning cruelly. Derek could see in his eyes— he thought he had won.

But anger surged through Derek. He pushed forward from the couch and drove his knife upward, jabbing it deep into the man's arm—the one cocked to swing the bat again.

At that moment, Herb charged into the room, sword in hand and raised in a front guard stance.

Both intruders froze at the sight of the weapon.

They panicked.

Without a word, they scrambled back through the broken window and disappeared into the darkness.

By then, it was growing hard to see inside the house—ash poured in through the broken window, swirling through the air. The mix of blood and ash clogging his nose sent Derek into a fit of coughing, his lungs seizing as he struggled to breathe.

Herb ran to the window, peering out into the darkness, trying to track the retreating men.

"You okay, son?" he asked over his shoulder.

Derek tried to answer, but the coughing overtook him, wracking his body until he couldn't speak—or breathe.

"Em! Come help the boy! I need to fix this damn window and keep the blasted ash out!"

Derek staggered, choking, his lungs burning as if they were swelling shut. He couldn't breathe.

He barely felt it when Herb caught him—everything was spinning. Then, everything went black.

CHAPTER THREE

Day Four

Location: Hidden Survivalist Compound, Central America

Marques had been lucky the day the meteors decided to strike and wreak havoc upon the unsuspecting and unprepared world. His job was not only his specialty but also his lifelong hobby. He and his family had always believed the world would end in a disaster. While others went about their days frivolously, he spent his time looking toward the future he hoped to control—one that he and his father before him had always believed would be dark and ugly.

Since he was sixteen years old, he had been working with his father. Back then, his father had believed the world would end in 2012. And believing that—like his father before him had—Marques' father had built an immense underground survivalist shelter, equipping it with all the tools, supplies, and aid kits he might one day need.

When his father was alive, he was the leading bomb shelter builder and contractor. He helped build or create more than two thousand shelters in four countries. And of most of those, Marques himself had helped in the design and construction.

He and his father had been fluent in six languages, which helped them immensely with their contracts in other countries. And just about all the money they made from building their shelters, they used to build their own and improve upon them.

His father had died nearly eight years ago, and Marques, now fifty-six, had taken over the entire bunker business. His shelter could now house—with food, water, and air, let alone other necessities—over two thousand people for a couple of years if need be.

The only problem Marques now had was one he had not believed possible: the loss of total power. He had planned for it to a certain degree. With today's advancement in technology, he had bought all the latest gear in stealth technology that any of the bunkers he had built had wanted installed. But he knew it was still possible that an enemy might be able to find his compound, using some kind of device that could detect energy use. So he had made plans designed around being unable to use technology for a certain amount of time.

But he had not planned for something on this scale. His backup generators had all exploded. No batteries worked anymore. He had absolutely no power. Gas seemed to explode with any heat or fire. And while he had plenty of candles for light, lighting them was a chore in and of itself.

He was lucky when the meteors fell because his government had informed him it was coming. He had been able to choose a thousand or so people he had wanted in his shelter, over half of whom were women and children, and those of the two hundred and fifty men whom he trusted the most. All of them were militants he had grown up around, and each knew how to fight, having pledged to him their loyalty in return for sparing them and their families. With these men, he had plans to make an army strong enough to rule all of America.

But he had made another mistake, too. Two days ago, one of his main men had challenged him for control, not liking Marques' plan. And of course, he had acted as he was used to. He had pulled his pistol, put it to the insubordinate's head, and pulled the trigger.

It had all happened in the blink of an eye, faster than a normal man could react. Only nothing had happened. No shot, no head exploding. Nothing. So he had repeatedly pulled the trigger, only to get the same result.

Dismayed and seeing the other men finally drawing their pistols, Marques had pulled his machete and ended it that way—a bloody massacre that left all of his men trembling in fear of him.

After that, it had taken some research to know that he had taken a significant blow. Gunpowder was essential in all of his plans, calculations, and simulations. Over the years, he had collected hundreds of thousands of guns, grenades, missiles, road and off-road vehicles, boats, and planes. All of it was now useless. His modern technology—phones and communication networks—were all just worthless hunks of junk now. He had spent millions upon millions on now-meaningless stuff. He knew he could find a way to use some things like gas, but it was so volatile now that using it for anything would be tricky.

So now he had to sit and recalculate and simulate his plans. The loss of firepower changed everything. For the last two days, he had been studying. During this time, his government's hidden shelter was ripe for the taking. It was only two miles to the east of his own, and he had already sent three of his men—equipped with survival gear, masks, guns, and machetes—to his government's shelter with a message from him, and he had just barely received word that his men had returned and were being escorted to him.

For this, all of his plans relied on surprise. If his government did not know their guns did not—and would not—work for them, then he would be able to capture their whole shelter with relative ease and add it and its supplies to his own. But with it, time was of the essence. The longer it took him, the more likely it was for someone to find out the same truth as he had. Then, the surprise would be a lot harder to obtain. If his men brought him back good news, he would send his troops tonight.

He watched with eyes like a predator as the door to his office slid open. It was so heavy, being of thick protective metal, that the sound of it sliding open on its tracks was almost like rolling thunder—a door he could easily lock from the inside, and with no more electricity, no one could get it open again.

His office, though, was sparse and devoid of too much stuff of personal value. He had stripped the room of anything electronic that no longer worked. Now it was full of atlases, books, and maps. Each wall now had a full-scale map plastered to it. They were marked with red circles and green writing. Each circle was a bomb shelter he had a hand in building, with or without his father. Some were marked in purple—those were ones he had nothing to do with but had found where they were hidden. The green writing was each shelter's logistics: how many people it held, how it was defended, and its weaknesses. All the stuff he had studied for years.

Most of the shelters had no relevance to his plans; some were so far out of his way that they made no sense to go after. But it was the limit of his accumulated knowledge. Now that every computer databank in the world was gone, this was the only record of his business and plans.

The other maps he had scattered around on desks were all local maps showing him all the areas of business that he needed to raid. For some of them, he had already sent men to raid; for others, he would have to wait. But so far, he had met no resistance on any of his raids. Everything was like a ghost town. Few people were still alive, and of them, they were sick.

Four heavily armed men came walking into his office. The least impressive-looking one left, shutting the door behind him at a nod from Marques.

Ringo was the most impressive of the three. He smiled with silver teeth at Marques, and Marques nodded for the man to tell him how it went.

"It went just as you suspected, Jefe. The government types were thrilled to see us alive and hear any communication. They have been in the dark since the storm. Not one has ventured outside. They all hope the power will be restored and have no inkling that their guns no longer work. But I am not sure for how long, Jefe. I believe we continue with the plan before they get wise to their true situation," Ringo told him, continuing to grin at the government's misfortune.

The other two nodded their agreement with Ringo's assessment. Marques leaned back with a confident smile.

"Good, good. Give the signal, then," he told Ringo before staring at the other two.

They both were guerrilla warfare commanders.

"Both of you, go back to their shelter and tell them you have an important message from me on restoring their power. I want you both inside before we strike so you can get in close with their commanders. After you have been inside for twenty minutes, strike. That will give us enough time to breach all the main areas and force their surrender. Don't kill those you don't have to, but none of their commanders can survive. We don't want anyone rebelling."

Just then, he was interrupted by the thunderous sound of his office door sliding open, and Marques stared in anger at the interruption as a young soldier entered, looking excited.

"El Jefe," the young soldier announced as he entered. "One of the scouts just returned with something so weird that you must see it." He began, then faded off as he saw Marques' face.

Marques raised a hand for silence that shut the young soldier's mouth. Then he turned back to Ringo, who looked amused.

"You all have your orders—see to them. Return when they are complete," he told them in the way of a dismissal.

Ringo nodded, looking serious, and the other two followed him out of the office.

Then Marques turned his whole, angry nature upon the young man who had rudely interrupted him. The young soldier went pale.

"The next time you show ignorance of your commands, it will be your head. Do not interrupt me when my commanders are in here," he threatened his young aide.

With a frightened look, the young soldier gulped.

"Yes, Jefe," he replied in a shaking voice.

Marques gave the boy a second to let it sink in, then gave him a deadpan look.

"Now what was so important that you had to interrupt my meeting with my commanders?" he demanded.

The young soldier blanched, then stuttered before he could control his fear.

"Jefe, a scout returned with an object that he swears fell out of the sky when the meteors fell. I have seen it, Jefe. It glows brightly and gives off heat, but it is so hot no one can touch it without protection."

Marques looked confused.

"A meteor?" he sneered. "You interrupted me for a stinking meteor?" he demanded angrily.

The young soldier's fear got the best of him again, and he began to tremble under his leader's look.

"Jefe. You must—" he started before he wisely changed the words he was about to say, choosing them more carefully as he continued.

"Let this meteor, if that is what it is, be brought to you, Jefe, so you can see it. It must be some kind of alien device. Maybe you see how it has power when nothing else works. I swear to you on my mother's grave, El Jefe, you have never seen anything like this."

Surprised by what he was hearing, Marques could not deny that he was slightly intrigued. Maybe it was an alien device. If he had a power source, he could figure it out. Perhaps everything he had would not be so useless after all. But he seriously doubted it.

"Okay, bring me this 'meteor' and the scout who found it," he told his aide curiously.

He watched his young aide, Dwain, leave his office, then return a minute later with one of his scouts. The scout was pushing a wheelbarrow that instantly lit up the office more than all of his candles did.

The thing in the wheelbarrow instantly stole Marques' attention. It produced light and heat, making his office quite cozy, bringing on instant sweat.

The scout who had brought it wore thick, sheet-metal gloves. They were singed and lightly smoking, and smoked even more as he picked up the glowing green object. The scout was covered in fine ash, and his face looked stark white from the protection of his mask, compared to the black ash that coated the rest of him.

When the scout picked up the glowing meteor, Marques did not fail to notice the scout's wince in pain as the thing burned him through the thick gloves.

Intrigued, Marques motioned his aide out of the office and got up, walking around his desk, thinking there had to be a way to use this to help him with his plans. He walked to his scout—a soldier he trusted named Julio.

The object Julio held was almost green with small silver strips, and to both of their amazement, it began to vibrate as Marques approached it. Curious about why it did so, he put out his hand to feel the fierce heat coming off the object. By the sizzle of the gloves, Marques could tell it was getting even hotter as he got closer, and he could only take that in one way: it was a warning for him to stay back. And that intrigued him more than it brought fear.

Julio looked positively scared as the thing vibrated fiercely in his hands. Marques could see he was straining to hold it away from himself without dropping it, even though it was obviously burning his hands through the thick protective gloves.

Seeing Julio's look was all the answer he needed to know that he was being warned to stay back.

"I take it this thing has not acted like this before?" he asked curiously.

His eyes wide and fearful, Julio shook his head. "Never!" he replied to Marques, wanting to drop the meteor so he could blow on his hands.

"Hmm," Marques mused as he moved closer, his hand hovering above it, feeling the now blistering heat that threatened should he touch it.

"Either the thing positively hates me or it is pleased to meet me," he told Julio with amusement as he studied the green and silver metallic object. "And seeing it vibrate like that, I will bet it is not the second."

To see what would happen, he took a couple of steps back, and like he had thought, the thing began to stop vibrating. Seeing it, he wondered if that meant this thing—whatever it was—was sentient and alive.

"Interesting," he mumbled as he studied it some more. "I don't think this is some kind of alien technology," he told Julio after a second. "If it is, then why would it act differently to me than it does to you?"

He frowned thoughtfully before continuing with his thoughts.

"No, its actions can only be based upon a discernible threat. Obviously, it doesn't feel threatened by you. But when I approach it, it feels threatened by me for some reason, so it warns me as I approach it."

"That is an animalistic behavioral trait—much the same thing a rattlesnake will do by rattling its tail when it feels threatened—to give you a warning not to threaten it, or it will defend itself with a strike. I think this thing is giving me a warning in much the same way as a snake would."

While he talked, he moved closer to the green, glowing metallic object. It instantly began to vibrate fiercely again. He leaned his head a little closer to it.

"But I do not take well to threats or warnings. A rattlesnake may be poisonous if it bites you, but all the same, it can only bite you if you do not kill it first," he said, sticking his face even closer to it than before, his voice turning deadly. "Don't you threaten me, or I will kill you like I have hundreds of snakes," he threatened.

As if it had heard and understood his words or tone, the metallic object stopped vibrating, and seeing it, Marques looked up at Julio with a smile.

"Not only can it discern a threat—it can understand what we are saying," Marques began.

Just then, Marques gasped in alarm and a little fear (though he would never admit it to anyone), for the whole top of the green, glowing object exploded outward. Something that Julio thought at first was a green and silver metallic snake launched itself out of the meteor—right at Marques' face—with its sharp, crystal-like teeth glistening as they tried to bite him.

Honestly, Marques had expected something to happen—just not what did. So he was not caught flat-footed; his hands streaked through the air as he jumped back. One hand closed around the hot, scaly neck of the creature that had launched itself at him, and the other caught the hard tail.

All he saw for a second were long, crystal teeth and claws trying to rip into his flesh, but unable to do so because Marques had caught it perfectly. Its teeth snapped while its four clawed legs raked the air ineffectively as he held it aloft so he could study it with a look of awe and amazement.

The creature was much heavier than he thought it should be for its size. It was almost three feet long, head to tail, stretching and growing a little as he held it away from him. It was the perfect replica of a dragon. It had one small nub of a crystal horn over each of its silver eyes and a row of smaller crystal horns that ran from its snout down the back of its head, and he could feel others down its spine and tail.

Its teeth looked lethal and were wickedly sharp crystals. Its skin was covered in shiny green scales, which were metallic silver under its neck and belly. Each of its four legs had four sharp crystal claws, and to his surprise, under each leg was a small crystal spur. Seeing them, he knew they were poisonous, and he was suddenly glad he had caught the creature as he had, because it was surely trying to use everything in its deadly arsenal to attack him.

The spurs reminded him of a platypus' spurs on their hind legs. And on the creature's sides, tucked close to its body, were two light metallic green wings with crystal nubs along the ends.

"So…" Marques drawled. "You have teeth and want to bite," he told it humorously. "So do I," he jested with a laugh.

Hearing him speak, the dragon viciously snapped its jaws and turned its head to face Marques fully. When it opened its mouth again, it spat sparks toward his face.

The sparks did not reach too far—at least not far enough to touch Marques. But seeing them coming toward his face almost made him drop the dragon. His eyes widened, and he tightened his grip on it instinctively, knowing that if it got free without them coming to an understanding, then in all likelihood, it would kill him. It was faster than any snake, and he had no gun to shoot it.

Seeing that the sparks could not reach him, he relaxed a little bit and gave the dragon one of his winning smiles.

"You're as vicious as I am," he told it in a flattering and approving tone, and looked it over in an admiring way as he turned it in his hands to face him fully, being careful not to let it catch him with its claws or poisonous spurs.

He spoke in a calm, commanding voice when he had its full attention.

"It's obvious that you feel threatened by me—that you feel I am a threat. Means we both have much in common. We are both vicious creatures that want what we want when we want it. But I will tell you this much, and I know you can understand me—you have already proven that. You don't threaten me or what I want, and I won't threaten you.

"You are very young in a world as harsh as I am, and it will kill you long before you can grow old enough to become its top predator like I am. But with my help, I will ensure you live to get old. I feel that you and I can become good companions. But first, both of us must have trust. I will keep you alive, and you will help me with what I need help doing."

Marques looked the dragon in the eyes and slowly loosened his hold. The dragon instantly clenched onto the arm holding its neck with all four feet of its claws. Once it had a good grip, Marques let go of its neck. It never took its eyes off Marques' own as the dragon grabbed onto him.

Marques broke the tension by ignoring the dragon and turning to the wide-eyed and pale scout.

"Have you ever seen anything so majestic?" he asked in an awe-filled voice.

Julio, who had not dared to move since the meteor he had found had exploded in his leader's face, now looked nervously from the mythical creature to his leader. His awe of his leader's unfearful handling of the dragon was plain in his voice when he answered.

"No, I have never seen anything like it, El Jefe," he replied.

"How did you find it?" Marques asked curiously as he felt the dragon moving around on his arm. He looked down at it to see it looking around the room. When it heard Julio's voice, it turned its head sharply and began to growl in a surprisingly deep rumble for how small the dragon was.

Seeing it threaten Julio, Marques snapped his fingers in front of the dragon's face to distract and get its attention. The dragon flinched, then glared angrily at him.

Feeling the menacing focus directed toward him made Marques smile at the dragon patiently.

The green and silver dragon snapped its teeth angrily but stopped its growling rumble and glared at Julio instead.

Julio ignored its look. "Jefe, it was easy enough to find with it glowing as it was. I found it close to a mile from Diara's place," he explained helpfully.

Marques smiled with a sudden idea.

"Alright, I want all of our scouts informed. Suppose they see anything unusual about any meteor. In that case, they are to notify me immediately, and if it is another of these egg things, they are to bring it to me without touching it," he told the scout in dismissal.

When the scout had left, shutting the door, he moved to his seat, staring down at the magnificent but very deadly dragon, envisioning the possibilities of a world without technology and guns being ruled by him with a giant, ferocious dragon by his side.

Not just one, he thought, shifting through his plans. There must be more than this one. Without guns, bombs, and planes, who could stop him with a full-grown dragon—let alone an army of them?

Catching his thoughts, the dragon clenched onto his arm and glared at him.

Seeing it made Marques laugh.

"Glare! That is your name. For your look does not just threaten—it promises death."

To his surprise, the dragon began to rumble—but this time not in a threatening way. This time, he was shocked to realize it was purring with contentment.

CHAPTER FOUR

Day Seven

Location: Pantier's Residence

The seventh day after the meteor storm, Derek felt much better; his eyes and chest no longer burned, and his coughing had stopped altogether. The Pantiers, on the other hand, were another matter. Both of them were so sick they could hardly get out of bed. So, luckily for Derek, while he was taking care of them, the two men who had attacked them days ago had never returned to try again.

The weather had continued to grow even colder. The sky remained pitch-black and full of soot and ash that seemed as if it would never settle. Walking outside was like walking through a thick, black, nasty fog that clung to you, getting everywhere, yet walking in it no longer bothered Derek. He kept the nose cleaners in and no longer had any trouble breathing. The air pressure was still very high, pushing in on his lungs, but it was as if his lungs had grown strong over the last few days, so he no longer noticed it.

During that time, he had rarely, if ever, been without the glowing meteor. And if either of the Pantiers thought it strange, they did not seem to notice it. They stayed near it for its light and warmth, but never once did they try to touch it after they saw it burn the man who had attacked them. They seemed to be almost as reverent with it as he was.

Right now, it was one of the rare times he was not holding the glowing meteor or talking to it, which he had also taken to doing a lot lately. Instead, the meteor was lying on the ground where he had kicked away a foot or so of ash. It was not too far from where he was, so he could still feel its warmth while he chopped up a small tree for wood. The tree had fallen during the meteor storm and was too close to the building to leave it be, so Herb had him chop it into firewood.

The exertion made his breathing a little harder, but Herb told him it would help strengthen his lungs so he could breathe the air while exercising without passing out from a lack of air to his brain—or so that was Herb's excuse.

Really, he thought, it was just an excuse to get him cutting firewood to burn. Not that he minded. They had plenty of firewood, but more wouldn't hurt. And to spice it up, Herb had told him that when he was done, he would start teaching Derek how to use a sword, which he was dying to learn.

He knew how to use a staff; it had been his preferred weapon in his studies of Jeet Kune Do. But his mother had never let him learn any other weapons, telling his teacher to teach him only practical skills he could use in self-defense. She had never understood the disciplined purpose behind learning the art of the sword. To her, Derek would never be in an encounter in his life where he would have and need a sword to defend himself. It was unrealistic to her, so she ensured that Derek was taught only practical things for daily life. Most of his studies focused on hand-to-hand disarming techniques.

Motivated to learn the sword now, he sent the axe sailing through the air to thunk and slice solidly into the tree. Over and over, the axe cut deep until his shoulders, back, and hamstrings were all on fire. It did not take him long to finish what he had started a couple of days ago.

Soon, all the trees were cut into two-foot squares that could be cut into four pieces, then stacked with the rest of the firewood to dry.

After a while, sweating pretty profusely, he forced himself to take a break. He picked up the meteor and held it, leaning back against a tree.

By now, he knew it was special, and he had no doubt it was alive. The mark on his chest was testimony to that. He had been careful to keep it hidden from the Pantiers. He did not understand it and was sure they would not either. The meteor's glow had not diminished, nor had the heat it gave off. And if he held the meteor still for a long time, now and then, it would feel like it had shifted slightly. The funniest thing he had noticed about it was that if he lightly ran his fingers over the top of the meteor, it would vibrate softly as if it enjoyed the feel of him doing so.

Another weird thing about it was how it kept him warm even when he was far away. No matter how far he got from it, he no longer felt cold. And sometimes, if he were away from it for too long, he would feel a weird need in himself to return to it until the need got unbearable, and he would have to go pick it up and feel its soft vibrations until the need went away.

Now, as he stared at it, he noticed something new. The silver had turned to gold at the bottom of the meteor, where the silver started swirling around it. Surprised, he stared at it, wondering what it meant, until he heard Herb call for him from the back door, seeing if he was ready to start his sword practice.

He almost felt too tired to want to practice. The way his shoulders were aching, he doubted he could even hold a sword up. That thought left him quickly enough, though, and he smiled, getting excited again. He did not care how tired he was or how tired he got; he would be able to learn how to use a sword!

The meteor must have somehow felt his excitement because it suddenly got brighter, lighting the way as he raced back to the house.

He took the meteor with him down the stairs to the basement door and shook off as much of the ash as he could before opening the door and quickly closing it behind him. Inside, the meteor brought instant light to the candle-lit room. He found Herb waiting for him as he shook the rest of the ash onto a garbage bag that was taped to the floor just inside the door. Herb, he noticed, looked pale and sickly as he stood next to a candle on a shelf, and his excitement turned at once into concern.

"Herb, are you okay? You don't look well; we can wait until you get better," Derek told him firmly in concern.

Herb gave him a half-smile and waved a hand as if to bat away Derek's concern. "Bahh, rubbish boy. I'm fine. Besides, I won't be the one holding the sword this time," Herb explained.

Derek nodded and fixed the garbage bag so no ash would get tracked in. Then he looked around the basement. Herb had cleared away a large area. A large circle was drawn in red tape within the room, and all around it, spaced evenly, were candles to give enough light to see. The floor itself was cement, and all the walls were plain and bare.

Herb took a seat on a desk to the side of the doorway; sitting next to him were three very different types of swords. One was a military saber Derek had seen him wield when the men had attacked. The second was a rapier, and the third was a katana. Seeing that the old man was waiting for him, Derek placed the meteor on the desk next to Herb to keep him warm. As he did, Herb caught his eyes.

"We will start today with the saber. It takes less finesse than the rapier and less overall mastery than the katana blade," Herb informed him, then bade him pick up the saber.

For the next couple of hours, Herb taught Derek how to correctly hold the saber and draw it. Once Derek's blisters began to pop, Herb called a break for the day, telling him that from now on, he was to keep the saber at his waist so it was close to hand whenever he needed it. And so he kept it close while he slept. He also made Derek promise to keep practicing drawing the sword whenever he found time, so it would come to his hand swiftly and without hesitation whenever he needed it.

That night, Derek spent again trying to nurse both of the Pantiers back into good health. He made them soup and kept the fire going so they would stay nice and warm. Emma had taken a turn for the worse after dinner. While Herb did another round of checking the house and store, making sure the building was locked and secure again, even though Derek had just done it, Derek sat by Emma, holding the meteor in his hands, running his fingers over the silver stripes right where they were turning gold.

"Em," he said after a while of thinking about what the gold might mean. "What do you think this means?" he asked, showing her where the silver was turning to gold.

"What's that, dear?" she asked, lost in thought, and turned to look at him.

"This on the... heater. See where this silver streak is? It is starting to turn gold. I noticed it for the first time this morning, just after I started chopping wood," he told her, showing her what he was talking about again.

"I don't know, hun. I'm no good with all these new gadgets that keep getting invented," she told him, giving him a serious look before continuing. "I've been meaning to talk to you about that thing. I ain't asking you to talk about anything you don't want to. What's your business is your business. But both Herb and I are expecting that ain't no heater. Though it has kept us nice and warm."

Derek frowned, feeling his heart speed up at the unexpected way the conversation had turned. And after a second, he nodded. "I was not meaning to lie to you and Herb. Just when you asked me, I had just been attacked for it. And, well, it kept me alive and warm, so I was not trying to lose it." He paused a second, feeling her eyes on him. He kept his eyes on the meteor, frowning down at it before continuing. "The truth is that on the night of the meteor storm, they fell around where I was trying to hide on the side of the mountain. Sometime that night, a huge meteor fell right in front of me, creating a big crater. I had been freezing cold, and for some reason, I was drawn toward the crater. It was like I could feel heat that way, and looking, I could see a faint light coming from the crater. When I got there, I watched as the meteor, the light was coming from, slowly dissolved in the heat until it left this. At first, I thought it was some kind of metal device. But over the last few days, I have come to know that it is not. I believe it is alive or is holding something that is alive in it," he explained to her.

"Or it is an egg of some kind," Herb volunteered as he came walking into the room. "Think about it; it kind of makes sense. The heat it gives off will keep it alive and warm while it is in space. And the light coming from it lets us know it's alive, or lets whatever it was that laid the egg know it's alive. For we know by now that it can think and protect itself. We have seen it when it burned the man who tried to steal it from you. Yet you yourself can touch it without being burned. And if it can think that much while in its egg, it must be pretty darn smart as an adult," Herb mused, studying the egg.

Derek looked down at it himself. Remembering the feel of it burning him made him touch his chest. The spot where he had been burned by it felt hot through his shirt. He ran his fingers lightly over the top of the egg, and for the first time in front of the Pantiers, the egg began to softly vibrate in his arms.

Seeing it made Emma smile, the first smile he had seen her smile in a couple of days. "Whatever it is, it likes you," she told Derek in an amused voice.

That same night, Derek had a horrible nightmare, and though he slept holding the egg to his chest, he suddenly felt a piercing cold surround his entire body.

In his dream, he found himself in pitch-black, fleeing for his life from the biggest human he had ever seen. He did not dare take the time to look over his shoulder to see if he was outrunning the giant human, for he knew if he hesitated at all, it meant certain death. For the giant human...

(*Titan!*)

...carried a very dangerous spear, which was ready to launch at him like a javelin. Instead, he picked up speed, flying faster and higher into the air, hoping to get far enough away with the eggs—all that were left of their kind.

Before he could get too far away, though, a pain ripped through him as the spear, having been launched with the full fierce strength of the Titan, slammed into, then through his hind leg, then up and across his stomach, slicing a huge, wide hole across it before the spear flew past and disappeared, falling back into the atmosphere as he fled with all his remaining strength.

Day Eight

Derek awoke with a start and realized he was no longer cold. In fact, with the egg to his chest, he felt hot. He was lying on his back, his mind now wide awake, and the egg was vibrating softly as he looked at it, pushing the stark terror of the nightmare from his mind.

He knew it was no dream now. It had been too real; the terror of the... Titan had been too real, and feeling the egg vibrating, he knew the dream had come from it. The terror he felt from the nightmare right now was coming from the egg. Even sleeping, he had felt the egg vibrating and had held it close, trying to comfort it. Looking at it now made him absently rub his chest where the egg had first touched, leaving its mark on him.

The dream was hard to believe. Dragon eggs, here on Earth? And one... what, full-grown female dragon? If it was still alive—something of which he truly doubted after seeing its injury caused by the spear—where had the fight taken place? In space? No, he remembered the female dragon leaving the atmosphere of some planet as it fled the Titan. And he did not think it could have survived in space.

The eggs, though, were a different matter. They were sealed solid to protect the unborn, and it seemed they survived space.

Then he stopped his train of thought. How had they survived space for so long? There was no such planet in their solar system that was capable of sustaining life, let alone complex life. And yet, he did not really believe the eggs had been in space for thousands to millions of years just to make it to Earth from another solar system in this galaxy or the next. Wouldn't they have hatched in space and died there?

A sudden cold chill pierced his mind. The cold was not painful. It felt cleansing and refreshing, like cold water when you're very hot. And with the feel came a thought of something he had learned in school: space is a vacuum.

And he understood what was being told to him. The eggs had acted like stasis while they were in space, preserving the unborn until they finally left the vacuum of space and entered a hospitable environment. Had the eggs landed on any other planet, they would have remained dormant, not allowing the hatchlings to hatch.

The cold feeling left his mind, and the egg stopped vibrating as Derek noticed something wrong. He had heard a noise that shouldn't be there.

He slowly got out of his makeshift bed, which he had made in the front room, hidden from the windows, and covered the egg with a blanket, then another, so he could hide the light coming from it. Then he placed it against the wall in the corner of the room, out of the way so no one accidentally bumped into it.

Then, as quietly as he could, he pulled his sword. The noise had come from the basement door. So, remembering the last bit of trickery the two men had used, he hurried up the stairs into the store where both of the Pantiers slept.

He quietly shook Herb awake, motioning that he was going downstairs, for Herb to stay upstairs in case it was a trap again. Then he was running swiftly and silently down the stairs. He checked all the windows just to be sure, and seeing nothing unusual, he again heard a noise downstairs, and he ran down to the basement and froze. It was pitch-black, and someone was in the basement already.

He started down the stairs even more slowly and saw a flickering light that had to come from a candle. That had to have been what he heard—the strike of flint to light the candle. Even so, his heart was thumping in his chest now. Remembering the last attack, he slowly inched his head around the corner of the stairs and was surprised.

There were four people coming in through the back door. The first was the tallest and was wearing the jacket of a park ranger. His face was wrapped tightly in cloth, and when he saw the garbage bag on the floor, he shook off all the ash and had the others do the same as they came in. The other three followed his example; they were kids about Derek's own age and were bundled up in clothes. One of them was holding the candle so they could all see.

In the Ranger's hand was a gun, and Derek could see it tremble from the cold as he motioned to the kids and shut the door nice and quietly.

"Stay here while I see if the owners are still here. There is smoke coming from their chimney, so I think they might still be alive. They know who I am, so they should let us stay here with them," the Ranger told them in a whisper that Derek could barely hear from so far away. He was kind of amazed that he did hear it.

Taking one last look at the kids, seeing them shivering and huddling together, he quietly retraced his steps up the stairs, feeling a little excited at seeing other people he wasn't threatened by. He was up into the kitchen and up the stairs before the Ranger even made it to the basement stairs.

"Herb," he said quietly. "We have visitors, a Ranger and three kids. The Ranger told the kids that he knew you. They all arrived on bikes."

Hearing Derek, Herb quickly came over to him, and Derek saw he was actually smiling in relief.

"Put up your sword, son. That should be Ranger Ellis. I'm glad to know he's still alive. We ain't seen him for nearly six weeks. You say he brought some young'uns, huh? Let's go see to them so we can let Em sleep this sickness off. She needs the rest," Herb said, motioning for him to lead the way.

They both walked downstairs to see the Ranger, who had now removed the cloth from his head, coming up the stairs from the basement. When he saw them, his eyes widened in surprise.

Herb, seeing it was indeed the Ranger he knew, put up his sword—his own military saber. Smiling in relief, Herb held out his hand. "It's nice seeing you again, Ellis."

Ellis quickly holstered his gun and shook Herb's hand with the same look of relief. "The same, Herb, the same. It's nice to see." The Ranger paused to cough a couple of times before continuing.

The cough sounded fake to Derek, so he bet it was a sign to the kids that everything was all right. "That there are other people still alive out here," the Ranger said as he gave Derek a studying look, seeing that he was someone he had never met before. "I see you got yourself a tag-along, too. I got three of my own. We were staying at the station when all the asteroids came flying in. They wiped everyone out. These youngsters and I are the only ones left. The rest all died of some kind of nasty sickness that's going around. Hell, it looks like you yourself got it, Herb."

Herb nodded and wiped a cold sweat from his brow. "I'm thinking I've about killed it; it's Emma I'm worrying about. She's come down with whatever it is, pretty hard."

Herb then gave Derek an appreciative look. "This here is Derek, and he's no tag-along. Without him, we would not have survived the last couple of days. He's a tough one; we've been attacked twice, and he saved us both times."

The Ranger stepped forward and shook Derek's hand with a grateful look, then he took in his looks and the small black eyes he still had from taking a bat to his nose. "Nice to meet you, Derek; seems I owe you for keeping the Pantiers alive. Man, it looks like you've been through hell and back," the Ranger jibed with a smile.

Derek smiled back, taking an instant liking to the Ranger. "You could say that. You can tell your tag-alongs to come upstairs. It's a lot warmer up here, and they look like they can use some heat."

Surprised to hear that Derek had seen them already, Ellis looked at Herb, who gave him a small smile.

"He misses very little," Herb assured the Ranger.

The Ranger turned back to the stairs. "You guys can go ahead and come on up here by the fire and introduce yourselves."

A second later, the three bundled-up kids came up the stairs. Two of them were twins who were either Derek's own age or a little older, though Derek was taller than all of them. All three had taken off the wraps around their heads, and just by their looks, he knew they were starving for some food, and all of them looked to be sick. They came up the stairs shivering, despite the warmth of the fireplace and the egg. He moved aside so they could go stand by the kitchen fireplace.

The two twins had brown hair and green eyes. One, he could tell easily, was a girl, having a pretty, if not beautiful, face with much longer hair and a delicate complexion. The other twin was slightly bigger than his sister, and the look he gave Derek was meant to intimidate him. The other kid was a boy, maybe a year younger than himself, and he was obviously the twins' younger brother with the same brown hair and green eyes. He met Derek's eyes with curiosity and looked at the sword he wore at his waist with wonder.

Once they were cozy by the fire, Derek went over, shook their hands, and introduced himself. "I'm Derek," he told them.

The boy twin tried to squeeze Derek's hand, but years of Jeet Kune Do had given Derek a killer grip, so much so that he barely even acknowledged that that's what the boy was trying to do. "My name's Nate Berger, this is my sis Nattalie, and my younger brother Nathan," he told Derek as he squeezed his hand.

Derek nodded and shook each of their hands.

"Derek, why don't you take them into the living room so they can get comfy by that fire? We are running a little low on water, but go use the rest to make some cocoa while I talk to the Ranger here. Then I will see to fixing something for them to eat while you go to the well and get some more water," Herb told him before turning back to the Ranger.

"We are good on water supplies. I was able to put a tent up over the well, not too long after the meteors kept falling. I still had to clean a lot of ash out before it was even close to drinkable, but it's clean now. I don't know, but I'm thinking that it's all this ash that has made us all sick. Well, besides Derek here, he hasn't gotten sick at all—just passed out once," Herb told the Ranger as Derek led the three into the living room.

The warmth they felt entering the room was really noticeable. Here, the fireplace was bigger; above it was the venting system that kept the whole building warm. As soon as they entered, Derek could feel the warmth of the egg, still a room away, as it sought him out.

"They are friends," he whispered to the egg in his mind, wondering if it would understand or not.

"Why are you wearing a sword?" Nate asked curiously as he let his brother and sister sit in front of the fireplace.

Derek ignored them for a second as he placed a pot on the pot holder over the fire, then picked up the last carton of water, pouring it into the pot so it would heat up. Then he turned back to them. "We have been attacked twice by two men who were desperate to take all of our stuff. Guns don't work anymore; nothing electronic does. So swords are probably the best defense we now have," he explained, fingering his sword hilt.

"Do you know how to use it?" Nathan asked in an awed voice.

Derek smiled. "Herb is teaching me; he's real good," he told him before disappearing into the kitchen to get some cups and the cocoa mix.

While he was busy doing so, he suddenly felt a flash of heat in his mind, then heard a cry of pain.

"Son of a bitch!" he heard Nate yell in pain.

Derek dropped the cups and ran into the living room, then to the front room where he slept. He found the room lit up brilliantly from the light of the egg, with Nate holding his hand to his chest, looking angry. The two blankets Derek had thrown over the egg were on the ground at Nate's feet, forgotten in his bewildered and awestruck look at the egg. Both Nathan and Nattalie were staring at it in wonder.

Derek rushed forward in concern, remembering the blistering he had received on his chest. "Are you hurt badly? You shouldn't touch that; it doesn't like being touched," he told Nate as he grabbed his hand to look at the burn. He was relieved to see that it was just a couple of blisters on Nate's fingers.

"Let me go!" Nate said angrily, snatching his hand out of Derek's grasp. "I was just trying to get some blankets for my brother and sister, and that thing burned me! What is it? I thought nothing electrical worked," he stated, glaring daggers at Derek.

Derek ignored him and bent over to pick up the egg. It instantly sent warmth through him and began to vibrate softly. To his surprise, it also gave off a slight rumbling sound, unlike anything Derek had ever heard before. He lightly touched the top, running his fingers over the velvet feel of it, and the rumbling grew even louder.

"It's not electronic," he told Nate after a second. "I owe it my life," he said seriously. "It's a meteor that fell during the storm, and without it, I would have died in the storm. It kept me warm for the three nights that it took me to reach this place. And it burnt one of the men who attacked and tried to take it from me."

"Really?" Nattalie said, talking for the first time. "You mean it's like some kind of alien artifact?" she asked curiously.

"How come it burned me and not you?" Nate demanded.

Derek smiled. "It did burn me," he replied as he picked up the blankets in one hand and gave one to Nathan and Nattalie.

Neither of them could take their curious eyes off the egg he was holding.

Derek walked back into the living room to check and see if the water was hot enough yet; he set the egg on the table and took the pot off the rack, seeing that it was hot.

The other three followed him, staying back from the egg, Nate still nursing his burned fingers. Derek motioned them all to the table. "Sit around the meteor, and it will keep you warm. Just think of it as a heater you can get close to—just don't touch it because it will burn you."

He left them to pick up the cups he had dropped, and when he returned, after assuring Herb that everything was all right, he found all of them sitting around the table, staring at the egg. He stirred in the cocoa mix and filled each of the cups, handing them all one.

"How did you find it? Are you sure it's a meteor?" Nattalie asked as she took a cup from him.

While they all drank, Derek told them his story—how he had been in the park when the storm came, watching his family's RV explode, hiding in the lee of the mountain, and the grueling task of following the road.

While he talked, the Ranger and Herb came in to listen. Mainly, the Ranger listened to his impressive story while Herb set about cooking a meal for everyone.

At first, he skimmed over finding the meteor, but when they kept asking him questions, he explained to them how he was going to freeze to death and how he had felt the warmth of the meteor attracting him to the big crater, how he had tied a sock over his face to keep from breathing too much of the ash, and then found the glowing meteor. He told them how he had used his shirt to help keep it from burning him and ran back to the mountain as the meteors began falling again. Then again, he told them of his three-day walk to reach here, only to be tricked by the two men who attacked him and tried to take the meteor from him. He had sliced one of their faces and the other's wrist before they ran off, after one had been burned by the meteor.

Nathan looked excited. "You said that it burned you too—where?" he asked curiously, interrupting his story.

Suddenly, Derek felt a little nervous and brushed his chest, feeling it hot beneath his shirt. He had not even shown the Pantiers where he had been burned by the egg. When he had first seen it in the light of the egg, he had been shocked, so he knew they would be too. Once the purple swelling had gone away, it had changed totally. But for some reason, he felt the egg wanted him to show them, and he began unbuttoning his shirt so he could show them where the egg had touched and burned him.

When everyone saw it, there was absolute silence.

"You're lying!" Nate accused angrily.

Where he had been burned stood a raised metallic mark. It was metallic red and gold in the shape of a magnificent dragon that covered most of his chest over his heart.

"Let me feel it," Nathan exclaimed in amazement. "It's a tattoo, huh?" he asked.

He let Nathan touch it.

"Wow!" he exclaimed wondrously. "It's hot and hard like heated metal."

"Let me see," Herb suddenly said with interest, stopping what he was doing.

He walked over and studied Derek's mark with a concerned look as he touched it and felt what the boy Nathan had described. He looked stunned.

"That sure isn't a tattoo. I have never seen anything like that. Why didn't you show this to us before?" Herb asked Derek in a confused voice.

Derek's face went red in embarrassment. "I... I guess I was just embarrassed to," Derek replied as Ellis came over to look at the mark himself.

Derek let the Ranger touch the mark and study it.

"It's real," Ellis said after a second. "Whatever it is, it is a part of his skin. And you say this meteor thing did this to you when you touched it?" he asked, looking at Derek seriously.

Derek nodded. "It did not look like this at all when it first happened, and it hurt like hell. I only touched it by accident, and it tore the skin from my whole chest, leaving a big, purple, bleeding wound. But afterwards, I was able to touch it without getting burned, and a few days later, it healed, and when the purple faded, this dragon mark was on my chest. I think it is what is in the egg."

"Egg?" Herb asked with a raised eyebrow.

"Yeah," Derek nodded. "I think the meteor is an egg."

"That's impossible!" Nate declared angrily. "He's obviously lying. There are no such things as dragons. I think the meteor storm messed with your head."

Derek felt a wave of anger flow over him and pushed it away; instead, he smiled at Nate. "We will see when it hatches. It will hatch when all the silver stripes turn gold," he announced smugly, though he had no idea how he knew that was true. He just knew with a certainty that when the silver turned gold, the egg would hatch.

Nattalie leaned over the table, looking closely at the meteor, seeing the silver stripes that were gold at the very bottom. "So you think it's going to hatch? What makes you so sure it's a dragon?" she asked curiously.

Herb went about finishing the meal he was making, and Derek rebuttoned his shirt before picking up the egg.

"I just know," he told her with a shrug, not about to tell them about the dream he had earlier, given to him by the egg.

The egg began vibrating the second he picked it up, and a second later came a deep rumble from it as he traced the silver and gold swirls with his fingers.

Everyone looked shocked at the sound, staring at the egg in his hands.

"I find it hard to believe," the Ranger said after a second, as Herb brought bowls for everyone sitting at the table.

Since there were only three chairs, Herb, Ellis, and Derek let the others sit in them.

"And was I not seeing all of this?" Ellis continued as he got a bowl. "For myself, I wouldn't believe it—dragons? How were they even in space? How can they live in space?" he asked incredulously.

"No," Derek said, shaking his head as he took a bite of the stew. "I don't think they can. The eggs could survive just because their shells protect them from the vacuum and cold in space. I think the eggs give off heat, so they will survive. While in space, I think the eggs kept the hatchlings in stasis so they would not hatch and die while in space."

"Eggs?" Herb asked again incredulously. He had only been jesting last night.

Derek felt his mind go cold. "About eighteen of them, depending on how many survived space," he replied before he could stop himself.

"How do you know this?" Ellis asked skeptically.

Derek just shrugged again, not sure how to explain it. "I don't know, I just do."

"How do we know you're not an alien like these dragons?" Nate demanded.

Next to him, Nattalie hit his arm, giving her twin a hard look.

"Ow," Nate complained, rubbing his arm. "Damn, sis, I was just kidding."

Quick to change the subject, Derek looked at Nattalie. "What happened with you guys when the meteors came?" he asked curiously.

Once everyone was eating, Herb handed Derek a sleeve of saltines to pass around.

Nattalie's eyes went wide at his question, and it looked like she did not want to talk about it. She was relieved when Nathan spoke up.

"Our van broke down before the meteor storm, so we and our parents were staying at a hotel while our dad waited to rent a car. Then the storm came and destroyed most of the town we were staying in," Nathan said as his eyes went red, and he wiped them with a forearm.

Nate continued for him. "Our parents and everyone else got really sick, not able to breathe," he said with a sigh. "The Ranger found us in the hotel… the whole town was dead like our parents, so when Ellis found us, he helped us survive and get over our own sickness, though it still lingers. Most of the town's supplies were ruined. We brought some things on our bikes, but we ran out of water quickly. So, Ellis said he had to gamble and found us the bikes. He told us he knew of a place here that might have all of the stuff we would need to survive. But none of us wanted to leave," he said, trying not to sniffle, though his eyes were watering. "Ellis, the Ranger, told us that if we did not leave, we would get sicker and die of disease caused by all the dead bodies, not to mention the lack of water and food. So we were forced to come here with him, and here we are."

No one said anything for a long while, just stared at their bowls and ate their stew.

After a moment, Derek finished his stew and left, taking a couple of empty water jugs so he could fill them up at the well. He put his nose cleaners in before going out the basement door. The bikes were leaning against the wall of the building.

All four of them were loaded with stuff. Two had extra baskets on the back that were also full. Derek could not imagine riding them all the way they had. Staying on the road in this darkness must have been a chore in itself. The bikes he saw were all connected by glow-in-the-dark rope, but still, he could barely see it. The journey from town must have been rougher than they had let on.

He walked around the back, then stopped in shock as he felt that cool feeling enter his mind again. A second later, he could hear the Ranger ask Herb a question, and it sounded as if he was standing right in the kitchen with them.

"What do you think of this boy? Is his story true?" the Ranger asked seriously.

A second later, Derek heard Herb's reply. "You can trust the boy with your life, Ellis. I have. His story is true; he is as stunned by all of this as any of us. He just has a good way of hiding it. As for this here egg? We will just have to wait and see what comes of it. There is no doubt in my mind that it is alien, and I've seen too many alien shows not to be wary. And if it is a threat to mankind, we will kill it. Yet I have watched the boy, and it seems genuinely attached to him. And Derek, well, he is one good-headed lad. We can trust him to know what is right."

Derek heard Ellis sigh in frustration. "What if the boy is too attached to this alien to see it for what it is, if it means us harm?" Ellis asked worriedly.

"Bah," Herb replied sternly. "If that egg meant any harm, it would have done so long before now. Instead, it has been a great help and a good distraction for a boy who just lost his parents in such a horrible fashion. Now, I'm not saying it ain't dangerous. If dragon myths hold true, then it is very dangerous indeed. But there are many dangerous things in this life; if it is more dangerous to those who mean us harm, then to us, it will make a good ally."

Surprised by the conversation, Derek thought of the dragon in its egg. "I will protect you," he said firmly. In his mind, a flare of warmth spread through his body, and he continued to the well, not even aware it was freezing out there until he had to take the pick and break the iced-over water.

While he worked, he half-listened to the other conversations around the egg, but none of them were really as interesting as the first one. When he returned, carrying the full jugs, everyone but Herb was trying consciously not to look at the egg in the center of the table, at least until it began to rumble at Derek's approach.

Derek put the water jugs by the wall and pointed to the egg. "I don't see how such a thing could be considered a beast," he stated, trying not to be angry about the way they talked about the dragon.

Herb laughed to break the tension that suddenly filled the room. "If it had a tail we could see, I would bet all I have that it is now wagging."

Nathan laughed, and Nattalie nodded with a small smile.

Derek went to the egg, brushing it with his fingers, and the egg quieted.

"I wonder what it looks like," Nattalie said, looking at Derek to see if he would know.

Derek just shrugged. "All I have is an idea. We won't know until it hatches."

Nate suddenly began to cough violently. When he stopped, Herb came and stood next to Derek, putting a hand on his shoulder. "Why don't you help them settle down and make some beds? They must be exhausted from the trip here. Now that they've eaten, I'm sure they'll want to rest," Herb said.

Derek nodded; it was just about the time he woke up anyway, and he wasn't tired, so he'd help them and go chop some wood. He led them into the living room and let the Ranger use his own bed in the front room so he could guard them should anyone break in.

That done, he picked up the egg and grabbed the axe that Herb had sharpened earlier so he could start his morning chores. Watching him made Herb smile.

"You didn't get much sleep. You can let the firewood go today," Herb told him kindly.

Derek hefted the axe to his shoulder, still conscious of the sword strapped to his belt. "I'm all right. There is no way I could get back to sleep if I tried," he said honestly.

Herb nodded. "When you're done, practice all of the techniques I showed you yesterday. I will be down later to watch you," he promised.

As Derek walked by the living room, Nathan sat up.

"Where are you going? Don't you need to sleep?" he asked curiously.

"I'm going to cut some trees down so we have plenty of firewood to keep us warm. As for sleeping, it's about five in the morning, which is when I usually wake up. I was sleeping when you guys came, so I'm not really too tired," Derek explained, repressing a yawn.

"How do you know what time it is?" Nate demanded, stressing the word *you*.

Derek just rolled his eyes. "I'm just guessing; I think the sun will rise in close to an hour if we could actually see it."

"I betcha it's like three in the morning," Nate said in a condescending tone of voice.

Derek shrugged. "Well, if it is, then it looks like I won't be getting too much rest today," he replied, then left before Nate could say anything else.

"I don't think he likes me too much," he told the egg as he made it outside and found a downed tree next to the house to start chopping up.

He set the egg down in a spot on the ground that he cleared of ash, then set to work in the egg's glowing red light. Halfway through with the tree, he wiped sweat from his face, leaving a black smear across his hand, and took a break. Hefting the axe, sighting a tree not too far away, he sent the axe flying end over end until it hit the tree, smacking into it with the flat of the blade.

"You know you'll ruin that axe like that," a voice told him from within the forest.

Derek jumped, his sword in hand, without having even remembered pulling it. He relaxed when he saw, to his relief, that it was just Ranger Ellis.

The Ranger was smiling as he studied Derek. "You got some good reflexes, I'll give you that," he said in an appraising tone as he walked closer to him.

Derek watched him curiously as he slid the saber back into its sheath at his waist. His heart began to slow down as he retrieved the axe from where it was buried under the ash. When he came back to the tree and the light of the egg, he found the Ranger studying him intently.

"Let me see the axe," the Ranger said, holding his hand out for it.

So Derek handed it to him and watched as Ellis studied it, hefting the axe, checking its balance, then its sharpness.

"This is not too good of an axe for throwing. It's too unbalanced and too large," the Ranger mused.

Then he turned, swiftly loosing the axe in an overhand throw that sent it smoothly through the air. It flew fourteen feet, only flipping end over end once before it sank hard into a tree, with a force that Derek was sure could take down a large animal.

He looked at the skinny Ranger with astonishment.

Ellis smiled at him, reaching behind his back and pulling out a hand axe. "Now this axe," Ellis told him with satisfaction, "is a perfect one for throwing."

He watched as the Ranger tossed it over his shoulder with a negligent toss. It sank head-high, almost twenty feet away, into a tree.

"Wow," was all he could say in amazement.

"I have had a lot of time on my hands being a Ranger. Learning how to throw axes, knives, rocks, and anything else solid has always been a hobby of mine to pass the time while I'm alone here in the park. I can easily kill a rabbit at thirty yards with a rock. I used rocks at first to better my aim. Then, years ago, a friend taught me the trick to throwing knives and axes. I once had to kill a mountain lion that had been terrorizing the park. I killed that one with a twenty-foot throw," Ellis bragged as he went to retrieve the axe.

"Can you teach me?" he asked the Ranger hopefully as he handed Derek back the long-handled axe.

Ellis gave him a thoughtful look, as if really assessing his potential. "I think we are going to need every skill we have to survive what's coming. I came out here today because I want you to convince Nate and Nathan to start learning the sword with you. It will give you competition, and it will teach them how to defend themselves. For I am sure the attacks you have had will not be the only ones, nor will they be the last. While I was bringing these guys here, I ran across tracks of at least three different groups of people on the roads leading to and from that town. Some of them were trails of fifteen or more people. I don't know why there are so many so close to the town. The town didn't hold that many people, and most of those died. So we will have to keep a good lookout. I don't think you will need to urge Nate too much; he seems to be jealous of you, so a couple of words from you should be all it will take to get him training. Well, a bit of envy never hurt anyone. So if you help them, I in return will teach you when there is free time," he promised.

Derek nodded. A little competition might help Nate out, but he suspected Nate would take it too far.

Hefting the axe again, Derek started back into the tree. After a second, he looked back over at Ellis, who was close to the egg, studying it.

"I don't know how good you are at hunting, but I saw some deer tracks in the ash a little deeper in the forest when I went to take a leak. I have never seen any during the last week until today. I think the deer are trying to eat the tree bark and leaves since ash covers just about everything else," Derek told him as he chopped back into the tree.

He saw the surprise and joy that lit Ellis' face, and in a second, the Ranger was taking off into the forest in the direction Derek had motioned towards.

Almost an hour later, Derek had finished and began stacking the wood into stacks when he suddenly felt cold chills run down his entire body. A second later, he felt a wave of warmth as if the day had brightened briefly for a second, then a sharp wind came howling through the forest. Then again, he felt the chills, and this time he recognized them. His heart began thumping frantically in his chest as he remembered the chills he had gotten just before each meteor storm.

"Ellis! Ellis! If you can hear me, you need to come back or..." Derek yelled as loud as he could. "Find shelter!" He then picked up the axe and the egg and ran to the basement, trying to hold back the panic that had seized him when he remembered facing the storm all by himself and the deaths of his parents. All of it came flooding back as he opened the basement door and ran inside. Not even a minute later, he heard the first screams of meteorites streaking from the sky.

* * *

Ellis, stalking a deer, suddenly froze as a voice pierced his mind and hearing.

"Ellis! Ellis! If you can hear me, you need to come back or find shelter!"

The voice was at once one that he recognized as the boy Derek's. At first, he had thought it was coming from close by, thinking the boy had somehow followed him in the darkness. But he realized, watching the deer, that they had not heard a thing. They did not move or startle at all, something that he knew would have sent any deer on edge or sent them running away. So he sat there watching them in confusion. That voice had been too loud not to have been heard.

But how? he wondered. He was at least a mile from the Pantiers, and there was no way he should be able to hear Derek from that far away, especially with how loud it was.

He knew he was too far away from the house to make it there quickly, and he knew Derek would not tell him something like that for no reason. So he began to look around for some kind of shelter and actually found a nice little gully just as the sky lit up with balls of fire that came raining down. And, like the deer, he scrammed, running toward the gully and got there just as the meteors began to hit the ground.

* * *

Once he was in the basement, Derek yelled again to get everyone's attention.

"Everyone to the basement! The meteors are falling!" he warned.

In seconds, he heard the commotion as everyone ran downstairs, just as he heard the piercing scream of meteorites falling outside.

CHAPTER FIVE

Day Nine; July 9th

Location: Central America.

It had all been going as he had planned it, all of them coming to fruition. The governmental takeover had gone flawlessly; all of the commanders who could not be trusted had been disposed of. His men had then raided all the supply businesses in the surrounding cities, taking anything they needed or wanted.

Survivors had begun trickling in, brought by his men, and depending on their use, he kept or sent them away to die. Each day, his army was growing, even though quite a lot had died from the sickness that seemed to hit everyone. Even he had not been immune to it. Though it did not really hit him badly, he had always been in good shape and rarely went outside now that the ash permeated everything.

So all in all, everything was falling into place just fine. Then all of his good luck turned to bad very drastically. He took his army of 380 men and launched an attack on the remaining governmental military bases. The attack had turned out just as he had planned it, and they were turning the bases into slaughterhouses when the meteor storm came again.

After the storm, only 215 of his men had returned to him. The military bases were in shambles, so he called a retreat.

He had returned to his office fuming at his turn of fortune. And what he arrived to find in his office turned him fuming with rage.

His office was shredded; maps, books, desk, floor, and walls (floor and walls solid stone!) were all shredded by Glare.

When he met the dragon's silver eyes, it screeched in rage at him for locking it in. He then watched as the furious green dragon launched itself from the desk towards him. Seeing that, his own anger snapped. A gloved hand snapped out, catching the dragon in the side of the head with its fist. The hit was so hard that the dragon was sent flying into a wall. Before it could get up, he had his thick leather boot pinning it down to the floor by its neck.

"Attack me?" he yelled furiously. "Your stupid damn meteors just destroyed my army! I kept you here to keep you safe so someone doesn't kill you. I feed you. Hell, had your stupid green snake hide been with me, you would probably be as dead as my army. And the thanks I get—" He growled, grinding his foot on the dragon's throat. "—Is you attacking me! Ruining my office! I should just kill you now and get it over with," he snapped furiously.

He felt a cold chill enter his mind, and a second later, a picture of a chain and collar appeared in his mind, along with the dragon's anger and terror of them.

"So?" Marques answered. "I put them on you for a reason. Why wouldn't I? You're too important to me to have you trying to escape or have someone else try to take you from me while I was away. I kept you here so you were safe, to keep you safe. So stop being so damn stubborn."

That said, he lifted his foot and carefully picked up the hurt and angry dragon.

"Trust me to know what needs to be done. I could not have had you trying to follow me. I cannot risk you getting hurt. One day, you will lead my army. Until then, you've got to live and grow into a fierce fighting machine. And I will keep you alive and teach you if you'll just do what I tell you without throwing a tantrum," he growled.

Then he set the dragon upon his ruined desk and grimaced as he looked at all of the damage Glare had caused. He knew he would have a hard time replacing all of the maps and information Glare had just unintentionally destroyed.

He looked down into his dragon's silver eyes. "Tell me I am wrong," he demanded. "Tell me you would not have followed me. Just tell me that, and I will apologize for putting the chain on you."

Glare snapped at him, and Marques laughed.

"Be angry all you like, but you know I am right all the same," he said as he took off one of his leather gloves and scratched the green dragon's head.

After a second, he took off the ruined collar and chain. The collar had heavy gouges and tears from Glare's claws, and the chain, what was left of it, had been snapped and chewed in half.

Surprised, he lifted the chain while studying it. He had thought for sure that it would hold the little dragon. But looking at the thick and heavy chain, he would bet Glare had snapped it as easily as if it were just a piece of annoying string, then chewed on it just because it was something to take its anger out on.

"How am I going to fix all of this damage that you have done here?" he asked in a wondering tone as he stared around again in dismay. He really had no choice; this office was no longer sound. He would have to move to another.

Frustrated, he picked up Glare. "You know you have really pissed me off this time. I am almost so furious with you that I don't want to give you the food that I so thoughtfully brought for you," he teased, the anger in his voice slowly fading away as he watched Glare react to his words. "Maybe I will just have to eat the juicy rabbit all by myself."

When he had first picked Glare up, the dragon was slumped dejectedly, beaten by Marques' anger. But when he mentioned food and a rabbit, all that dejection left the dragon, and in a second, he was perked up, looking once more like the very dangerous predator he was.

Glare crawled up his arm to sit perched on his shoulder, his tail wrapped around Marques' neck as Marques opened the door to his office and walked out.

"Clean this up and save the things that are salvageable. Have some of the women try to piece together the maps and find me another office," he told his aide as he walked by.

There was a candle every four feet in the passage of hallways and rooms he was walking through. Thankfully, candles were one thing he had plenty of, so he did not have to worry about living in the dark. The walls also had glow-in-the-dark markings along each passage. They didn't shed much light, but they kept people from getting lost. As he walked through each passage, men and women stepped aside for him, eyeing both Marques and his green dragon with both fear and respect.

Marques deemed it not to even notice any of them, but Glare lived up to his name, looking like he wanted to attack each and every one who even looked at him and Marques.

It made Marques smile. He had told the dragon over and over that these were his people and not to frighten them too much. So instead of Glare growling like he did at first every time he saw someone, now he just glared at them like he would have eaten them if they got too close.

Something that really would not have surprised Marques. In the days since the green dragon had hatched, Marques had come to realize the dragon had an unquenchable hunger for meat. And while he fed it constantly, as much as possible on the low meat rations they had, he could not seem to feed it enough. Still, with all the dragon did eat, it had not gained an inch of height or length. Instead, it got heavier, its scales hardening even more, its horns, claws, and teeth growing a little but gaining an even deadlier sharpness.

When the dragon's hunger continued to grow, he tried to feed it dried meat, which he had plenty of. But Glare would not touch it unless he soaked it first. And then he ate only because he had to. But rabbits, squirrels, rats, and cats, the dragon ate with abandon, killing them and swallowing them in halves, bones and all. And because of that, the women and children had taken to hiding all of their pets. Not that it helped; pets still came up missing.

Sometimes, he had to admit that it was his doing just to keep Glare satisfied; the last thing he needed was the report of a child going missing. But other times... the dragon somehow slinked away for minutes at a time without him even noticing. And he had a good eye. He wasn't sure how it did it until it came back looking very satisfied. It never took Glare more than a minute to eat, and sometimes it took the dragon less time to locate, hunt, and capture its prey.

Thankfully, no child had come up missing yet; he'd had a serious talk with Glare about it, but though the dragon seemed uninterested, he couldn't help but remember how it looked at people, not him. So, to make sure he avoided such an unpleasant thing, he made sure Glare was fed, even if he had to steal a kid's pet to do so. His men and their families were already scared to death of Glare; the last thing he needed was for them to really have a reason to be scared—another reason to keep Glare chained when he was not around to keep an eye on the sneaky dragon.

Marques took Glare down to a lower level in the shelter, where he could see some of his most trusted men gathered around a cage.

When Glare saw the cage and what was in it, he instantly came to attention upon Marques' shoulder. It was no soft furry rabbit; it was a huge, muscled raccoon. Marques could feel the dragon tense upon his shoulder with eagerness. He had never given Glare such big prey before, but he guessed it couldn't be worse than one of the tomcats Glare had taken to eating.

"Ten Cigars says it killed the raccoon within ten seconds," Marques told his men.

Three of his men instantly took that bet, happy to have something to bet about, and all of them knew Marques' cigars were the good ones. The men all gathered around the cage in a circle, and Glare jumped to the ground, his claws scarring the concrete as it landed, then kneading them against the cement in excitement.

One of the men instantly pulled the cage door open while another jabbed the raccoon with the end of a stick. The raccoon instantly burst out of the cage, trying to get away by running through the men's legs. And when that did not work, it jumped upon one of the men.

The man cursed, his eyes wide and face suddenly pale as he saw Glare pounce. The raccoon saw it at the same time, and it twisted in the air, its claws trying to hold Glare back as the dragon tackled it. They landed on the concrete, and Glare's wings spread out around the raccoon like a cocoon, holding it in place while Glare attacked it.

With Glare's wings all the way around the thicker raccoon, no one could see anything but a ball of green wings. A second later, the ball opened up, and they could all see Glare happily crunching on the dead raccoon's head, which they all saw was no longer attached to its body.

The three men all groaned at having lost. But otherwise, no one took their eyes off the green silver dragon as they watched it crush the raccoon's head and swallow it whole before moving to the body, gnawing and crunching its bones until it swallowed it whole too.

The silence was finally broken sometime later as men came running down the corridor, obviously looking for Marques with excitement on their ash-covered faces.

"Jefe! Scouts have returned, and they want to see you. They say it's something important, that they said you sent them to find," one of them said, out of breath as they entered the room.

Marques waited until Glare had finished swallowing the raccoon like the dragon was a snake. Then he looked up, excitement filling him. This could only mean they had found him another egg that had fallen in yesterday's meteor storm.

"Glare, come," he said quickly as he tried to decide whether or not to take the dragon. As the full dragon got to his feet and walked to him, he decided that he might as well take Glare, just to see its reaction.

Once the heavy Glare was on his shoulders, he was led to where the scouts were waiting for him. As soon as they saw him, they stood up, and one smiled at him, stepping forward.

"During this last storm, a huge meteor was sighted to have struck down west of here. We traced it down and found it two miles out, next to the ocean. It was that meteor that shook the ground so hard yesterday. When we got close to it, we saw it was larger than any we have seen fall so far; the crater it created was enormous. Most of the meteors melt or evaporate after they fall to Earth, but what is left of this one is not what we expected it to be," the man told Marques seriously, and his voice lowered as he looked at Glare sitting upon Marques' shoulders.

"What we found was a giant dragon—" When Glare heard that, its head perked up. "—we are not totally sure that it is dead. We did not dare get too close to it because of how big it actually is and because we saw movement from it. It hasn't got up, so it might be too hurt, but we didn't want to take any chances and decided to let you know so you can decide what to do," the man explained carefully, trying not to seem scared or unnerved by the sighting of the huge dragon.

Marques was already moving. "Take me to it," he told them over his shoulder. "Krevas, go get me the supplies that I will need. Bring me a crossbow. You will find me in my armory."

Marques left in a hurry. He could not believe his luck, especially after yesterday's devastating storm. A live dragon? Most likely, if it was still there, it was really hurt, and if so, it might be easy to capture or kill if he had to.

Once in his armory, he motioned for Glare to jump to the table. And once the green dragon was out of the way, he unlocked his secret safe. In it were two things no one even suspected he had. One was an air cartridge tranquilizer rifle. The second was an air pistol, pump, or cartridge. Neither were effective at great range, but at close range, they could be lethal. He had already proven it with the pistol. A headshot with it would kill. He did not want to waste the cartridges he did have, as they were practically irreplaceable now. So he had only used the pistol twice, once with the pump and once with the cartridge. Both worked fine.

The rifle was in a case that held quite a few different darts. He chose four of the most lethal. He loaded the rifle and put the other darts in a container meant for them and slipped them inside his jacket. He then grabbed an extra cartridge for both the rifle and pistol and put those in his pocket, too.

He strapped the pistol to his waist right next to his machete, then loaded the gun and put away some extra ammo. The crossbow would be just extra protection in case one or both air guns somehow broke—not really likely, but he was not going to take any chances. Both guns were at their maximum settings, which would use the cartridges fast, but it would ensure that what he shot at got hit with enough force to be effective.

Both of the guns had taken him some research to find, and it had been done with the help of a man already dead, so no one besides him knew about them. The rifle was the only one of its kind he had been able to find. He had found plenty of BB guns and rifles, which he had stashed away because, for right now, he did not trust anyone with them, and needful things brought you power over others. He had learned that at an early age. They would be worth a lot more than gold in the future.

He looked thoughtfully at Glare; it was time to test the dragon. "Light a couple more of those candles so I can see," he told Glare nonchalantly.

The green and silver dragon gave him an indignant look, then rumbled a complaining growl as he moved around to an unlit candle upon the table.

Glare opened his mouth, his crystal teeth glistering as he took a deep breath. The sparks swallowed the whole candle, turning it into a melted pile of wax before it took flame.

"Careful," Marques told Glare with a chuckle of amusement. He had never tried to get the dragon to light anything before. Yet it was obviously something Glare needed to learn, so he decided to teach it so the dragon could practice and get better at lighting things on fire.

The next three candles melted the exact same way, and as the dragon's anger began to become apparent, Marques started laughing, which made Glare all the more furious, and he roared a growl, melting yet another candle.

"Aim higher. Aim for a place just above the candle where you can see that little white string sticking out. That string is what needs the fire, not the entire candle itself," he explained, noting the dragon believed the whole candle needed to be set on fire.

The next candle lit easily under the shower of sparks unleashed above it. Seeing it light on fire excited Glare, and he gave a victorious roar, just as a soldier was coming in carrying the crossbow for Marques, causing the man to jump back out of the armory.

The roar surprised even Marques, who had shut and hidden his safe again. It reverberated in the room and made Glare's last roar sound wimpy.

He watched with a smile as the soldier who had jumped back, thinking he had angered the dragon, poked his head in the room to see if it was alright for him to enter. While Glare lit the other candles around the room, Marques laid the rifle on one of the desks and motioned for the soldier in the doorway to bring the crossbow in.

He gave the crossbow to Marques, who took it over to a large mirror hanging on the wall and looked at his reflection in the candlelight.

He was a big man, and the clothes he had on to stay warm made him look even bigger. His hair was short and black, matching his black eyes and standing out from his tan, sun-colored skin. All of his clothes were dark, and he gave off the air of a predator ready to take down prey. Looking at himself, he slung the crossbow and its quarrels over his shoulder, using the shoulder strap attached to both. It rested easily on his back. It was an old crank model, which made it a lot easier to lock in place, but still made it hell to reload.

Turning away, he snatched up his rifle, ignoring the confused look of the soldier who had brought him the crossbow, and motioned for Glare to get on his shoulder as the soldier handed him a ski mask and a filter mask.

He put them on and found the scouts waiting for him just outside the armory, along with twenty other men armed with similar crossbows. If they noticed anything weird about him carrying the rifle, none of them deemed it worth voicing.

* * *

It took them a little over two hours on foot across some pretty treacherous areas to reach the gigantic crater. It was almost a mile across, not to mention pretty deep. And when Marques finally got close enough to see what lay in the center of it, he caught his breath in surprise. Never in all of his thoughts did he believe it would be this big.

It was a dragon, alright, and it was a mountain in size. He could not see any movement, but he could see the wound. It was a giant slice that cratered across its stomach. It was hard to tell its color in the dark haze, but if he had to guess, it was red with a gold belly.

When Glare saw it, Marques felt the dragon tense for a long time. Glare was but an ant's eye to this one in comparison. The little green began to tremble upon his shoulder. Before Marques could stop it, Glare jumped off, launched into the haze, and let out a piercing, deep keening sound that Marques was surprised to hear with both his ears and his mind.

The sound was at once beautiful and terrible, and it invoked an immediate response from the mountain in front of them. Or so he thought at first. He saw the dragon's belly ripple and heard a second keening sound. This one was deeper, louder, and even more hypnotic, filling the dark sky with noise.

A twelve-foot dragon ripped out of the mountain's stomach a second later, black as night with golden horns, teeth, and claws. It was almost too dark to see, but it announced its presence by opening its mouth with a burst of fire that filled the darkness and showed off its terrible beauty—black scales glistering all along its head and back, and red scales shining beneath its throat and stomach.

The dragon shot like a bullet towards Glare, and though Glare was smaller, he rose into the air, sounding off what Marques could only guess was a battle cry, and shot at it, sending Marques' heart thumping in his chest with fear.

The black dragon heard the cry and gave off a sound that sounded to Marques like a chuckle, then it tackled the smaller green dragon.

Seeing all of his plans about to unravel, Marques signaled his men. Crossbows came up, sighting on the bigger dragon, as he aimed with the rifle. But to Marques's relief, the black dragon did not hurt the little one; he just tossed him through the air as it somersaulted in the air itself.

Glare let out another piercing keening cry like his first, and the black answered again with an even grander one that shook the air.

And that led Marques to understand what they were doing—sharing their grief over the death of the mountainous red dragon. Both the dragons tumbled in the air a couple more times, then the black one shot into the dark haze and flew off with incredible speed.

Marques was tempted to shoot it, but doubted he could pierce those black scales. Likely, all it would do was piss it off and likely get them all killed. Either way, as he watched it disappear, he knew he wanted it.

When Glare tried to follow after the bigger black one, Marques called out, stopping him.

"Glare, let it go its way, get back here," he demanded sternly.

Glare growled and, to Marques' relief, began to fly back to him. He stared at the dead dragon for a long time, making plans, the foremost of which was to capture the black dragon.

CHAPTER SIX

Day Eight

*Location: **Pantiers' residence.***

The meteor storm only lasted an hour, but the devastation it created was widespread. More meteors fell this time than in the first couple of days, and they sent the Earth trembling with each gigantic impact.

Still, when all was said and done, those in the Pantier residence were alive, if a little shaken by the close calls. The building remained intact, almost escaping the meteors' wrath. They were missing some shingles on the roof from a real close one that took out an entire section of the rain gutter, and Ellis was going to have to check it out to make sure the roof was still sound to live under.

Beyond that, only trees had been hit around the Pantiers. And the storm had laid the trees flat; almost one in every four had fallen to the meteors' onslaught. Most were burned, though thankfully, none of the fires had really spread, and all of them had died pretty quickly.

The storm brought a new wave of coughing and hard breathing to all of them but Derek, who seemed to weather the lack of oxygen just fine. It hit Emma hard, though, and they had to watch helplessly as she tried to choke down each breath.

Two hours after the storm ended, Ranger Ellis returned. He had to wait for all the fires to stop before he could return, and he did not mention hearing Derek's call to anyone but the strange boy. And all he said to him was, "Thanks for the heads-up."

Derek had looked at him in confusion with a silver-eyed glance before he nodded.

While everyone was sleeping, Derek was in the basement practicing drawing the saber from its sheath. The only other person awake was Ellis, who was double-checking the building again to ensure they had not missed anything on his earlier inspection, where he had determined the building was livable.

Not far from where Derek was practicing, the egg sat on the table, shedding light for him to see by. He practiced every move Herb had shown him and was at it for almost two hours before Herb walked into the basement and sat beside the egg to watch him, studying his form and balance.

"Remember what I told you about your grip," Herb reminded him sternly. "You're grasping the sword too hard with your thumb and index finger. Hold the sword firm with your pinky and ring finger."

Derek nodded and corrected his grip, drawing the sword one-handed into the two-handed grip.

After a second, Herb coughed and looked as if he was debating how to say something before he spoke up.

"We need to talk, Derek," Herb told him quietly.

Surprised, Derek sheathed the sword and turned to Herb, who looked pale and sick in the egg's light. In fact, he was seated closer to the egg than Derek had ever seen Herb get before—probably soaking in the egg's heat, Derek thought. *He looks cold.*

"What's wrong?" Derek asked with concern.

Herb waited until Derek got closer, then studied him intently in the red light of the egg, taking in everything about him. Since Derek had first come to them, he had thickened up. Normally, he would not think it was too weird; he was young, only fourteen, so he was still growing. But Derek had not just gained weight and muscle; the boy had also grown taller. And in only the short time he had known the boy, that was amazing. The most surprising change that had come over the boy was not normal, though. When he had first met Derek, his eyes had been sunken blue with an occasional silver shine that vanished the instant he saw it.

Now, looking at the boy in the light of the egg, his eyes were more grayish than blue, and the whites of his eyes were all silver. Had he not known the boy's age, by looking at him, he would have guessed he was sixteen or older. He was tall enough and broad enough. He would be surprised to learn that Derek had just turned fourteen, especially if he compared him to Nate, who was a year older than Derek, yet looked younger than him.

Derek's hair was blondish-brown and needed a cut. And as he looked at Herb, he pushed it out of the way of his eyes and gave Herb a questioning look.

It took Herb a second again to get to the point.

"The egg is changing you in ways that… are, I guess, incomprehensible," Herb began.

Derek gave him a puzzled look. "Changing me? What does that mean?" he asked in a shocked voice.

Herb smiled to lighten the mood that had just come over Derek; he did not want the boy thinking he was accusing the egg.

"What color are your eyes?" Herb asked curiously.

"Blue," Derek said instantly.

Herb held up a mirror.

Derek looked in the mirror, seeing his face in the egg's light. And when he saw his gray, silver eyes, he gave Herb a shocked look.

Herb nodded. "That is not the only thing, though it is easily noticeable. Since arriving here, you have put on a lot of muscle and are taller, too. I would not even mention it; the others won't have noticed since they arrived. But whether they know it now or not, they know what happened today. They just have not realized it yet.

Derek, you spoke to us all in our minds when you warned us about the meteors. I don't think they realize it because they could also hear your voice at the time. But Emma and me? There was no way either of us could have heard your warning. We were both sleeping upstairs in our beds—no way to hear your voice from down here in the basement. To us, you spoke in our minds. So I want to talk to you before it happens again, so you know what you can do and guard it against those you don't need to know, you can do it."

Derek listened to him in silence, shocked to realize what Herb was saying was true. Then he remembered the Ranger thanking him when he returned and realized there had been no way for the Ranger to hear him.

"The Ranger knows," Derek told him seriously, now a little worried. "I warned him right before the meteors came; he was too far away and could not have heard me—"

"Yeah, I heard you," the Ranger said, coming down the stairs and into the light of the egg. "Damned near startled me. I was chasing down the deer you saw tracks to when your voice told me to find shelter. I knew it had not been out loud because it did not startle the deer, and it should have. When I heard it in my head, it was loud enough to."

Ellis then walked in to study the egg. "I've never felt anything like it, no offense," he told Derek quickly. "Your warning helped me find shelter just in time. But how did you know?" he asked curiously.

"I felt a sudden chill as if the wind had changed. It grew warm for a second, and then I felt the fridge cold, which I had felt just before the first meteor shower. And I just knew they were coming again," Derek explained, a little uncomfortable under their glances.

Ellis shook his head. "I didn't feel any change in the air; there was no warmth or cold. Well, besides the freezing temperature, it is right now. The meteors just started streaking down out of the sky. I would have been caught flat-footed with nowhere to run if you had not sent that warning, though."

He then gave Derek a long, hard look. "But I think Herb is right about this. There are certain things that are best not to let other people know. We are entering a very touchy, troubling time, and troubled people do very desperate things when they can't understand something. In the last dark ages, people ganged up and killed all those they thought were different or possessed. The fewer who notice these things about you, the better it will be for you," Ellis warned seriously.

Derek nodded thoughtfully, then smiled as a thought came to him. "I think the strangeness about me will be overshadowed by the company I will keep," he told them seriously as he looked down at the egg.

As his eyes met it, the egg began vibrating as if in answer.

* * *

Day Nine; July 9th

The next day passed quickly. While the others all slept in, Derek kept chopping wood, only stopping when the Ranger stopped by to teach him a little about throwing a hand axe and the proper releasing technique. Ellis watched him practice in the light of the egg, but Derek could only make it stick in the tree once.

Before he left, Ellis gave Derek a small throwing dagger in a sheath, showing him how to strap it to the back of his belt so it would be hidden from sight, and told him to practice throwing it while no one was around. On the sheath was a small sharpening stone, which he also showed Derek how to use correctly, because throwing the knife would dull it a lot.

Once Ellis left, Derek again started back into the tree, chopping it into blocks to dry for firewood. He had been doing so for a while, lost in his thoughts about the egg, when he felt rather than saw people leaving the building from the basement. Surprised that he felt people coming, something he had not been aware he could do, he turned, looking through the darkness to see the three Bergers approaching the egg's light.

"Don't you rest?" Nathan queried curiously. "You got up early again and have been chopping, eww—" he spat, whipping off a chunk of ash that had floated to his face. "—Yuck. You've been out here for hours, like half the day," he continued in a muffled voice as he pulled his scarf over his mouth to stop the ash from getting in when he talked. All of them were wearing nose cleaners now.

Derek laughed, lifting the axe. "Are you saying you want to give me a break? You can cut some if you want."

Nathan dropped the scarf with a grin. "Sure," he replied, eagerly grabbing the heavy axe from Derek. "Whoa, this thing is heavy. How can you hold it for so long?" he asked curiously as he hefted it over his shoulder and slammed it down into the wood that Derek was splitting. The axe sank deep, and Nathan gave it some tugs but could not get it out. All he did was make himself start coughing as he ran out of breath, trying to pull it free.

Grinning, Nate bent over, yanking the axe out with a hard tug and hefting it to his shoulder. He looked at his brother with a bit of surprise. "You're right, this thing is heavy," he told his brother as he put a block split into the split Nathan had made, then hit the block with the back of the axe, splitting the wood all the way down.

They all watched in silence, hearing Nate's heavy breathing as he chopped and split a couple more. Derek sat next to the egg, lightly touching it, noticing that the gold had not moved up the silver stripe at all.

As if reading his thoughts, the egg vibrated as she reassured him it would happen soon.

He knew it instinctively. "It's a girl," he told the Bergers out loud.

"It is?" Nattilie said in surprise. "How do you know?"

He just shrugged, realizing he should have kept it to himself after his talk with Ellis and Herb yesterday.

"I can't wait for it to hatch," he told her. "Seems like I've been waiting for a long time, but it has only been a week or so."

Nate looked over from the woodpile he was leaning on to catch his breath again. "I noticed the gold has not risen. How long will it take?"

"Maybe weeks or just days. I don't even think she knows how long before she hatches," Derek told them as he stroked the egg.

"I want to find one," Nattilie said suddenly in a hopeful voice.

"Yeah, me too. I think we should go look for one. They can't be hard to find, glowing like that," Nathan agreed, suddenly excited.

Derek froze, knowing it was too dangerous to have them running around the woods in the dark. He quickly looked at Nate and made a calculated risk, thinking to him softly, 'Nate? We can't let them go off by themselves in the dark forest. They won't find anything and will only get lost. I can't go with them because I've got sword practice with Herb, and I want you to come with me. I think you know how important it is to know how to defend not just yourself but your brother and sister as well. Tell them maybe if they go find Ellis, he will take them with him when he goes looking around, and that will give us time to practice with the swords.'

When the first words were heard in his mind, Nate's eyes widened in shock, and his mouth moved as if to speak, but he listened, and after a second, nodded.

"I bet Ranger Ellis would know all the spots to look; he knows this land well, and maybe with his help, he will help you find an egg," Nate told them, joining their conversation.

Surprised, Nathan looked at his older brother. "You're not going to come hunting with us?" he asked curiously.

Nate shook his head, hefting the axe. "Someone has to chop wood," he replied, chopping another piece. "But go to Ellis; you know he will take you searching, and he knows all the best places to look."

Nathan shrugged. "Your loss, then, brother. I'll find a dragon first," he bragged.

And for some reason, Derek knew it was the truth. He shook his head as a cool certainty filled him. The world they had known had ceased to exist the second the meteors came. A new age was dawning, one in which doom loomed over all.

He watched Nathan and Nattilie leave to find the Ranger and shook off the looming doom he felt by picking up the egg. He watched as Nate put down another piece of wood to chop and hefted the axe to his shoulder, walking over to Derek and standing in front of him, staring up at him with a frown upon his face.

"Thanks for doing that," Derek told him.

Nate shrugged, his questions plain on his face.

"You will find a dragon," Derek told him with certainty. "Or it will find you. You will have to have patience, though, because unlike your brothers, your dragon has yet to be born."

Nate looked stunned, almost disbelieving, as if not understanding what Derek was trying to pull on him.

"What?" Nate said after a second. "How do you know that?" Again, Derek just shrugged, not sure how to answer. "I just do; you will understand when your dragon comes."

Nate looked perplexed. "Why did you choose me to spar with? Why not, Nathan? He likes you a lot more," Nate demanded.

Derek smiled. "For two reasons. One, Nathan will be great, but never as strong as you. I need someone strong, fast, and cunning to compete, train, and fight beside. Not that your brother cannot do any of these things. You're just older and more experienced than I am, and if we want to survive what's coming, all of us will have to push each other to our limits."

There was more he wanted to say; his mind felt crystal cool, but even what he had said shocked him. He had predicted the future with a certainty he could not shake. He knew it was true, and that scared him.

"If we don't, we will all die," he added quietly.

Suddenly anxious to leave before Nate asked him even more questions that he was afraid to answer, he walked to the house with the egg in his hands. A second later, Nate followed him.

Inside the basement, they found both Herb and Emma looking a little better, sitting at the table waiting for them, their faces lit by all of the candles around the room.

Next to Herb on the table lay four wooden swords with leather grips that looked extremely old and quite battered. Derek had seen ones just like them in the Bushido classes taught in the dojo he went to. They were called Bokken, and he wondered where Herb had gotten them.

Emma smiled at the boys as they came in, shaking off all the ash onto the plastic garbage bag. When they were done, she gave them both a cup of hot cocoa, then sat close to where Derek placed the egg so she could keep warm.

They both drank in silence while Herb studied them. When they finished, Emma took their cups.

Herb then looked Nate over critically. "So you have decided to learn as well, huh?" he asked as he picked up a bokken and turned back to Nate.

"Learning the sword takes a lot of time and dedication. Are those two qualities you have or wish to have?" Herb asked seriously.

Nate looked determined. "I can learn. I won't quit," he replied.

Herb nodded thoughtfully. "The Ranger tells me your family has all studied taekwondo?"

Nate smiled confidently. "I was two weeks from taking my black belt test."

Herb looked over at Derek, who looked surprised to hear that. "Take off your sword for right now. It will just get in the way," Herb told him.

Derek undid his belt, setting his sword aside and laying it next to the egg, as Herb handed the bokken over to Nate.

"Nate, I want you to strike, one strike at Derek," Herb told him seriously.

Derek, hearing it, became alert, his eyes tightening so he could see without blinking, his senses heightening as his body loosened and his heart sped up. His training coursed throughout him as Nate took the Bokken and looked skeptically at Herb.

"He is defenseless. I won't strike him if he does not have his own sword," Nate told Herb outrageously.

Herb smiled, looking proud but stern. "I applaud your morality, and it tells me I was not wrong about you. But never underestimate any of your opponents. He might not have a weapon in his hand, but that does not make him weaponless. Look at Derek, assess him. Is he weaponless?"

Nate turned to study Derek closely, but Derek saw how he only looked for a visible weapon. He did not look deeper to see his stance, eyes, or bearing.

"He doesn't have a weapon," Nate replied confidently a second later.

Herb frowned in disappointment. "Don't just look for a weapon in sight," Herb chided. "Look deeper. What does his stance tell you? His eyes? The way his back is set and the emotional play on his face? Does he look scared, wary, angry?"

Frustrated, Nate studied Derek again. "He looks, I don't know, willing for the challenge."

Herb smiled teasingly. "And what does that inform you? If he is willing for a challenge and you have a sword bokken, which he doesn't have, why would he be willing without a weapon of his own?"

Nate frowned at Derek. "So you have a weapon?"

Derek smiled. "I have one, but it's not what I would use if you attacked me." He then showed Nate the throwing knife hidden in the small of his back. He saw Herb's surprise. Herb gestured, and Derek handed it to him.

Nate then looked at Herb, starting to understand. "It tells me that for some reason, he is confident that he can take the challenge."

Herb nodded, looking up from the throwing knife. "Knowing that, strike at him. From now on, while we are here in this practice room, leave morals to me. I don't mean try to hurt each other; what I mean is if I tell you to do something, then do it because there is a reason for me to teach it to you, and in doing so, you will learn the lesson I am trying to teach you. I won't ask you to do something like this without a reason."

Herb then sat back to watch.

Derek kept his eyes upon Nate, seeing his determination, his stance, and the whole of his body, looking for the tell-tale signs of an imminent attack. He waited until right before Nate decided to strike and sprang forward. Nate's response was the natural one—torque, so you can strike. He cocked the Bokken back above his shoulder. But Derek had already stolen the initiative; he knew that by how Nate held the sword, it could only come down or down to the side. He closed the distance, using an upward cross-block to catch Nate's wrists just as he brought it down, trying to hit Derek before he got too close. Derek used that rushed momentum and twisted his hips, still controlling Nate's wrists. He applied pressure, then bent a little and sent Nate flying over his shoulder as the motion of the move put his back against Nate's stomach.

Had it been real, Derek would have let him slam hard and taken the Bokken from him; instead, he used the control on Nate's wrists to pull up on Nate's arms and keep him from slamming full force upon the concrete. Nate's feet hit the concrete, but Derek's grip on his wrists kept anything else from touching. With a little jerk on Nate's wrists, Derek hauled him back to his feet.

Emma clapped, and Herb nodded to Derek to thank him for breaking Nate's fall, while at the same time teaching Nate not to underestimate his opponents—something Herb wanted to get out of the way really quickly, so Nate would have more caution when being rude to Derek.

Nate's face was red with anger, embarrassment, and bewilderment. And Derek could sense he was on the verge of attacking him again. Instead, though, Nate lost his temper and gave Derek a questioning look.

"How?" Nate asked instead of demanding like he usually did. Derek could see a reluctant respect in his eyes.

"I guessed your intent. I have studied Jeet Kune Do since I was eight, learning the keys to initiative. I was able to see when you would strike, where and how, then I chose a move capable of defending and attacking that line of attack you chose," Derek told him seriously.

Herb stood up from the table. "Strap your sword back on, Derek," Herb told him before handing Nate Derek's saber, trading him for the Bokken.

Surprised, Derek looked to where his sword had been and saw it had been switched to the katana blade. As Nate strapped on the saber, Derek touched the katana sword reverently, knowing it must have history. He had never held a samurai sword before, though he had tried over and over to get his mom to let him join a kendo class his teacher taught. Several times, though, he had been able to stay late practicing staff techniques against some of the kendo students.

Because of his interest in swordsmanship, he had studied a lot about them; he knew just by how this one was made that it had distinction. Herb had to accomplish something of importance to have been given this sword. It was a family legacy that had to have been passed down generation to generation, and he felt honored that Herb was letting him use it.

He bowed to Herb before he picked it up, and Herb smiled and bowed back before letting his natural demeanor fall back in place. It had been years since he had studied under the Yahawa family, almost a lifetime ago, Herb thought as he watched Derek strap it on his belt.

Derek and Nate spent the next two hours learning from Herb how to hold and draw the swords, perfecting and learning their balance and stances. Both of whom took to the teachings easily. When their hands had blistered and their muscles ached, Herb finally dismissed them, telling them they would start all over tomorrow after the wood had been chopped. He also told them he expected Nathan to join them for both.

An hour after he had eaten, Derek took the egg with him into the darkness of the forest. He knew instinctively that the sun was setting even though there was no trace of light in the sky. He set the egg down, wondering when the sky would actually clear. Being careful not to cut his back, he pulled the throwing knife, holding it like the Ranger had shown him, which was hard because of his tender blisters. He threw it at the target tree he had selected, doing it exactly as Ellis had shown him.

The point hit but did not stick in the tree.

He was on his seventh try when a cool feeling entered his mind. Then the strangest sound he had ever heard in his life sounded within him. It was beautiful and eerie at the same time, and it brought chills across his flesh with the feeling of deep sadness.

A second later, a second more powerful cry pierced his mind. This one was a lot louder. It was beautiful, but it had a deadly edge to it that was primal and savage, and the hurt, sad feeling pierced his mind deeply as he heard it.

Dragons! He thought in amazement. He was hearing dragons! Not just one, but two of them. Then he felt her coolness enter his mind—his egg calling to him as if lonely and sad. And he knew the two dragons were mourning the loss of something.

He picked up the egg after putting away the throwing knife, and holding it close, he ran his fingers over it in a way it seemed to like, calming it as it vibrated in his arms.

"You're safe with me," he told her softly, wondering what the dragons were mourning.

In answer, coolness entered his mind, showing him a picture, and as he saw it form in his mind, he gasped in disbelief and amazement. There was a huge red-gold dragon lying on its side, a gigantic wound across its stomach. It was the same one from his dream, only this time, he could actually see how huge it really was. It had been bigger than the Titan by far, but next to Earth standards, it was monstrous. In front of it flew two different dragons; the smaller was green and silver, the bigger one was black and red. They were both tussling with each other.

"Where is this?" he asked the egg in his mind.

His question to this surprise was heard by the black and red dragon, startling it from its play with the green, and it abruptly broke off its contact, flying off as fast as lightning.

He shook his head as it cleared off the coolness that had filled it.

"Your mother," he stated in understanding as he stroked the egg. "Those must have been your siblings," he said in wonder.

Eighteen dragons, he thought in surprise. Then a thought came to him, *no, nineteen, eighteen eggs and one hatched already.* The black one had hatched sometime in space, living inside its frozen mother. He shivered at that thought. The black was a female, given life by the queen dragon to make sure all the dragons did not die off.

He tensed as he felt someone approaching him, then relaxed when he recognized the footstep pattern as nattalie's, dumbfounded by that recognition. He did not think he had been around her long enough to be familiar with her footsteps. Surprised at himself, he ignored her approach as if he did not know she was there, and sat looking into the dark forest, his fingers drawing a soft rumble from within the egg.

When it seemed like an eon had passed, she finally walked into the light of the egg, like she had just found him.

"It's so quiet out here now," he told her as she came into the light. "There are no crickets making noise, no bug sounds, and all of the birds are still hiding."

"When will they return?" she asked while studying his face.

"In a day," he told her without thinking. "They need to eat," he explained quickly, realizing that coolness of certainty was in his mind again.

"Do you know your eyes are silver?" she asked hesitantly.

He smiled! *"It's just the light from the egg that makes them look like that,"* he told her quickly and looked for a way to change the subject. "Your brothers are both going to learn the sword. What about you?" he asked curiously.

She gave him a shy smile and shook her head. "Taekwondo was enough for me. Besides, I would be no good with a sword. I don't like sharp objects — I mean, like swords. I can cook and cut food with a knife, but swords make me nervous. I only took martial arts because my dad made me. 'Learn how to fight, Nat.' 'Don't let others take advantage of you, Nate.' 'Bullies only respect force, Nat'—every day, I would hear it. So I took the classes with Nathan. But martial arts never helped me much. And it didn't save my dad," she said with a sad sniff.

Derek knew she was going to cry, so he tried to lighten her mood. "Of course, martial arts never helped you; you never had to use it because the bullies were scared you were taking it. Plus, then the bullies would have to take on your brothers," he told her with a laugh, motioning for her to sit down beside him on the log when she cracked a small smile.

"Maybe you're right, and a sword is not right for you. But you cannot turn a blind eye to the world when it's about to burst into anarchy. It is just changing too much, too quickly, since the meteors fell. Maybe it's not on you to fight, and your brothers and I will try our hardest to help keep it that way. Only the world will take things into its hands as it wills. What happens if you are chosen by a dragon? Will you then regret not taking the chance to learn how to protect it? Your weapon may not be the sword, but who is to say that it is the best weapon for you? It may be the bow and arrow or the staff. I've fought with the staff and am pretty advanced with it. It is very effective even against swords if it's wielded right, but until you do find that right weapon, use the ones you now have the opportunity to learn. For you will never know when that knowledge will save your life," he told her seriously as he struck the egg with his fingers.

She studied him for a long time before nodding in agreement. Then she smiled. "You speak as if you've had a world of experience." She touched his arm. "I don't mean that in a rude way. It's just you speak of things with a certainty of knowledge that I have only heard people my dad's age speak with. I will think about what you've said. If I had a dragon, I would want to be able to defend it. But aren't dragons invincible?" she wondered curiously.

Derek frowned sadly, shaking his head as he remembered the dream. "No, they have their strengths and weaknesses like all other things. These ones that came are the very last of their kind. They were brought here by their queen. They have been hunted and eradicated from their own planet. They came to this one hoping to survive, only they brought the meteors somehow, and while few people know that now, that will change when people start hearing tales about and seeing dragons. Then they will come in droves to hunt and kill them. All of our myths claim heroes slay dragons. Well, dragons are here now, so men will try to become heroes. Those men will think there must be truth to the myths and won't stop until they slay all our dragons. But I won't let them," he told her fiercely, all the while knowing men were not the only fear they would face.

She looked up at Derek, caught up in his fervent words. "I won't let them either," she replied with a wistful look.

CHAPTER SEVEN

Day 10; July 10th

Early the next morning, four people huddled together next to the egg, each with an axe in their hand. A smaller axe had been found by the Ranger when Nattilie had told Herb the night before that she, too, wanted to learn the sword so she could defend herself better.

That had surprised both Herb and Ellis, but Emma smiled when she heard it while taking their dishes away.

"You know why Herb has us doing this, right?" Derek asked Nathan now as they stood around.

Nathan looked both sleepy and grumpy at being woken up so early. "So we have enough firewood?" Nathan quipped, hopefully. Nate smiled at his brother's naivety. "Look at all of the firewood Derek has already cut. It would last us a very long time. There is no way that we need more anytime soon."

Nattilie, who was looking at her axe in the light of the egg, nervously looked up. "He's right. There must be a reason behind it. There has to be. I've seen how many supplies we have left, and I overheard Emma saying we only have enough to last us a couple more months. Ellis says he can bring some more in from town, but Herb told him we will have to leave here within a month if things stay the way they are now. That way, if it takes us a long time to find more, we have enough to get by while we look," she explained.

Derek nodded. "There is no way we will use all of this wood. The reason he has us do it is so we build up the strength in our arms and wrists. That strength will make us better with our swords. Everyone, go pick a downed tree, and stay close so you still have enough light to see."

At first, Nattilie and Nathan stayed close to Derek and Nate, watching what they did until they got the hang of it. Then, they started chopping trees into sections nearby.

Within a couple of minutes, everyone but Derek had stopped to take a break and catch their breath. Then they started up again. As the minutes passed, their breaks got longer and longer.

By then, Derek was already on his second tree. He was used to the weight and the feel of the heavy axe; his blisters from yesterday's practice did not even hurt today, though he knew on some level that they should. And his muscles did not burn like they used to. Never before had he finished a tree without needing a break. In fact, today he seemed energized and did not feel the muscle burn or cold chill that made the others keep taking breaks. And his breathing was not strained at all. He could still feel the heavy pressure in his lungs, but now it was like breathing came as easily as blinking his eyes.

While he continued chopping, he felt the cold sensation of the egg entering his mind, refreshing him even more as he actually realized this time it was his dragon's presence he was feeling. Suddenly, he began to hear voices in his mind that there was no way his ears could hear because of the distance his second tree was from the others.

"He's like a machine," Nathan said with awe.

Then "Owe!" Nathan complained. "What was that for?" he asked.

"For being a doofus," Nate scolded him.

Nattilie laughed. "You're starting to like him," she teased her twin brother.

"He's just like us; he wants to survive, and he knows the best way to do it," Nate replied before Nathan suddenly interrupted them.

"Guys, I just saw something moving in the trees," Nathan said in a suddenly scared, hushed voice.

Derek instantly snapped back to attention, and for a second, he felt lightheaded as his senses suddenly amplified by ten. His hearing and sight were magnified, and with his senses, he could suddenly sense presences all through the surrounding forest.

"Run!" he yelled, pulling his sword as he turned and saw two men charging him.

Pain suddenly shot through Derek as he was jerked to the side when a crossbow bolt took him in the left arm. He panicked, trying to hold back his fear.

"Help Ellis! Herb!" he yelled as he managed to block a weird-looking staff that had a knife blade on its top. The force of the blow almost drove the katana blade from his hand. Instead, he rolled to his left with the force, pushing the staff away from him.

Pain again shot through him as the bolt in his left arm snapped as it hit a tree. He forced himself to continue the turn. Going down on one knee, he sliced the blade low, going right under the spear-staff and slicing into the man's arm, then stomach. At the same time, he saw the other man trying to reload the crossbow.

Jumping forward into the man he had just sliced, Derek knocked him backward hard, slamming his right shoulder into the man's chest. The move took the man's wind and slammed him back into the crossbow man, who was just raising it to fire. That close, the crossbow bolt went right through the Spearman and sliced through the side of Derek's neck.

As he felt the pain, he heard a vicious roaring in his ears, and in his mind, he saw the red egg explode outwards.

The dragon, fierce in its anger, sprang free of her egg, stretching and growing as she did. By the time she was biting into the man who had grabbed Nattilie, she was four feet long. That man dropped like a stone, the back of his neck where she bit him ruined and squirting blood as he fell. Then she was flapping her wings furiously as she flew towards Derek, and blood was gushing from his neck when she reached him. By then, she was over five feet long, and her furious roars trembled all the trees in her outrage.

The crossbow man had pulled a knife after he pushed the dead Spearman off of him, and he came at Derek, trying to stab him with it. As the boy was wobbling on his feet, his sword barely came down in time to block the knife and send it flying from the man's hands.

The man, though, had lost interest in Derek; he was staring over Derek's shoulder with a look of grave terror in his wide eyes.

That was when Derek heard the roar and saw the red dragon shoot past him, its claws, wings, and jaw enfolding the man, killing him effortlessly.

Derek stared in shock, his vision playing tricks on him, and he felt very lightheaded. He fought to keep his eyes open and saw her about to take a bite of the dead man she had just killed.

"No, Spring!" he yelled, or tried to yell. "Not men."

Then he fell to the ground, blacking out.

Spring, surprised by the command, swirled around. Dragons always ate their kills! She wanted to retort to him. Then all thoughts disappeared as she saw and felt the pain in him as Derek fell to the ground. That painful, fearful feeling filled her again, the same one that had made her hatch early. Fear. A feeling no dragon had ever felt.

Spring roared as he fell, the dead man forgotten as she drove forward, curling around him, feeling helpless about what to do. She could feel him dying, and she roared again, anger and anguish filling the sky with her voice as she stood guard above Derek.

Around her, men ran in fear for their lives, their objectives forgotten in their fear, six of them dead left behind.

Ellis and Herb had both heard Derek's plea in their minds. They had come rushing out of the basement in the last of the light left by the egg. They saw Nathan on the ground with a deep head wound, Nattalie being grabbed by another man, right as the egg exploded in a burst of light. Ellis used that light to throw an axe at the man standing over Nathan's prone body, trying to take the axe from his limp hand. Ellis's axe caught him in the forehead, killing him cold as the light of the shattered egg began to fade, and as more men rushed from the trees, Herb engaged them, seeing to his astonishment, the dragon kill the man holding Nattalie.

By then, Nate had killed one of the men facing him, kicking the knife from his hand before thrusting his sword into his chest, then fought desperately in the fading light to hold off the other knife man, receiving cut after cut to do so.

By then, all the men had lost the urge to fight in the aftermath of seeing the dragon. As Herb killed one of the men who had rushed from the forest, the other four turned away and ran off, fleeing in terror of the dragon's rage.

Ellis and Herb quickly checked all of the Bergers, seeing that Nathan would have a big scar on his forehead, but should be alright. That's when they noticed Derek missing. Ellis used a cloth to grab a fragment of the still-glowing egg that was slowly fading, and they left Nathan with Nate and nattalie and ran towards where the dragon had charged.

In the remaining light of the egg, they saw the dragon soon enough and flinched, fear flowing through both of them as it roared angrily. It was standing over Derek's prone body. Fighting their fear, praying Derek was right in trusting the dragon, they both ran forward, stopping only when a low, vicious growl cut through their nerves, stopping them both cold and making them break into a sweat in the freezing air.

Herb put up his sword, holding his hands out for the angry dragon to see that he was weaponless.

"Put your weapon up, Ellis," Herb whispered quickly.

As soon as he did, the growling stopped, and the dragon stepped hesitantly back, but not very far. It seemed very reluctant to move from Derek, and it was a lot bigger than they had thought it would be from just hatching from a tiny egg.

The dragon was red with a yellowish-silver underbody. It had two sharp crystal horns over each of its silver eyes, long crystal teeth, and claws that, like the horns above its eyes, were flecked with gold. And those silver eyes never left theirs.

"We will help Derek if we can," Herb said, addressing the dragon.

Then he slowly walked forward, hesitating no longer and hoping the boy was still alive. He felt uncomfortable being so close to the dragon and the fierce heat coming from it, but it would not back away any further. He motioned Ellis a little closer with the eggshell so he could see better, then bent forward, turning Derek over. As he did, the boy gasped in pain as the bolt in his arm snagged in the ground, causing the dragon to snarl as she too felt it.

The pain jerked Derek to semi-awareness, and he could feel the world reeling around him as he gazed up into Herb's face. "My neck," he tried to tell him, trying to grab it.

Herb forced his hand down. "I am seeing it, son. Don't you be moving!" Herb muttered, turning to Ellis, who placed the fading shell by Derek's head. "If not, it is going to get them and bring medical supplies."

Then, Herb bunched Derek's shirt, pressing it to the wound. "Damn, that's a close one," he told Derek.

"Don't let her eat them," Derek whispered worriedly. "But she needs food. She should not have hatched so soon."

"Shh, boy, I know," Herb assured him. "Don't waste your strength; I'll feed her."

The her that he was talking about startled the daylights out of him as she nudged him aside gently with her head and looked down at Derek.

Derek felt her cool awareness enter his mind, and a picture of him—whole and healthy—appeared for him to see. It had a worried feel to it. He looked up at her. "I'll be fine in no time, don't worry," he assured her.

And Herb almost laughed when the dragon made a sound that sounded very humanlike for "I don't believe you," replying by huffing out air.

The sound brought a smile to Derek's face before he passed out again.

Herb looked at the red dragon, which was almost four and a half feet tall while sitting. "He will be okay; he just lost a lot of blood," he assured her, wondering if she actually understood what he was saying.

It seemed like it, though, because the dragon did not look away.

"But he is right, men are not food. Dead or not," Herb told her sternly, biting down his fear as he did.

Spring snapped her jaw in annoyance, showing him she understood. Suddenly, she looked up, and a second later, Herb heard the sound of birds—thousands of them. Spring looked at Herb enquiringly.

Surprised, he nodded, wondering how he knew the dragon was asking if it was all right to eat them.

Then Spring was gone, darting into the air right out of the trees and in front of the birds. Feathers went flying in a flurry through the black haze-covered air as birds squeaked and broke from her in alarm, trying to get away.

By then, Ellis had arrived with Emma, holding candles with Nate, who stood watching the dragon take off over the trees with awe.

"So it hatched," Emma stated in astonishment as she saw it flash by chasing birds, while she bent over, checking Derek's neck.

"His arm, too, looks," Nate told them, lowering the candle so they could see the broken bolt sticking through his left arm.

While Emma cleaned and patched up Derek's neck the best she could, Herb looked over the wound in Derek's arm.

"Damn, it's only a flesh wound," he told Emma. "But you're going to have to slice it all the way open to clean out the ash," he growled angrily. "Damn, ash is everywhere."

Emma nodded, seeing his anger was truly at the boy getting hurt. "This will have to do for now. Help me get him back into the house where there is light, warmth, and no ash," she told them, shaking in the cold air.

Nate and Herb picked Derek up and carefully began to carry him to the house.

"Who do you think those men were?" Nate asked angrily.

"Just desperate men," Emma replied while holding a candle and making sure Derek's bandage did not come off his neck.

"But that many of them? There were ten of them. Where did they come from?" Nate asked in a perplexed voice.

"Probably from a bunch of towns. Now, when we get Derek in there, you take off his shirt, then your own. I want to see all those wounds you are pretending you don't have." Emma told him in a stern voice.

They fell quiet as Derek moaned, then he laughed weakly.

"Of all those birds, she only caught two," Derek whispered in a weak, amused voice before he slipped back into a deep sleep.

They got Derek into the house. Then Herb went to help Ellis make sure the building was still secure and to keep watch of it, while Nate and Nattalie helped Emma with Nathan and Derek.

When Spring returned to the house, Herb was waiting for her at the basement door. He watched her land, seeing that she had grown even bigger in her flight over the forest chasing birds. From head to tail, she now had to be over six feet long. She landed and walked warily towards him.

"Derek's inside resting. We fixed him all up, though it will take him some time before he heals. I will let you inside, but be careful not to make a mess of the house," he told the red dragon in a hopeful, understanding tone.

The dragon made a noise that Herb had no doubt meant something like, "Who me, never," and looked up at Herb expectantly.

Herb smiled. "Go in then, and I will see what we have for you to eat."

Spring gave a contented soft rumble, just like he had heard it give Derek whenever he had stroked the egg. And as he opened the door, she walked softly into the house, followed by Herb.

Spring could sense right where Derek was, so she went up the stairs, following her senses until she entered a room she had seen only through Derek's eyes before.

It was filled with people, all of whom froze in shock and a little fear as she walked in, going to where Derek was lying in his makeshift bed of blankets. Once there, she curled herself around him, laying her head upon her claws next to his own head, then shut her eyes, trying to ignore all of the humans who were looking at her, just as she had felt Derek do a time or two.

"Look how beautiful she is," Nattalie exclaimed excitedly in a whisper to Nathan.

Nathan, his head now all stitched and wrapped up, smiled at his sister. "Did you see her rip that guy off of you? It was amazing!" Nathan told her, his voice tinged with awe.

She nodded with a shiver at remembering the foul-smelling man. "Did you hear her name? Derek called her Spring."

"I hope my dragon is half as beautiful and daring as she is," Nathan whispered fervently.

Nattalie gave him a confused, quizzical look. "Your dragon?" she asked in surprised disbelief.

Nathan nodded with a smile. "Derek told Nate yesterday that I would have one."

Not quite believing him, Nattalie smiled. "I hope you do, I hope we all do."

* * *

Sometime later, Derek woke to warmth surrounding him comfortably. He popped open one of his eyes to see red, glistening scales close to him. He lifted a hand and, with a small smile of awe, touched her warm scales. They felt like polished, smooth metal, and the touch sent a shock of warmth through both of them, scales rippling underneath his unexpected touch.

A warmth spread deeper within his body as he felt the coolness of Spring's mind enter his own. And again, he saw a picture of himself whole and healthy with that questioning feel to it. He ignored it as her head swooped around to look at him with her liquid silver eyes.

He gave her a teasing smile. "I see you made it back. You didn't eat too many birds, did you?" he teased.

The picture of the two delicious ones she ate floated through his mind, and with it came a feeling of vast disappointment at how quick the birds were.

He laughed softly. "They are not that fast; you're just not totally wing-savvy yet."

She chuffed sarcastically and showed him a picture of her flying with perfect grace in his mind.

Amused, Derek rubbed her scales, bringing an instant low rumbling sound that rattled the front windows. "Shh, you'll wake everyone up," he teased her.

The rumble quieted, but not by much, as he kept rubbing her scales.

"You're a lot bigger than I thought you would be," he told her as he touched his bandaged neck, then moved the blanket to look at his bandaged arm.

Again, the picture of him whole and healthy flashed with concern in his mind.

"Soon," he assured her as he felt Ranger Ellis approaching the room.

"I thought that was you," Ellis said as he came in.

Spring sat up and put her tail protectively upon Derek's chest. Seeing it, Ellis smiled and walked to Derek. He sat resting on his heels and looked Derek over.

"So what happened?" he asked.

Derek carefully sat up. "Nathan saw a shadow, and while I was distracted, men somehow snuck up on us."

Ellis frowned. "Distracted? That is not like you. I have seen how tense you get when anyone approaches you. What had distracted you enough not to sense the men coming?" he asked, trying not to make it sound like an accusation.

Derek went red in embarrassment and looked at Spring.

Spring chuffed and looked at the roof as if ignoring Derek's look.

Seeing the two made Ellis smile. He did not understand it totally, but he had a feeling Derek's distraction had something to do with the dragon, so he let it go. At least everyone had survived the attack. But he and Herb would have to teach Derek how to be vigilant at all times. The boy had super spooky senses, and if they could, they would work to enhance them.

"So what happened?" he asked Derek in a lighter tone.

Derek looked back at him. "When I heard Nathan, I suddenly felt them. I turned right into a crossbow bolt that was meant for my back. I was able to block the spear thing before it put a hole in me, and I called you and Herb. Then I killed the spear wielder and saw the crossbow man raising to take aim again, so I jumped into the dying Spearman, sending him back into the crossbow man. The crossbow went off, went through the spearman, and caught my neck as it flew by.

By then, Spring had erupted from her egg to join the battle. I was able to block a couple of knife swipes and sent the knife flying from the crossbow man's hand. Then Spring took him down," he explained, rubbing Spring's hard tail.

Ellis listened thoughtfully before nodding. "There are six bodies; four of the attackers escaped, running like hell once your dragon showed up." He paused with a half-smile. "You know your eyes are as silver as your dragon's now? They even glow a little in the dark."

Derek had not known that, but he knew he could now see a lot better in the dark. The candles around his room were like flares in his eyes, and even though Spring did not glow, she was like a bonfire when he looked at her.

He looked at Ellis seriously. "We need to find Spring some meat. She only caught two birds, and that will not be able to sustain her. She hatched way too early and has grown too much. Her hunger hurts her more than my wounds do," he told the Ranger seriously.

Spring sat watching them both and butted her head affectionately against Derek's shoulder.

"Can she eat a deer? They are out there. Like the birds, they broke shelter looking for food, trying to strip the trees of bark," Ellis told him.

Spring gave Derek a look that told him she did not know what a deer was. So he formed a picture of a group of bucks and does in his mind. Spring instantly bent forward, snapped her jaw, and shook her head, miming ripping something apart.

Derek laughed at her eagerness. "Deer won't pose her a problem, but she's never hunted. She acts all sure of herself, but her tiredness is there with her hunger. Can you show her where they are and maybe bring one down for her? One of those crossbows will come in handy."

Ellis looked over at the dragon doubtfully. "On the ground, she would make too much noise for us to get close, and her scent might give us away. Tell her to follow me in the air, and if she can, watch me, and as I bring one of them down, she can pounce upon it."

Spring again mimed tearing something apart, and they both laughed.

Derek patted her leg. "Go get something to eat," he told her.

He watched them go as he lay back down and closed his eyes. And for the first time, initiating it on his own, he sought the coldness of Spring's mind. It wasn't long before he was watching them approach the forest. In his mind, seeing out of Spring's eyes was a weird feeling, and it tripled as she took to the air, flying higher and higher, testing her wings and the feel of the air beneath them.

Her eyesight was phenomenal. She could see through the clouds and haze of ash that had enveloped the world as easily as Derek now knew he could. Nothing was hidden from their vision. From over a thousand feet in the sky, she could make out Ellis' slow-moving body. Then she saw the deer—hundreds of them combing through the dark forest. Around them, stalking silently, were cats and wolves; some were already eating, while others stalked with the hopes of catching prey. Derek gave her a name for each one she saw.

Seeing the deer, though, had started a fierce hunger within her that then slid into Derek, making them both grow excited. And when Derek noticed she was panting, he calmed her down.

"Not yet," he whispered soothingly in her mind. "Give Ellis time to bring one down!"

It was hard to tell her that because he, too, felt that excitement crushing him. He was the only reason she was reining it in long enough to wait for Ellis, and only because he asked her to.

Soon, her impatience was growing by leaps and bounds. The Ranger was moving slowly so as not to spook the deer while he got close enough to strike. But to her, it seemed like he was a snail who would never reach the deer.

When she saw Ellis lift the crossbow, excitement flowed through them both, and no longer able to wait any longer, she dove from up high, her wings and legs tucked to give her greater speed. Derek heard the crossbow lose its bolt, and Spring saw a deer stumble and slam into it, all four claws gripping and pushing viciously down. Derek heard the sound of its backbone snapping like twigs beneath the pressure. He knew it was dead, and so did Spring. She let it go as another deer flashed by, and instantly, Spring latched onto it with a claw, jerking it back, and her teeth latched onto its neck as they both tumbled to the ground. Derek felt a brief wave of pain as the deer landed upon one of her wings, which had not tucked properly.

A second later, the deer fell still, and Derek left her mind so she could eat. Before he left, he noticed just how happy she was at her first successful hunt.

He returned once she was finished eating, busy licking her claws, with the Ranger not too far from her. She met his mind with a wave of warmth and happiness that he had returned.

"You ate everything," he heard Ellis exclaim in wonder. "Derek had said you were hungry; I guess he was right."

At the sound of Derek's name, Spring turned to pay attention to Ellis.

Ellis gestured to the deer with its back broken. "You brought down the wrong deer," he told her humorously, pointing to another dead deer with a hole in its heart.

She snapped her teeth and made the ripping gesture. Ellis laughed. "Well, we got extra deer meat now, so if you're still hungry, eat this one," he told her, pointing to the one she had crushed.

Derek could tell she was full, at least for the time being. She walked to the deer and grabbed its neck in her mouth, then flexed her wings. Feeling a sharp twinge of pain in the one the deer had fallen on, she knew she could not fly with the deer in tow.

Seeing her intention, Ellis nodded. "Wait a minute, and let me clean this one. Then we will take them back so Derek can eat some, too."

Confused and not quite understanding what he said, Spring let go of the deer and sank to the ground, waiting.

When Ellis began to cut and clean the deer he had shot, he tossed the insides to her, which she eagerly snatched from the air and swallowed. When he was finished, he hauled the deer to his shoulders, and Spring got up to follow him, dragging the deer by its neck to catch up with him.

CHAPTER EIGHT

Day eleven, July 11th

Derek woke to the smell of deer being cooked over the fire somewhere in the building. The smell made his mouth water almost immediately. Next to him, he could feel the comfortable warmth of Spring, content for the time being, sleeping with her head next to his own. He realized he was using one of her legs as his pillow, as his cheek scratched against one of her polished, metallic-looking scales.

He knew the room was empty before he even opened his eyes, having to squint in the bright light of the candles. He felt a throbbing in his left arm and neck as he slowly sat up, leaning back against Spring's full stomach.

Spring gave a little rumble, then faded back to sleep.

He was still sitting, in the process of waking up, thinking about getting up, when he felt Emma and Nattilie approaching.

"Don't even think about getting up," Emma warned him with a tender smile as she came into the room carrying a cup of warm cocoa.

Nattilie came in behind her, carrying a tray full of food.

Stew, meat, and crackers. *He thought as he took a whiff of it.*

"I thought you might be awake by now, but you still need your rest," Emma chided as she handed him the cup while Nattilie carefully placed the tray over his lap.

Smelling the food, Spring's eyes opened, and she lifted her head, studying the food before turning her face away as if she were not interested. A fact Derek knew was a lie.

"I did not want to give you any anyway," he teased her as he sipped his cocoa.

Spring let out a breath that sounded like a chuckle, and Derek patted her shoulder, amazed at just how big she was.

"Why did you name her Spring?" Nattilie asked him curiously, her eyes looking at the dragon with interest.

"Because it means a new beginning, and besides that, did you see how she popped out of her shell? She launched out of there like a spring," he told Nattilie with a laugh.

She nodded with a smile. "The name fits her. Her scales are almost gold now. They were yellow when she hatched. Do you think her hatching so early will have any ill effect upon her?" she asked worriedly.

Derek looked at Spring. "No, if anything, it just made her a lot stronger. And she will need it so she can grow faster. Two other dragons that I know about have hatched. So far, one is a small green that is not even half her size. The other one is a big black and red female; she is over twice Spring's size," he told her as he started into his stew, not believing just how hungry he was.

"You've seen other dragons?" Nattilie exclaimed in surprise.

Derek ate a couple of bites of the stew as he considered how best to answer her.

"In a way," he told her after a second. He looked over at the sleeping dragon. "Spring can hear them far off when they want to be heard. The two I mentioned were at the site where the queen had fallen. They were both grieving her loss, and I think they passed on their knowledge of her death to all the other eggs wherever they were. And Spring received it. We have no idea where they were, though."

His hunger got the best of him, and he began to eat again. In between bites, Emma and Nattilie filled him in on how everyone was doing. Nathan had received twelve stitches to his forehead, and he himself had six on his neck and ten across his arm. Nate had received several knife wounds in a couple of different places, but luckily, none of them were serious. Nattilie herself had a nasty bump on her head.

Looking at her, he saw she now had a rapier sword sheathed at her side. Emma, he saw, had a large knife at her own waist. His own sword, he saw, was leaning against the wall, not too far from his reach, and next to it was the weird-looking spear that had almost killed him.

Emma saw him looking at the weird spear. "Ellis brought it in last night when he came back from his hunting expedition. He said it was yours if you wanted it."

"How long was I asleep?" he asked as he finished his stew, and Nattilie brought him some more.

"All last night and today. It's close to night again," Emma told him as she grabbed his empty cup and watched him eat some more of the stew. "I don't want you getting up and risking opening any of the wounds I closed on you. You get yourself some more sleep and take it easy for the next couple of days so you can heal and get better," she scolded him as she left with his cup.

While he ate some more, quenching his hunger, Nattilie watched the sleeping dragon.

"I see you're wearing a sword now," he remarked casually.

She turned to study him. "You were right. I did not have a chance to do anything. I saw them attack Nate and Nathan, trying to reach the egg, and I froze. I swung my axe as a man got close." Her voice broke. "But he just took it from me."

She drew in a deep breath to keep the tears from falling, which he saw in her eyes. "They could have stolen your dragon and killed all of us. But it won't happen again," she assured him fervently. "I won't let it happen again."

Derek nodded. "Next time, all of us will be ready."

Days twelve – seventeen.

The next week passed horribly slowly for Derek, making his days feel boring. Emma had relented to let him move around, but he could not leave the house. She did not want any chance of ash getting into his wounds until they healed. So in secret, at least to her, he practiced almost all day long, every day he was stuck in the house, drawing his sword and learning to handle it one-handed so he would not stress the stitches in his left arm. At times, he even toyed around with the spear, trying to wield it correctly.

The spear looked like it had come from a museum. It was obviously old, but the wood of it was solid. The blade that topped it was a foot and a half of sharp, etched metal. On the flat of the blade was a crown with a snake's head. The spear with the blade was just a little taller than he was, and the shaft of the wood was almost two inches thick. It was a lot heavier than any staff he had ever used.

Spring was nearly always with him, going outside for brief periods of time to stretch her wings. Then she was back watching him, stretching, or sleeping. By the end of the week, her scales were a pure red and gold. Her horns had grown a little larger and were flecked with bright gold, as were her claws. Her teeth were crystal with only tiny specks of gold in them, but they, too, had grown a little, looking razor sharp.

He could feel it every time her silver eyes set sight on him, and if he ignored her for too long, she would grow playful and bump into him as if by accident. She was always careful of his arm and neck, but wanting to tussle all the same, she tried to wrap around him so he would play back and scratch her scales until she was rumbling a contented purr.

Then he would go back to whatever it was he was practicing, which was usually the sword—drawing and one-handed strikes. He learned quickly how to hold and use the sword one-handed, and his strength kept up with him, allowing him to practice with one arm for longer without fatiguing.

At the beginning of the week, Herb busted him practicing one-handed and showed him the proper techniques for one-arm strikes. Then he just sat watching him, correcting Derek whenever he needed to. After that, Herb gave him a book to read that had been written a long time ago by a man named Musashi, telling him that Herb's own teacher had made him read it.

So when Derek was not practicing, he was reading and studying the writings of Miyamoto Musashi, who he learned was a famous Japanese swordsman who founded a two-sword fighting style. The writings corresponded with everything he had ever learned studying Jeet Kune Do. Reading it, he found himself no longer so bored.

* * *

Day Seventeen – July 17th

After a week of sheltering, he decided it was more than time for him to go outside. He snuck outside through the basement with Spring in the middle of the night. A surprised Ellis met him at the door as he was walking out.

Ellis smiled. "I was wondering when you would venture out again. You have a lot more patience than I do. How are you feeling?" Ellis wondered as they walked outside, shutting the door.

Spring bolted past them, stretching her wings out long and flapping them a couple of times.

"I'm feeling a lot better," Derek assured him. "My arm is not even sore, just a tiny scratch that won't even leave a scar," he said, demonstrating by moving his left arm around.

Ellis frowned. "Are you sure? I saw that cut; it must be a scar," he said in disbelief.

"Look," Derek replied, pulling his shirt off so the Ranger could see by the light of the candle he was holding.

The dragon on his chest sparkled in the light of the candle as he showed Ellis his arm. All that could be seen was stitches with a tiny scab—no scar at all.

"What about your neck?" he asked Derek curiously, surprised at just how quickly the boy healed. Not to mention the boy had his shirt off in this freezing weather and did not look even a little bit cold.

Derek removed the bandage that was merely for show now. "The same thing, a tiny scab—no scar."

"You're a tough kid, I'll give you that," the Ranger told him in a surprised voice.

Derek put his shirt back on, then turned to Ellis. "Have you seen any sign of those four other men?" he asked curiously.

"Not a sign," Ellis said with a shake of his head. He then gave Derek a hard look. "When was the last time Emma looked at your wounds?"

"Yesterday," he replied. "But that was before the scab fell off. The full scab was still there this morning, but as I stretched my arm, the scab just started to crumble away," Derek explained, looking away from the candle as it gave his sensitive eyes a headache.

Spring was waiting excitedly. He could feel it in her eagerness to reach the forest and how hungry she was again. He sniffed, catching the same scent that she did. He could smell the deer through the ash and his nose cleaners. And when he looked into the forest, he could catch the shadow movements just at the edge of his sight within the trees.

"Put out your light," he told the Ranger quietly.

"Why? Is there somebody out there?" Ellis asked quickly, his hand going to his ax, pulling it.

"Not someone, deer. They are in the forest, but the light is keeping them away," Derek explained.

Spring, they could both see, was tense with excitement.

Ellis damped the candle wick with his fingers, wondering how the hell the boy could see in the dark when he could not see a blasted thing. But Derek and the dragon's eyes were both tracking movement off in the forest—a forest Ellis could no longer see anymore.

Spring looked at Derek anxiously, and he nodded, watching as Spring crouched and began moving softly forward without a sound.

Realizing that Ellis was now blind in the darkness, he reached out and touched the Ranger's arm to get his attention. "Get your axe ready, and we will test your skills. The deer are all heading this way. Spring is going to slip off to the side and get behind them, then slowly start heading their way. When they are close enough, I will let Spring know, and she will flame—ah, spit fire, or so she tells me she can do, though she has never tried it. Anyway, if it works and she does, you will have light to throw by. She will be behind them when she does this, so it will make them all turn towards her to see what caused it, which will give us the best chances to score direct hits—you with your axe and me with the crossbow you have. Then Spring will take one down herself."

Ellis, already tasting deer, smiled in the dark. "Sounds like a plan," he said, handing Derek the crossbow.

Derek looked it over, putting a bolt in it. "I just point and shoot?" he asked in an unsure voice, having never fired one before. Though over the last week, he had heard Ellis had been teaching all the Bergers how to shoot it.

"Aim just behind the shoulder. Give me your knife in case I get the chance for two," Ellis told him quietly.

Derek handed over the throwing knife, then silently led Ellis by the arm through the darkness and as close as he dared to get to the forest.

Derek then reached out to the Ranger with his mind and told him, "We will wait here. They are coming, but they are relaxed, so their pace is unhurried. Spring is almost beside them now. I think she will wait for them to pass her, then start following behind them until they are close enough for us to get."

Derek could see Spring like a shining glimmer in the darkness. She was slinking through the trees deeper and deeper into the forest.

Ellis nodded to Derek and shivered in the cold as they both hunkered down to wait a couple of feet from each other. Almost fifteen tense minutes passed, and with each one, Derek could feel Spring's excitement growing. The feel of it pumped up his own excitement.

"Soon now, so get ready; they are only thirty yards away," he thought to Ellis.

It wasn't but a minute later when a bright light breached the dark forest. Derek saw Spring burst forth from behind the deer, spewing fire from her mouth.

The deer all turned as one, then broke in fear, fleeing before the flame-spewing dragon.

Derek aimed right before she leaped. He could already see the huge buck in the dark, its broad left flank exposed right as Spring exploded from the trees. His mark was a little high as he rushed to load another bolt and fired again while they ran off.

It was over in seconds—five deer down, though Spring had to leap upon the first one Derek had shot to keep it from running too far away. Then she let off a victorious and thunderous roar.

"Oh no," Derek thought, hitting his forehead, knowing that she had just woken everyone within the house. True enough, he could feel them all coming.

When they came, Ellis was already dragging the deer towards the house to be cleaned, and as Herb gave him a surprised look, Ellis grinned hungrily. "We got fresh meat now," he told Herb happily.

CHAPTER NINE

Stalker

Day 11: July 11th

Location: Arizona

Ken Callay was a very worried man. For the last week and a half, he had been living off of cactus and lizards. And because of that and the meteor storm that had so disrupted his life, he no longer looked like his normal cheerful self.

He still stood six feet tall, but he no longer weighed 210 pounds. Nothing of his usual broad face could be seen, wrapped as it was to keep him warm and to keep him from breathing the fine ash and dust that now permeated the air. Nor could his brown eyes be seen, hidden as they were behind a pair of dark wraparound sunglasses. Wearing them made it all the harder to see, but it kept the constant blowing and floating ash out of his eyes.

Not that sight was that much of a problem when it was so dark that you could not see anything anyway. He had no choice now but to rely only on his senses of what was around him; thankfully, his senses had been developed strenuously under the watch and teaching given to him, courtesy of the United States government.

He was twenty-two years old and a top graduate of the Green Berets. He had been driving from Yuma, Arizona, to San Diego, California, when the meteors had fallen from the sky. He'd had no warning of their coming, nor was it broadcast over any news program. It just happened, and the Hummer he had been driving blew up in his face. Since then, it had taken every last ounce of his energy and will to survive the freezing cold and lack of food and water.

His first mistake, but one he could not have avoided, had been to leave the road in the middle of nowhere to find some kind of shelter from the falling meteorites. Doing so, he had somehow gotten himself lost in the darkness with no stars, no light, and no damned working compass to guide him out of the desert.

Skilled from all his training, he was not really worried; he had lived off the land before, been frozen until he could barely move, let alone think, and he had survived that with less stuff than he had now. At least now he had some supplies in the Hummer and his knowledge of survival skills. So, he gathered the supplies he deemed useful in his military pack—a K-Bar knife that was now at his waist, an empty canteen, some dry rations, extra clothing, boots, and shoes, anything not electronic, since it had all shorted out on him. He had even discarded his useless gun when it had failed to fire at a coyote who had thought he might be lunch, forcing him to break its neck when it had attacked him.

So, in reality, he should not be so worried or even bothered by a few inconveniences, like this infernal ash and almost blistering cold. He knew how to stay healthy enough to keep mobile, so he did not freeze to death or get frostbite.

Two things worried him, though. The first was only a niggling worry because he knew he was lost but would eventually find his way out. There were too many cities around where he was not to run into one of their roads, eventually. The second worry stood at the forefront of his mind. He was being followed. Had been for the last day and a half, if he was keeping track of the time correctly. And whoever was following him was good. None of his evasion tactics or crossbacks had worked to either lose, show, or engage his stalker.

And he had no doubt it was a stalker. He was prey. He could feel it down to his bones. Whoever was after him was one of the best he had ever seen, or really not seen. It was as if Ken's every move was noted and seen through the impossible dark haze surrounding everything.

Twice now, he had tried to shrug it off as just his imagination. He could not see or hear anything different; he had found no tracks, besides maybe those of a bigger lizard, not even tracks of a coyote or wolf. There was nothing out there to find, and he had convinced himself of that, telling himself it was all just a trick of his mind when he had felt the heat of some living presence close to him. And in the cold, frigid air around him, there could be no doubt. Yet he had seen nothing, so he had again passed it off as nothing, only later to have seen something in the darkness that had looked awfully like a pair of silver eyes studying him. After that, he knew he was being stalked, no doubt about it.

Now, he was lying under ash-filled ground, trying to sense or hear anything out of the ordinary above or below the ash. He had not moved in over an hour. Sand and ash had begun to cover him the instant he lay down, which helped to insulate what little heat he had. He had his knife in his hand, buried right next to his head, so there was no chance of it being seen at all. All of his clothes were camouflaged, so he knew even if there had been any light to see by, he would be a difficult target to find and nearly impossible under all this ash.

This time, he was the Stalker; he was tired of being stalked, and if those silver eyes could somehow see through this darkness, they had lost him long before now. He just hoped the thing stalking him got curious soon. He had not slept since he had gotten the first inkling that he had been followed. And lying here like this in the freezing cold was making him even more tired. He knew he could go a while longer without sleeping, but the last eleven days had taken their toll upon his mind and body; he was now running on fumes.

Because of that, he'd had no choice but to become the Stalker, hunter, killer he had trained for. He needed sleep, and he could not do so with whatever was following him. And if his Stalker had managed to see him go down, maybe it would think he was sleeping. Either way, with the ash covering him, his Stalker had to be good to find him. The hour of shifting sand and ash, with no single movement on his part, would change the whole power balance of who was now the prey.

Time passed by, and true enough, he finally felt the warmth of a presence come near him. Over and over, always cautious and slow, searching meticulously for him. Had he had any doubt in his mind, it was gone now. But the heat of the presence was intriguing; what had such heat to give off like that? He went over every predator it could be, and none could fit that category, not here in the desert anyway. It could be a very big wolf, but he heard no paw scrapes in the ash, and neither had he seen or felt any on his double backs. He was stumped. He waited patiently, hearing no footsteps, paw treads, nothing!

He did learn more about his Stalker, though; whatever it was, it was sly, patient, and very careful. And to top it off, it radiated heat. He grew to want his Stalker near him if only for that extra warmth, and as it got closer to him, he could feel it in the warmth it gave him.

Thinking of that heat made him sleepy, though, and he had to focus all of his remaining energy on keeping his prone, still body from trying to sleep. He also did not like the fact that his mind and body were betraying him by finding comfort in the warmth the Stalker brought with it when it was hunting him down, most likely for its next meal. Because when he felt the heat of his Stalker's silent return, his body almost cried out in relief at the feel of its warmth. He fought hard not to grit his teeth in frustration, and he hoped his Stalker made a deadly mistake this time.

A little closer, a little closer, he thought, using it like a calming litany. Just a little closer, Stalker, and you're mine.

And as if having heard those thoughts, his Stalker stopped.

He wanted to scream in frustration; why had it stopped! He just knew that it had finally found him.

Then he felt it begin to withdraw again, taking its warmth with it as it left his vicinity, and he growled—actually growled in frustration.

"Stop!" he thought fiercely. "Don't leave!" Not wanting to wait again for its return.

To his amazement, the Stalker did just that; it stopped.

Stunned and a little shaken at the realization that the thoughts in his mind were being read as if they were a book, he made himself stop thinking. No more litany, nothing, dead silence as if he had suddenly died. His senses were on high alert, higher than they had ever been. Ten minutes passed without his Stalker's warmth moving an inch. Then twenty. Neither of them was moving. Then, slowly, he felt the heat start to get closer.. But he held onto his thoughts, clamping them down, not thinking, just feeling, his senses tight as his body grew warmer with the Stalker's approach. It came closer and closer until finally, for the first time, he heard a noise above the sound of the wind and shifting ash above him.

The noise itself was peculiar, and he had a hard time keeping himself from thinking about what could be making such a noise. The sound filled him. He knew it and recognized it, but it made no sense to him whatsoever, and he wasn't about to think about it, to make sense of it. The warmth of the presence got closer and closer to him, and the sound coming from it was nearly right above him now. When it was, he launched himself into action, shooting out of the ash and sand like a big bullet.

One of his hands grabbed at the thing in the air while the other slashed viciously with his knife.

His eyes went wide beneath his glasses as sparks shot at him. One of his hands closed tightly around what felt like hot metal through his leather gloves. The other arm was racked in pain as claws gripped onto it tightly, holding the knife back.

Even grasping onto it, he could not believe his eyes, seeing it as it spat sparks at him for grabbing its silver tail. A mistake he realized as all four of its clawed legs and arms snatched onto his arm, holding it with its crystal-looking talons. Then its crystal-like teeth opened, and its head thrust forward.

Overwhelming pain filled Ken. He had felt things pierce his arm and thought it was the talons. Then the creature—for he could only think of it as a creature, having never seen anything like it before—snapped forward, biting into the left side of his chest.

Surprised by both its looks and the pain it had brought to him, he automatically let it go. But by then, he knew it was too late; he could feel a hot, poisonous sensation crawling up his arm and knew he had made a mistake.

The creature, surprised by his attack, roared out a challenge, swirling like a silver dervish in the air before turning to stare at him with its liquid silver eyes from five feet away.

The pain in Ken's chest was nothing compared to the poison he felt coursing up his knife arm. Fire seemed to burn all of his nerves raw, and his vision, what he could see, began to distort and waver as if he were in water. A fierce cold seized his chest suddenly, and fire flared in his brain as the poison spread up his arm and throughout his system. He roared back at the creature, his roar one of pure pain. Then his ears were throbbing, heart and head pounding, his nerves alive with lava. He fell to his knees, then onto his face, sending up a bunch of ash to cover him as he blissfully but painfully passed out from the intense pain.

* * *

His body alternated from raging fever to freezing cold, from seizures to shakes to paralysis. He had never in his life been subjected to such pain, never believed it possible. His eyes had turned into burning orbs of fire while his skin and muscles clenched tightly, spasmodically.

And through it all, he felt the presence of his Stalker right next to him, as if trying to give him comfort. A weird thing when he thought about it, because it was the reason he was in so much pain.

Dark and mysterious dreams assaulted his mind when he fled the ongoing pain of his body. Dreams of dragons, big and majestic, fighting humans. Only they were not humans; they made him seem like a tiny ant. They were huge and magnificent, and they hated dragons. And he felt the dragons' own hate of them as they killed the dragons one by one. His own soul rebelled and recoiled at the horrible things his dreams showed him that were done to each of the dragons caught, young and old alike.

He saw the queen dragon's retreat, her eggs the last of her kind, one from each remaining species of dragon. He then saw the two dragons mourning her death. And last, he saw his Stalker, felt its hunger, pain, and loneliness, how it had followed him for days, a lot longer than Ken had even suspected. It watched him, learning from him, copying his survival techniques, feeling cautious of him, but also its curiosity.

Day Twelve – July 12th

When he was finally able to open his eyes, he had to squint because everything seemed so bright. He could, to his astonishment, see through the black clouds of haze all the way to the horizon without straining his eyes. He almost thought at first the darkness had left, but when he looked up, he could see far; the sun was still blocked from view by all of the ash in the air. But he could sense the heat of it and knew it was up.

His left arm and chest still burned with fire, and he was a little surprised when he saw he was still holding his knife. His stalker, he knew, was still close by but hiding from his sight. When he had first been attacked, he had believed it would eat him while he was helpless, but now, he knew that was never true. It was out there somewhere, watching and observing him from a safe distance.

Choosing to ignore the baby dragon, he slowly stood up, shook ash off of himself, and put up his knife. Looking around, seeing nothing of a threat to him, he began to check his wounds.

Deep breaths steadied him as he lifted the sleeves of his jacket and shirt to see the throbbing puncture wounds in his left forearm. Four of them. They were swollen and red, but he did not think he needed to lance them. It seemed his body was already fighting off the poison that had been injected into him through each wound. He then lifted his bloody shirt from his chest, seeing a huge purple bleeding welt. But to his ultimate surprise, there were no teeth marks at all, which he thought was weird because he distinctly remembered the feel of teeth ripping out a big chunk of his chest.

He sighed, pulling down the blood-soaked shirt. It could have been worse; it could have eaten him while he was out of it. He was still mobile, though he needed to find a cactus so he could get some water. He was dehydrated and hungry. He could also feel that his stalker was just as thirsty and hungry as he was.

Then he paused, realizing what he had just felt. He could feel what the baby dragon was feeling, he thought with amazement.

A little stunned, he turned to it. He could not see it; like him, it was excellent at hiding, but he could feel right where it was. "I'm going to find some food. You can come with me if you want," he told it out loud, not really believing the dragon could understand him.

He then looked around, trying to find the best way to travel to a cactus he saw far off in the distance. Then he set off softly, his ears attuned to the desert, listening to the shifting sand that would announce the hidden presence of animals or larger insects, sounds he had become accustomed to over the last week.

As soon as he moved, he heard the telltale sound of wings moving through the air. They were not noisy, but now that he knew what to listen for, it was easy to pick them out. He turned and waited for the baby dragon.

The dragon was pure silver with gold under its jaw and stomach, and it stopped well back from him, as if unsure of his intentions now that it was in the open.

The sight of it stunned him. He had never seen anything so majestic in his life. To think, a live dragon! Just like some kind of myth come to life. He studied it intently, meeting its silver eyes.

"Well, are you coming or not, Stalker?" he asked quietly. "Because if you are, it won't be by stalking me anymore. So get over here or leave. Your choice."

The dragon chuffed as if in amusement. *Chuffed!* He thought, with a smile. It could definitely understand what he was saying. He watched it fly over to him, stopping about three feet in front of him.

The dragon had liquid metal silver eyes with two rows of crystal spikes that ran back from each eye all the way to its tail, which ended in a spiked ball. The four horns above its eyes were the longest, a little more than two inches tall. And its teeth, when it opened its mouth in a stretching yawn, were long and sharp, as crystal-looking as its horns, spikes, and claws. It had four long crystal claws on each leg and arm, with a hidden smaller one on the back of each leg and arm. It was the hidden ones he knew instinctively that were poisonous and had been what had punctured his arm.

The dragon let him study it while it too studied him, noticing his short brown hair under his wrap, his once brown, now silver eyes (unknown to him) with the same liquid metal silver look to them as Stalker's own. The whites of his eyes were still white, though they almost glowed in the dark. He was tall and thickly muscled, unlike most of the humans Stalker had seen in Ken's memories.

Suddenly, Ken heard a scurry on the sand. They both plunged into action simultaneously, driven by a fierce hunger that sharpened their reflexes. Ken was faster.

"Ha!" he laughed, having beaten the dragon. A jackrabbit pinned to his K-Bar knife. "Too slow," he taunted as the dragon gave off a grumble while looking hungrily at the rabbit.

He knew he needed water more than food, so he sliced the rabbit's throat and forced himself to drink its blood before tossing it to the starving dragon.

He watched with dumbfounded amazement as the whole rabbit went down the silver dragon's throat.

"Good gods, you just swallowed it whole!" he exclaimed in astonishment as he glanced at the dragon again. It was only three feet long, but if it kept eating like that, it would be big in no time flat.

He turned back to the way he needed to walk. "After we get ourselves something to drink, we need to find a way out of this oasis," he told Stalker with a little sarcasm. "So if you know a way out, lead on because I seriously believe I have been leading us in circles."

Stalker perked up and began looking around as if to see a way out that it could not find.

Ken smiled. "Stalker," he said to get its attention. "It's alright if you don't know a way to get us out. We're both survivors. Eventually, we will venture out of here. Until then? We'll hunt this desert dry," he told it with a chuckle.

Stalker snapped its jaw, and Ken got the feeling Stalker approved of his plan.

Ken then began the slow walk towards the far-off cactus, still amazed at how well he could see in the dark. Both of them remained highly alert for the sound of anything moving, and neither of them seemed to make a sound, so they would not alert anything to their own presence.

Twice more, they caught food, a snake and a lizard, both of which he gave to Stalker, snacking a little on his dry rations as the dragon ate. Once at the cactus, he carefully began draining the pulp for water until they both had enough, and his canteen was full. Then he oriented himself by the sun, the ability to sense it giving him a way to sense directions, something he had not had over the last week and a half.

That sense of direction gave him hope that he would soon find a road and follow it to a town or city just by traveling north. That night, still no road in sight, Stalker slept next to him, and for the first time, he really came to understand he no longer felt the cold; he had not since he had woken up. The wounds on his arm were all but gone already, but his chest was still a gigantic purple welt.

Day Thirteen; July 13th

"What the hell did you do to me?" Ken asked curiously when he woke, knowing he had slept a long time, and touched the slightly hot wound on his chest, sending a tingling through his body.

Suddenly, he felt his mind grow cool, and a picture of Ken and Stalker flashed through his mind. The picture made them both seem larger than life and nearly invincible. Stalker was gigantic with horns and teeth that were long, sharp, and wicked-looking, and Ken looked big and deadly.

He looked over at Stalker and rubbed his silver head with an amused laugh. "Is that how we will look?" he asked teasingly. "If so, then there is nobody who could beat us."

He had meant it as a jest, while Stalker let out a pleased grumble when Ken tousled his head affectionately. It gave Ken a serious look at his statement.

Another picture entered Ken's mind. This one was from the nightmare Ken had while dreaming. It was of a gigantic Titan gripping a spear, and the caution he felt from Stalker told him just how deadly the Titan was.

But he shrugged, looking at Stalker seriously. "There are no Titans here," he assured the silver dragon.

Another picture formed in his mind. First, a desert with nothing but rabbits, snakes, and humans. The next picture was the same, only now, Stalker was there. The third was the same, but now with a Titan.

And Ken suddenly understood what the dragon was trying to tell him. There had been no dragons, but they appeared. There were no Titans, but they were coming.

"How? There is no way for Titans to come here?" he told Stalker confidently.

Stalker gave him a frustrated look, as if the dragon knew what to answer, just not how to tell him.

A picture of a dragon entered his mind, and with it, a feeling that Ken knew what a dragon was. It was not an individual dragon he recognized; it was the fact that it was a dragon that he recognized. And Ken knew what the dragon was telling him. He knew a dragon when he saw one. He knew Stalker was a dragon.

A picture then came to him of a Titan, as Stalker realized Ken was starting to understand and got excited. Ken again felt that recognition and then fear, which Ken quickly got rid of, understanding fully what Stalker was telling him. How did he, Ken, know what a dragon was by sight? How did he know what a Titan was by sight?

He thought about it for a minute. He had obviously believed they were myths of some kind. But if Stalker was right, then somewhere in Earth's past, the two species had been known, which could only mean they had been to Earth before, for the story to be passed on to humans. And that meant there was some way for Titans to come to Earth. The dragon queen had made it, though she died in the process, but if Titans had a way, there was no wonder Stalker was so cautious.

"How, though?" Ken asked again.

Stalker just looked away, uninterested, as if all that mattered was that they would come.

Ken tousled the silver dragon's head playfully again until it lost its seriousness and began a pleasant rumble.

Day Fourteen, July 14th

The next day, they both got up early, and Stalker lived up to his name, wandering farther and farther out ahead, trying to track, hunt, and catch anything that so much as moved above or below the ash. A few hours later, Ken was surprised to find Stalker had stopped hunting and was just waiting for him. The silver dragon's eagerness was written all along his tense body.

When Ken caught up to him, it did not take him long to figure out why. Up ahead was a flat of ash that must be a road, and following it with his eyes, he saw a gas station.

"Stalker," Ken told him seriously. "I want you to hold back. If someone is alive here, I don't want them to see you. It is safer that way. You hide, stalk, and watch me without being seen," he instructed.

All of Stalker's enthusiasm melted off his silver body, his head dipping, and Ken could not help but smile as he lifted Stalker's head with one finger so the dragon was looking him in the eyes.

"Cheer up. If there are other people here, they are most likely the type neither of us would care to meet. You and I are loners because there are so few like us. Not all humans will like you. We have a lot of myths about dragons, and very few, if any, are good. Humans will be scared and afraid of you, and if they believe or really fear you mean them harm, they will attack you unhesitatingly, even if it means their certain death. And since all of our myths talk about dragons as killers and firestarters, there will be few humans like me who will give you a chance. Most will not, and even more of them want to blame you, dragons, for the meteor storm. But don't let that give you a bad picture of humans. Respect them, and they will come to see reality from myth. Don't harm a human unless you have no other option. But never trust them either. You trust me, and any that I trust."—then he laughed—"which will be few enough that you could count them on one hand—or claw in your case."

He looked towards the gas station, seeing no sign of anyone, then turned back to Stalker to make sure the silver dragon was still paying attention to him.

"So hide and watch, and if no one is there, I will call for you to come," he assured Stalker.

Stalker gave him an uncertain look, then bumped his head affectionately against Ken's shoulder, careful not to poke him with his horns. Then he flew off into the haze.

Ken watched Stalker until he was out of sight. Then he slowly and carefully made his way towards the road and its gas station, the K-Bar held firmly in his leather-gloved left hand. When he reached it, the place looked abandoned. It looked like a meteor had knocked a good-sized hole in its roof.

All of his senses were amped up as he approached the door. There were two cars; both were burned, and he knew someone had been here trying to start the cars. That made him even more cautious. He glanced through the store's windows, but his senses could not reach beyond them. Inside, the place had a slight glow to it, almost as if there was a small fire still going from when the meteor smashed through the roof. Yet he could not see any sign of smoke inside and none coming out, just the regular ash haze that surrounded the gas station and filled the air with darkness.

He cautiously and quietly slid the door open and let himself in, trying to quest out ahead with his senses for anything alive, and halted as he felt something warm yet cool just ahead of him. Inside the store, most of the shelves had been knocked over, with packages of food covering the ground. Some had been opened and neatly piled by the trash, but others were unopened, and the sight made his stomach grumble in hunger. Seeing food he could actually use just lying about surprised him when he knew by the neatly piled bags and wrappers, someone was still here or had been here.

He went deeper into the store, smelling a horrible smell, and saw a horribly burnt dead man lying in an aisle, and next to him, to his surprise, was the thing making light. It must have been what had made the hole in the roof—a glowing metallic meteor or, as he knew what it was, a dragon egg.

As he walked curiously closer to it, feeling its cool presence with his mind, it began to vibrate in warning.

"I would not touch it. It will burn you badly," a young female voice told him, nearly startling the hell out of him.

He felt slow and stupid to have been startled by a girl. He had put too much attention on the dragon egg and had not even noticed her crouched with a metal bar in her hands right next to the counter. He turned slightly to look at her, in no way at all showing she had even startled him. She was shivering in the cold, wrapped in a blanket. All that could be seen of her was her face and the surprisingly steady hands holding the metal bar.

"Are you the army? Have they come to help?" she asked hopefully as she took a good look at him in the light of the egg and noticed the camos he was wearing.

He shook his head slowly. "I seriously doubt there is an army anymore," he told her quietly before turning back to study the egg. It was sun-yellow with bluish-silver strips around it.

Ignoring her, he turned, bending over the egg. "If you burn me, I will feed you to your brother," he warned the egg seriously before gently lifting the egg off the ground.

It continued to vibrate in warning, but it did not try to burn him. With his other hand, he put away his knife.

"What? Why did it not burn you?" the girl asked, incredulously as she came a little closer, her eyes pleading desperately. "Please, sir, don't take it. It is so cold and dark, and it has kept me warm, or better yet, take me with you, yeah, please take me with you." She motioned to the dead man.

"My dad was all I had. I ran the store for him. Then,"—she gestured hurriedly outside—"all this happened, and he got burnt when our car exploded, then became sick when I tried to take care of him. Then the second storm came, and this fell through our roof. The shock of it must have killed him, and since then this"—she motioned to the yellow egg in his hand—"has been keeping me warm. But it burned me when I tried to move it away from—" She went to motion to her dad, then instead, she showed him the palm of her hand, which had a huge purple bruise that covered the whole inside of her hand. It was just like the one on his chest. "See," she said, showing him. "It burned me badly."

Ken looked down at the egg, his face angry, "You marked her," he stated, incredulously.

The egg stopped vibrating, and Ken shook his head in surprise before turning to study the girl more intently.

"No," he told her after a second. "I cannot take this. Here, it's yours if you want it. It won't burn you now that you've been marked," he told her softly as he held the yellow egg out to her.

She gave him a skeptical look, then looked down at the metal bar in her hands, a little unsure, and judging whether or not to let it go and grab the warm object he held.

"Why are you talking to it? Can it understand you? And how do I know for sure it won't burn me again?" she demanded in a voice that showed she was trying to hide her fear.

He lifted a hand, taking off the sunglasses so he could see her even better, to look in her eyes so she would know he was telling her the truth and not trying to trick her. But whatever he had intended to do wasn't what happened.

She gasped in fear as she looked at him, holding the iron bar up protectively in front of her so she could strike him if he tried to attack her.

"Stay away!" she demanded fiercely.

"Whoa," he told her in a calming voice, holding the hand with his glasses up in a calming gesture. "What's wrong? Don't you understand if I had meant you any harm, your dragon here would have warned you or hurt me by now?"

"Dragon?" she asked, like he was crazy and confused. "What, are you crazy?"

Ken lifted the egg. "This is a dragon egg," he explained patiently. "Inside of it is a dragon, your dragon, since it marked you. Like my dragon marked me. See—" He put his glasses in his jacket pocket and opened his jacket, pulling his shirt down, showing her the purple welt identical but a little bigger than hers.

"Your... your eyes are silver. And there is no such thing as dragons," she exclaimed nervously, staying well away from him.

"Stalker, come here," Ken commanded lightly.

Waiting on the roof, next to the hole the egg had made its entrance from, Stalker eagerly dropped through the hole and flew in.

The girl screamed in fright, then watched with shocked awe as the silver dragon flew to the yellow egg, giving off a loud rumbling purr that was answered by a quiet rumble from within the egg a second later.

"A dragon," she whispered softly, not truly believing her eyes. "A real dragon."

Ken watched as she slowly lowered the iron bar and came towards him hesitantly.

"Don't try to touch Stalker," he warned her seriously, seeing her giving the silver dragon an awed look.

Stalker studied her just as intently before he dropped to the ground right next to Ken's leg, his eyes silver like Ken's, never leaving the girl.

The girl, Ken noticed as she got closer and was lit by the egg's light, had shortish black hair, blue eyes turning silver, and Ken thought she would be rather beautiful once all the ash was off her. He wasn't certain of her age, maybe seventeen. And despite a store full of food, she was gaunt and pale.

Ken held the yellow egg to her. "It won't burn you," he assured her confidently as she hesitated to grab it.

When she finally did, taking the egg gently from him, it began to vibrate softly in her arms, not the violent vibrating it had done to warn off Ken.

"What's your name?" he asked her after a second, putting back on his glasses because the bright light of the egg was giving him a headache. "My name is Ken Callay," he told her in introduction as he reached down to stroke Stalker's horny head. "This is Stalker."

She looked up from the yellow-blue egg. "My name is Kate Fox, but everyone calls me Katty," she told him nervously, then whispered in a wondering voice, looking at the egg, "It's alive!"

Ken nodded with a soft smile before looking down at Stalker with a worried expression.

"Our problems seem to have just multiplied," he told Stalker in his mind.

Stalker grumbled in reply, acknowledging their new predicament.

CHAPTER TEN

Day 15-27

They ended up staying in the gas station for a week. Ken moved and buried Kate's father to make the place semi-livable while they ate and drank from the store. Ken stayed there long enough to nurse Katty back to health, then with two packs of food and canteens, they set off with the egg and silver dragon.

This time, cutting through the desert was a lot easier as Ken now had a map that showed him the safest cities and towns to the north, which he decided to keep traveling towards.

His week with Katty had helped him come to a better understanding of the egg's choice. At first, he had thought that maybe it had chosen her just because she was the only human around at the time. But getting to know her, he quickly realized she had a hidden layer of iron inside her. By the time they had left, he had grown fond of her.

The morning after he arrived, both of their bruises had cleared up, and to their surprise, they were left with identical marks. His was just bigger because it was on his chest, and hers was on her palm. Where the bruises had been were now metallic marks of a red dragon's claw, with crystal gold talons tipping it.

Ken knew the mark must symbolize something, but Stalker, in his smug way, refused to tell him. By the time they left, Katty's eyes were as silver as his own, and she had little trouble seeing through the darkness.

As soon as they left, he began teaching her how to survive in the desert. A skill he assured her she needed to know because of their dragons. He doubted very much they would ever be able to stay long in any city for the safety of their dragons and themselves. He'd also had her wear a pair of sunglasses so if they did run into other humans, they would not see their eyes and be overly suspicious of them.

The day after they left the gas station behind them, the sun-yellow scaled dragon with a blue-scaled belly hatched from his egg, and Katty fussed over him for nearly three hours. Unlike Stalker, the yellow dragon only had two horns above its eyes and a row of smaller horns running down its back to the end of its tail.

Katty named him Keen, a name the sun-yellow dragon took to liking instantly. But whether she meant it for its voice or its intelligence, Ken wasn't sure. It did seem to be a fitting name for the dragon. It could hunt better than all of them put together, digging under feet of ash and sand to find snake dens, lizards, and a lot of things Ken himself would never have suspected were there. And the yellow dragon was brassy, teasing Stalker over every catch that Stalker had missed.

Stalker, Ken knew, really didn't mind. He would tussle the younger, smaller dragon and pretend to maul it. But he knew Stalker just liked hunting warm-blooded and larger prey, so he let the younger dragon hunt the smaller, harder-to-find prey.

Katty, for her part, listened very attentively to him, learning the best plants for food and where to find water beneath the sand. Most things were hidden under the large layer of ash, but Ken could always find them. It was a slow process, but in the horrible conditions they faced, he taught her the best he could. Thankfully, like him, she no longer felt the cold, so he did not have to work too hard to find them shelter at night. Once he had picked a spot, he started teaching her the basics of hand-to-hand combat mixed with knife fighting. He put aside an hour or two each night for it before they got some rest. And while they played and fought, so did the two dragons.

They would pause at times to watch Stalker teaching Keen, pinning the yellow dragon down easily and miming mauling him. One time, Keen got so angry that he bit or tried to bite Stalker's tail. They did not know what happened, but afterwards, they heard Keen's anguished roar. The yellow dragon hid for a day after that until he returned, his wounded pride healed, to start it all over again. And afterward, he never got angry at Stalker when the silver dragon was teaching him.

Meanwhile, Ken's senses seemed to be heightening to even higher levels of awareness. He could sense the magnetic north easily without trying. He could find and sense water or water-soaked plants. He could sense with his eyes closed where animals, even insects, were without them even moving. In his mind, they became flares of warmth. It was easier when they were close, but he could sense stuff far off as well and tried to teach Katty to sense them, knowing that with her growing senses, she should be able to do so as well. But after days of trying, he came to realize the most she could sense were large things, like animals and the dragons, when she was close to them. She couldn't sense north, water, or bugs.

Both their strength and endurance were also growing by leaps and bounds. Ken noticed it quickly because he had been trained to learn and know his limits, and he had easily surpassed every single one of them. His speed and balance were better than they had ever been in his life. He had run miles chasing and pushing Katty without even breaking a sweat. So he was casual about testing himself, almost scared. He at one time held his breath for over fifteen minutes without struggling, so he had spent his time pushing Katty, testing her almost nonstop, watching as she grew stronger and stronger and more confident about herself with each passing day. He soon realized she could easily pass any test he himself had ever taken to become a Green Beret.

That seriously surprised him, seeing as he had only known her for two weeks, and of that, he had only been training her intensely for one week. And if she continued to learn as quickly as she was, then he could only imagine her potential, let alone his own.

When a change suddenly came over Stalker, they both noticed it. The silver dragon began to get short-tempered with Keen and began spending more and more time by himself or only around Ken. And his scales began to take on a glossy look.

Wondering if his dragon was getting sick, he tried to keep near him and gave the silver dragon what comfort he could.

Day 28, July 28th

When Ken awoke the next day, it was to find that Stalker, for the first time in weeks, was not next to him or even close. When he got worried, he closed his eyes and sensed that Stalker was a mile away and flying off. Surprised, he alerted Katty that he would be back and took off after the silver dragon, knowing something was wrong, just not sure what it was.

Which led him to stalking the silver dragon. When he caught up to it, he was out of breath. The dragon had flown for miles with Ken hot on his trail. Where the dragon had stopped was a huge sand-rock cave in which it had hidden itself. And as Ken quietly got closer, he could see that Stalker was twitching every now and then, and unnoticed, Ken slid deeper inside, getting closer to his dragon. Surprised, Stalker had not sensed him there. They had played hide and seek in the desert, and Stalker had very good senses, though for some reason, not as good as his own were now.

The weird thing was, as he slid closer to Stalker, the silver dragon was looking right at him without seeing him. Stalker seemed to be in silent agony, but all he could feel from the dragon was as if Stalker had a fierce itch. Seeing him like that made him all the more worried. How could he be so close to Stalker, and the silver dragon not even see him or sense him? He didn't seem to sense the silent agony the dragon was in, but he could see it, so somehow it meant Stalker was masking it from him.

When he got close enough to touch Stalker, and the silver dragon still did not know he was there, he really got worried. Something was definitely wrong with his dragon.

"Stalker, are you alright?" he asked in concern, no longer able to hold back his worry.

The sound startled the dragon so badly that it roared in defense, trying to lash out blindly at the sound of his voice.

Ken quickly slid back out of the blind dragon's path of fury and away from the sparks that lit the little cavern they were in. Then he tried to soothe Stalker with his mind.

"It's okay, Stalker, it's just me, Ken. You're safe, no need to try and eat me," he teased soothingly, then more seriously. "I'll protect you. Just tell me what's wrong. Did you eat something poisonous, or are you just sick?" he asked in his mind.

As he continued to soothe the silver dragon, it began to calm down and go out of defense mode. But now he began to twitch even harder than before, Stalker's scales rippling in a painful-looking movement that made Ken flinch as he watched it.

The silver dragon either couldn't answer or deemed not to and just ignored Ken. Not to be deterred, Ken continued to soothe and reassure the dragon, getting closer again now that Stalker had calmed down. He sat next to the dragon, determined to sit with him through whatever it was Stalker was going through.

What he saw next was not something he expected to happen; it shocked and amazed him. Stalker arched his back like a blind cat, and there was a sudden tearing sound as the scales on Stalker's back split wide open, right down the middle, revealing shiny new scales that slowly pushed up through the old ones like an armor plate. Stalker's head popped off, revealing a softer one that beat softly in and out with Stalker's heartbeat, and Ken knew it would harden, but Stalker was at his most vulnerable right now.

A second later, Stalker began to emerge slowly and painfully from his old hard scales, and as he did, the soft-scaled silver dragon began to stretch and lengthen, doubling in size. By the time Stalker had finished, he was six feet long, a lot thicker, and looked even deadlier than before, with all of his horns lining his body now a little bigger.

"Wow," Ken said appreciatively as he looked at the new and improved silver dragon over, and Stalker looked at him, turning his large, soft head his way. "You should have told me!" Ken reprimanded him. "Do you know how vulnerable you were? Are?" he asked, incredulously.

Then, as the silver dragon wilted a little, Ken reached forward, touching the soft scales that had yet hardened. The touch made Stalker shiver slightly and sent a blast of warmth up Ken's arm.

"Next time, you tell me so I can guard you. I snuck right up next to you without you even knowing," he scolded him.

Stalker made a noise as if amused, and a cool feeling entered Ken's mind as a picture of Stalker as a fierce predator, unscared of anything, formed for Ken to see.

Ken laughed and gently pushed the soft, larger dragon. "Whatever, look at you, you're all soft and cuddly," he teased, and to prove a point, he tussled with the silver dragon, holding him down and rubbing his soft scales until Stalker succumbed to a deep rumble of pleasure.

Ken could still feel Stalker's itchiness in his mind, so he set about scratching all of the silver dragon's new soft scales—his back, head, legs, wings, and tail—until smoke was issuing from Stalker's nostrils in uncontrollable pleasure.

Once all the itchiness had gone away and the silver dragon faded off to sleep, Ken studied the remains of the Stalker's shedding, scales, and claws.

The scales, he felt, picking up the heavy skin, were still harder than iron, yet a lot lighter. And after a minute of debating, he decided they would keep them. He could think of a couple of things they might be useful for.

Two weeks later, on August 11th, Keen shed.

CHAPTER ELEVEN

Day 18; July 18th

Location: Pantiers' Residence

The night and day after the deer hunt were long for Derek. He had stayed up the rest of the night helping cut up deer meat because, with Spring's excitement from the hunt still flowing through him, there was no way he would have been able to get any sleep. Not long after that was done, he found himself holding an axe again for the first time in a week as he helped chop wood with the Bergers.

Meanwhile, as he chopped wood, the Bergers stood watching him, in the light of butter-wick lamps, (A trick Emma had found worked for fire since oil and gasoline seemed to explode when lit. So Emma had figured out all kinds of things that worked in lamps and had lamps hanging all over the back of the building, so they had light to see while they chopped wood.) with growing surprise. They were once again huddled close together around Spring to keep warm as they took a break. Each of them was wearing heavy clothes to stay warm, ski masks over their faces, and leather work gloves to prevent their hands from freezing to their axes. At the same time, Derek was comfortable swinging his axe in jeans and a t-shirt, with only sunglasses on to cover his face. And those he was using because the light of the lamps glared brilliantly in his eyes, giving him a nasty headache. Yet, for some reason, the light from the lamps did not bother Spring. She just sat and studied their surroundings for any intruders.

"Em removed his stitches; there was not even a scar!" Nattilie exclaimed to her brothers in astonishment.

Nathan grimaced and rubbed his still sore head. "I wish I healed like that."

Nate smiled, stretching and shaking his head in wonder. "We've rested long enough," he told them with a weary sigh. "Any longer and none of us will be able to stay close to him in strength."

Both Nathan and Nattilie groaned, neither of them wanting to leave Spring's warmth yet. But they both hefted their axes, as Nate did himself.

Not too far off, Derek watched them with a smile as he easily sliced through the wood of the tree he was chopping up. The axe was now just an extension of his arm, which did not even feel the strain of hefting it for so long. Every now and then, at even intervals, he would switch hands, learning how to handle the axe ambidextrously, just as he was learning the sword.

"Stay close to them, Spring, so they don't get too cold," he told Spring in the coolness of her mind.

He knew the Bergers had been out chopping wood for the last week, but they had never been out this long. And the last thing he wanted was for them to get sick because they wanted to compete with him.

Last night, he'd had a long conversation with Emma as they cut up the deer meat. At first, she had been angry at him for leaving the house and risking an infection. But she had quieted down when he had shown her his wounds had all healed. She had checked them thoroughly, to her surprise, before she had cut off the stitches that were no longer needed.

"A week," she had exclaimed incredulously when she was done taking the stitches out. "And not even a scar."

She had then begun hounding him with questions about anything unusual he could do, and as he dodged each one, she made him promise to tell her if he noticed he could do other things that were out of the ordinary. That had made him smile because he had known right there and then that she had been writing down everything out of the ordinary that she knew or suspected he could do. He even knew what she had written about his all-seeing eyesight and senses, immunity to the cold, weird communication with his dragon, suspected mind communication, etc.

Knowing that she had written everything down, when he could not possibly know that, startled him. He realized immediately that he had read it unintentionally from her mind. He kept his surprise to himself and off his face as he reviewed everything she knew and had jotted down. The list was surprisingly long, and the things she had noticed about Spring were even longer, he had noticed with amusement.

Thinking on it now worried him. He did not mind them studying him and Spring. What bothered him was that she was writing it all down, and if someone else besides Em ever read those notes, it might spell disaster for both of them. He would have to find a way to broach the subject without letting her know how he knew about what she was writing.

When he noticed later that the Bergers were getting exhausted and cold, he put down his axe and took a break.

They all straightened as he approached. "I think Herb should be waiting for us," he told them as he rubbed Spring's head affectionately.

Spring let out a loud rumbling purr before butting him playfully with her shoulder, trying to knock him back. Feeling her playfulness, he wrapped his arms around her neck and began wrestling with her. She instantly mock-growled and rose onto her hind legs, trying to tackle him onto his back while her front claws tried to wrap around behind his legs to pull him off his feet as her chest pushed against him. It would have worked had Derek not sprawled, pushing his hips back from her before she could take his balance. He was amazed by her strength and weight and strained with all his might to push her back as she tried to keep him close, careful not to let her claws dig into his back and legs.

Putting a little muscle into it, he got leverage and used an arm to lift her claw off his back long enough for him to spin under it and around to jump on her back, tackling her to the side and sending ash flying around them. He felt her surprise and excitement at his move as they tumbled on the ground, him on her back, holding her head by her two small horns, keeping her from dislodging him. At least until he felt her sneaky tail try to wrap around his own neck. Then he realized she'd be able to pin him if he did not let go quickly.

So he let go of her head and began scratching her sides. Her mock growl turned into an instant loud rumble, and her back legs started kicking in the ash as the scratching pleasure became unbearable.

The others watched them both with amusement until ash began to fill the air, and laughing, they backed away from the ash cloud Spring was creating.

"See what you did?" Derek accused playfully after a second, standing up and brushing ash off his clothes, face, and hair, with false indignation. "Now I'm covered in this grime that I can't even wash off," he complained with a smile.

Nathan laughed. "You were already covered in grime."

Nattilie nodded. "The only one who isn't is Spring," she said, looking at the sparkling clean red and gold dragon.

Nathan coughed, whipping ash off his face. "I will be glad when all of this ash is gone," he told them as he headed back towards the building's basement and began stomping and brushing ash off of himself in a clear spot Em kept free of ash, at least as much as she could, so they could get most of it off of them before they entered the basement door.

All around the door were wooden planks, and Herb was making an area to tarp off to keep the ash from getting by the door, so it was easier to dust off the ash and sweep it out of the tarped area before entering the house. It would be like a semi-clean room before entering the house, and it was only half built so far. Derek would help Herb finish it later.

His brother and sister followed him as Derek brushed off even more ash from his clothes, then retrieved his axe.

When the Bergers were all in the basement, Derek looked over at Spring, who was busy inspecting one of her claws. "Nate seems more determined than ever," he told her in a musing voice.

Spring looked at him, and he felt a mixture of emotions come from her as she showed him what Nate felt: courage, determination, jealousy, and admiration.

He frowned thoughtfully at those feelings before shrugging them off. "Come on, let's go join all the others before they eat without us."

At the mention of eating, Spring suddenly lost interest in her claws, and he could feel her hunger.

He smiled and led her inside.

Day 18-35

The next few weeks flew by for all of them. Derek and the Bergers continued to gain strength and train. Herb now had them each sparring with each other or with himself with the bokken. Sometimes, even Ranger Ellis stopped in to practice with them, but he was mainly foraging, hunting, and trying to gain information about other places and towns that might have survived. Once he disappeared for five days, and when he returned, he was frozen and exhausted, but he brought back three extra bikes along with some other supplies.

While the Ranger rested, they began to plan where they should try to head, or if they should even risk traveling now. They were running out of supplies, but with Spring, they could get enough meat, and they did not have to fear going without water because the well was remaining full and untainted by ash—a risk they would have to take if they decided to leave.

Aug. 4th

Towards the end of the fifth week after the meteor storm, the air began to lighten slightly during the day, and a shadow of the sun could finally be seen in the sky. It did nothing to warm the air, though.

During the last week, Derek had also noticed a sudden change in Spring. Her mind began to feel all itchy to him. She began to get grumpy around others, and her scales all began to dull in color. Instantly worried, he had gone to Herb and Ellis, worried she might be sick. But when they even got close to her, she tensed up, growling fiercely, smoke oozing from her snout.

Derek held up a hand for them to stop and went to her, soothing her by scratching her dull scales, even though he knew it did nothing to soothe her itchiness. And when he looked into her eyes, he grew even more worried when he saw they too were glossing over.

"It's alright, Spring. I know you keep telling me you're not sick, but I know something is wrong. Let them take a look at you. Maybe they can help," he told her in a calming voice.

A picture of Spring, gigantic and awe-inspiring, whole and perfect, floated through Derek's mind as she tried again to reassure him she was fine, but just itchy.

"All the same," he told her lightly, trying to keep the worry from his voice. "Let them look, if only to reassure me."

He watched Spring turn her head towards them and noticed that she could barely even see them. That made his worry all the more pronounced, and he motioned them forward.

Smoke still oozed from her, but her growl stopped, and Herb and Ellis quickly came over to study her intently.

After a second, Herb shrugged. "I don't know what's ailing her," he told Derek, sounding as confused as Derek felt.

On the other hand, Ellis was studying her thoughtfully, and as if coming to a conclusion, he nodded to himself, not looking so worried anymore.

"Spring has not grown an inch since she hatched and attained her full size. She has eaten a lot and gained plenty of weight, filling out a little more and getting thicker. But she is generally the same size," he said, looking at Derek. "She does not seem worried?" he asked curiously.

Derek rubbed her neck. "No, just easily aggravated, as you can both see, and…" He frowned. "She feels itchy," he told Ellis with a shrug.

"Itchy? What do you mean?" Herb asked curiously.

"All of her scales itch and burn. She hides most of the pain from me, but I still feel it," he explained.

"Feel it?" Ellis asked in surprise. "In what way?"

Derek suddenly wondered how much he should tell him about how closely bound he and Spring were. Then he decided he might tell them a little since they were trying to help him figure out what was wrong with Spring.

"I can feel everything she feels. Her emotions, pains, hunger, anything she wanted me to feel, and sometimes stuff she doesn't want me to feel, like her itchy sensation now. She can feel the same from me. That is why she hatched like she did. She felt me get hurt and knew I was dying. Hatching like she did was the only way she could keep me alive, so she did it," he told them with a smile of affection for Spring as he rubbed her neck. "But now she has found a way to block parts of her mind from me," he continued, sounding annoyed. "I wouldn't mind if I didn't think she was just trying to hide her pain."

"You mean you can read her mind?" Ellis asked in an astonished voice.

Derek frowned, knowing this conversation was getting close to an area that he did not want to pursue. "It's just my link with her," he told them seriously. "What she thinks I know, what I think she knows. Only now she's trying to hide her pain from me."

Herb nodded as if he had just confirmed something he had already suspected.

Ellis turned back to Spring. "I don't think anything is wrong with her. In fact, I think she is just growing," he assured Derek with a smile. "I think she is getting ready to shed her scales, much like a snake does. I would like to see it, but I think it would be too risky to watch closely. She's rather likely to get even more aggressive because she will be completely vulnerable to attack during her shedding. So I would advise you to stay near her during those times so she will be protected."

Surprised to find out that Spring was going to shed, Derek looked at her to confirm Ellis' words. Spring, though, was occupied, ignoring all of them as she gnawed on one of her particularly itchy claws.

Aug. 5th

The next day, Spring began to twitch violently and went down to the basement to be alone. Derek stayed with her, watching over her nervously as she arched and stretched her jaws violently, looking as if she were in intense pain.

While he reassured and kept Spring calm, the others, seeing them rush downstairs, all came to watch from the stairs, staying as quiet as they could so they didn't make Spring feel threatened. They were all curious to see what happened and how she would look after she shed.

Suddenly, a picture formed in Derek's mind, showing him the door and the outside of the house. Then Spring was blindly moving around, crawling towards where she thought the door ought to be. Another frantic picture showed Spring as a gigantic dragon, much too big for the basement.

Derek hurriedly ran to the door, opening it for her, and helped guide her through the tarped tented area they had finished last night and into the sparsely lit backyard.

Spring looked around, searching for some kind of shelter, something to hide under, and Derek could feel her aggravation as she saw nothing but downed trees and the forest. Her frustration at not finding shelter hit Derek hard, then another violent spasm hit her, causing her to arch in pain.

Derek ran to her. "It's okay, Spring, trust me, I will protect you," he told her, forming a picture of him standing guard with his sword in hand.

She made a soft chuckling noise, then arched again. This time, though, Derek heard a ripping sound and watched in shock as the top of her head popped and peeled off her like an armored plate. The scales upon her back split down the center, and she began to arch and stretch out of her dull-colored scales, revealing a bright red head as it came out first, followed by her back, wings, and legs.

Derek was forced to step back in astonishment as she began to grow, unfolding and stretching her new scales, soft and slick, huge compared to the little dull ones she was stepping out of. Her wings opened into the air, stretching themselves out towards the dark, hazy sky. He could not believe his eyes. She was tremendous, as big as, if not bigger than, the black and red dragon he had seen in his mind. And she was still growing bigger. He could feel the others inside the tarped-off area watching her grow with the same awe he himself felt.

Realizing he was suddenly feeling their emotions, he closed his mind to them, feeling uncomfortable reading their minds, as if it were a violation of common courtesy.

When Spring was done, she stood tall, glistening in the light of the couple of lamps and the faint light of the sun. In his eyes, she beamed with radiant light as she stared down at him with her soft, liquid silver eyes. Her scales were lightly trembling and rippling, and he could feel how much they itched her.

He stepped forward, touching her front leg, which was now as thick as he was. A feeling of warmth traveled through him, and he felt her hot and slick scales beneath his palm.

"Wow," he exclaimed as he began scratching her soft-feeling scales.

She grumbled appreciatively, leaning into his hand. He grinned and began scratching a little harder, causing her tail to slam into the ground, swirling up ash through the air as her grumbling purr grew to even greater heights.

For the next hour, he scratched her scales as she lay upon the ground, rumbling affectionately as he took away her itching. The Bergers slowly came from the tented area and began to help him, timid at first because of her size, then more excitedly as Spring let them scratch her.

While they helped scratch Spring, Emma, Herb, and Ellis looked at the dull scales left behind. Herb held up the top plate of what used to be Spring's head. He studied it in the light of the lamps, then gasped with astonishment when he looked through the eyeholes.

Amazed, he held it out for Ellis to look through.

Ellis paused what he was doing and looked through the eyeholes in what was left of what used to be Spring's head. He sucked in his breath. Everything around him lit up brilliantly; he could see deep into the forest with no problem.

Ellis handed it back, and they both just stared at it in wonder.

"Think you could make a helmet out of it? Its eyes are perfectly spaced, maybe line it with some leather..." Ellis asked as he thought it over.

Herb looked at it. "It's possible," he replied quietly. "If Derek approves. I don't think he will mind, though."

Herb bent, studying the dull scales. "These would be perfect to make an armor suit out of. The gold scales are small enough to make gauntlets with, and they are so strong that only a very strong, well-placed blow with a katana blade would be able to pierce them. They are even lighter than metal."

Emma watched them curiously before speaking. "Armor? Like olden-day armor?"

Herb nodded. "There are enough scales here to make a full suit and probably two pairs of gauntlets. If a way can be found to line them with leather so they won't bite into the person wearing them."

While they sat musing about how it could be done, Spring finally stood up and stretched.

Derek and the others all took a step back from her as she spread her wings out. A picture of her flying gracefully filled Derek's mind, and he smiled, touching her leg.

"Go," he told her gently.

Spring hunched to the ground, then launched herself off it. Her wings beat a couple of times, fanning and catching air, scattering ash, then she was in the sky.

Derek closed his eyes and felt her coolness, seeking her mind so he could watch out of Spring's own eyes as she flew. The feeling of air coursing over her wings and scales as she sliced through the air made Spring happy, and she soared effortlessly through the sky.

"She is so big!" Nattilie whispered with awe, touching Derek's arm.

Her touching him was so shocking, he opened his eyes, pulling his mind from Spring's, as a weird tingling went through him. He shook it off and looked at her.

"She's bigger than the black and red dragon," he told her with admiration.

"She's big enough to ride now," Nathan exclaimed happily, and not a little louder.

Derek shook his head. "I don't know," he began, until Spring's emotions broke through his mind.

He felt anger at him doubting her ability and strength, and a picture of her carrying him in her claws easily and gently while flying appeared firmly in his mind.

He smiled, shaking his head, and sent a picture correcting her of him sitting upon her back as she flew.

That picture brought back a rush of excitement and amusement from Spring. A second later, he felt her approach, diving down to land lightly on the ground right next to them.

Derek smiled at her excitement and shook his head as he looked up at her. "Not right now," he told her patiently, rubbing her snout. "Wait until your scales harden more, then we will try it. And we will have to make sure we have some kind of saddle to sit on and hold me in place until we are both used to it. Your scales and horns will cut me to shreds if I try sitting on you without one," he explained.

Spring looked down at him with an upset expression and grumbled before stretching again, hunger overriding all of her emotions in Derek's mind.

Just sitting, she was over twelve feet tall. He knew she had to be close to or over sixteen feet long. The two horns over her eyes were only a little longer, as was the row of spikes running down her back and tail. While he studied her, he noticed the spikes stopped on her lower neck and upper back, right where he would be sitting if he rode her. That kind of surprised him, as did the fact of how little her claws and teeth were compared to her new size. He had no doubt they would grow quickly now that they had room to grow. Her horns, spikes, and claws all glittered with more gold streaks, and her liquid silver eyes seemed to be lit from within by a silver fire.

Seeing his appreciative look, Spring bent, touching his forehead with her snout. A burst of warmth, like a breaking dam, filled his body; it was so hot it almost burned, causing him to gasp. The mark upon his chest lit up fiercely through his shirt as if it were on fire. Affection filled his mind, and as he caught his breath, he reached up, scratching her neck, ignoring the heat coursing through his body, causing his heart to thump erratically and sweat to form all over his skin.

He looked up a while later as he felt Ellis approaching with a cooler full of deer meat.

"We have enough to feed her a little, but she's going to have to hunt for more," Ellis told Derek, handing him the heavy cooler of meat, then hid his surprise as the boy took it easily, as if it weighed nothing.

At the smell of all the meat, Spring, now totally sapped of strength from what she had done to Derek, perked right up, hungrily looking at Derek expectantly.

Derek set the cooler down, opening it, and began tossing her pieces after piece as he unwrapped them.

"This will have to hold you over until we can go hunting for some more deer," he explained as he fed her.

"I hope it's enough to hold her over? She is a lot bigger than I even imagined she would get this shed, and I remember how much she ate when she first hatched," Ellis mused as he watched her swallow all the meat.

Derek tossed her the last piece. "This will give her enough energy to wait until tomorrow, when her scales are hard enough to go hunting. I think she ate enough the last couple of days to be okay even if we don't hunt tomorrow."

He then turned to Ellis as Spring began to groom herself and continued stretching. "Can you help me make a saddle for her? She wants me to ride her tomorrow, and I will need something to hold me down and keep her scales from slicing me up."

Ellis frowned in surprise as everyone gathered around to admire Spring.

"You're going to ride her?" Emma asked in a shocked voice.

Surprised by the incredulous note in her voice, Derek turned to her. "Spring insists that I try. She was a little offended when I thought she might not be able to."

Behind him, Spring made a loud, indignant noise as if in outrage at such a weakness.

"While she flies?" Emma asked in a stunned, disbelieving voice.

Derek nodded. "Spring can carry my weight easily, but I would need a saddle. Her scales are too sharp for me to sit against while she moves. I would also have to be able to tie down my legs so I wouldn't fall out of the saddle if she made an unexpected turn-"

Suddenly, both Derek and Spring came alert, tensing. Derek's hand went to his sword as a low, dangerous growl began to issue forth from the sparkling red and gold dragon. Neither of them knew what they had just felt, but they had felt it at the same time, assuring them that something was there.

"What's wrong?" Herb demanded as his own hand went to his sword, seeing Derek's look.

Derek sent his senses outward, as he had learned to do when searching to see where one of the Bergers was while he had been stuck the whole week in the house. Whatever was out there fled from his senses, but not before he noticed there was something trying to flee.

He looked up at Spring, and a feeling of excitement came over him as Spring recognized what he had sensed as another dragon. She wanted to take off after it, but he put a restraining hand upon her leg.

"We don't want to scare him off," Derek told her calmly.

Spring settled, looking excited.

"Scare who off?" Ellis asked nervously.

"A Dragon," Derek said with an excited smile.

"A Dragon?" Nathan exclaimed in shock. "Another dragon?"

Derek nodded. "It's young and very hungry. I think it smelled the meat we just fed Spring. Go get some more and bring them out. Let's see if we can't get it to come to us."

Nathan happily ran inside to get more meat.

Derek pulled back his senses, knowing that somehow the dragon could feel him searching for it, and he did not want to scare it off. It did not seem scared of Spring at all, but it felt very wary of him.

"A dragon," Nattilie said, wondering. "I wonder what it looks like? You said he, so it's a boy?" she asked curiously.

"That's what Spring senses. The dragon won't let me sense it. It's too wary of me. But I can feel the hunger it had right before it fled."

Nate stepped aside as Nathan came from the building carrying a couple of packages of deer meat.

Spring stared at it hungrily, licking her teeth, watching as Nate and Nathan both unwrapped the meat, giving Nattilie herself a package to unwrap. When they all ignored her, Spring let out a whimpering rumble full of hunger.

From the forest, in response to the sound, a little deeper in than either Derek or Spring could see, came a rumbling growl in answer to Spring's whine.

Spring instantly perked up, her whine gone, and a short, loud roar of indignation came from her.

Then Derek felt the dragon; it came charging through the forest in a flash and an answering roar, louder than Spring's, filled the air. Surprised birds broke cover from the trees with piercing cries of alarm as they fled their cover. The dragon ignored them, flying right through the bunch as it charged.

Derek's first sight of the dragon was a surprise. It ignored the birds, intent on answering Spring's roar, and though it glowed in his eyes like Spring did, it was not as brilliant. The dragon was all black with a silver underbelly, making it blend in perfectly with the dark forest around it. It was small, only about three feet long, but it looked dangerous, with long, sharp crystal teeth and claws. Three long, sharp horns upon its crested head made it look almost like an ancient Triceratops with wings. But its whole body, wings, and tail were covered in little spikes, and its tail ended in a spiked ball. Derek could only imagine how it would look full-grown.

The only thing that stopped the little dragon from answering Spring's challenging roar was all the humans. As soon as it saw them, it stopped its charge dead still, right at the edge of the lamp's light, but close enough that everyone held their awed breaths when they saw it.

Frustrated and a little unsure of what to do, the dragon roared a challenge at all of them. And for some reason, that challenge heated Derek's blood, almost drawing a growl from him that he had to hurry and calm himself to keep it in so he would not scare it away.

Surprisingly, he felt Spring behind him, giving him a little rumble to help calm himself down.

Nathan, unlike the others, was undaunted by the roar. He walked towards the black dragon, holding the meat.

The dragon froze, unsure. And Derek felt two entirely different feelings come from the dragon. The first was its awesome hunger that tried to override everything. The second was a deeper yearning that Derek could not understand.

Everyone watched, holding their breaths in fear, as the dragon flew right at Nathan, and it was so fast that before Nathan could move, the dragon had snatched the meat from Nathan's hands, eating it and drawing a surprised cry of pain from Nathan, one that instantly had everyone on edge.

"Son of a bitch!" Nathan cried, holding his hand. "It bit me!"

Then he looked angrily at the dragon, who was busy swallowing the big chunk of meat. "You bit me," he accused in surprise.

The dragon looked at him, making an indignant sound. Then turned, growling at Nate and Nattilie, who were walking forward holding out pieces of meat.

"Give the meat to Nathan," Derek warned them before they got too close. The dragon continued its vicious growl until Nathan pushed it out of his way and grabbed the meat from his brother and sister.

He then turned back to the dragon, holding out the meat. "Don't bite me this time, Charger."

Amused, Charger delicately snatched the meat from Nathan, then sat at his feet, working on swallowing both big pieces down.

A loud roar came from Spring as Charger was swallowing the last piece. And swallowing it, his hunger abated. He stood up next to Nathan and drew in a deep breath before he roared loudly and fiercely, the sound shaking the trees.

Derek was surprised by how loud the roar actually was for such a little dragon, as was Spring, as she tried to roar louder and failed by comparison.

Hearing it, to all of their surprise, the little dragon chuffed in amusement, then charged Spring.

Cold flashed through Derek's mind, and he saw Nathan stagger as he too saw the flashes of images both of the dragons relayed to each other while they tussled together. Spring, he noticed, was gentle with the little dragon, catching it at once as it tried to zoom around her. She pinned it down and mimed tearing him apart.

That was when Derek noticed the extra claw on the back of each of Charger's legs. He felt from Spring that they were poisonous, and Charger never once tried to use them on Spring.

After a second, Spring let him up, snapping her jaws at him. Charger stood up with dignity, then shook off the ash, proudly walking to Nathan, at least until it saw it had somehow forgotten some meat. Then it pounced upon it, and everyone laughed as it tore into it.

"Charger's a good name," Nate told his brother, who was busy examining his wounded hand.

Nathan looked up excitedly. "Oh, it's perfect! He has no fear, nothing! Yesterday, he chased off a huge bear! As if he could eat it!" he told his brother with admiration for the black and silver dragon.

Nattilie laughed. "Look at him. There's no way the bear was going to eat him; Charger would get stuck in its throat, and the bear would have died of bad indigestion," she said with a laugh.

Derek came over to take a look at Nathan's hand, whose whole palm was covered in a purple, bloody bruise.

"You've been marked," Derek told him. "I wonder if it's the same as mine?"

Behind him, Spring made a noise that said she was not amused by what Derek had just said.

CHAPTER TWELVE

Day 37; Aug. 6th

The next day was one of excitement for Derek. That night, he slept outside with Spring wrapped around him. This time, he did not feel the cold or dread he had felt the last time he had been forced to sleep outside. Emma had tried to talk sense to him about sleeping inside, but Derek had not spent one night away from the dragon since he had found her egg, and he was not going to stop just because she was now too big to enter the house. So he reassured Emma that he no longer felt the cold and that the air did not bother him; he had not worn nose filters since he had healed from the attack.

All through the night, though, that hot warmth Spring had given him had made him sweat and ache in a weird way. But he woke early feeling nice, warm, and cozy against Spring's scales. And as he stood, she stretched, nudging him affectionately with her head before lying back down while he went to fetch his axe.

To his amazement, he found Herb, Emma, and Ellis huddled inside the basement over a candlelit table covered with leather hides. They all glanced up as he entered, then glanced again in shock.

"Good God's boy! Did you grow even bigger?" Herb exclaimed with vast astonishment.

Looking stunned, Ellis stood up and walked to Derek. He had been taller than the boy before yesterday; now the boy was almost an inch taller than him.

"I'll be damned. He's taller than me!" Ellis muttered in disbelief. "Over two inches in one night? That has to be some kind of record."

Concern all over her face, Emma came around the table. "How do you feel?" she asked worriedly. "Are you sick, tired, hungry?" she asked, reaching up to gently feel how hot his forehead was.

Derek smiled. "I feel fine, in fact, I feel great," he assured, though he could feel his stomach growl in need at the mention of hunger. "I am hungry, but really no more than I usually am at this time of the morning."

Then he stared at Ellis as if just realizing he was taller. "I am taller," he said in amazement. "I didn't even realize it."

Shaking his head carefully, remembering the feeling of warmth Spring had passed into him, he decided to change the subject, wondering just what Spring had done to him. "What are you guys doing up so early?" he asked to change the subject.

Herb sat in a chair by the table, pulled out a pipe, and lit it with a candle, then sat puffing it as he studied Derek. Finally, when neither Emma nor Ellis answered him, Herb spoke up from around the pipe.

"We are finishing the saddle you will need to ride on Spring. But if you grow any bigger, you won't be fitting it," Herb replied in an amused voice.

Herb then reached across the table and picked up a measuring tape, tossing it to Derek. "Go and measure Spring. I will be needing to know her length, girth, and so much more, so I can fit the saddle to her properly."

Derek went and did as they asked, making Spring wake up so he could get the right measurements. When he returned, Ellis had left, and Emma was busy punching holes through the leather and binding pieces together, while Herb sat studying the bottom of a leather saddle horses wore.

"She's sixteen feet, eight inches long-" Derek told him as he entered and gave Herb the other measurements for the girth of Spring's neck, chest, and leg span.

He then watched as Herb slowly designed the saddle so it would fit Spring perfectly. There would be four straps that had to be cinched tight, and two straps for Derek's own legs. One strap would go around Spring's chest, one around each of her two front legs, and the last around her lower neck, so the saddle would be held securely in place without imposing upon Spring's movement and keeping her wings free from hitting him or the straps. His two leg straps would be loosely secured to cinches on the strap around Spring's chest.

As Herb and Emma began measuring out and securing the straps to the saddle, Herb also began instructing Derek how to cinch them down, check the girth so it wasn't too tight or too loose on Spring. And he also warned him to always check the straps for wear or tears because even though the leather they were using was tough and thick, it wouldn't be able to sustain the continued stress of Spring's sharp scales, and eventually, it would wear thin, and that's the last thing he would want to happen when he was in the air.

Derek listened, and when Herb was finished talking, turning his attention back to the saddle, Derek went back outside to see the Bergers all chopping wood, while Charger and Spring both tussled in the ash. He watched it with a smile as he lifted his own axe to join them.

"Nice to see you join us," Nate teased, then paused with a "gawf" and an incredulous look as he saw Derek in the lamplight.

"No way!" Nate exclaimed in disbelief. "You're taller! How?"

Embarrassed, Derek could only shrug. "I'm not sure, but I can't wait for breakfast because I am starving!"

Behind him, Spring and Charger rumbled their agreement.

Derek turned to Nathan, looking at him seriously. "Did Charger explain to you about why they are here?" he asked hopefully.

Nathan nodded. "It is amazing how they communicate," he replied, then he frowned. "But some of the things I have seen, like the…"

Derek reached out to Nathan's mind before he spoke too much. Doing so, he realized Nathan's mind felt different now; it was a lot cooler, like a dragon's mind, than the hot minds of other humans. "Don't speak of the Titans to anyone yet; neither your brother nor sister is ready. Also, how good are your senses? You need to start training and practicing them every second you can spare. That way, nothing will be able to get near you, Charger, or any of us. Spring and I are going to hunt in a couple of hours, and it will be up to you and Charger to protect everyone here. So keep your senses sharp and alert so no one can even get close again," Derek instructed Nathan in his mind.

Nathan struggled for a second before figuring out how to speak into Derek's mind. Derek felt Nathan's mind reach for his and realized he could easily block it if he wanted to. Instead, he sealed off anything personal in his thoughts and let Nathan speak in his mind.

"Senses?" Nathan asked in confusion. "What do you mean?"

Seeing that their silence was unnerving Nate and Nattilie, Derek turned to watch the dragons and laughed as he saw Charger, with his boundless energy, fly circles around Spring, annoying her. "Look at him, doesn't he ever get tired?" he asked Nate and Nattilie, distracting them while he spoke to Nathan in his mind.

"Close your eyes. Feel with your mind. Where is Charger? Spring? Both of them should be cool flares of fire that you can sense easily. Where are your brother and sister? Both of them will feel hot in your mind. Where am I, Em, Herb, Ellis?" he instructed.

Derek then waited a minute, watching the dragons, before he again continued. "Do you feel them?" he asked Nathan curiously.

A minute later, he felt Nathan's reply. "I can sense the cooler flares in the minds of Charger, you, and Spring, but everything else I feel is confusing," Nathan replied in frustration.

Derek smiled and let Nathan feel his approval as he replied. "Our minds are now different from theirs. In order to sense your brother, sister, and the others, you have to recognize their minds. They are warmer, more frantic, and confused compared to ours or our dragon's minds. Keep your eyes closed and sense for your brother. He's right next to you; recognize his presence. Do the same with your sister and the others. Learn the feel of them so you can keep them in your mind at all times. And that way, you recognize who they are, so when anyone else comes around, you will instantly know it is not one of us and be alerted to that fact. Tell Charger to help you; he will be very eager to test and help you become as territorial as he is, and he is very territorial. If he knows no one else but us is supposed to be in Spring's territory, he will make sure it stays that way."

After a couple more minutes of watching Spring catch and toy with Charger, they all began to finish their daily chore of chopping wood.

Derek had a hard time concentrating through his growing hunger. It racked his body, and he could feel an answering feeling gnawing at Spring as she mock-fought the energetic little black and silver dragon.

As the sun came up, the day actually lightened a little bit, and in that light, as he looked around, he caught the beginning, telltale sign of silver appearing in Nathan's eyes.

"One last thing," Derek told Nathan aloud in a very serious voice for his brother and sister to hear as well. "You must make sure Charger knows the difference between men and food. Much like Spring, Charger holds the belief that prey is simply prey. If they kill something, dragons eat it. But Charger must understand that if he kills or hurts a man, he must not at any time eat it. Men are not food."

Nathan looked confused, and Nate and Nattilie, hearing it, came over to join them.

"Why?" Nathan asked.

Derek looked over at both of the twins. "You will both have to do the same thing with your dragons. If even one of our dragons ever eats a man, they will be doomed. It will spread to other people, and they will seek to kill all dragons. Our dragons are different from some of the others," Derek explained. "There will be savage dragons that hatch; I have felt the minds of two so far. They are not like our dragons at all. They are wilder, more aggressive, and feel chaotic compared to ours. They will eventually see men as prey, if they don't already."

He looked over at Spring adoringly before he continued. "Our influence changes our dragons, and a time will come when we will have to prove that the dragons who are bonded to humans are not savage. That won't be possible if your dragon ever eats a human."

"I will have a dragon?" Nattilie asked with excitement.

Derek paused, not sure of how to answer her because he knew she would; he just did not know how he knew it.

He gave her a reassuring smile. "Spring seems to draw certain dragons to her."

Nathan nodded sagely. "Charger flew a long way, like an arrow straight towards us, towards Spring. Something about her pulled Charger here. So much so that he didn't even hunt as much as he would have liked to."

Just then, Herb came out of the basement carrying the newly made dragon saddle.

"You're going to have to strap this on yourself," Herb told Derek as he carried the saddle to him, "so you know how to do it right. First, see if it fits right, and make sure that it is snug on her."

Seeing the saddle sent Derek a feeling of excitement.

He listened and nodded to Herb, and as he took the saddle from him, he was surprised to note there were extra saddlebags attached to the sides of the saddle as well as a small one on the back.

Herb smiled as he saw Derek study the saddle and admire his handiwork. "Those are just in case you guys need to carry things. There is also a place for that spear of yours, so it will fit right next to you on the saddle. I don't know how you guys are going to hunt; there is a place for a crossbow and a quiver of bolts behind your saddle, and plenty of room in the bags to put meat in once it's been cut. There are also plastics to put the meat in."

Herb then looked up at the sky, and a smile broke out on his old face. "Ah, I see it is finally lightening up a little. Good weather for hunting."

Derek looked worried. "Herb, why hasn't it rained?" he asked as he motioned for Spring to come to him, while Emma came out carrying a crossbow, quiver, and some other things for the saddle.

Feeling Derek's growing excitement, Spring easily pinned down the elusive Charger and then trotted over to Derek proudly.

Herb frowned at Derek's question. "There ain't been any lightning either," he said, wondering before he just shrugged. "I'm expecting these meteors have just dried up the air. But once the air clears up again, I believe it will come down with an almighty vengeance. Best we get our hunting done now, cause we might not be able to later. Ellis has gone south to hunt and search. So you should go north if you're still set on trying this."

Derek nodded, and with Spring waiting for him, he picked up the saddle again to start strapping it down. It was a lot heavier than he thought it would be, but Spring was missing spikes in the perfect place for him to put it on, though she looked and felt uncomfortable while he did.

"Derek, huh," Emma told him, carrying a blanket over to him. "Put this under the saddle spring; it will help keep her scales from chewing up the leather so quickly, so it will last longer."

Derek nodded thoughtfully and loosened the straps he had already put in place, then slid the blanket under with Nathan's eager help. Then, taking his time, he cinched everything down.

"How does it feel?" he asked Spring, patting her neck.

Spring stood, stretching, then she unfurled her long, spike-tipped, metallic red wings and walked around for a second.

When she lowered herself to the ground again, Derek adjusted a strap that was too loose. "Fly around a little bit and get used to it while I go get my spear," he told her as he ran his hand along her flank.

Eager, she disappeared in a swirl of ash that made everyone but Derek cover their eyes, since he was the only one with sunglasses on.

When he returned, he found everyone trying to watch Charger chase Spring through the dim light of the sky, which was hard since Charger was so small compared to her.

"Make sure you tie down your sword so you don't lose it by accident," Herb reminded him as Derek came back.

Seeing him, Spring dove to him; he could feel both her hunger and excitement as she zoomed towards him. And it grew as she softly landed in front of him. Derek went to her, pulling a leather thong from within the saddlebags and tying his sword to its sheath in a way that would hold it secure but still be easy to get off if he needed it. He was going to tie a loose loop on the bottom of the sheath to hold it to his leg to keep it from flapping around, but then he thought better of it and took off the sword, tying it to the saddle next to the spear as he put it on the saddle too. When he returned, he would find a way to belt the sword across his back so it wouldn't get in the way while he was on Spring, and so it would still be at hand if he needed it.

Then excitement coursed through him as he stepped onto Spring's leg, and she helped him into the saddle, where he got comfortable and slipped his legs into the tied-down stirrups and cinched them tight.

He saw that everyone was watching him with fascination as he finished checking everything. Spring looked back at him expectantly as he rubbed her neck, and he nodded to her; he was ready.

"Be careful!" Emma and Nattilie both said at the same time, and Nattilie blushed as everyone looked at her.

"I will," he assured them, getting ready.

Then he forgot everything as Spring gracefully took her first steps with him on her back, and vertigo hit him as she launched herself into the air, making him grip one of her neck spikes directly in front of him so he could keep his balance as the air pressed in on him.

Spring's cool mind touched his own, and a picture of her flying easily and gracefully with him on her back filled his mind with the feeling of reassurance as the vertigo hit his stomach and she rose easily into the sky.

Then Charger came charging out of nowhere with a loud, vicious roar. Hearing it boiled Derek's blood so quickly, he couldn't stop the growl that came from his throat.

He reached out to Charger in his mind, his blood hot. "Stop issuing me challenges!" he growled angrily. "I know you're just playing, but my body takes it the wrong way," he snapped.

Instantly, he felt Spring trying to soothe him with her mind. And Charger, stunned by his reaction, gave off a little whine that seemed to cool Derek's blood even more.

"Sorry," he told Charger in his mind as his blood cooled again. "We can play when we get back, right now, though, we need to find food."

Charger grumbled in a hurt way and flew back to Nathan, his usual energetic excitement gone for the time being.

Then the Pantier residence was far behind them as Spring shot north, her wings beating a slow, majestic beat in the air.

"Why do his challenges make me so angry?" he asked Spring in an irritated voice. "Especially when I know he is just playing?"

Spring dove over the dark forest, and he could feel her trying to answer him in a way he might understand. The picture of him with his dragon mark flickered for a second, uncertainty in his mind, as if she was not exactly sure the why of it, but the mark had to be the how. Then all kinds of things filled his mind: the dragon mark and Spring's warming touch had both changed him, made him more dragon-like. All dragons felt a certain way when they heard certain roars—the mourning and challenging he had heard before, but there were others: territorial, victorious, death, vengeance, and mating. All of which evoked emotions they all carried. And he was unused to all of them, so he felt them more keenly until he could learn to control all of the emotions they invoked within him.

All of this Spring tried to relay to his mind emotionally. Then, amusement filled his mind from her. *He was Spring's. The strongest and greatest, unconquerable!* Spring told him lightly with affection.

They had been soaring over the forest for a little over ten minutes when they finally spotted the first deer.

Derek barely had time to grab, cock, and load the crossbow before Spring dove down from the sky and swooped carefully through the treetops. Derek aimed at a huge buck to the side of Spring's own target as she closed the gap and flew upon them. They hit the deer by surprise, the bolt leaving the crossbow a mere second before Spring pounced.

The force of it surprised Derek, and he almost lost the crossbow as Spring's coiled legs snatched out. He heard the buck's back break. Then Spring was flying through the trees, the dead buck in her claws as her wings beat hard, pushing down through the air to gain height.

"Don't lose sight of the one I shot," Derek told her as the buck he shot bounded off. Again, he had missed a direct hit. *He would have to practice with it more,* he scolded himself as Spring, flying, tore viciously into her buck.

Spring gave a little growl, then whipped around a tree back the way they came, shattering the buck's antlers as its head slammed into the tree, causing Spring to almost drop her huge meal. She landed on the ground, fiercely chomping into the buck.

With his senses following the deer he had shot, he felt the wolves in the forest just as Spring landed. And they were going after his kill. Untying his feet, he jumped off of Spring, his spear and loaded crossbow in hand, he went after the deer.

"I'm going after my buck before the wolves get it," he told Spring as he ran off into the forest.

Spring ignored him; he could feel her pleasure at enjoying her meal. So with a smile, he set off on a run. Though he sensed it, spotting its blood was enough with his eyesight as good as it was. The blood left a slightly glowing warmth in the cold air of the forest's ash-covered ground and trees. He also noticed the wolves were a lot closer than he had thought, and there were a lot more of them. They all had blood in their noses and were gathering quickly to take down the wounded buck.

Feeling all of them about to take his kill, a slow heat began to build in his body, and it grew, as did his anger, when he saw the first of them through the trees. His anger soared as he realized he might lose his kill. It boiled his blood, making him run even faster, passing the wolves, and he growled as they gave chase.

His growl stopped them cold, making them back off and hesitate before their own hunger made them continue to chase him.

Feeling their savage hunger emanating from them tripped him up. Surprise filled his mind as he realized he was reading all the wolves' minds.

Within a second of his slowing, he was surrounded by the growling wolves—too many of them for his frantic mind to count—and again, anger and heat swept through him. He reached towards their minds with his own, sending them a fearful warning in a picture of himself, big, vicious, and very deadly.

The wolves all yipped in surprise, and a few whined, shaking their heads and backing off. But the three biggest leapt forward undaunted, flying at him with snarls of rage.

Those snarls brought on the full force of his rage. His blood boiled, and roaring, he met all three of them in the air. His spear, when he thrust it, was glowing brightly. He did not have time to really notice it, though. The closest of the three wolves dodged to the side, snapping at the spear as it missed the wolf's neck by less than an inch. Seeing it try to bite the spear with its teeth, he pulled it back, thrusting it viciously at the next while ducking under the third, who went for his neck and ended up sailing past him.

The second wolf tried the same trick as the first one had, only this time, to Derek's surprised eyes, it seemed that somehow the spear in his hands grew longer and sliced the wolf's neck as it tried to leap back.

As the third wolf leapt over him, he released the crossbow bolt, which slammed into the wolf's chest, causing it to release a surprised and hurt "yip."

Having killed two of the wolves, Derek let out a victorious roar, jumping forward towards the first and last one who dared to face him.

He did not get the time to kill this one, because there came an answering roar, this one full of a dragon's anger. Wolves cried in fear and pain as Spring ripped into them from behind, just killing and tossing their bodies.

As the one facing Derek turned to flee, suddenly all panic-filled, Spring pounced through the trees, her jaws snapping viciously down upon the wolf's back, killing it with a snap of her jaws.

Then, in his head, Derek felt a piercing cold barrage through his mind and every mind close by. A picture of him and Spring was sent from Spring into the minds of all around, and with it came a challenging territorial roar that shook the forest as Spring laid claim to all the territory around.

In answer, everything froze, then ran. The once seemingly empty forest came alive as big and small animals fled for their lives. Seeing it, Derek smiled and hefted his spear. That was when he really noticed it was different. The haft was glowing with an inner fire, the color of charred wood. And the blade that topped it was longer and sharper. Where the snake crown had been etched into the metal was now the same dragon mark that was upon Derek's chest.

Then he noticed that Spring was frozen in place, the wolf dead at her feet, uneaten. Which, judging from her earlier hunger, was not like her. She was too hungry to ignore a kill she had just made, and that alerted him that something wasn't right. Instead, Spring just sat, her head cocked as if seeking or listening for something.

Concerned, he let his senses grow, feeling the entire forest around him. But with all the fleeing animals, he could not sense anything alarming. He walked to her, touching her shoulder.

"What's wrong?" he asked in concern.

Spring unconsciously let off a reassuring rumble at his touch, then looked down at him and sent a question to him.

Dragon?

"You think you felt a dragon? Near here? Or was it just Charger?" he asked, sending his senses out even further, searching for the feel of a dragon. He did not feel anything near them.

As if unsure, Spring sent him the same question.

He shook his head. "I didn't feel it. I can feel everything fleeing before your roar," he told her proudly as he scratched her chest. "But I never felt a dragon. Keep your senses open, though. Yours are stronger than mine, and if you felt it, then it must be out there somewhere close by."

Reassured, Spring bent and began to eat the wolf at her claws.

Derek checked on his buck, setting his glowing spear back in Spring's saddle. He dragged the buck closer to Spring and the wolves so he could skin and clean it. The buck was a huge six-pointer and heavy, but to him, it was easy to drag.

"I want to skin these wolves for their pelts, even some of the ones you killed back there. Then you can eat the rest," he told Spring as he set to work skinning and cleaning the buck.

It took him hours to get it all done. When he was finished and had stored the wolf pelts, deer skin, and the buck's meat, he climbed back into the saddle, looking at the now full red and gold dragon.

"Have you felt the dragon again?" he asked her curiously. To his vast amazement, Spring shook her head negatively, and seeing it made him smile.

"See," he teased her. "You are already learning simple answers," stroking her neck scales affectionately.

Spring chuffed loudly, and he felt sarcasm fill his mind from her, making him laugh humorously.

With the saddlebags full of meat and six skins upon his lap, Spring started back to the Pantiers, going a little slower than when they left because they were a lot heavier.

CHAPTER THIRTEEN

Day 37, Aug. 6th

On their flight back, Spring stopped twice to look around. And the second time, he had to keep her from roaring out in frustration and challenge as she kept feeling the sneaky, elusive dragon. The last time, Derek felt the sly dragon himself. He knew it was following them, but like Spring, he could not feel where the dragon was. None could be absolutely sure it was a dragon they had both sensed. It was that cunning, and Spring wanted to double back, knowing she was faster and stronger. She could fly faster and further than any dragon and could catch whoever was following her. Derek had smiled and rubbed her neck, keeping her on course. They had been gone long enough. He was starving, and he knew the meat he was bringing would be a relief to everyone.

Spring let out a roar to announce their arrival. Herb and Nate met them in the back of the building as they landed upon the ground, most of which was now clear of ash. It seems Herb had the Bergers busy freeing the yard of as much ash as they could. Sighing and very hungry, Derek untied his legs and tossed the skins down to Nate, who almost collapsed under the weight.

Herb looked at the wolf skins and raised a questioning eyebrow, then he saw the glowing spear as Derek pulled it from the saddle, about to hop down. Herb's eyes widened in shock, while Nate gasped in disbelief.

Meanwhile, Spring sat with her head cocked to the side, trying to sense the dragon who had been following them. Derek climbed off the saddle, resting the glowing spear upon it as he opened the saddlebags.

"I had a little problem with some wolves as I was hunting," Derek explained to Herb. "It seems they thought I would be a good meal when I would not let them eat the buck I killed, which happened to be the biggest one there. As for the spear?" He just shrugged. It seemed to him he had been doing that a lot lately when he could not explain something. So he changed the subject, feeling uncomfortable. "You should have seen the size of this buck. It was a splendid, huge six-pointer. We got plenty of meat, and Spring ate good herself."

As he talked, he began uncinching all the straps on Spring, then slid the saddle and blanket off of her, grabbing the spear so it wouldn't fall as he did.

In his hand, the spear felt warm; the shaft was solid and smooth. Feeling its warmth with his mind, it flared brightly for a second, then its glow slowly began to fade.

He put down the saddle and studied the spear curiously. It still felt warm in his mind, but beneath his palm, it was already cooling in the freezing air. The shaft was a reddish-black, and the mark upon the blade was a vivid red that stood out in contrast to the silver metal. A tinge of gold outlined the red dragon mark, and Derek could really feel a warmth in it. It was unlike anything he had ever felt, and it radiated only from the mark on the blade.

"Can I see it?" Nate asked curiously, trying to keep the awe he felt from his voice.

Startled out of his reverie of the spear, Derek looked into Nate's eyes. "Are you sure you want to try to touch it? It is not an ordinary weapon now, and I don't know what all it can do," he told Nate in a voice full of warning.

Startled to hear that, Nate drew back. "Why? Do you think it might hurt me?" he asked Derek cautiously.

Derek paused, unsure. "I don't know. I know it helped me kill a wolf that was out of my reach, yet somehow it still sliced the wolf's neck."

"What happened?" Herb asked in a concerned voice, interrupting them.

As Derek began to pull all the meat from the saddlebags, he explained to them exactly what happened, how he had shot the buck from Spring's back and slightly missed the mark, letting it run off into the forest, so he had gone to chase it down while Spring was eating her kill and ended up surrounded by a bunch of wolves who wanted his kill for themselves. He replayed how they had surrounded him and then how the three had attacked him. Nate hung on his every word.

"I don't know how or when it happened, but as I thrust the spear at the first wolf, I noticed it was glowing in my hands-" He then explained how the second wolf had been too far away for the spear to reach as it jumped back, but how the spear had seemed to stretch the distance to kill the wolf before it returned back to normal.

"It must be magical," Nate said in an excited, musing voice. "How else could it have glowed like it was when you got here?" he asked with certainty when both Derek and Herb gave him questioning looks.

"I guess that could explain it-" Derek began.

He stopped speaking as a scream of pain pierced the air, and all of them, hearing it, began running around to the front of the building, where Nattilie's voice had come from.

* * *

Nattilie had been replacing candles in the front room for Emma. She had almost finished when she got the weirdest feeling that she was being watched. She had quickly looked around and, not seeing anything, continued what she was doing, wanting to hurry so she could go see Derek, who had just returned.

Derek, she thought with a smile. He was so different from anyone she had ever met. She almost could not believe she was a year older than him because he seemed so much older than he was. Just thinking about him got her heart fluttering in a weird way.

She changed the last candle and felt a cool chill of being watched again. This time, she swiveled around, looking out the front window, but she could see nothing out there but sooty darkness. As she was looking hard out the window, she saw a shadow ripple across the plastic covering the broken window.

She quickly stepped outside and stuck her head out of the tent cover that kept the ash out, her hand resting lightly upon the rapier on her waist. Again, she saw nothing but darkness, parted only by the setting of the sun.

She was about to go back in when she saw a flicker of movement out of the corner of her eye, and with it came the cool feeling of being watched again.

She shut the door and carefully left the tent, pulling her sword a little as if uncertain if she should call for help. But she would feel stupid if she did, and there was nothing there. Most likely, she told herself it was just the shifting sunlight she had seen moving.

Off the front porch, she began to walk slowly to where she had thought she had seen the movement. She was almost twenty yards away from the house when Charger came flying out of nowhere, flying right past her, and slammed viciously into something hidden in the ash right at her feet.

It was so close to her without her realizing it that she cried out in surprise and fear as she watched the dragon appear from the ash. It was almost twice Charger's size, and it pinned the little spiky dragon to the ground, its jaw wide, thrusting towards the little dragon's soft neck.

"No!" she screamed, lifting her rapier angrily. "Leave Charger alone!" she said, running to it, hoping to scare it off from Charger before Charger was hurt.

The dragon was a little over five feet long. It had two silver horns, one above each silver eye. All of its teeth, claws, and spikes were just as silver. It was a dark blue metallic color with silver under its jaws and stomach, and hearing Nattilie, it paused, mauling Charger.

It then burst towards her with frightening speed, so fast that she was astonished, then yelped in pain as fire raced up her hand. The rapier she was holding dropped to the ground as a bloody purple welt formed over the top of her hand.

She was stunned, for when she looked up again, the dragon, *her* dragon, had vanished from sight.

Charger got shakily to his feet, breathing heavily, then angrily let out a loud, thunderous roar that belittled every roar he had let out before. It was so loud it left Nattilie's ears ringing.

From somewhere in the darkness came a chuffing sound that repeated itself like a funny chuckle. Then another roar filled the air as Spring flew over the house, and the chuckling sound abruptly stopped.

Nothing answered Spring's angry, challenging roar.

The big red and gold dragon landed next to Charger, touching him with her snout, causing the still-shaking dragon to calm down and let off a grumbling purr.

Seconds later, Derek came around the house, running towards Nattilie. "What happened?" he asked her in concern as she picked up her fallen rapier.

She sheathed the sword, then looked at the big, ugly purple mark that covered the entire back of her hand. She then smiled, showing it to him. "I found my dragon," she told him happily, no longer feeling burning pain in her hand as it was overwhelmed by her happiness.

Surprised, Derek looked around, but neither his sight nor senses could detect the dragon who had marked her.

Herb, Nate, and Nathan came running up to them, Nathan looking a little worried and sick. They all listened while Nattilie explained what happened, Nathan and Charger standing to the side as Nathan made sure his dragon was okay.

"What does it look like?" Nate asked as Nattilie finished.

"A little smaller than Spring was when she first hatched, with two silver horns, dark blue scales, and a silver stomach, claws, and teeth," she told them as she looked around for her dragon.

When it became obvious the dragon was not going to show itself with all of them around, Derek and Nathan took their dragons around the back while everyone but Nattilie went inside to watch her from the window.

Determined to wait, Nattilie just stood where she had last seen it. After a while, she realized she had been staring at it the whole time. The dragon was only five feet in front of her, again hidden upon the ground under the ash. It was hidden so well that even after she realized she had spotted it, she could not tell it apart from the ash and ground.

She sat on her heels and smiled tentatively at her dragon. "So are you going to introduce yourself, or was burning me enough?" she asked quietly in a wondering voice.

The dragon didn't move, but a cool feeling like the one Nathan had described to her entered her brain. A picture of himself floated through her mind, and the feeling of vast contentment filled her as she saw him in the mountains, hunting. Then a regal, awe-filled picture of Spring entered her mind. In it, Spring was the vision of terrifying might and beauty, and it had pulled him from safety and food upon the mountains where he had claimed his territory. A feeling of loneliness overcame her, filling her, and with it, the wariness of humans, dragons, and populated areas.

"And me?" she asked, a little disturbed by the dragon's feelings that had overcome her dragon.

In answer, the dark blue dragon moved slowly, effortlessly forward until it touched her hand with its snout. Warmth filled her instantly, and to her amazement, she watched the dark purple welt disappear upon the back of her hand until what was left was a metallic red dragon claw with gold claws that covered her entire hand. With it came the feeling of contentment from her dragon.

Smiling, she reached out, scratching his neck. "Vex," she whispered, naming him, and he grumbled a deep purr in answer.

"Come, meet the others. They are not like other humans, and though you like your own territory, for now, we must share it with everyone here," she told him as she touched the dragon mark upon her hand. It was warm to her touch and felt smooth as metal.

As she walked back towards the house, she felt Vex's reluctance to come out in plain sight, as well as his apprehension about being around other humans and dragons. But he came, walking into the lamplight on the porch, and she saw the large scar of broken scales where a mountain lion had tried to kill it while Vex was still in his egg. The scar marked him from neck to tail, and half of his tail was missing, eaten by the mountain lion, whom he had later tracked down and killed. From the images flashing in her mind, she knew Vex had been very bad off and had healed a lot when he had shed for the first time. But the horror of that attack could still be plainly seen in the scars Vex had.

As she opened the tent, the others came to the porch to take a look at Vex and meet him. "This is Vex," she informed them, waving a dragon-marked hand at her dragon.

Vex eyed them all warily until he saw Derek follow everyone out of the house and onto the porch. Then Vex puffed up as tall as he could stand and moved closer to Nattilie. Derek, who missed very little, noticed it immediately, and he reached out to Spring, letting her see it through his eyes.

"Why is he doing that?" he asked Spring curiously in her mind.

Amusement filled him as he felt Spring's silent approach. None of the others even noticed her until she dropped out of the sky behind Vex.

Vex did not seem surprised, though; he steadfastly ignored her, but everyone heard his contented rumble as he moved closer to Nattilie.

Derek watched it with surprise. "He didn't challenge you like Charger did," he mused lightly in her mind.

Again, amusement filled him, then came a flickering of different emotions. The first was directed at Derek, and it was jealousy, and it was deep. Vex was very jealous of him.

"Why?" Derek asked in confusion.

Two pictures formed in his mind. The first was of Spring, and the second was of Nattilie. Not understanding, Derek just gave up and turned his attention back to Vex.

Vex let Nate, Nathan, Emma, and Herb touch him, but when Derek moved forward, Vex puffed up again, this time giving a warning growl.

It set Derek's blood on fire and confused him. The feeling he got from Vex's growl was that Nattilie was his, and Derek could not have her.

Finally, Derek understood what was going on, and he smiled down at the dark blue dragon, his blood still boiling. He bent down, pulling off his glasses so he could see clearly into Vex's silver metal eyes.

"I'm not a threat to you or yours. As you know-" Derek reached over, touching Nattilie's hand, startling her as he lightly traced a finger over her dragon mark. "-Each of us must work together, and while we are here, this is all of our territory. And everyone in it will abide by the rules that have been put in place to ensure our survival. That means you do not attack men unless they attack you or one of us, and no matter what, no matter how hungry or angry you are or get, you will not and must not eat men."

Vex looked at him intently as if measuring who he was, then he chuffed his agreement. As he did, Charger flew out of the house and tackled the bigger dragon with a challenging roar.

Everyone froze in shock until they realized the two dragons weren't really fighting each other, or maybe Charger was trying to get revenge for earlier. But Vex easily and quickly pinned Charger and mimed shredding him to bits, then, grabbing the little dragon by its spiky tail, he threw it into the air.

Charger then issued an indignant, challenging roar, and Vex, following him into the air, answered with a roar of his own that shook the house windows before he stalked after the smaller dragon and tackled him in the air.

Everyone was amazed. Charger was fast, but that speed did not help him when Vex could easily outguess and outfox him at every turn.

Soon, the day's excitement mellowed down, and Derek, starving, finally got to eat his first meal of the day.

CHAPTER FOURTEEN

Day 38 – 40

The next few days were frantic for Derek. He spent them hunting with Spring, gathering as much meat as they could. So he did a lot of cleaning, skinning, and cutting. He did not have to worry about being attacked by anything, especially the wolves. They all ran in terror when Spring flew over the forest.

In the mornings, instead of chopping wood, he sparred with Herb, Nate, Nattilie, and Nathan. Herb left him black and blue with the bokken. The old man really was a master swordsman, and he proved it daily as he pushed Derek to his limits, then set the others upon him to push him farther. Herb's only problem was that, despite his mastery, he fatigued easily. He just wasn't young anymore, and with the haze still in the air, it made his breathing difficult when he really got into it.

That little time sparring with Herb each day was enough for Derek, though. He had never taken to being humiliated easily, but he ate it up, learning everything Herb showed him in seconds if not minutes. Totally astonishing his teacher, and he used it all as he sparred against Nate and Nathan. But against Nattilie, he went further; his form perfected, he moved smoothly, quickly, and was therefore a lot softer. Herb instantly berated him for it, telling him that if he fought her brothers that same way, they would not be able to hold their swords as long against him as they did. And Derek understood; it's just with Nattilie, he had to fight his best to teach her to fight her best. With her brothers, he fought more powerfully and with more aggression. But his thoughts on the subject soon changed as Herb thrashed him soundly in their next match, and Derek vowed next time, he'd fight her brothers like he did her.

Day 41; Aug 10th

Everyone was in a near panic by the end of the fourth day after Vex's arrival. Ellis had been gone for four days and had not returned.

When Derek returned that night with meat and found out the Ranger still had not returned, he had a hurried talk with Herb and decided he and Spring would go south and try to find the Ranger.

Not wanting to delay, he gave Herb the meat, then he and Spring took to the air again, flying south over the route the Ranger had told Herb he would follow.

As each day passed, more and more of the sunlight could be seen, turning a cloudless day into a heavily overcast day. And now, as the sun was setting, it looked much like the moon seen through clouds. To Derek's eyes, though, the light given by the haze-covered sun was brilliant, and it left no shadow upon the ground that he could not see into or in the trees as they flew over them. He could clearly see and follow the bicycle tracks still visible in the ash-covered road.

Close to an hour later, he felt a faint presence. It was in the forest to the left of Ellis' bike trail, and just by the feel, he knew it was the Ranger. But he wasn't exactly alone. Both he and Spring felt the presence of something else. Both were dying.

Spring dove down, gathering speed as they felt the Ranger's life ebbing; the trees whipped beneath them. He could spot smoke through the ash in the air, letting him know there was a fire burning nearby, but he urged Spring past it and towards the Ranger, who was farther in the forest. They passed right over the ashes of a campfire and, to his surprise, the still-warm bodies of three dead men.

Derek reached behind his back, loosening the strap upon his sword, making sure he could draw it if he needed to. Then he loaded the crossbow as Spring, urged on by his worry for Ellis, sped through the trees.

A quick scan of his senses showed no one was near Ellis, but that other faint presence they had felt. As Spring landed, Derek untied his feet and jumped off of Spring, landing next to Ellis' crumpled form. With the spear and crossbow in hand, he knelt by Ellis, who was lying on his side, curled around a dragon egg that was a dull copper color and not shining.

"Ellis," Derek said, dropping his spear to turn the Ranger over.

The Ranger was out cold, and what he saw confused him when he turned Ellis over. Ellis had two wounds, and both looked suspiciously like gun wounds. One was below his eye, which had swollen his face grotesquely, deforming his cheekbone. The other wound was in his chest, and his shirts were covered in blood.

"Shit," Derek whispered frantically.

Putting down the crossbow, he began to feel a weird warmth burning through his blood as he looked at Ellis and the egg in frustration. He ripped open Ellis's shirts, then ran to grab some bandages from the saddle where Spring was looking as worried as he was. He carefully cleaned the small wound in Ellis' chest. It kind of looked like it had been caused by a BB, then he bound it. The whole time, that fierce burning spread through his body, building within him just as it had when the wolves had attacked him.

He lifted Ellis onto Spring's back and tied him to the saddle, facing down. "Spring, take him to Em. He is going to die of blood loss, so please hurry. I will see if I can find out what happened here," he told her firmly as he finished tying the Ranger to the saddle.

A picture of the egg and concern formed in his mind. He nodded. "I will keep it with me, but it doesn't look healthy. It is not shining, and look how it's cracked," he said as he paused to look it over. Then he looked back at her. "Go, I will do what I can," he assured her confidently, though he didn't feel that way.

Spring took off, sensing how urgent it was to get the Ranger to Emma, and Derek bent over the copper-colored egg. He could feel that burning sensation run through his body, building to a greater level as he gently picked up the cracked egg. He sent his mind gently into the faint, calm presence inside the egg.

"My name is Derek, I am bound to Spring," he told it and sent a picture of him and Spring into its mind. "If you can hold on, I will take you where you need to go."

At first, he thought there would be no response, but as the fire raged higher within him, lifting the hair on his arms, the egg slowly began to glow in his hands, and a wave of warmth passed from him into the egg.

The energy that left him dropped him to his knees, leaving him breathless for a second as a sudden fatigue hit him. He stayed on his knees like that, straining to even catch his breath for close to a minute before he found the inner reserves and strength to gain his feet again. In his hands, the egg was glowing faintly, and its crack was all gone. Relieved, he smiled tiredly and reached with his mind towards the egg.

"Just hold on," he told it reassuringly, showing it a picture of Nate Berger. "Soon you will be where you belong."

The egg responded with a soft vibration before he felt its own tiredness, and it stilled in his arms, glowing faintly.

Holding the egg in one arm, he hooked the loaded crossbow to his belt and picked up his spear. He had to move slowly because his muscles were too drained to move fast. Then, with those in hand, he began walking towards the camp he had seen as they flew over it. By the time he got there, he was moving a little easier, and in his mind, he felt relief because he heard Spring's roar that announced she had landed at the Pantier's.

The camp he saw was a disaster and a trap. He noticed it too late. He had been too tired to extend his senses, wanting to save and gather what energy he could, and he regretted it now. For he had been watched, followed, and surrounded by others who were now hiding all around the camp.

Carefully, he let the hand holding his spear drop on it to get it closer to the crossbow at his waist. All around him, he felt men getting closer.

"Just let that hand stay by your side," a voice behind him said, nice and loud.

Derek gritted his teeth, but he didn't move a muscle. He could feel Spring's sudden alarm and panic, leaving the Pantiers with a roar of anger. Behind her, he felt Charger and Vex following, but he knew whatever happened here, it would be too late for them to arrive.

Frustration and anger gave him strength, burning through him. His senses exploded. He felt a man two feet behind him and two more right behind that man. Six others were spread out through the woods; all were facing him, and in their minds, he saw they all held different kinds of BB and pellet guns. A couple were spring-action, but most were pump.

Shit, he thought. He had already seen what the guns had done to the Ranger.

He turned slowly, eyeing the man who had spoken angrily. "I don't know who you are or what business you think you have pointing those weapons at me-" he began, only to get interrupted.

"We have the right of the United States government," the man holding his gun on Derek said, interrupting him. "Now, I suggest you put down what you're holding and slowly put down your weapons. If you make any sudden moves, my men will shoot you," he warned.

Rage filled Derek; he knew by reading their minds that they were not government men. They were just trying to lull him into a false sense of safety. With the rage growing in him, knowing he was likely to be shot either way, he moved.

His spear flashed brilliantly as it sliced cleanly through the wrist of the arm closest to him, holding a gun. Then he was diving forward in a side roll, passing the man whose hand he had just severed, and left the slightly glowing egg by a tree, and was back on his feet, spear flashing and crossbow aimed. He fired as BBs and pellets filled the air where he had just been. His spear caught the gun hand of the next man as he turned to find Derek right next to him. And like the first guy, the spear left the second man with no hand. The third guy was not so lucky; Derek's crossbow bolt took him right in the chest as he tried to fire at Derek.

The crossbow bolt had a chilling effect on the men. The other six, seeing three go down just like that, all turned and ran or tried to as another man appeared, stopping them in their tracks and turning them around.

Derek didn't waste any time; he reached towards the egg with his mind. "If you can, if it won't hurt you, turn off your glow," he told it hopefully and felt relief when he saw its glow leave out of the corner of his eye. He ran forward, hooking the crossbow back to his belt, and kicked ash over the egg without anyone the wiser. Then grabbed the first man he had injured, who was too busy holding his bleeding stump to put up any resistance at all. Using him as a shield, he walked towards the seven gathering men, his anger burning through him at the thought of them trying to take the egg.

From their minds, he knew the man he was using as a shield was their leader and the seventh man's brother. When that man met Derek's eyes, which, like always, were hidden behind sunglasses, Derek held the glowing spear to their leader's throat.

"Drop your guns, or I will kill your leader," Derek threatened viciously.

The seventh man smiled. "He's as good as dead now," he replied lightly, trying to bluff Derek. "He only has one hand now and no medical supplies to kill off the infection this infernal ash brings." Then the man grimaced angrily, worried for his brother. "No, you put down your weapon, and I won't shoot you, but boy, I promise you will pay for cutting off my brother's hand."

Derek smiled grimly. "You threaten me and expect me to put down my weapons?" he asked sarcastically. Then he laughed. "No, I'm not scared of your little pee shooters. I have already done and proven that. A shot from them is not likely to kill me. But I guarantee you, my spear and sword will kill. No ifs, ands, or buts about it."

The man Derek held was trembling, and he spoke up. "Josh, damn you, I'm bleeding to death. Either kill him or let him go."

At his words, Derek pressed the spear tighter to the man's neck, drawing a gasp from him as it punctured the skin and drew blood.

"Easy now, easy," Josh said calmly, holding a hand up. "It seems we have a little standoff here. Why don't you just let my brother go?"

While he talked, Derek sensed the other handless man sneaking up on him.

In a quick, unexpected move, Derek pulled back with their leader in front of him a couple of feet, stopping the man who had been trying to sneak up on him and putting him firmly in Derek's sight, in front of and to the left of him. The move was done so smoothly that no one expected it. Even their leader was surprised because he had been lifted as if he weighed nothing. And he was sure he weighed at least fifty pounds more than Derek, who had moved him without a problem.

"How about you and your men begin leaving, and I will let your brother follow. I don't want to hurt anyone, so why don't we each go our separate ways?" Derek asked, even though he had a feeling things were going to get a lot worse before the sun fully set. He could feel all of their greed for the egg and now for his spear. And he knew they were not going to leave without them. His only hope was to maybe stall them long enough for true darkness to set in or for Spring to arrive.

Worried there might be even more men he had overlooked, he widened his senses and felt other presences, but he realized after a second they were only horses, twelve of them, no more men.

The one-handed man who had been trying to sneak up on him, seeing he no longer could, suddenly dropped to his knees, pointing, aiming, and then shooting his spring-loaded BB gun.

He was close enough that he might have killed Derek, aiming for his eye as he was.

Derek was not caught slipping, though, for as the man determined his action, Derek moved. His hand holding their leader snapped behind his back, finding, securing, and then throwing his knife at the same time as he pulled the leader in front of the gun.

The BB grazed their leader's face, drawing a line of blood from his cheek to his ear as Derek's knife slammed butt-first between the man's eyes, dropping him like a stone to lie face down, unconscious from the force of Derek's throw.

"Son of a bitch!" their leader cried out, then went still as the hot spear again was held firmly against his neck.

"Either you are very good or very lucky," Josh whispered to him nervously.

"I told you, I don't want to kill any of you," Derek told them as his mind frantically searched for a way out of this situation. "All of us have been made desperate in the last weeks. Like you guys, I have had to survive, and I plan on surviving. Your men are desperate, but you have horses, food, and guns. That is more than most who have survived. Yet you attack and try to kill a decent man when you come across him."

Josh interrupted him. "So you're a decent man?" he asked with a wry smile.

"Not me," Derek growled angrily. "Your men shot and almost killed a man I know, Ranger Ellis."

"Ranger Ellis?" Josh asked in confusion.

A man behind Josh stepped forward. "He's the one I told you about, Josh. He killed Mike, Stern, and Crab. All over that stupid rock they had found," he explained angrily.

"What are you talking about? That glowing rock the kid was carrying when we arrived?" Josh asked in confusion.

"Damn it, Josh. I'm bleeding to death over here, so is Devan. Stop this stupid conversation and help him," their leader said sternly.

Josh looked at Derek questioningly.

Derek did not want anyone closer to him than they already were. But he also did not want any of the men to die; that would turn this situation even worse. He pointed to a man trying to hide behind a tree and out of his sight.

"You come bind Devan's wounds, then cut some strips so your leader can bind his own," Derek told the man he pointed to.

They all watched Josh as he motioned for the hidden man to obey. Some minutes went by while the man Derek had knocked out had been helped up and his arm bound.

Then, when the man tossed the leader some bindings, Derek watched as the leader carefully bound his own arm, making no move at all to distress Derek. His mind, Derek felt, was more than intrigued by Derek, the glowing rock, and his glowing spear. And the leader concentrated on these things rather than his own pain.

Once all that was done and someone had made sure the man who'd been shot with the crossbow was still alive and breathing, Josh turned back to the man so he would answer his question.

"It's the same rock, only it was not glowing when Mike found it," the man said, then gestured over to the Ranger's bike, which was leaning against a tree, full of packages. "Then this Ranger came upon us, and well, Mike was trying to open the rock when the Ranger came. Mike told us that the rock was hollow and that there was something in it.

He figured maybe it was crystals or gold, but nothing he had tried over the last couple of days could crack it open, had not so much as dented it, being all metal like it was. So when this so-called Ranger joined our camp, telling us he had some meat to share if we would share our fire, he saw Mike slamming an axe into the rock, and he and Mike got into an instant argument in which the Ranger took the rock. And why Mike and I, we all pulled our guns. This Ranger—" the man said after a second of looking at Derek. "—He was tough. Mike tried to shoot him, but the Ranger knocked the gun out of his hands and whomped him a good one. Then Stern shot him, and the Ranger went berserk. He killed Stern, Crab, tried to kill me, and when Mike shot him again, he killed Mike. They're all dead. I went to get you."

"Where is the rock now? I don't see it," Josh asked.

"This kid, he is fast; it disappeared somewhere before he attacked us," another man said quietly, his gun still pointing unwaveringly at Derek.

"Why does your spear glow?" Josh asked Derek curiously.

Derek smiled pleasantly. "I have no reason to tell you that. You got me between a rock and a hard place. If you want me to volunteer any information that I have, then you'd better make this a more hospitable environment. Tell your men to put down their guns. It's obvious your men and the Ranger had a misunderstanding, and I don't see your men as highway robbers. They may be desperate, but I don't think most of you have lost your sense of morality—"

"A misunderstanding?" the man who had been at the camp when the Ranger arrived blurted out angrily. "He killed Stern, Crab, and Mike— that is no misunderstanding!"

Anger made Derek's sight go red. "Had they not shot the Ranger, he would not have killed them. Had they actually listened to him, it never would have happened. Mike was about to kill something he knew nothing about, and the Ranger was trying to keep him from unknowingly killing it."

"How could he save a rock?" Josh demanded with angry sarcasm.

"It's not a rock," Derek growled fiercely, his anger at the dragon's treatment and almost death exploding from him. "It's a dragon egg, and your men almost killed it!" he snapped before he forced himself to shut his mouth, knowing he had to learn to control his anger more. Having said what he had, he knew his fate was now tied to these men.

There was stunned silence, then laughter filled the air as they all thought Derek had lost his mind in the meteor storms.

"A dragon?" Josh asked with amusement. "Boy, you need to be in an institution for the mentally ill. "The meteor sickness must have soured your mind," he began to rant, until his brother and leader raised his hand to silence him.

CHAPTER FIFTEEN

Day 41; Aug. 10th

"Alright," their leader said in a calming voice. "So the glowing rock is a dragon egg? What about the spear you're holding that is not hot against my throat?" he asked curiously in a placating tone.

"Look at it," Derek told him wryly. "What is the symbol upon the blade?" he asked.

"A dragon," the leader said after hesitating and straining his eyes to see down so far without alarming Derek. "But why is it glowing? And why does it burn my skin?" he asked calmly, though now Derek could feel the man's mind racing, trying to put logical explanations to what he was seeing.

The man's thoughts surprised Derek; they were all very scientific, considering what elements could possibly do such things, but the man could find absolutely no explanation. A coating on the blade could make it hot to the skin, and a mixture of certain ingredients could make the spear glow. Yet all were things no boy could find, and he had no doubt Derek was young, just did not know how young.

"The answers will have to wait, Jean," Derek told him and felt the man tense incredulously when Derek spoke his name, for he knew no one had said his name at all. "Now I will release you if you will assure me no one will try to take what is mine and what is not theirs."

Jean Perry paused in shock, trying to figure out how this boy, no man, had known his name. Then he forced his mind to focus on something else.

"You're talking about the glowing rock, right? If you are talking about the rock you call an egg, then by rights, it is mine. One of my men found it and died for it," Jean replied firmly.

Keeping his senses wide for any sudden movement or treachery, Derek slowly lowered the spear, knowing that this man, their leader, was too curious about him now to let any of his men attack him. And he was right when he saw Jean motion to his brother, a motion that halted all attacks upon Derek.

"If it were just a rock, then yes, I would agree with you," Derek told Jean as the man turned slowly to face Derek and get a closer look at him, a look that the man's curiosity could not help but take. "But it is not a rock; it's an egg. And I can no more claim it as my own than you can. It claims the man it binds to. And at the moment, that man is not here. So I will take the egg to him," Derek told the scientist in a voice that left no room for compromise and left no doubt at all that he meant what he said.

Jean studied the mysterious man intently, gesturing openly for all of his men to put up their guns. And as they did, he saw to his surprise, the glow of the spear slowly fade, leaving them in growing darkness. He had a hard time seeing, but the man, with sunglasses on, seemed to pierce the darkness easily, watching each and every man until all the guns were put away. The man, he had to admit, had a very frightening quality to him, one that promised a very quick end to violence, something he had shown beyond doubt already.

"Elk, check Mark and make sure he's not going to die on us," Jean said over his shoulder before turning back to the mysterious man, giving him his whole attention.

From what Jean could see, he was young, tall, and pretty thick-set. He moved with a grace that belied his size and surprised Jean. On his person, the man carried an arsenal of weapons: a spear, a crossbow, a knife behind his back, and a Samurai sword strapped across his back. All of which the man seemed easy and familiar with using. His eyes behind those glasses unnerved Jean. He could not understand how the man saw everything with them on. His hair was semi-long, with blondish-brown streaks across his face.

Derek watched the man named Elk check the guy who had been shot with the crossbow. Derek knew the man was still alive, but he had not moved since Derek shot him.

"He's still alive, Jean. The bolt went right through him, near the shoulder. He's bleeding, but I don't think anything vital was pierced," Elk told Jean, sounding relieved.

Jean sighed in relief himself. "Well, at least no one is dead," he muttered before studying Derek. "I find it hard to believe there are dragons. And this egg thing? I don't know what you mean by it claiming a man to bond?"

Everyone's hands went to their guns or pulled them as Derek bent down, retrieved his knife, and placed it in its sheath. Jean quickly waved everyone to calm down and put their guns away. They did, but they watched Derek like a hawk as he checked his crossbow to make sure it was hooked firmly to his belt.

Derek, meanwhile, kept his senses on full alert; he could feel Spring urgently getting closer as the minutes passed. And she was flying faster than she ever had before, screaming through the sky.

"Your men seem to get more twitchy the darker it gets. So why don't you have the fire rebuilt so they can see better and not mistake any of my moves as doing something I'm not?" he suggested as Spring met his mind, showing him a picture of the Ranger being helped by the Pantiers.

Jean nodded at the suggestion, and Josh sent two men to rebuild the fire before walking slowly to his brother.

"Do you mind if I check his arm?" Josh asked, doing it anyway.

Knowing what he was doing and trying to do, Derek just ignored Josh, letting him check his brother's arm. Then, right before Josh could signal his men to attack, Derek stepped forward, his spear glowing brightly, the very image of impending violence.

"It won't work," he warned Josh coolly. "I will kill a couple of your men and you two, and my dragon will kill the rest."

His words froze Josh in a panic. For some reason, as unrealistic as it seemed, he believed the man.

"Your dragon?" Jean asked curiously, looking around in surprise. He had tried to warn his brother not to try anything until they knew more about the mysterious man, and now they were going to get a lot more than they bargained for; he could feel it. Despite being as scientifically minded as he was, he somehow believed the man was not lying at all.

Derek smiled. "Come, Spring!" he called loudly.

A fierce, vicious, deadly roar sounded in the air, followed by bright light as fire spewed from her jaws. Then, two more roars followed that, still far away but getting closer. One was so loud and vicious it seemed close, and suddenly, men were frozen in fear, shaking with it.

"Spring," Derek informed her quickly in his mind. "I am unhurt, but I can barely stand. I have no energy. Everything I have, I have used to show them I am strong, unbeatable, so they won't attack me. Come land by me. Tell Charger to get the egg and fly it back to Nate. Have Vex stay hidden; then if these men attack, we will kill them, and Vex will hunt those who try to flee!"

Spring growled fiercely, scattering men as she landed right behind Derek, who had his glowing spear still pointed at the two brothers, keeping them from even thinking of moving.

"Tell your men not to run; if they do, the other dragons have my permission to kill them outright," Derek threatened in a stone-cold voice.

"There are others?" Jean gasped in astonishment, his eyes full of disbelief as he stared at the big red and gold dragon, who looked very angry, her silver eyes flashing with violence.

At Derek's nod, Jean shouted out fearfully. "Stop! Hold your places. There are other dragons out there, and they will kill you if you run!" Jean yelled frantically at his men.

As if to prove the point, Charger burst through the trees, chasing a man who had tried to run, then dove back toward Derek as if to reassure himself that Derek was okay. He hovered in front of Derek for a moment, studying him carefully.

"I'm fine, go get the egg out of here," Derek said, reassuring the spiky dragon.

Charger gave him a rumbling welcome, then dove to the tree where the egg was hidden. Everyone watched in silence as the dragon picked up the heavy egg, and it began to glow faintly again. It looked like metal and was the color of copper. The spiky dragon then flew off, carrying it in all four of its claws. Derek heard Charger rumble to the egg and heard its tired response. Then Charger was gone.

Spring continued her deep, loud growl as she eyed all the men who had tried to hurt Derek viciously. Her growl was answered by a louder, fiercer one from Vex, hidden somewhere in the trees.

Hearing it, Derek saw Jean shiver again.

"Dragons," Josh whispered in disbelief.

"Spring, light that fire so they can see you clearly," Derek told her in a soft, appreciative voice.

Spring turned to the pile of wood Jean's men had stacked, and flames roared out of her mouth, engulfing it from ten yards away. The heat of it made the brothers wipe sweat from their faces.

There were gasps of fright and awe as everyone saw her fully in the light of the raging fire. Then Derek gasped as Spring loomed over him, touching Derek with her snout and sending flaming hot warmth coursing through his body, filling his body with much-needed energy and making the dragon mark upon his chest flare up brightly beneath his shirt, and his spear glowed even brighter in his hand. Derek's breath caught in the force of the energy Spring gave him, his heart beating erratically as if it would explode in his chest. Then the flood of energy stopped, bringing everything back to normal. Derek let out his breath and ran his free hand through his hair, smoothing it down because it had poofed out of control at Spring's touch.

Watching them closely, Jean finally took his eyes off the dragon to look incredulously at Derek.

"It can understand you?" he asked in amazement.

Derek nodded and rubbed her neck affectionately. Spring did not stop glowering, though. Her silver eyes were menace-filled; she looked at Jean and Josh as prey. Her worry for him made her want to tear them apart in frustration that she had not been there when he needed her.

"How many?" Jean asked as he held his bloody, bandaged stump.

Derek just smiled and ignored the question. "All of these questions can be answered in time. Right now, though, I have medical supplies, so if any of your men know how to use them, they can see to your wounded."

Derek went to his saddlebag and pulled out his medical box. Spring snapped her jaws viciously at Jean as he tried to get closer to her to inspect her and the curious saddle, where he had no doubt the mysterious man rode.

Unperturbed by the vicious dragon, Jean stopped where he was, but he continued to study the saddle with intrigue.

"You ride upon it?" Jean asked in an excited voice.

Derek set the medical box on the ground and looked up at Jean. This time, there was no hint of a smile on his face. "Her name is Spring," he told Jean, then looked over at Josh.

"Does he always ask so many questions? He should be worried about having lost a hand, but he ignores it as if it is irrelevant." Derek asked in surprise.

Josh laughed nervously. "He's a scientist, what do you expect?" he replied, then came as close as Spring was going to let him; he looked into the medical box with hope filling his face for the first time. "Do you really have supplies?" he asked cautiously.

"Peroxide, alcohol, numbers, needles, thread, pills, cotton, bandages, anything useful, I have," Derek replied as he brought the open box to Jean. "Have your men help those who need it, and don't let them take anything they don't absolutely need to do so. These supplies are not the easiest things to get, so we have to use them sparingly."

"We?" Josh asked.

As the rest of the men began to slowly come to the brothers, bunching around them while eyeing the dragon, who eyed them back viciously.

Derek, seeing Spring getting amped up again, lightly rubbed her neck. "Spring is, as you can see, very fierce," he told all the men looking at her. "And she will kill without hesitation if she is attacked. But she is not a beast or a creature, and she won't eat men. She won't even harm them unless they mean me, her, or those in her territory harm." He gestured around them. "All of this is her territory. Even the other dragons acknowledge it, and every dragon in her territory is like her. If you don't attack them, or theirs, then they won't attack you. Without her, I would have died a long time ago. So before you try to judge her a monster, listen to my story of how I met her, and then you decide if she isn't a worthy companion to have."

While the men began tending to their wounded, Derek told them about being caught in the meteor shower, how he found her, and how she had kept him alive. He left out the names of everyone but told them of the attacks on the Pantiers and how they had survived.

The men all listened in silence, and from their minds, he saw their wonder and amazement. All of them felt staunch disbelief when they found out he was only fourteen. They were willing to believe in dragons more than that.

"And so you taught her not to eat men?" Josh asked as Derek finished his story, his eyes moving back and forth from Derek to Spring standing behind him.

"Yes, and she understands the reasons. I have told her of our myths about dragons and explained how men are scared of things that they cannot understand," Derek explained.

"So they came from space?" Jean asked tiredly, speaking for the first time since Derek started his story. "Did they bring the meteors, or did they just happen to be in them?" he asked seriously.

Derek paused. He knew if he spoke wrong, the men would all condemn the dragons, no matter what he said. All of them suffered irreparable damage and hurt because of the meteors, and if the dragons were to blame for the meteors, they would be condemned. He looked up at Spring, touching her hot scales gently.

"I cannot say exactly what happened, nor could I put it into the right words, but Spring can if you will listen to her. But I have to warn you, she doesn't communicate like we do. So Jean, would you be willing to listen to her? She will show you what happened. Then, if you approve, she can show the rest of the men," Derek told the scientist, knowing his curiosity would make him listen. And Jean, he now knew, was the one he must convince. For a reason he was not sure about, he knew this man would either help men accept the dragons or condemn them.

Jean looked up at Spring nervously. Derek described her in an affectionate and loving way, describing qualities desirable to him. Yet she looked so vicious and angry. And in a way, he guessed he could understand it. If their bond was as tight as the mysterious man suggested, then he could see why the dragon wanted to rip them apart. They had tried to kill the man.

"What do I have to do?" he asked Derek, a little unsure if he wanted to try it. But his scientific mind was leaping for the chance, just as Derek had known he would.

"Nothing," Derek replied and looked at Spring. "Spring, if you would."

Jean suddenly gasped as his mind was pierced by coldness. He clenched his brother's arm before slowly relaxing again and closing his eyes.

Derek touched Josh's arm, seeing his apprehension and concern for his brother. "It's alright. Spring communicates through images; your brother is just seeing the memories she has, which were passed to her by her mother, the queen dragon," Derek explained quickly.

Jean sat still for a long time, watching and trying to understand what he was seeing. When he opened his eyes, he saw his brother's anxious face. He gave him a look that told him he was fine, then he turned to study Derek, his face thoughtful.

"What I have seen is very disturbing and interesting, to say the least," Jean told him after a second of contemplation. "But it does not answer my question, just makes them all the more pressing. It doesn't exactly claim the dragons are innocent of the meteors, but it doesn't condemn them either—"

Spring could feel how important it was for Derek to win over this man. She did not like it, but she too felt the truth of it. So while the man mused over what she had shown him, she sent a thought to Derek.

Surprised by the picture that formed in his head, Derek turned to Josh. "Have someone find your brother's hand, as well as that of the other man's."

Josh gave him a weird look before stumbling around in the dark himself to look for the amputated hands.

"Where did they come from?" Jean asked Derek seriously.

Derek just shrugged. "I have been trying to find that out myself. I have gone over and over Spring's memories, for wherever they did come from, it had to be close or at least relatively close. It was out of this solar system because there was total darkness around the planet they came from. The heat, what heat they had, came from within the planet itself. But before the queen died, I think she caught a glimpse of our solar system and headed towards it. Because I'm sure that was the light she was heading towards when she died."

Jean frowned, then, after a second, he looked thoughtfully at Spring, who, for once, did not look like she wanted to kill him. "You can share your memories with the others," he told her respectfully.

Spring looked down at Derek, and he nodded.

There came the startled sounds of gasps of fright as pictures began to form in all the men's minds.

Derek, concerned for the Ranger and the egg, sent his mind searching north. He felt Vex and ignored him and kept going until he felt Charger.

"Everything has calmed down here," he reassured Charger quickly as he strained his mind further, trying to reach Nattilie or Nathan's mind. But without Spring there, for some reason, he could not reach them, so he gave up with a sigh as Josh returned with the amputated hands.

"Why do you want these?" Josh accused angrily, suspicion crawling through his mind that Derek must want them for trophies.

Derek looked him in the eyes, tempted to take off his glasses, but decided against it for now. "Spring thinks she might be able to fix or heal them," he told Josh seriously.

The men, hearing that, looked stunned.

"You mean, like reattach my hand?" the other man, whom Derek had cut off his hands and knocked out with his knife, asked in a stunned voice. "How?" Then he shivered. "No way, man, how can she reattach my hand?" he asked in a suddenly panicked voice.

"Calm down, Dev," one of the men said calmly, putting his arm around the man's shoulder to help calm him down.

Jean walked to Derek, grabbing his brother's hand delicately and looking at him curiously. "Can it be done? Can she do it?" Jean asked interestedly.

A picture of Derek floated through Derek's own mind. And confused, he turned to his big red and gold dragon. "Me? I can't do it. It's not like I can just put it back upon his arm and tell it to heal," he told her in a surprised, ridiculous voice.

Spring bent, touching him affectionately with her head, filling him with the confidence that she had in him, and a picture formed in his mind of the cracked egg. Then again, it is whole and glowing. Then the feeling of intense heat surged through him as she helped him remember the feeling that had been coursing through him when he had healed the egg.

Derek looked in her eyes. "Are you sure I can do it? You've seen what healing the egg did to me. I couldn't move for a long time, and it sapped me of all my energy," he told her in her mind.

She pushed him gently with her head and rubbed up against him affectionately when he rubbed her neck.

Derek was not as sure he could do it as she seemed to be that he could. He turned back to Jean. "Spring herself cannot do it, but she thinks I can. If you're willing to try, I will see what I can do to fix your hand."

Jean frowned. "She thinks you can? How? By magic?" he asked sarcastically, his disbelief written all over his face.

Derek gave him a serious look. "If that is what it is, then yes, by magic," Derek replied before sighing. "Take off your bandage, clean your hand, and hold them together."

As if amused to see this fail, Jean sarcastically did as Derek told him to, not even wanting to hope that his hand could be reattached, so he did not feel let down when whatever this was did not work. While Jean unwrapped his arm, his brother began to clean his bloody hand with alcohol.

Derek closed his eyes, trying to remember the warmth he had felt healing the egg. But just remembering did not seem to help him at all because he could not feel that feeling in him now. Frustrated, he tried even harder to find that feeling; since remembering did not work, he searched his mind and body and found two focus points for the warmth that came to his mind: the dragon mark on his chest and the dragon mark upon his spear in his hand. The spear flared up brilliantly when he focused on it. It grew warm in his hand. But he knew instantly that was not the warmth he needed. The spear's warmth was savage and destructive. So he let it go and watched the spear's glow dim a little. Then he focused on his dragon mark. Suddenly, a gust of warmth filled him, like a lightning strike, leaving his ears ringing and his body trembling.

Spring behind him yipped in pain before lunging forward to catch Derek softly by clamping onto the back of his shirt with her teeth to keep him from falling.

A second later, his ears stopped ringing, and he pulled his hands from them and noticed both of his palms were damp with blood.

"What happened?" Jean asked as Derek finally opened his eyes.

"I'm okay, Spring. You can put me down," he told her reassuringly and got his feet under him. Then he looked at the surprised brothers, both of whom had scrambled back like he was going to blow up.

"You sure you're okay?" Jean asked in a shaking voice, surprised if not awed by what he had just seen. "You lit up like a Roman candle about to explode," he said, trying to keep his wonder from his voice. Nothing he knew scientifically could explain what he had just seen. The boy had lit with an inside fire, like he was a god.

Derek ran a hand through his hair, flattening it again. His head was pounding, even though he did not show it. "I just learned something never to try again, kind of like putting your finger into an electrical socket. If you're ready, I think I know how to do this, if it can, in fact, be done. I'm not saying it can. I've never done it before, but if it works, you do get your hand back."

What he had just seen scared Jean, but again, his curiosity had him moving to the man with a dragon.

Derek felt his sudden fright and touched both the man's hand and arm as they were put together in front of him.

"No fear," he told Jean with a smile before closing his eyes in concentration.

Derek sent his mind towards the dragon mark, and this time, he drew the power from it instead of trying to enter it. Slowly, that strange warmth began to fill him, coursing through his body, building until it raged inside of him. He could actually feel its whole complexity, so many of them: destructiveness, creativeness, and parts he recognized, feeling when he healed the egg. He pulled upon them until it raged in his body for release.

"Grit your teeth," Derek whispered to Jean.

Then, not a second to spare, he released the warmth boiling within him and opened his eyes.

Jean gasped, going still as bright light surrounded Jean's amputated hand and arm.

Derek felt the warmth leaving him as visions filled his mind. They were of veins, tendons, muscles, cells, and skin, all reforming into one again. Then he sank to his knees, trying to capture his breath as his energy drained from him. This time, it was not nearly as bad as when he had healed the egg, and almost instantly, he was back upon his feet to see Jean and Josh staring at him with awe and amazement.

Derek grabbed Jean's hand to study it. It was totally healed. Where it had been cut by Derek's blade was a silver scar, and to his surprise, though he didn't show it, on the outside of Jean's hand was a small red and gold dragon head. Derek ran a finger over it, feeling the warmth in it.

"This is a gift from Spring and me, in thanks for understanding the dragons' plight," he told Jean as Jean clenched his fist and moved his wrist to see if he had total movement and feeling.

Then Jean laughed. "It's perfect!" he said in astonishment. "It damn well worked!" he exclaimed to his men, showing them his hand to their amazed looks.

After everyone had seen his remarkable recovery and he had shown Dev, Jean walked back to Derek, who was busily eating some jerky Herb had dried. Behind Jean, Dev followed him nervously.

Feeling a bout of starvation, Derek ignored them and concentrated on chewing the tough meat. He did not like the feel of Dev's mind, but he had already told him he would heal him.

Dev, whose name was Devan Hill, had a lot of things hidden in his mind, and all of them had a very unpleasant feel to them.

A picture formed in his mind from Spring, and it showed him not healing Devan.

Derek stroked her scales. "If I don't," he told her lightly in her mind, "we will lose these men. We can't risk it. We need them; they will be the first men who know about us and will spread tales. The good kind, tales that show men the good dragons can bring. If I heal him, he will be one of the miracles you worked. If I don't, they will slowly turn against us, and I can't take that chance because I refuse to heal one guy," he told her, feeling frustrated.

Jean was studying Derek and smiled when Derek turned his attention back to him.

"I saw you fall after you healed me. Are you okay? Can you heal Dev still?" he asked in surprising concern.

Derek wished he could lie and say he couldn't. But he could envision them turning against him in some way if he didn't, and he needed to put Spring in their good graces so there was no ill-will towards her. He could not and would not allow that. He had been the one to cut off his hand, be it that the man had been trying to kill him at the time, but still, he had to lay the bridges to keep Spring and the other dragons as safe as he could. So he nodded to Jean.

"I am okay, just a little tired. Give me a second, and I will heal Dev. Make sure to clean his hands well," Derek told him, eating more jerky.

Derek then reached into Spring's mind. "When I healed Jean, I left a mmm… magical mark. I don't want to leave one on Devan. What can I do differently?" he asked her, hoping she knew a way.

He got the feeling from Spring that she was unsure.

"Maybe," he mused to her, "if I try to pull the magic back, I won't leave a mark?" he asked.

Again, a picture of him not healing Devan filled his mind. And chewing jerky, he sighed. Walking to Devan, who was looking at him expectantly, yet very close to panic again.

Just wanting to get it over with, Derek touched his hand and arm.

"Grit your teeth," Derek told him before drawing upon his dragon mark.

This time, the warmth filled him faster as if it had created a path now for its easy passage. It filled him fast and a lot more forcefully.

This time, he swooned when he released the magic. But he stayed on his feet as he envisioned all of Devan's veins, muscles, tendons, cells, and skin forming as one, and as soon as it was finished, this time he pulled the magic back into himself. A bad idea, he realized as the magic raged throughout his body, he could feel it doing stuff to him, healing him, then no place to go, it blasted out of him in a burst of light, like a lightning strike, that blew out of his feet sending him flying back into Spring, who again caught him as softly as she could so he wouldn't get hurt.

The unexpected blast caught everyone by surprise, but when they saw no one was hurt, they forgot about it, staring at Devan's hand.

Devan himself stared at his hand with wonder and awe as he flexed it. It looked perfect, like nothing had ever happened to it.

Only as Derek looked at it, he could see a glowing dragon mark, the same as Jean's, but only this one was invisible to anyone's sight, but his and Spring's. Derek could not feel the magical warmth in the symbol like he could in Jean's. But then neither could he sense Devan's mind anymore. It was like, to his senses, even though his and Spring's eyes could see him, Devan was no longer there.

And that gave Derek a bad feeling in the pit of his stomach. He hid it well, smiling at Devan, who thanked him gratefully for fixing his hand.

Jean patted Derek appreciatively upon the back with his now healed hand.

"You look positively tired and hungry now, sit, and we will make some supper," He began, but Derek interrupted him.

"Not yet," He told Jean with an appreciative smile. "I still got one more person to heal, then we can sit, eat, and discuss all of our futures."

Derek walked steadily through the men, who gave him a wide berth until he reached the man he had shot with the crossbow. A man Derek knew was more dangerous than all the others, a reason he had shot the man instead of chopping off his hand. This man was just too well-trained and deadly.

The man smiled up at him. "No explosions?" He asked Derek hopefully.

Derek laughed, relieved he felt an instant likeness to this man. "No explosions, just grit your teeth, and it will be over in no time," Derek told him as he knelt next to where the man was lying.

He put his hand on the man's chest over the wound, and Derek's mind touched his. His name was Mark Dresa; his friends all called him Firebrand. He was younger than the others, being only 24. He had served in the military, and Derek was surprised to find he was a trusted friend of the president and a new recruit to the Secret Service, set to watch and protect Jean Perry.

All of that was interesting, telling Derek how the man had been trained to be as dangerous as he was. But what surprised Derek the most was the awe in which the man held for Derek and Spring.

Derek lowered his voice so only Mark could hear him. "I think you've served our president well in protecting Jean; he's a good man." Then, his hand still on the amazed Mark's chest, Derek sought the magic in his mark again.

He knew this one was going to empty him as he felt the warmth rage inside him, and he released it into Mark. This time, he did not pull the magic back, and when the wound disappeared, a small red and gold dragon head appeared on the man's chest.

Derek touched the hands holding his arm tightly. "My lips are shut," Derek promised in a reassuring voice that relieved Mark instantly, who released his arm when he realized he could trust Derek.

Exhaustion hit Derek like a rock to the head. He tried to force it back so no one could or would see it. But Mark did, and he was quick to help Derek straighten up when he almost stumbled.

"Gods, do you feel like I do?" Mark asked curiously, rubbing his suddenly rumbling stomach. "You must be starving. You just healed three of us, and if my body is crying out from just being healed, I can only imagine what it's doing to you."

Derek smiled good-naturedly. "I'm starving, alright. All I have eaten today is some jerky. I've been hunting buck all day—"

Suddenly, Vex growled viciously, and a man's terrified voice spoke up in a panic.

"Calm down, dragon. Calm down, I'm not food."

Then, a chuckling sound filled the air, and Derek felt amusement from Vex. This was followed by the picture of a man trying to sneak off with one of the horses.

Derek turned to Jean with a smile. "I see you tried to send someone to warn your family that you would be out all night?" Derek told him in a musing voice. Though he knew exactly what Jean had done. It was written all over his face and mind.

Jean's jaw dropped in amazement. "How do you know?"

Derek shrugged. "Lucky guess, and it is what I would have done in your situation."

Derek then looked into the trees. "It's okay, Vex, you can let him go," he called out to the dragon.

He heard men all around let out breaths in relief and turned back to Jean. "How many survived the sickness?" he asked curiously as they walked to the fire.

"Let us eat first, then I will tell you how we survived," Jean said, gesturing for him to take a seat near the fire.

Jean sat right next to him, and they both watched as men moved around the camp, being careful not to get close to Spring. And as a man brought some food from the horses and began to cook it on the fire, Jean studied Derek in the firelight.

"I take it you know my name is Jean Perry. What's yours?" Jean asked after a moment's deliberation.

"Derek Grisbe," Derek replied, studying the scientist in return. Unlike his brother Josh, who had black hair, Jean had long grey hair. They both had hazel eyes and were inches smaller than Derek's tall frame.

"Derek," Jean said again in a musing voice as if contemplating the name itself. "Why the sunglasses? You can obviously see perfectly with them on, but they are an oddity in the dark."

Derek nodded. "Being bonded to a dragon changes you," he replied after a second of deliberation. "Part of the change is my eyesight. In the dark, any source of light is very powerful and tends to give me a headache."

Jean frowned when Derek did not remove his glasses, and he realized he would have to make his request out loud. He wanted to see Derek's eyes, watch what he watched, and see just how good he could see.

"Can you take them off while we talk?" Jean asked politely.

Josh sat down next to his brother, and Derek lowered his voice so that only they could hear it. Mark was not far off, watching like a hawk and probably could hear him too.

"When I said my eyes were changed, I meant literally. Seeing them might unnerve your men more than they already are," Derek warned Jean seriously.

Josh smiled kindly. "They are going to see them sooner or later, Derek," he replied.

With a sigh, Derek reached up, pulling his sunglasses off. He heard the intake of breath from all around as men saw his pure, liquid silver, metal-looking eyes. Eyes that matched his dragon's.

Derek squinted in the light from the fire, being careful not to look right at it. The light did not actually hurt his vision; it was just brilliant to look at as he saw it in all its beauty. No definition of light or darkness in the flickering flames was left out.

Every set of eyes was now upon him as he folded up his sunglasses and hooked them in the collar of his shirt so they would be out of his way.

"Do your eyes actually glow? Or is that just the light from the fire?" Jean asked him in a stunned, curious voice.

"I think it's just that they reflect light when it is dark, no matter how much light there is, my eyes will find it and magnify it so that no matter what I will always be able to see as if it was as bright as day time," Derek whispered uncomfortably as he felt the weight of everyone's awed and stunned gazes.

"Are there other humans that are bound like you are, as you call it, to dragons?" Mark asked him curiously as he came to take a seat next to Josh so he could face Derek.

CHAPTER SIXTEEN

Day 41; Aug. 10th

At the Pantiers, everyone was in the front room, listening to the Ranger's quiet voice. He was awake but groggy from the pain medication that Emma had given him, so she could dig out the BBs. Taking one from his face that had been stopped by his cheekbone, and another from his upper chest that had luckily been stopped by his muscles, but not before the BB nicked a couple of veins that made him bleed out.

"So there is another egg?" Herb asked as he helped the Ranger drink some water.

Ellis nodded with a sad look. "Only I got to it too late. When I finally got the egg, it was cracked, and before that... I don't even think it was shining like the other one. I think it was dead or very near it before the men found it and began trying to open it with brute force. When I got there, one of them was taking an axe to it until it cracked."

Nathan suddenly sat up, and after a second, he smiled in relief. "If it was close to death when you saw it—" Nathan told the Ranger happily. "Well, it's glowing now. Charger has it, and he is bringing it here. He also says Derek is okay, that Vex and Spring are protecting him from the ten humans with him."

"Is it still alive?" Nate asked in relief.

Nathan nodded. "Charger says Derek healed it. I saw it. Charger got the picture of Derek healing it from Spring and passed it to me. The egg is whole again. Derek lit up in a fierce light, and suddenly the egg began to glow and heal. It was awesome."

Nattilie touched her brother. "Show me, I want to see it," she said excitedly.

Nathan frowned before nodding. "I'll show everyone, watch," he told them as he closed his eyes, reaching for all of their minds, then showed them everything Charger had shown him.

He heard Emma gasp, but the others all remained silent as they saw the images of Derek being watched and protected by Vex and Spring. He then showed them the glowing egg that Charger carried. Then, in Derek's eyes, a picture from Spring shows Derek glowing and healing the egg.

Nattilie nodded thoughtfully. "Vex says Derek just healed three of the men he had hurt. He says Derek chopped off two men's hands and shot another in the chest with a crossbow."

Then she gasped as Spring entered her mind, sending pictures to her.

Everyone watched her as she fell quiet, then sat looking intently at the dragon mark on her hand. After a second, she smiled, and the dragon mark suddenly lit up with light.

"Of course," she whispered to herself. "That's how Vex healed my hand."

Nattilie got up and walked to Ellis, studying him intently. "Can I heal you?" she asked confidently, though she rubbed her dragon mark nervously.

"You can heal me?" Ellis asked in surprise, studying her face intensely. "You mean like Derek healed the egg?"

She nodded. "And like he healed the three men, look," she told him before showing him in his mind everything Spring had just watched Derek do.

Nathan then gasped as she shared it with everyone. They were all stunned by the pictures of Derek healing the men perfectly. Then they saw Nathan's palm light up as Nattilie's hand had as he learned how to use his dragon mark.

"You can really do it?" Ellis asked her seriously, no longer doubtful.

She did not answer this time. Instead, she put her glowing hand on his chest, and following Spring's instructions, she began pulling warmth from the mark until she could feel it filling her up like a balloon. When she could not hold it back any longer, she released it into the Ranger.

Nate caught her quickly as she fell, and Ellis' wounds sealed shut, and a small red and gold dragon head appeared upon Ellis' chest. Nattilie collapsed into Nate's arms as all of her energy was drained from her.

"Nat! Nat! Are you okay?" Nate demanded in an upset voice as he caught and laid her gently upon the ground, finding her unconscious.

Emma and Herb both ran over with worried expressions, quickly huddling over her, checking her pulse, and trying to see if they could gently wake her up.

"What's wrong with her?" Nate asked Nathan angrily.

Looking scared, Nathan closed his eyes and reached his senses out to Charger, relaying pictures of what had happened when Nattilie had healed the Ranger.

In answer, he heard a roar announcing Charger's arrival. He ran to the front door and tarp, opening them to watch Charger fly while carrying the egg. Smoke was puffing from the small dragon's mouth from the effort of flying so long, carrying the heavy egg. He dove in, forcing Nathan to step out of the way as he flew by.

Charger flew right to Nate, who gently grabbed the egg from him. Everyone heard the sound of tearing flesh over Charger's breathing, but Nate never even reacted to it. He just held on tighter until the egg was in his hands.

Then, huffing and puffing, the black and silver dragon dropped to the floor and made his way wearily to where Nattilie was lying while Nathan shut the door.

Herb and Emma uncertainly made room for Charger as he walked around her prone body as if looking for something he could not see.

A picture filled with frustration from Charger suddenly formed in Nathan's mind.

Nathan looked at Herb. "Charger needs you to expose her hand that has her dragon mark. He cannot touch her to heal her with his power unless it is on her mark. He's not her dragon, so anywhere besides her mark he touches her with his power will hurt her worse, or he could just touch her like he would me," Nathan explained to Herb.

Herb moved Nattilie until her hand was exposed, and Charger touched her dragon's mark with his snout. Her mark lit up brilliantly, and Nattilie's eyes fluttered as she gasped for breath. Her weak pulse suddenly became strong again. She looked around in shock until she saw Ellis crouched down next to Herb, his face full of concern.

"It worked!" she said excitedly with a joy-filled smile, ignoring the hot, fiery feeling now running through her body.

"Yeah, and you almost killed yourself doing it," Nate growled at her angrily, drawing her eyes to him and the copper egg vibrating gently in his hands. "You are not as powerful as Derek. None of us is. So next time, think carefully before you try something he does," he warned his sister, scared she had almost drained herself of energy.

Nattilie frowned as she sat up with Herb's help. "But he healed your dragon and three men that were hurt a lot worse than Ellis was. I thought I would be able to heal Ellis if he could heal all of them," she tried to explain to her twin.

"Charger indicates that Derek received assistance from Spring after he healed the egg, she infused him with renewed energy," Nathan explained to them."But even so, Charger says it would have taken more energy than all three of us have to heal the egg. And in doing so, Derek didn't pass out," he said with awe for Derek's power.

Charger, happy to be near Nathan again, began rumbling loudly as Nathan rubbed his scales.

After everyone was sure both Nattilie and the Ranger were okay, Herb turned to Ellis, looking at him seriously.

"So who are these men that attacked you and Derek?" he asked the Ranger, sounding displeased.

The Ranger was busy studying and feeling the warm dragon mark on his chest, and it took him a second to answer.

"I'm not totally sure. I heard some talk right before I saw them trying to pry the egg open, and they tried to kill me for protecting it. They said something about a bomb shelter they had paid money to live in, in case anything like this ever happened. Whoever they are, I think all of them are or were powerful men in their own right. Powerful enough for the government to warn them of the meteor shower heading towards Earth. And powerful enough to get to the shelter with all of their supplies before the meteors actually began to fall," Ellis told him.

"A bomb shelter? Near here? I guess that makes a little sense. There would be plenty of places to hide one here," Herb replied thoughtfully.

He turned to Nattilie. "How is Derek?" he asked in concern.

Nattilie closed her eyes and listened to her dark blue dragon, who had not taken his eyes off Derek.

"Vex says he's fine. He's sitting with two of the men he healed earlier. One who Vex thinks is the men's leader. They are all eating," Nattilie said, watching from Vex's eyes.

"What do you think the boy is doing?" Ellis asked Herb curiously.

"I think he is trying to win these men over to keep us safe," Emma replied as she began putting out bowls of stew she had been cooking in the living room fire.

Ellis chuckled. "I bet they got a surprise, one of their lives, when they faced that boy."

Herb nodded with an admiring smile for Derek. "Ten to one odds, and the boy comes out the victor. Without Spring beside him to even things up," he chuckled to himself. "I can just imagine their faces when Spring showed up. She left here like a furious hurricane."

Nate laughed. "With how angry she was when she left, I'm surprised they didn't die in fright. I sure would not have wanted to face her."

"Vex! No!" Nattilie said angrily in alarm.

It was so loud it drew everyone's attention, though. When they looked at her, she had her eyes closed and did not realize she was speaking out loud.

"Leave these horses alone! If you're hungry, go find a sleeping deer. I don't care if they look juicy, and you're tired of hunting. If you eat one of those horses, Derek is going to be mad, and those men will never trust us. So get away from them before they run off," she scolded her dragon.

Nathan and Nate both smiled at each other, and Charger imitated Vex's chuffing chuckle of amusement.

Seeing them laughing at her, Nattilie growled. "It's not funny! He could upset everything Derek is doing," she complained vehemently.

Nathan looked at Nate. "Nattilie loves Derek," he told his older brother in a teasing voice.

Nattilie went bright red. "No, I don't! You little lizard!" she said defensively.

"Nattilie loves Derek, Nattilie loves Derek, Nattilie loves Derek," Nathan teased in a chant that Nate quickly picked up, chanting and teasing his twin.

Nattilie started towards her brother furiously until Herb stopped, hiding a smile.

"Boys," he told them in a scolding tone. Then, seriously, "Your sister is right. Derek is going to need all the help he can get to win these men over. And I have a feeling they're going to want to meet all of us. Ellis tells me they are only about ten or so miles away on horseback. Most likely, Derek will bring some or all of them here in the morning. I want you all to get some rest. We will have an early morning tomorrow so we can help them clean up; that way, we can make a good impression on them."

Herb then looked at Charger. "That means you, too." The black and silver spiky dragon tried to look both innocent and indignant, giving Herb a wounded look.

As the Bergers settled down for the night, Emma began to clean the house of all the ash that always seemed to find a way in. While she worked, Herb and Ellis began to talk quietly.

CHAPTER SEVENTEEN

Day 41; Aug. 10

After Derek had eaten his fill of instant beans with chopped-up deer meat, his tiredness began to drop away. He spent most of that night talking with Jean, Josh, Mark, and Devan, getting to know them and how they had survived the meteor storms.

Jean Perry, as Derek had read from his mind earlier, was the leading scientist in America. He headed the government's NASSP facility (North American Space Science Program). He was also the first person to have noticed the quickly appearing meteor cloud, which he had sighted coming out of the asteroid belt past Mars. Originally, that is where he believed the meteor cloud had come from, and he informed the president. Now he was no longer sure of that.

After the sighting of the approaching cloud, he had stayed in contact with the president, and when all had seemed lost, he had been flown from his home in Vernal, Utah, with his family to a private bomb shelter in a military plane. And right after they landed at the bomb shelter, the meteors began to fall.

Josh Perry was younger than his brother by ten years. He had done six years in the service before taking over the family ranch in Vernal.

Mark Dresa told a story that was far from the truth, claiming he was from a rich family who had bought him room and board at the bomb shelter here in Wyoming because he had not had the time to travel to the one in Virginia where his family was currently staying. He made no mention of his military training or secret service recruitment, let alone his friendship with the president.

Devan Hill had created a rich family, though technically, he had no wife or kids. He had a fiancée who had died of meteor sickness. He was a self-proclaimed oil tycoon, one of the richest men in America, and sitting next to Mark, he looked fat. Whereas Mark had short brown hair with light brown eyes, Devan had thinning blond hair and icy blue eyes. Mark was three inches shorter than Derek's over-six-feet frame, and Devan was a couple of inches smaller than Mark, yet easily outweighed him by fifty pounds. Devan had been warned by the owner of the bomb shelter and had flown his family and fiancée to the shelter, arriving just minutes before the meteors struck.

After listening to their stories, Derek stayed up listening to Jean, who told him about the shelter, its conditions, and the people who had fought the meteor sickness that killed most of those in the shelter. Only one hundred and seventy people remained of those who had made it to the shelter before the storm. He knew by reading the scientist's mind that the shelter only had thirteen pellets and BB guns, and those they had raided from a sporting goods store in a nearby town they had passed through.

The shelter itself had plenty of provisions of almost every kind. Only medical supplies were off-limits, and that was only because so many of them had been used up trying to help everyone through the meteor sickness. The shelter had provisions for over three thousand people to be housed in it, almost all of whom had died from the illness that had spread like wildfire the first week after the meteors had fallen.

Since then, only fifteen people had left the shelter at a time, and those were mainly to scout out nearby cities and towns, trying to find other survivors, food, supplies, and anything that might be useful, like horses, bikes, certain oils, since some, like gas, just exploded instead of lighting. So they mainly looked for lamps, candles, and strikers because matches hardly ever worked. Jean explained that some kind of chemical in the air kept them from igniting, so flint and stone became the preferred lighters. Anything they could find that could be used and hoarded that kept flame was now a valuable commodity.

Derek listened to him for hours, and before they separated for the night, it was agreed that Jean, Mark, and Devan (who Derek had only reluctantly agreed upon) would follow him in the morning to meet the Pantiers and see if the Ranger was alright. With that agreed upon, Derek took Spring and Vex deep into the forest away from the camp, and there he curled up next to Spring and fell asleep.

Day 42; Aug. 11th

Derek only got an hour's worth of sleep before rousing, to his surprise, full of energy. And he knew he had grown again from Spring's touch. His clothes felt tight, as did his shoes. That didn't so much amuse him as it worried him. Over the last week, he had already noticed other changes brought on by Spring's last touch; he did not need much sleep, he slept less and less each night, yet what little he did sleep refreshed him deeply. And while that may not have been a bad thing, growing bigger so fast that people noticed it made him stick out even more, which to him was a bad thing.

Spring was curled up contentedly around him, awake and staring at the dark blue dragon, who Derek could see was ignoring her as he cleaned his scales.

When Derek stood up, looking at her, his annoyance went away, and he couldn't stop himself from rubbing Spring's neck, drawing a loud rumble of affection from her. She looked calm, but he could feel her wariness as men began moving through the forest and around the camp, taking down their makeshift lean-tos and rolling up all the bedding.

At Spring's rumble, the birds in the forest chirped warmly in surprise, and men from the camp, hearing it, froze, looking into the forest, reminded that there were dragons there.

Derek reached into Vex's mind as he felt Jean and Mark begin to make their way deeper into the forest, trying to find Derek.

"I want you to follow the men on the horses to wherever it is they are going. Stay out of sight so they don't see you or suspect you might be there. That means no eating their horses," he teased before he continued. "If you eat on the way, don't let them hear it, but don't lose them. I want to know where this shelter of theirs is and the easiest way to reach it."

Vex's calm mind touched his own, and he felt the dark blue dragon's concern and anxiousness to get back to Nattilie and knew the dragon was itching to return to her.

Derek smiled. "Soon," he told Vex out loud as the dragon swirled and disappeared through the trees. Even Derek's own eyes had difficulty trying to see and follow the dragon through the forest. Vex's hiding skills were tremendous.

A second later, he had put on his sword and sunglasses and grabbed his spear, turning so he could watch as Jean and Mark slowly made their way deeper into the trees.

Jean, he saw, was carrying a lantern, and they were both going the wrong way.

Derek touched his mind to his spear, making it light up brightly in the morning darkness so Jean and Mark could see where he was.

"I'm over here," he told them, catching their attention.

Startled, both of the men looked around, seeing the light, and hurried over to him before gazing in awe at Spring in the light of Derek's glowing spear. Her red and gold scales glistened as she stretched and studied them with her silver eyes, and the same intensity with which they studied her.

Jean walked to Derek as Mark tried to look at the ash-covered ground unobtrusively. And Derek, missing nothing, knew the man was looking for the marks in the ash of the other dragon everyone had heard but not yet seen.

"We just wanted to make sure you did not want to take a horse," Jean explained as he looked at Derek with a friendly smile. "I know you told us last night you would lead us there by flying ahead of us with your dragon. But we do have an extra horse here, three of them in fact. So, if you want to ride one of them with us, we will be happy to oblige you. And it will make it all the easier for us to follow you in this infernal darkness. With you on horseback, seeing your spear glowing in front of us will be easier than straining to see it over the trees."

Derek thought it over quickly, and doing so, he could feel Spring's instant dislike of the plan. She wanted to be with him at all times. As for himself, he had never ridden a horse before, and he was sure riding the merry-go-round as a child didn't count. He wondered if it was any different than riding Spring.

Behind him, Spring made an indignant noise at Derek's thought.

He smiled, reaching back to stroke her shoulder scales. "It would be easier to lead them, though," he thought to her. "And you can watch over and protect me from the sky if anything does go wrong."

Spring grumbled, letting him know she was not happy, then, without any preamble, she jumped into the air, sending ash flying with her wings as she took to the sky.

Derek watched her, feeling both of the men's eyes upon him, and after a second, he turned towards them again.

"She doesn't like the idea, but you are right, it will be easier for me to lead you in this darkness if I am riding beside you," Derek told them.

They both smiled, and Jean nodded thoughtfully while Mark continued to study Derek.

"How did you let the dragon know you would ride the horse? You didn't even say anything," Mark asked in an intrigued voice.

Derek glanced up at Spring adoringly and motioned for them to lead him to a horse, his spear losing its bright glow. "The bond between me and Spring does not need words; we know what the other wants, needs, or feels without having to communicate it to each other," Derek told them seriously.

Jean led him through the trees and back to the camp, where there was an already saddled horse waiting for him. Derek frowned at the saddle thoughtfully, and as men began to leave the camp, following Josh back to the shelter, Derek tied his spear to the saddlebags, which would be easy to grab but would be out of his way until he needed it.

Out of the corner of his eye, he saw Devan ride his horse over to him. Derek only realized he was there by that flicker of movement, and he turned to meet Devan's gaze.

Devan lifted his healed hand in greeting with a troubled expression on his face as he met Derek's eyes. "Derek," he said in greeting before dropping his hand and looking at it as if it were weird to him. "I was wondering... I noticed that both Jean and Mark... well, they have those metallic dragons where you healed them, and I was wondering if I have somehow offended you because I don't have a mark like that. Not that I am ungrateful for what you did in healing my hand, I just don't understand how they have been marked and I haven't," he said in a worried, complaining voice.

Unable to sense or read Devan's thoughts, Derek ignored the man while turning to make the stirrups a little longer so he would be comfortable when he sat in the saddle. When that was done, he looked up at Devan, studying the man intently, and wondered what the man's mind was hiding and had hidden from him when he had healed him.

Derek smiled politely. "Devan, you have done nothing for me to take offense at. Everybody is different," he said, quickly coming up with an excuse that might satisfy the man. "Your body just responded differently than theirs did. But I can assure you, you have a mark just like theirs. I can see it glowing right now. Why is it not visible? I would have to study it to find out."

His response was rewarded with a deeper frown from Devan, and he knew the man did not like the thought that Derek would study him, so he let the issue drop.

Derek was in the middle of hopping into the saddle when suddenly he froze, getting a bad feeling inside of him. He felt an answer to the feeling from Spring.

"What's wrong?" Mark asked in concern as he rode his horse over to where Derek was mounting his, having seen Derek's pause in the light of the lantern Devan was holding.

Derek felt a chill cross his skin, almost like the one he felt when the meteors came. Only this one was different; he did not feel that vast panicking feeling as he did with the meteors. He shrugged it off as he mounted the horse. It was a big brown, and it moved nervously under his weight. He put a calming palm to its neck and reassured it gently with his mind. The horse calmed instantly.

He then looked at Jean seriously. "You'd better tell your men to push their horses. Something just changed in the atmosphere, and I think something is going to happen. It would be best if we all hurry."

"What about the Ranger's bike and provisions?" Mark asked Jean. "Do you want us to load them on the horse? We won't be able to take the bike."

Derek looked at the man. "We will need them where we are going."

He quickly sent his mind to Spring. "Can you carry the bike and supplies to the Pantiers?" he asked silently, knowing there was no way Vex could carry such a bulky thing for that long.

Spring dove down, scattering ash and frightening all of the horses. She looked at the bike as she landed and settled next to the tree it was leaning upon. And a picture came to Derek of supplies falling from the bike.

Derek shook his head, telling her they were all tied down and wouldn't fall out as she flew. They all watched as she grasped the bike with her hind claws and took off, flying and scattering ash as she flew off with the bike.

"Take it to the house. I will be close behind you," he told her out loud.

Then he reached for Vex's mind. "Fly back with Spring. Something is going to happen, and if it is a storm, I don't want you stuck in it so far from Nattilie. It will worry both of you unduly. We will have to find their shelter some other time."

In reply, he felt a welcoming feeling from Vex as the dark blue dragon changed directions.

"Come on, we should hurry," Derek told them, urging his horse towards the road Ellis had been following to get back to the Pantiers.

"What do you mean something is going to happen?" Mark asked worriedly, his horse following next to Derek's as Jean said goodbye to his brother, urging him to hurry back to the shelter.

"I'm not exactly sure what I feel, but I can still feel the air pressure changing. Can't you feel the rising pressure in your ears? It has been slowly growing. Why I didn't notice it before, I don't know, but I have been suspecting a large storm coming for the last week, wondering why it hasn't rained. And I think that is about to break. When the sun is up fully, this dry spell we have had is going to change violently. So we have to hurry, or we're going to be caught right in the middle of it," Derek told them urgently as he led them from the camp at a trot and onto the ash-covered road.

He realized quickly that riding a horse was both easier and harder than riding upon Spring. But he would prefer to be on Spring. He felt uncomfortable sitting upon the back of a beast whose mind was so simple compared to Spring's own. The feeling of sitting so close to an animal he couldn't and wouldn't blend minds with was appalling to him.

They all rode in silence for the first couple of minutes, then all three of them began pestering him with questions about Spring and the other dragons, about the buildings they were going to, and about everyone who would be there.

Not too long after they set off towards the Pantier residence, a brisk wind began to pick up, scattering ash to further darken the air around them. The men instantly reached into their saddlebags and pulled out their gas masks, putting them on, while Jean motioned to a pair in Derek's saddle for him to put on.

Instead, Derek just put a couple of nose filters in. His glasses would protect his eyes from most of the ash, and he was so used to the ash now that it rarely even bothered him when he did breathe in huge lungfuls of it. All it seemed to do now was inconvenience his body until he coughed and spat it out.

He felt the air pressure start to really build and urged his horse to an even brisker pace, using the light from his spear to help guide the men behind him. Then he felt Vex just on the edge of his perception and could sense that the dark blue dragon was trying to hide from him, while Vex kept a careful eye on him to make sure nothing bad happened to him.

He reached for Vex's mind. "Vex, unless you want to walk the rest of the way to the Pantiers, then you'd better follow Spring. The wind is going to pick up, and you won't be able to fly in it."

From far off in the trees, there came an annoyed rumble from Vex as he was caught, and all the horses' ears perked up and back as they got suddenly nervous.

"What was that?" Mark asked, a little agitated, his hand holding the butt of his BB gun.

Derek turned back to see them all watching him nervously; he just waved it off. "It was just one of the dragons. Seems he wanted to stay behind and travel with us," Derek explained as he looked around, following Vex's dark shadowing movement with his eyes and senses. "He's gone now, though."

After that, it was a quiet ride as they pressed their horses harder. The wind really began to pick up and started howling around them, blowing ash, dust, pebbles, and sticks into the air.

Thankfully, it was blowing at their backs, making them all grateful they did not have to run into it. Ahead of them by miles, Derek could sense Spring struggling against a crosswind that was blowing high in the sky.

Seeing her struggle with the bike worried him. But she gently assured him by sending him a picture of her being strong, quick, and graceful to him. Letting him know that this little wind was no problem for her.

When she finally did reach the Pantiers, he sighed in relief. The wind was moving so fast and blowing so much ash that it turned even his eyesight dark, and he had to stop and wait patiently a few times for the men to keep coming, making sure no one got lost, which was hard because he could not sense Devan like he could Jean and Mark. So several times, he had to circle his horse to go find the man in the darkness swirling around them.

Mark found a solution a short time later, tying all of the horses to each other on a rope he pulled from his saddlebag. After that, they made a lot quicker time.

In the growing darkness, Derek was forced to untie his spear and force it to light the darkness around them as brightly as it could until it was so bright, it began to vibrate softly in his hands, growing white hot. Doing so, he could feel his energy beginning to sap from forcing it so powerfully. Yet even though the longer he held it lit, the weaker he got, he did not dare lessen the light. He could barely make head or tail of what was road and what wasn't. He did not want to get lost in the storm, and the last thing he needed was for one of the horses to break its leg.

They were still a little bit away from the Pantier's when they all heard a crash that shook the ground. At first, Derek thought it was just a tree falling in the wind, but he felt a vague sense of pain. Feeling that pain, he automatically thought it was Spring, and fear lumped up in his throat as he forced his horse to a sudden stop. Not wanting to stop in the raging wind, the horse neighed and pulled against the reins until he put a hand on its shivering flank and forced it to calm down.

"What's wrong?" Jean's muffled voice yelled in concern. "Why have you stopped?"

Derek held up a hand to halt their questions and sent his senses questing out into the woods to the side of them, where the sound had come from, with the feeling of pain. His thoughts instantly slammed into the frantic and panicking mind of Vex.

The dark blue dragon had been following them, and the wind had tugged his wings, making him clip into a huge tree, which had been broken or weakened because when the dragon hit it, the tree had fallen on Vex, pinning the dragon's neck and wing under it while its roots ripped out the tree next to it and sent it crashing down on top of the other. The weight crushed Vex into the ash-covered ground. Derek reached Vex's mind just as the weight of the combined trees cut off its circulation, and it passed out.

"Stay here, I will find you in a minute," he told them firmly and sliced the spear through the rope tying them to him. Then he frantically kicked his horse into a gallop off the road and into the trees. The already tired horse struggled to obey him, hooves flying across the forest floor, trying to balk, but Derek kept a firm hand on its neck, keeping the horse calm so it would not panic.

"Stay!" he commanded the horse forcefully as he jumped off of it, using his senses to find the dying dragon. He landed right next to the trees, pinning the dragon. He dropped his still-glowing spear and, growling, bent, trying to move the trees forcefully. They wouldn't budge, and he could feel Vex dying.

Frantic now, he grabbed the tree above Vex's neck, getting a firm hold on the trunk, and yanked with all of his might. He could feel the strange warmth from his dragon mark filling his body, and he pulled upon it as frantically as he pulled upon the tree's trunk. He groaned as the tree started to budge and tried harder.

"Lift!" he growled fiercely, commanding his body to lift the tree. And to his amazement and relief, the tree did just that. The tree pinning Vex and the one pinning it both lifted in Derek's trembling arms until it was off of the unconscious dragon.

"Vex! Wake up!" Derek demanded in a strained grunt, unable to move the trees aside or to let them go until the dragon was out of the way.

The dark blue dragon was beyond hearing him, though, and he feared the worst when Vex didn't move at all.

"Wake up, Vex!" he screamed fiercely.

He could feel his energy draining from him by the second, his arms, chest, and legs shaking violently with the effort to hold the trees off of the dragon, which again did not hear him. He tried to think of a way to move Vex. In his mind, he could feel Spring in full panic mode, flying towards him as fast as she could. And surprisingly, he could see Nattilie lying unconscious. He was not sure how that happened, but he growled, straining even harder.

He did the only thing he could think to do; he pulled fiercely upon the warmth of his dragon mark until it went cold and sent his mind into Vex's.

"Wake up!" he commanded with the last of his strength.

The loss of energy in doing that was staggering; the trees slipped a couple of inches before he caught them again. And they grew so heavy in his arms that he put everything he had into holding them. Panting frantically for breath, he could feel his heart beating outrageously hard in his chest, so hard that he thought it might explode.

Vex's head snapped up and around to his vast relief, and when its silver eyes met his, Derek growled. "Move!"

Vex moved as if bitten, and Derek just collapsed. The trees slammed with a thud into the ground. Derek's head and vision were spinning, and he felt a presence near him as he toppled headfirst right over the trees he had just lifted to save Vex. He never felt his face hit the ground. He was unconscious before the trees hit the ground.

* * *

As the brilliant glow from the spear on the ground began to fade, the three men who had just witnessed yet another impossible feat from the boy Derek all looked at each other from atop their nervous mounts with shocked expressions. Then their eyes went back to the dark blue dragon, which curled protectively around the boy and let out a vicious roar as it touched the boy with its snout, trying to wake him. When the boy did not respond, the dragon touched him again with its snout, this time creating a brilliant flash of light, and again let out a booming, fierce roar so loud the horses all panicked. Only the big brown horse the boy had been riding stayed where it was, as if rooted to the ground. Though it was too panicked, bucking and rolling its eyes in terror. The other horses all bolted with their riders trying to flee the angry dragon.

Far away, the three men heard an answering roar respond through the darkness as they each tried to regain control of their mounts. When they did, all the horses still tied together, they returned to see the dragon's silver eyes looking at them expectantly as it curled over the prone boy.

Despite his bulk, Devan moved quickly. He was off his horse and running through the furious ash-blowing wind, stumbling around as he tried to remember where the boy had fallen because he could not see a thing. He did see those silver eyes flash menacingly upon him as the dragon turned towards him with its full attention. The growl it gave him was so devastatingly threatening that it froze him in place and almost stopped his heart from beating. His hair rose, and goosebumps rose upon his skin as fear filled him from just hearing the frightening sound.

Devan felt a hand grab his arm, pulling him back and nearly startling him even worse. "Stay here, I don't think the dragon likes you," Mark's voice yelled to him over the sound of the howling wind.

The truth of that was in the fact that, as Mark moved forward towards the silver-eyed dragon, it kept its venomous eyes upon Devan, never once looking at Mark as he moved to Derek's unconscious body.

"Put him over his horse!" Jean screamed over the wind. "The storm is getting worse!"

"Damn it, I can't see a thing in this damn darkness!" Mark growled angrily.

Fire suddenly shot from the dragon's mouth, scaring all three of them as it set a tree on fire.

"Thanks!" Mark yelled to the dragon appreciatively, surprised that it had understood what he was saying or needed.

He bent, checking Derek. "He's still breathing, but his heart is pounding erratically. I'll be damned if it doesn't feel like he's having a major heart attack, and he is cold to the touch," he yelled at Jean.

Then lifted Derek's body and stumbled. Oh damn, how much did he actually weigh? He thought as he strained to run with him to his big brown horse, which surprisingly didn't move as he approached in the flickering flame of the tree. Instead, the horse whickered and tried to nuzzle the boy as he approached him.

He almost fell a couple of times under the big boy's weight, and he did stumble as a huge roar sounded right above them. And the boy's big red and gold dragon landed hard upon the ground to the side of Mark and the horse. The horse, terrified of the dragon, reared in panic, but it did not budge; it stood its ground, its terrified eyes rolling wildly at seeing and scenting the dragon.

As the dragon landed, it gave off a fierce growl, warning Mark to back off. And he wisely lowered Derek to the ground and moved away. She didn't stop growling until Mark was well away. Then she bent, nudging Derek with her snout, sending a brilliant light throughout the boy's body, which in turn caused the red dragon to slump tiredly over the boy.

A second later, sparks filled the air as the dark blue dragon touched the red one, who turned upon it with a fierce, angry look and roar.

The dark blue dragon gave the red one an indignant look, then, to Mark's amazement, it began to laugh, or it made a sound imitating a chuckle that kept repeating itself as if the dragon was amused about something.

In answer, the red dragon just ignored the blue, and, not looking so tired anymore, she carefully pulled Derek to her chest, cradling him and struggling against the wind. She powerfully took to the air, not letting the wind buffet her at all until she got higher, then the wind slammed into her, tossing her into the air, where she just barely missed the top of a tree as she gained height and was then lost to all of their sight.

"Come on, we've got to go now!" Jean yelled fiercely. "It is only getting worse, and still, the rain has not started. Believe me, we want to be out of it before it does."

"How?" Devan demanded angrily, running back to where his horse was visible through the raging tree fire. "We don't even know where we are going!"

In answer, the blue dragon got their attention by issuing a small roar. When they all turned to look at it, the dragon bent its nose carefully, pushing Derek's spear towards Mark, who carefully picked it up.

As he touched it, he felt an electrical shock sting his hand, and a flash of heat flared inside of Mark, making the symbol upon his chest light up fiercely.

The blue dragon then walked into the wind past him and towards the road.

"I think the dragon is going to lead us!" he yelled to them as he carried the spear to his horse and mounted up.

They watched as Devan mounted and then grabbed the big brown's reins. But as he tugged to get the horse moving, it resisted. It wasn't until Devan got frustrated and shouldered his own horse into it that it finally began to move, hesitatingly at first, but as Devan kept tugging its reins, it followed with more vigor.

They found the blue dragon waiting for them on the road, and once there, they realized the wind had changed its direction. Now it was blowing right in their faces.

The dragon started out down the road, blowing the flame every couple of breaths so they could see it through the pitch-black, ash-filled air.

Their horses balked at facing the wind head-on, but they were eager to run, and as the dragon ran ahead of them, the horses kept pace. The dragon, they saw, tired quickly; it didn't dare try to fly; one of its wings, though tucked, looked to have a wicked gash in it. Then a small rain of sparks appeared in the road ahead of the blue dragon, and a second later, they saw a small black dragon on the road.

It roared loudly in greeting to the larger blue, who was too tired to do more than rumble back.

Jean, Mark, and Devan watched the little black dragon struggle against the wind, being blasted around by it. But it was a game, and it encouraged the bigger blue to charge at it or try to snatch its tail to make it run faster.

What seemed like an hour later, they could all see a large flame appear ahead of them. From behind the flame, they saw the big red dragon sitting impatiently in front of a building and looking into a window with what Jean thought had to be frustration because she could not fit in. She roared when she saw the men, and they saw a tent in front of the building's front door open, sending light into the darkness as people came out of the house.

The blue dragon struggled exhaustedly to the front steps, then, out of energy, it just collapsed.

"Vex! Oh, Vex!" a young girl's voice cried out in anguish, and as the men all dismounted, they saw a young girl come running from the house, crying heavily as she met the blue dragon on the steps.

There was a flash of light as they touched, then the girl had her arms wrapped around the dragon's neck and was talking to it softly as her tears kept falling.

Then Jean's attention was grabbed by two men who came out and met them on the tented porch. One of them, the oldest, turned back towards the door.

"Nate, get those saddles off the horses. Nathan, help him out," the old man said.

Before turning to study all three of them carefully, "My name is Herb Pantier, and this is Ranger Ellis. You guys are welcome, please come in out of this hostile storm and introduce yourselves."

Jean, Mark, and Devan shook off their ashes and shook each of their hands, following them into the house as the two boys ran out to unsaddle the horses.

"How's Derek?" Jean asked in concern as he took off his mask.

Herb led them into the living room, where Emma was leaning over Derek, who they saw was still unconscious. But he did seem to be breathing a lot easier.

"He still has not woken up," Herb told them with a worried frown. "What happened?" he asked in concern as he studied each of the three men in the light of the lamps strung all around the room. And in the light of the fire in the fireplace.

Before he answered Herb, Jean turned to the Ranger, whose eyes he could feel studying them all warily.

"Ranger Ellis, I am glad to see that you are alright. We feared the worst after what Derek told us," Jean told the Ranger sincerely as he shook his hand again. "We are truly sorry for the misunderstanding."

Ellis nodded, some of his tenseness leaving as he took Jean's measure and noticed the dragon head mark like his own, upon Jean's hand.

"If I had been able to explain myself quicker or better, maybe there would have been no misunderstanding at all, but the egg was already cracked, and I feared it might be dead," Ellis explained with no regret in his tone.

Devan took his mask off and gave Ellis a tight smile, hiding his anger. These men had been his friends and companions over the last couple of weeks, and that misunderstanding had cost them their lives. But he did not let his anger show as he talked to the Ranger. "I doubt any explanation involving the real truth would have been believed by any of the men. Hell, I've seen it. I've seen stuff I don't rightly believe myself, and I saw it with my own two eyes, which gives me no choice but to believe it," Devan explained to Ellis with disbelief.

Beside him, both Jean and Mark agreed. For Jean, it was even harder to believe. He had grown up his whole life relying only on science. From the building blocks up, everything could be explained. But this was hard to swallow, even though he had seen and experienced it firsthand. A dragon was hard to believe, but it was possible. It was just a living, breathing organism built of nature's building blocks. Having his hand reattached without surgery defied all logic he knew and believed in. Yet, his hand was on and in fully functioning mode.

With a sigh, Jean turned to Herb. "What happened?" he stated with awe mixed with disbelief, turning to stare at Derek's prone, unconscious body. "Is that we just witnessed the impossible, again!"

As he spoke, a young woman came walking into the room; by her side walked the dark blue dragon. A second later, a young man came who could easily have been her twin. He was carefully carrying a glowing copper and gold egg in his hands. Following him came a boy with a black silver dragon lying upon his shoulders. All three of them went to sit right next to the old lady, taking care of Derek.

After a minute, Jean continued, but his eyes did not fail to notice that the marks upon their hands were different and bigger than his own. Nor did he fail to notice the dark blue dragon, though a little deformed, now looked healed, and the girl had dark black circles under her eyes.

"What we saw..." he continued. "Well, we were coming here as fast as we could, Derek leading us with the light coming from his spear. "He explained and turned to look at Mark, who was holding the spear, and he watched as he put it where Ellis told him to, against the wall. "When suddenly Derek stopped, we had all heard the crash of falling trees. Derek told us to wait and took off like the wind, bolting into the forest. Well, since he had our only light, we really had no choice but to follow after him. And when we did... we saw him trying to save that dragon," Jean said, pointing to the dark blue dragon.

Seeing it, Vex gave a little growl before he buried his head behind Nattilie.

"It was pinned underneath a gigantic old tree. And I mean gigantic. It had to have been twenty feet around. And that tree, when it fell, pulled another huge tree right on top of it. I don't know how the weight of both those trees did not kill the dragon. But I guess we now know how hard their scales are," he told them, and wonder filled his voice as he looked over at Derek again. "Derek, I guess he saw that the dragon could be saved. We saw him grab that huge tree trunk in both hands and haul himself up on it. We could hear his tendons straining from where we were on our horses, over the sound of the howling wind. And before we could see why he was doing it or even try to help him, he lifted both of those damn trees right off the ground. And then just held them, screaming at the dragon to wake up, when it finally did, maybe a minute later, he just collapsed, slumping over the trees, and that's how we reached him."

While he spoke, Emma got up and walked to Herb. "Derek should be fine now. His heartbeat is back to normal, but his skin changes from hot to cold in flashes. I think with a little rest, he should be okay."

Outside, the howling of the wind picked up, whistling through the chimney and fluttering the tarp that covered the broken window and the tent outside the door. They could hear both of them thrashing loudly in the wind from the next room.

"Nate, what did you do with those horses?" Herb asked in concern.

"I took them out back so they could find what shelter they could behind the house," Nate told him seriously as he looked up from the egg vibrating under his palms, one of which had a huge purple welt upon it.

Herb nodded and introduced Emma to the three men. While they talked, Herb turned to Nathan. "Go tell Spring that she better find a place to hole up in, this weather is getting even worse, and when it finally crests, water is going to burst forth from it like a dam that is going to explode."

Jean smiled as Herb put his own thoughts into words.

CHAPTER EIGHTEEN

Day 43; Aug. 12th

As everyone began to settle down, Devan began to feel like he was an outsider, something he was not used to in any kind of social gathering. He had always had a talent for being charismatic. But here? He noticed quickly that any conversation he had or started was polite but short. And everyone seemed nervous to talk with him, but the Ranger. Ellis, he felt, disliked him as much as he disliked the Ranger. The sharp-eyed Ranger studied him in a very assessing manner, as if waiting for him to dare to step across an invisible line just so he could forcibly haul him back, which made him nervously avoid the man.

The others, Jean and Mark, he noticed, had no such problems. They were both accepted easily into the group, and there was no nervousness when either of them talked to someone. Noticing that, he knew something was awry. No one here seemed to trust him. The dragons all stayed away from him, yet they were curious about Jean and Mark. And somehow Devan knew it was because of Derek. That boy did not trust him, and somehow everyone knew it. It had to be the reason he did not have a mark like Jean and Mark did. And as he watched, all the others ignored him yet welcomed Jean and Mark. A slow anger began to build within him.

But why? he wondered vehemently. What did the boy know about him to make him not trust good old Devan? A sudden thought filled his mind, and with it came a cold chill that stayed on his skin like a sticky sweat. What if Derek had somehow read his mind when he was healing him? Was it possible? Or did the boy just not trust him because he had tried to kill him twice instead of just once, like Jean and Mark had?

Frustrated, he began to recall every mysterious thing that Derek had done since he had met the boy, and there were a lot of them. Thinking on each, one led him to a certainty that he just knew Derek somehow knew about his past, or suspected something. A deeper anger began to fill him, and he forced himself to hide it deep. If Derek could read his thoughts, and given the way he was with his dragon, he could, then maybe so could the dragons and the other kids who were bonded to them. That must be why they stayed so far away from him. That made him wary, and he began to get the itch to leave.

An hour later, there was a loud rumbling sound that shook the building. It took them a minute to realize the sound was coming from hail slamming into the building and the ground.

Herb had them all begin checking the building, making sure there were no leaks that had started anywhere. Then, just as a precaution, he had everyone move upstairs and bring the most valuable stuff up with them in case it did flood. Jean was quick to assure him that while it was a good precaution, it was so cold out there that he doubted any of the hail would melt. He believed it would just freeze into ice and be the beginning of a new ice age.

Derek slowly came aware as he felt himself being moved, and he groaned in pain as fire filled his body and mind. Everything around him was spinning, both his sight and his senses. And he could not make heads or tails of where he was or what was going on around him. For a moment, he felt so confused that he could not remember who he was, let alone who the concerned-looking faces were that were carrying him up some stairs.

"He's awake," a voice said next to his throbbing head, drawing his eyes to an older face that seemed somewhat familiar to him.

"Derek, can you understand me?" the old man asked after seeing the confusion on his face.

Derek, he thought. Yes, that was who he was, but what was he doing here? Where was he, and why was he being carried? He tried to ask those questions, but he could not seem to force them through his lips.

Then he felt a blessed coolness enter his mind, and the raging fire that had been frying him slowly dissipated.

A picture formed in his mind of a tall, well-built, dangerous-looking man holding a shining spear who was standing next to a huge, beautiful, red and gold-scaled dragon, who, in comparison, made the man seem small. But together, they looked unstoppable. With the picture came the feeling of a question, and it took him a long time to realize the picture was of himself, and the dragon was Spring.

Spring! He thought suddenly.

And he remembered, sending his mind to her cooler one. "Spring! What happened?" he asked her in her mind as his memory was all hazy due to the pain, making his mind burn.

Pictures began to form in his mind, helping him remember, as well as a vast sense of relief from Spring that he was now able to talk to her.

After a second, he reached out to Vex with his mind and grunted as fierce pain, burning red hot, scorched all of his nerves. It was quickly doused by Spring's cool mind, and a concerned picture formed in his mind again of him, whole and healthy, with that questioning feel to it.

"Are you okay?" Herb and Emma both asked him in concern as they laid him on Herb's bed in the back room of the store.

Derek smiled tiredly through the pain to ease the old man's concern. "I will be," he muttered as he struggled to sit up. "You need to rest, dear," Emma told him as she urged him to stay lying down.

Derek reluctantly agreed when fire branded all of his nerves for even trying to move. And with a nod, he remained lying on the bed.

"How is Vex?" he asked as he gathered his thoughts. "And how did I get here? Did Jean and the others make it here safely?" he asked in concern.

"Vex is fine, shaken up a little. He won't leave Nattilie's side now that he's back," Emma told him with a reassuring smile.

"As for me," Jean replied from where he was standing in the doorway with Mark and Devan behind him, "we made it right ahead of the storm of hail that you can now hear pounding upon us. Your dragon grabbed you and flew you here, and the blue one led us here," Jean explained.

"I'm glad you guys made it okay," Derek told them as another bout of fire raced over his nerves as he tried to look at them. He squeezed his eyes shut, trying to fight it off, his body trembling in pain.

"Derek?" Emma asked in concern as she touched his forehead and again took his pulse. "Are you okay?"

Derek did not even try to answer. He sent his mind immediately to the cooling mind of Spring, seeking refuge from the fire on his own. Her mind quickly curled around his, soothing the pain.

"Why the pain?" He asked her worriedly, his mind feeling all confused.

She showed him a myriad of different pictures in his mind. Of him expending all of his energy trying to free the trapped Vex. Vex was trying to revive him with his own energy when Vex felt he was dying. Then, when that did not work because Vex had not been strong enough, he sent energy into Derek's body without touching his dragon mark. Something that almost killed him as surely as his lost energy, then Spring herself gave him more energy to revive him and keep him alive.

Then Spring sent him a picture of his energy, Vex's energy, and her own energy, and of all of them now mixing inside of his own body. She sent him the feel of Vex's energy, then the feel of Spring's, and a feel of his own. She showed him how all were a little different. How Spring herself was more powerful, but Vex's was more complex and defined in certain aspects, in which he exceeded even Spring's power. Then came the feeling of his own energy, changing and growing after both Vex's and her touch. And a feeling of her anger at Vex for almost killing him by not touching his dragon mark when he gave Derek his energy.

"Derek, can you hear me?" Emma asked in a slightly scared voice if he was no longer responding to her.

Her voice pulled him back from Spring's protection, and pain ripped through him, causing him to arch and grit his teeth.

"Fine…" he managed to say. "Needing rest."

Then he fled his body to Spring's protection, unable to bear the fierce pain any longer.

They all watched as his eyes closed and his body just stopped trembling.

"Vex says Spring is helping him, sheltering him from the worst of it. He says he is burning, and if he remains conscious of it, he might not survive, so Spring is keeping his mind sheltered in hers until his body changes and cools," Nattilie told them as she walked into the room. The dark blue dragon looked around the door at Derek, almost guiltily.

Nattilie almost unconsciously inched away from Devan, not liking the fact that she could not sense him or that she could always feel his eyes upon her in a way that made her very uncomfortable.

Emma walked to her. "You need to get some rest yourself. Go look in the mirror; if you think Derek looks bad and tired, you are a matching pair. Go get some sleep."

Nattilie was too tired to argue with her. Having healed Vex had drained her more than she was willing to admit, especially after having healed the Ranger last night. While Charger had revitalized her, healing Vex had drained it all. She was just lucky her dragon had not been hurt worse than he had been. Wounded pride and a couple of torn scales upon his wing, let alone his exhaustion from giving energy to both Derek and

Spring. Had the dark blue dragon been any worse off, she would now be as dead to the world as Derek was.

Before she left and took Emma's advice, she looked down at Derek. She did not know what she would have done had he not saved Vex. She had felt as if she herself was dying when Vex got pinned under the tree. Unable to breathe, her head pounding, she had passed out right after her dragon had. It was a feeling she never wanted to feel again. The bond between her and Vex was a lot stronger than she or even Derek had suspected; she was now sure. If Vex had died, she would have too, and that was scary. And definitely something she would have to warn the others about. Their dragons had to be protected at all costs because if they were killed, they would most likely die themselves.

The look she gave Derek was tender. She had never, in her life, met anyone like him. He was daring, courageous, and everything a fourteen-year-old boy wasn't. Both Spring and he had saved her life, and now Vex's. And while that affected her feelings for him, she had other feelings she tried hard to hide or ignore whenever he looked at her or touched her.

Just thinking about him, she could feel Vex watching her at the doorway, staring with jealousy. She reached down, touching Derek's hand affectionately, and her mind sought his.

"Get well," she told him warmly.

She wasn't sure he heard her, but he mumbled something and lightly squeezed her hand a second before going still again.

Herb and Emma smiled at each other as she left.

"We could all use a healthy meal," Herb said, leading them out of the room and back down the stairs to the kitchen. "Hopefully, this storm isn't going to be as bad as we all believe it will be," he said, listening to the hard pounding of hail outside.

Jean nodded in agreement as he too listened to the sound of hail filling the house. "We can hope."

CHAPTER NINETEEN

Day 44; Aug 13th

For the next couple of days, Devan sat trapped inside the Pantiers' residence. And with each passing day, his anger and frustration at being isolated grew. Everyone pretty much just ignored him when they could. They were nice and polite to him, or at least the adults; none of the young ones even acknowledged his existence, especially the young, pretty woman named Nattilie. She spent all of her time in the basement training with her brothers or up in the room with the weird boy Derek, who had still not gotten any better. *With any luck, he never would,* he thought glumly.

It was Nattilie, his eyes always followed. She reminded him of a butterfly, innocent and beautiful. She was trim and fit with wide, curvy hips, long legs, and small but very attractive breasts. And her silver eyes were so distracting. He had to always force himself to look away from her when she caught him taking peeks at her. He had tried a couple of times over the last couple of days to talk to her and get to know her. Had he met her before the Meteor storm, he could have easily won her over with all his money, no matter her affection for the weird boy. But now he was hard-pressed to think of a way to woo her. He could never get around her alone; she was always with her dragon or with her brothers. That was when she wasn't with the weird boy, Derek.

All of the dragons seemed aggravated when he was near them after his first night there; he made sure he kept his distance from all of them. He had walked into the kitchen, talking with Mark, and almost run into the smallest dragon. It had swirled around like lightning with a heart-stopping growl that made his heart jump in his chest as it snapped its razor-sharp teeth at his healed hand. Only quick reactions on his part kept him from losing his hand again, but it was a close call and almost seemed intentional, as if his healed hand somehow offended the dragon.

That had served to make him even angrier, and he had stayed away from everyone in a brooding mood, just listening to their conversations when they all forgot he was even there. That was when he had heard the oldest boy, Nate, talking to the Ranger, showing him his now healed hand and dragon mark, which was the same as his brother's and sisters'. As they talked, Nate showed the Ranger how to make his dragon mark glow and talked him through how to use it to heal.

Devan had listened to them with interest, focusing his anger to make him understand what Nate was telling the Ranger. Derek had assured him that he, too, had a dragon mark that he could see, but Devan couldn't. He doubted it; he was sure Derek knew something about his past, and if so, the boy had deliberately not marked him. So he listened at first with only half interest, but as Nate broke it down to Ellis how to use it, he filed it away to try later, just in case Derek had not been lying. But either way, he would make sure Derek was paid back for chopping off his hand, making everyone, even his pals Mark and Jean, treat him as if he were somehow diseased now.

It wasn't until halfway through the next day, full of anger at being treated like a social outcast, that he went to vent his growing anger outside. He stumbled out into the icy hail from the front door, which he noticed no one used. Everyone always used the basement and never even went around the front. Ice was covering everything, coating the outside of the tent over the porch with ice, and he had to be careful as he walked into the hailstorm so he didn't slip. It was pitch dark out, the lamp on the porch hardly giving off much light. But much to his surprise, he did not really feel cold, though he knew it must be freezing. He stared off into the darkness for a minute before heading off into the storm to vent some of his anger.

He was instantly assailed by chunks of hail. Some were quite large in size and stung when they pelted into him, driven hard by the fierce wind. One big chunk bounced off his chest, and he automatically caught it before it fell. It was almost three inches around, and the force of it hitting him damn near stole his breath. But as he looked at it in his hands, a weird feeling began inside of him, stirred by his anger. The healed hand was warm and tingling as it held the hail ball; his other hand just felt fine, not cold at all, even though he was holding onto a cold piece of ice.

It was then that he remembered what Nate had told the Ranger about activating the mark. So, staring at his warm hand, he decided to experiment. They had used it to heal; could it do more? Could it be used for other things as well? Feeling the warmth in his hand, he studied it with his mind, and remembering the warning Nate gave the Ranger, he did not let his mind center on his hand; he pulled the warmth from it. Instantly, his hand heated, and the chunk of ice in it melted into water, dripping off his hand.

Seeing it made him smile. He held out his hand, staring at it, and pulled warmth from it, thinking what he wanted. A wave of heat hit the ice on the ground in front of him, and to his satisfaction, it melted for a good five feet, causing water to flood into the ash-covered ground and around his boots.

Curious, he tried something else. If he could melt the ice so easily, could he freeze it? Concentrating, his mind began to boil with the warmth he was pulling, and a wave of exhaustion pounded into his body as the water refroze. He knelt, breathing heavily; at least with the ice holding down the ash, the wind was semi-free of it, and it felt nice breathing cold, fresh air, though being pelted by hail was not so refreshing. As he stood back up, he noticed his boots were now stuck in the ice. He tugged on them to get them out, and when that did not work and he kept getting pounded by hail, he growled in pain and used his remaining warmth to heat his boots.

Within seconds, he was free. He also noticed that the more he used the mark, the easier it was to use, leading him to the thought that if he kept learning new things with it, the quicker it would work and the less energy it would take for him to do something.

He made his way back into the house feeling tired and very hungry. Entering, he saw Nattilie and one of her brothers talking in the kitchen. They saw him and hurriedly walked the other way. He couldn't help but stare at her. She was wearing tight jeans and a loose shirt. Neither of them was actually wearing their swords, probably thinking that no one in their right mind would attack their place with the hailstorm pounding furiously around them. He watched them leave and couldn't believe how snobby she was. He knew instantly they were going to check on Derek.

Both of them, he thought angrily, *I'll make them both pay*. And until then, he would learn to use his mark in ways they would never even expect it could be used. With that thought, he headed back outside after grabbing some food to eat.

August 13th

It wasn't until the next day that he saw the opportunity he had been planning for. He had thought it out all day yesterday and most of the night. And though he had not expected the opportunity to come so quickly, he was not going to let it pass when it literally fell into his lap.

There was some kind of commotion going on in the basement, and everyone but the still-sick Derek was down there. He had gone down for a second himself, but lost interest when he heard it was just Nate's dragon egg hatching. So he went back upstairs, growling under his breath about another damn dragon in the world, wishing Mike had killed the damn thing with his axe. He was sitting at the table brooding over it when he saw Nattilie come up the stairs by herself, her dragon obviously wanting to watch what was going on.

She walked right by him as he sat drinking coffee, without even noticing him. And that brought his anger to a boil. He had thought it out perfectly on how he would get Derek back, make him pay. It had been obvious that the young woman, Nattilie, was too good to even deem him worth noticing.

The problem when he planned it was how he could take her without the dragons knowing? Without her own vicious dragon finding her? And how could he get her out of the house without the big dragon seeing him?

That, too, had been simple to work out; the dragons, he had learned and tested, could not sense him for some reason. He remembered how Charger had snapped at him when he had almost run into it, surprising the dragon. And he knew the big dragon stayed around the back of the house, and no one used the front but him. So if they couldn't sense or see him leaving, that only left tracking him. And with the magic he was learning, he doubted if they would be able to find him, and if they did? He had learned some dangerous tricks to stop them that he was sure they would not like.

So as Nattilie walked by him, not even noticing him, he reached out quickly with his hand and tried the magic that he had worked successfully on a horse last night.

"Sleep," he muttered softly.

Nattilie gasped in shock at the unexpected touch to her arm, then collapsed right into Devan's lap.

Devan bounded out of the chair with her, pulling leather cords from his pockets and quickly and expertly tying her wrists behind her back, gagging her just in case she did wake quickly. Then he hauled her onto his shoulder, a little surprised at her weight, and left by the front door, picking up a bundle of food and supplies he had stashed away after gathering them in secret last night.

With her on his shoulder, he ran through the ice storm. He knew he had to be fast, and in no time, he had reached the horses he had experimented on last night. He quickly tied her to the saddle of one, and once mounted himself, he set off at a trot.

He thought about an umbrella to protect them all from the ice storm, and using his mark, a wave of dizziness hit him, but suddenly, the hail did not. It stopped pounding into them, and after that, the horses were a lot easier to handle.

A mile from the house, he felt strong enough to finish what he had started last night with one of the horses and used magic on the other to make its scent and hoof prints disappear. He watched the horse carrying Nattilie for a second, making sure its trail could be spotted like the one he was riding. Then, with a boot to his horse's side, he changed directions, riding hard towards an abandoned town the shelter had already scouted and looted a week back.

As he did, he put his mind to the last of his problems: how was he to keep her from contacting her dragon when she woke? Because even gagged, he had no doubt she could and would. The last thing he wanted was to be found yet, though he had laid plans just in case. He was still unsure if his plans would work.

He used his magic on Nattilie, then slowed the horses and used a little strengthening magic to keep them going when they had gotten really tired. Then, forcing them on, he ate, starving after using so much energy. He knew he had to be careful; he might need to use some in an emergency and did not want to come up short, because then he would be dead. He did not have a dragon to revive him. He was so busy thinking and eating that he almost didn't realize Nattilie was waking up and saw her struggling. With a growl, he reached out, touching her, and put her back to sleep.

As the hours passed, he began to worry that maybe he had been going the wrong way. Everything was the same: swirling hail, ice, and trees. With his eyesight now, he could make out most things in the dark, but hour after hour, mountain after mountain, it all looked the same. So it was a great surprise when he came across a big cabin in the mountains. By then, the horses were trembling in exhaustion, both near dead.

Luckily again, there was a barn in the back. The door was locked, but as he dismounted and led the horses to it, a quick touch of his hand had it open, and a minute later, he was hauling Nattilie into the cabin. He tossed her onto a couch in the front room and looked around. Part of the cabin was missing its roof from the meteor showers, but the bedroom was a nice room. He took Nattilie to it, putting her on the bed. He smiled, looking down at her. Even tousled, she was extremely beautiful. He set to work, tying her to the bed, her hands together above her head to the very sturdy, heavy wood headboard. Then he went to make preparations in case he was found and to try to find rope for her legs.

* * *

Nattilie woke up feeling groggy and having trouble breathing. She tried to sit up, but it failed when she noticed her hands were tied together above her head. Fear instantly shot through her as she tried to remember how she had gotten here. All she could remember was the shock she felt when Devan had touched her.

What had happened? And where was she? She wondered fearfully as she looked around, not recognizing anything around her.

"Vex," she cried in her mind, growing more scared by the second. She tried to reach out to him with her mind, but she could not feel or sense him. She couldn't sense anything. And that really made her fear grow.

She struggled fiercely to free her hands, knowing she was a lot stronger than anyone knew. But her hands were securely bound, and the bed's boards were so thick she couldn't break them. She tried to scream, but found her mouth gagged. Her heart began to beat wildly in her chest. She flipped over onto her knees, facing the bed board, and began to yank on the bed until it and she were shaking, but still, she couldn't tear her hands free.

Devan walked in to see her on her knees, her shapely rear in front of him as she tried to break the headboard. He wanted to stay and watch. It was an enticing view, only he thought she just might break free.

"Ahh, you're awake," he told her with a grin as he walked into the room holding a rope.

Nattilie scrambled and wound up on her back, looking up at him with wide, scared eyes upon seeing his leering smile.

"I bet you regret acting so high and mighty now, don't you? Go ahead, scream all you want. Beg because I promise, you will be begging by the time I am done with you," he taunted with a smirk.

His voice sent a chill of horror through her, and she screamed in her mind for Vex, throwing her body hard against the bed, yanking on her hands.

Devan laughed cruelly and stood over the bed. She tried to kick him, and to her dismay and fury, he caught her leg, and before she could yank it back, he had a rope secured around her ankle. She screamed, fighting hard in a panic as he pulled the rope hard with both hands, forcing her leg tight and to the side on the bed. He then yanked the rope around the bedpost, securing it tightly, tying her leg down.

She felt his lecherous touch on her ankle and tried to kick his hand with the heel of her other foot.

Devan smiled at her deviously, moving his hand at the last second, so she kicked her own skin hard. Then he jumped forward, catching her ankle in both hands, and she fought him fiercely, screaming and crying as he roped and tied her other leg down to the other bedpost so she was stretched out upon the bed, only able to move her head.

He was breathing hard when he finished. Then he stood over her, feeling dominant but very tired. He was excited, though, glad he had saved some energy because after the last thing he had done, he had almost died; it had been a lot harder than expected, and he was still surprised it had worked. *Hopefully,* he thought, looking down at Nattilie, *he wouldn't have to use it.* He could see Nattilie's furious, tear-streaked silver eyes glaring at him as her chest heaved while she tried to free herself.

"You thought yourself so safe and protected by your dragon, your brothers, and oh yeah, your boyfriend 'Derek'," he said the boy's name sarcastically. "Well, your dragon is dead," he lied to her cruelly to see her cry even harder. "And one day after I kill you, I will kill Derek too."

Hearing his taunt bit Nattilie to the core. She screamed in fear and pain. "Vex," she tried to cry out through her gag.

Devan stared down at her, his lust for her plain in his eyes, and when his hands touched her ankles, she tried to kick or jerk them off of her. She struggled, tears pouring down her cheeks as she felt him get on the bed between her spread legs, and his hands trailed up from her ankles to run softly up her jeans to her calves in a caressing gesture that left her panicking, then slowly up her trembling and jerking legs to the inside of her toned thighs. He watched her fear and panic as his hands slid up slowly higher, sliding tenderly up her inner thighs as her body jerked and bucked to get away from him. Then she froze, her eyes wide as his hands slid higher still, rubbing harder up the inside of her legs until she felt his fingers touch her pubic mound, running over it, feeling and caressing her.

Devan's fingers pressed against her mound, feeling her trembling beneath him. Her head turned away as she cried, her breasts heaving frantically at his violating touch.

"Do you like that?" Devan asked cruelly. "Is that why you stopped fighting?" he taunted, his fingers pressing against her soft mound. When she ignored him, his fingers moved to her jeans, and she tensed as he snapped them open and jerked her hips back as his hand touched her soft, trembling stomach. His fingers found and slid under her panties, sliding over her smooth lower stomach until he could feel the hair of her mound against his fingertips. But when she continued to ignore him, he removed his fingers. "Or maybe you stopped fighting because you fear you'll like it?" he asked with a sneer. "Hmmm, wouldn't that be great, the ice princess loves my touch and caress," he taunted with a smile.

Again, she ignored him, her eyes closed tightly, and turned away from him. Seeing it, he frowned. *Well, this is no fun if she won't fight,* he thought.

Then something came to him. With all the stuff he had found, he could do if she wouldn't fight, what if he could make her want him? Wouldn't that be something? To make her want him against her will? Oh, that would be great. How would her boyfriend Derek react to that? She was cute, well, no, beautiful, and if he could make her want to be with him even though she didn't want to? Well, that would make it all the more enjoyable. But first, a test to see if he could make her like his touch. Then he would go from there.

He felt the warmth grow in him as he pulled on it and looked down at her. She had opened her silver eyes and was shaking as she looked at him. He got off the bed and walked around it, and as he tried to touch her face, she jerked back, her eyes full of fear, tears, and panic.

"Would you rather me touching you elsewhere?" he asked curiously as she again jerked away from his touch.

She froze at his words and flinched as he lightly stroked the tears from her red cheeks and looked into her brilliant silver eyes.

"Forget your fear of me when I touch you. Where I touch you, you will burn with pleasure so much so that you will want to do anything and everything to please me," he thought to her fiercely as he used his mark.

The rush of dizziness hit him harder than he had expected. He had used too much earlier, and he stumbled back to slam into the wall, out of breath, his heart pounding in his chest. He sagged against the wall, and before he could fight it, he passed out.

Nattilie watched it in shock, surprised that Devan had just collapsed to the floor. Instantly, she began struggling, yanking, pulling, tugging, bouncing, anything to break the bonds holding her. She didn't know what had just happened, but she could still feel his violating touch and wasn't about to feel any more of it. She struggled with all of her might, calling for Vex, Derek, Spring, her brothers, and could feel nothing at all.

She didn't know how long she had panicked. By the time she gave it up as hopeless, she could feel her torn wrists bleeding and see blood through her jeans on each of her ankles. The pain didn't stay long; she could already feel them healing when she was calm enough to think. She tried to remember what had happened and how Devan had caught her.

She remembered walking up the stairs to check on Derek and tell him about Nate's dragon, Cyclone. She had never even seen Devan sitting at the table; she had just been so excited about the baby dragon. It had been so big for a male, a foot and a half bigger than Charger's three feet. Unlike the copper gold of the egg, the dragon had emerged all shadowy grey and silver, with huge wings that spread out really long. His eyes, though, were not a pure silver like all the other dragons; his were a dark blue with silver pupils. And unlike any of the other dragons, he had come out of his shell really weak, struggling to lie in Nate's lap.

Then she remembered Devan's touch. It had been so surprising and shocking to be touched by someone you didn't know was there. All he did was touch her arm, and she could remember nothing more until she woke here on this bed and shivered at what he had done to her.

She must have fallen asleep because she was jerked awake with a gasp to a feeling that sent tingling through her body in a weird way. It was a touch on her leg. The touch was so alarming, and yet it was unlike anything she had ever experienced before.

She opened her eyes, curious to see what it was, and her eyes widened with alarm when she saw Devan leering down at her. She knew she should fear him, but she felt no fear. Instead, she gasped as the feel of his fingers touching her calf sent her pulse racing in a peculiar way. The feel sent a fire through her body in a way that was definitely not unpleasant.

She felt his fingers graze up her leg, spreading that feeling, and she was shocked to hear herself moan as a tingling started in the pit of her stomach, then it rushed down her body with a feeling of pleasure that widened her eyes. Alarmed, she looked at Devan, and when she met his eyes, that feeling in her doubled, causing her hips to actually raise up off the mattress, and this time she did moan as she felt his fingers move over her knee and trail lightly up her inner thigh over her jeans, sending the feeling up between her legs again until she was breathing hard.

Her back arched as his fingers slid up her inner thighs to touch and softly press against her mound between her wide-spread legs. Her whole body clenched with desire, her back bowing off the bed to deepen the touch, but it was gone, and she moaned, breathing fast, looking up at him in surprise that his touch could do that to her body. She had never felt anything like that before; her stomach was shivering with shocks of pleasure, and between her legs, she felt a soft ache she had never felt before.

"What was that?" Devan taunted with a leer, having heard her moans. "Did you like my touch?" he asked lightly, trailing his fingers over her shirt.

Nattilie closed her eyes; she couldn't think. His touch was doing something to her that—ohh—she moaned, opening her eyes in shock as his fingers lightly brushed over her breasts and sent a fire between her legs to replace the ache she felt there. She gasped as his hand softly cupped her firm breasts, squeezing them lightly until she was moaning in pleasure and breathing hard.

She knew something was wrong, but at the same time, she was defenseless against his touch. She could not figure it out. His touch unraveled her thinking brain into something else that actually wanted to feel more. She watched him uncertainly as he looked at her, then bent, his hands loosening her gag. Her eyes widened as he bent over her, and she lunged, trying to bite him. He pulled back, and she missed, but followed her back, and as his lips touched hers, her stomach swooned in a feeling that made something between her legs clench tight. She moaned in pleasure, her eyes rolling back as he kissed her lips lightly over and over, making pleasure inside her grow until, to her shock and embarrassment, she was kissing him back.

He leaned back with a smile, and his hand landed upon her stomach, causing it to tremble as he slid it up to her breast, feeling it beneath her shirt and bra, making her moan as his fingers found her nipple and grasped it lightly, causing her to arch up to him.

"You have never kissed anyone before, have you?" he asked her in an excited voice.

"No," she whispered, her head going back as his hand rubbed and caressed her breasts, rubbing them both thoroughly until she was moaning and looking excited.

He kissed her lips again, slowly, teasingly, licking them, and she could not believe the pleasure it gave her.

"Oh, stop," she moaned, and his hand caressing her breasts moved down over her taut, trembling stomach, causing her hips to rise up on their own to meet his hand as it slid lower over her open jeans.

"Are you sure?" he asked seriously.

She felt herself crying. She knew this was wrong, but the feel of his hand sliding over her stomach, hips, then down to touch her lightly between her legs, where she felt so tight and achy and burned to be touched, made her want to feel more, to her shame.

"No," she said in an unsure voice.

And her hips arched higher as his fingers slid between her spread legs and pushed gently against the softness of her mound.

"Ohh," she moaned in shock and pleasure.

He leaned, kissing her again, and she hesitantly kissed him back as his fingers pushed where she was burning with pleasure. His fingers pressed softly, then harder, creating a rhythm that her hips picked up, arching up to his hand with each hard push, drawing moan after moan from her as his tongue pushed inside her mouth.

He smiled, teasing her lips with his, pushing his fingers against the building warmth and wetness he felt growing between her legs, learning her soft, accepting virgin body as his tongue thrust in her mouth. Her mouth opened, accepting him in shocked pleasure, kissing him enthusiastically, her hips jerking as her pleasure soared even higher with his teasing fingers.

His hand then moved over her open jeans, pulling her shirt out so he could rest his hand flat on her bare stomach and feel her hot flesh beneath him.

She gasped at the raw feeling that sent moisture between her legs.

"Oh, stop please," she whispered in a scared voice, trying to deny the pleasure his bare hand on her stomach gave her.

He stopped and walked around. She watched him curiously as he got on the bed between her spread legs.

"What are you doing?" she asked breathlessly, wanting him to touch her again and yet worried that he would. She knew she should be afraid, but she wasn't. The look he gave her as he kneeled between her outstretched legs sent a spike of pleasure between her legs that rose drastically when both of his palms slid onto her bare stomach, touching and feeling the trembling hot flesh. They slid over her sides, slipping her shirt up higher, exposing her bare flesh as she moaned and began to pant at the pleasure storming her body.

She watched as he pushed her shirt up over her white lace bra.

"Do you want this?" he asked as his hands lightly trailed over both of her breasts, making her nipples throb, and her back arched as his palms closed over her bra-clad breasts, cupping and caressing them, causing her to cry out as a wave of fire burned through her. Her head went back, eyes rolling as his hands slowly caressed and rubbed both breasts until it brought small jerks to her hips in uncontrollable pleasure.

"Oh my," she cried out in pleasure as he bent, touching his lips to her stomach.

"Do you?" he repeated, this time kissing a little lower.

The feeling of his lips against the soft skin of her lower stomach was unlike anything she had felt yet, and with each little kiss that moved down lower and lower, it just built within her. And though she knew it was wrong, she wanted it to go on.

"Yes," she whispered. "Yes, yes, yes," she cried loudly and louder as each kiss moved lower and lower until his lips were grazing her open jean waist.

He kneeled above his and grabbed the waist of her jeans, tugging them down side to side until they were down around her ankles, then again between her spread legs. He looked down at her like a conqueror about to enter her sacred temple. Her legs were perfect, white, toned, smoothly muscled, and long. His gaze followed them up to her panties. He could see her bushy mound beneath the damp white cotton lace.

His hands moved to her wide-spread thighs, and her eyes widened at his electrifying touch. His fingers slid over her hot, smooth thighs until he grazed her mound through her panties.

"Ohh my," she cried out in pleasure, her whole body tightening at the feel of his fingers grazing her now swollen, aching mound. She could not believe how sensitive she was there. All her inner muscles clenched tight with pleasure at the feel.

How was he doing this to her? she demanded in a daze. *Why did it feel like this?* She heard of sex, of course, but she'd had no idea it could be like this. And while she was revolted by Devan, his touch made her beg for more. She did not fear for her virginity; he made her want it all.

Especially when his fingers cupped her sensitive mound. Then her whole back bowed in delight.

"Oh please," she moaned, delirious in pleasure.

Devan smiled, his fingers pressed against her soft mound. "You want me? Don't you? Right here?" he asked as his fingers moved over her panties, pressing against her, feeling her open a little as his finger pushed against her as far as her panties would allow.

"Yes!" she begged, her hips arching to push her virgin flesh hard against his pressing fingers. Each press of his fingers left her breathless and needing more, her hips rocking in time with his presses.

"You must earn it," he teased her.

She looked at him, pleasure filling her silvery eyes, making her look like a beautiful goddess.

"Oh, please," she begged as his fingers left her mound to find the waistband of her panties. "Tell me how?" she panted.

"You must do anything I want," he told her firmly as his fingers toyed with the elastic waistband of her panties.

"Anything!" she promised quickly as her hips arched up, arching for his touch again, and her legs widened as she felt his fingers slide under her panties and over soft, smooth skin until they found and slid through her bush.

"Anything?" he asked as his fingers moved lower, lightly touching the top of her mound.

She gasped in pleasure. "Anything!" she promised breathlessly as his fingers slid lower to find her silken, swollen lips and slid lightly down them, causing her eyes to widen and her hips to arch up.

"Oh," she moaned, her head going back as his fingers slid slickly over her before gently pushing one inside the velvet tightness of her virgin mound.

The hot, wet feel of her tight lips parting around his finger as he pushed it deeper inside her trembling heat excited him, as did her moan.

"Oh," she moaned. "Oh, oh, oh," she cried softly as his finger slowly pushed in and out of her tight, slick pussy.

"Anything?" he demanded, pushing his finger deep inside her.

"Yes! Yes! Yes!" she cried out, her hips meeting each thrust of his finger, forcing it inside her deeper and faster.

She didn't know what happened. One second, she was tied, spread out upon the bed, and the next she was in his arms as he moved over her. It was shocking, but the pleasure building inside of her made it hard to think. He leaned over her, kissing her while his finger pushed and felt inside her mound, causing her hips to jump up, sending fire through her as it penetrated her wet, swollen pussy.

She moaned in his mouth in near panic, her hands on his chest trying to push him back or off her, but then the feel of his stomach on her own made her arch against him, her legs widening for him as his finger continued to push deep inside of her, pulling her to the edge of something building in her.

She got a second to think as he removed his hand and knelt above her, his hands on her spread thighs, spreading them wider as he then pushed down his jeans.

His hand, she thought in a daze. He had waved it to make the ropes let her go. Was he using magic like she did to heal?

She was so distracted she didn't realize he was on her again until his hands cupped her breasts, squeezing them and sending fire between her legs. She watched, panting, as his hands undid her bra, freeing her breasts. She knew she should be ashamed, but the look he gave her made her lay back, and she moaned, biting her lower lip as his hands found her soft breasts and cupped them softly, rubbing them until her nipples were each sending a sizzling heat between her legs that grew as Devan laid fully upon her, and she felt his now naked, hot hardness brush the inside of her thighs. Then its heat moved up between her legs to press hotly against her panties.

No! she cried in her mind, trying to stop the pleasure building inside her, but the hard feel of him nudging up between her legs had her hips pushing up to meet it until she was panting. Instinctively, her hand heated, and she pressed it against him. But nothing happened, and her will to fight flagged as a rush of pleasure filled her as she felt his hardness twitch against her virgin mound. She cried out.

"Oh god," she moaned as his hands caressed and tweaked her nipples, and his hardness pushed up hard against her mound, making her back arch up. And annoyance filled her. What was stopping him from entering her? She could feel him hot against her, her legs wide, and as he pushed again, nudging hard between her legs, she panted.

"Oh," she cried as he began to rub his hardness all over her mound. Her mind clouded, kissing him hard, then he was kissing her throat to her chest, then covered her breast with his wet, hot mouth, his tongue tasting her nipple.

"Ohh my," she moaned as he sucked on her nipple and breast, then moved to the other, making her hip jerk up against his arousal to feel it push and press against her until she just needed to feel it push inside her where she ached for him to be. Her hands moved to her hips.

He looked up from her breasts and smiled.

"Do you want me?" he asked, licking her nipple.

And to her ultimate dismay, she nodded.

"Then pull down your panties for me," he ordered, and watched as her hips raised and her hands grabbed the waist of her panties and slowly pulled them down.

He stared down at her, gloating at the beautiful sight of her spread out before him. Her silvery, pleasure-filled eyes, heaving breasts that were perfect and firm, the smooth, silky skin of her taut stomach, her golden bush hiding her swollen, red pussy, and her wide-spread, long legs. The sight entranced him so much that he almost didn't feel his mental alarm go off about someone fast approaching.

Nattilie looked up, seeing the alarm on his face, and reacted instantly, leaning forward. She found his balls and squeezed hard.

He jerked back with a hiss of pain, and she used her other hand to poke him hard in the eyes. He howled and tried to hit her, but she jerked on his nuts hard. He screamed, and she scrambled off the bed as he tried to hit her again to get her to let go. He caught her on her shoulder with a backhand, and she again yanked hard, as hard as she could. She had to struggle to fight him, and the pleasure of touching him caused her to feel all at once. But she felt the heat of her mark and pulled on it, touching one of the ropes. She didn't have the time to think; he was about to hit her. She released the warmth, and the rope came alive instantly, and before he could move away, he was tied to the bed.

"You stupid bitch, you think I can't get out?" he snarled viciously as the ropes came loose.

Scared, Nattilie looked around and yanked one last time on his balls before jumping away from the bed and scrambling for his belt knife. She then turned and threw it as he lunged over her, tackling her to the floor. Luckily, the knife took Devan in the throat, and she pushed him off of her in a panic, realizing she was naked, and found her clothes, running out feeling dirty and violated.

She stopped only to dress, then ran out through the ice storm for the barn she saw, knowing there had to be a horse there. She ran back to see a horse, then froze.

"I'm going to make you regret you were ever born," Devan's voice snarled.

She turned from the horse in a panic to see Devan at the barn door, blood covering the front of him, a knife in his hand.

"Surprised to see me alive, bitch?" he asked calmly, walking into the barn. "I can heal just as quickly, if not quicker, than you can, only I can do so much more," he told her with a smirk as he waved his hand, and a flame appeared in it. "Now we are going to finish what we started, only this time I will not be nice, undress!" he demanded with a growl.

Her heart in her chest, Nattilie froze, not understanding how his neck wound had healed instantly. There was no way he had that power. She looked around, trying to find a way to fight him. She knew if he touched her, she would unravel again, and she could not let that happen. Then her eyes flicked past him. Behind Devan in the ice storm came Derek.

CHAPTER TWENTY

Day 44; Aug. 13th

Derek was not sure how long he had slept; his mind stayed nuzzled in Spring's while his body fought the ice and fire that flared along his nerves. It was Spring's own anxiety that made him snap his eyes open to feel the chaos of emotions brewing downstairs below him. Outside, he could hear the continuing onslaught of hail, which should have kept anyone from attacking them. But from the emotions coming up to him, they were under attack somehow.

"Spring, what is going on?" Derek asked in growing worry when he felt she was very aggravated and out flying in the hailstorm.

Spring's reaction was relief that he was awake, but also furious. And her mind barraged him with a bombardment of pictures, telling him that Nattilie was gone, and so was the evil man. Vex could not find her and believed the evil man stole her away on a horse.

That woke Derek up instantly, and though his body felt scared from the inside out, he got up angrily.

"Come get me," he growled to Spring.

"Nattilie!" he cried out with all the power in his mind.

When there was no response, he sent his senses out, searching for her. His chest shone brightly as he pulled upon his mark. His mind soared; in seconds, he was farther away than he had ever been able to sense before. And he was not even straining as he had to before. All around him, he sensed life, animals, and insects, all of which were hiding from the hailstorm. But the only horse he sensed was around the Pantiers; he sensed something far off to the east, but it was so far off he was not sure what it was.

He struggled into clothes that seemed too small for him, belted on his sword, and grabbed his spear before hurtling downstairs and out of the house before anyone could stop him. He saw startled faces in the basement as he snatched up his saddle and headed out the door.

"Do you know where she is?" Emma asked hopefully as he stormed past her.

He shook his shaggy head. "I might have felt something to the east. Spring says there is no trail or scent after the horse left here. He will have to take her somewhere nearby that he knows about. How long has she been missing?" he asked, feeling a weird feeling in his gut.

"No one is sure," Emma replied in a shocked, scared voice. "It has been hours since anyone has seen her. Everyone has left to search for her in different places. Herb and Mark took Nate, and Ellis left with Jean and Nathan."

"It's all my fault, Em," Derek growled to his shock, close to tears. "Spring warned me not to heal him—"

Emma touched his broad arm calmly. "Hush now," she replied softly. "It's not your fault; that man is just plumb evil."

Just then, Spring roared to announce her arrival in the backyard.

Derek knew, though, as that feeling in his gut grew, it was he who had brought Devan to their place. And now, Nattilie was missing because of him. A picture of her silver eyes filled his mind, and he couldn't fight the guilt he felt.

"I'll find her," he growled in a very determined voice as he moved to the door.

"Watch out—" Emma began hurriedly.

Derek grabbed his head in pain as he walked through the door and ran into the top of its six-and-a-half-foot frame. He swore and closed the door.

He instantly felt Spring's cool mind try to soothe his fears while he moved to her, strapping on her saddle.

In seconds, they were in the air.

"Go east," he told her as he finished strapping his spear to the saddle.

While she did, he sent his mind and senses roaring out of him and almost immediately felt Ellis, Nathan, and Jean.

Upset, he pulled his mind back and had Spring turn before they went too far.

"Go where the horse was lost," Derek told her, hoping he might find a clue everyone else had missed.

A second later, Spring was landing again, and Derek jumped down to study the ground, being pelted by ice. It was almost impossible to see anything with dancing hailstones flying all over the icy ground. But he worked quickly and, within a minute, found a horse's hoofprint in the ice. Just as a big piece of hail smashed into his glasses, knocking them askew and making him stumble, more in shock than in pain. Though it did feel as if someone had thrown an ice ball right at his face.

Frustrated, angry, and scared for Nattilie, Derek felt his blood boil, and as he fixed his glasses, his chest lit up brilliantly. What he needed was something to keep the ice and wind out of his and Spring's way. And with that thought, a huge dome surrounded each of them. Ice and hail pelted right off of it; not even the wind got through it.

Derek gasped as a burning pain speared through his still raw-feeling mind as he lost some much-needed energy. But Spring was quickly by his side, touching him again with her snout, sending warmth through him, making him almost growl at her. He knew she meant well, but damn it, every time she did it, he grew taller. The energy flowed through him fiercely, and he saw a picture of himself whole and healthy in his mind as Spring asked him if he was alright.

In answer, he reached up, scratching her neck affectionately. Now was not the time to have that conversation with her. Right now, he was too worried about Nattilie. He searched the ground, trying to find any other tracks, but could not find anything. The tracks had completely disappeared. He looked around in frustration, trying to figure out how to follow the tracks; he knew they could not have just vanished, so how had Devan hidden them? He bent, studying the last hoofprint, and he could feel warmth gathering in him again, growing with his frustration. Touching the hoof mark, he got an idea.

"Show me where you have gone," he whispered, releasing his warmth.

To his relief, the hoofprint lit up beneath his fingers, then suddenly began to glow, revealing tracks that had been invisible before.

"He hid it in magic," he growled worriedly to Spring. "He knows how to use the dragon mark in ways we have not thought of."

He jumped onto her back. "Can you follow this from the air, or will we have to follow it from the ground?" he asked, hoping she could make out the faint glowing marks from the air.

"Ground it is," he answered as she began to run along the trail.

"We are too far behind," he told her worriedly.

In his head, Spring sent him an image of Nattilie, beautiful and furious, big and strong. But it did not stop the sick ache he felt in his gut. If Devan knew how to use the dragon mark, Nattilie was really in trouble. All she knew how to do with it was heal. None of them had even expected it could do more than that, but him. And even then, his suspicion had been small because of his spear. He'd had no idea it could create a dome to protect him and Spring from ice, let alone hide or reveal trails. Whatever else it could do, Devan obviously was more advanced at it than he was. Is that how he had caught Nattilie? He had to know Derek would follow him, and this time, Derek would kill him, and if Devan had not counted on him coming, he had to know her dragon would.

As if that thought had summoned Vex, the angry dark blue dragon dropped out of the sky, smoke issuing from his nose. Vex was so furious he could feel the danger radiating from the dragon as it ran next to them.

"We found the trail, go let the others know and lead them to it before it totally fades," Derek commanded Vex.

Vex looked around anxiously, and Derek knew he did not want to leave now that the trail had been found.

"They are nowhere close yet," Derek assured Vex and watched as the dragon took off into the sky.

It seemed to Derek that the trail went on forever. He had no idea how the horse had survived carrying two people over mountains, through the forests, pounded by hail, and the freezing wind. They followed the trail hour after hour, with Spring running fast and tirelessly.

Vex followed, trying to keep up, but he got tired as the day turned to night. Spring herself ran until she almost collapsed. Derek gave her a little energy to keep her going awhile, but they were both growing weary, and Derek knew he had to have energy left to fight Devan. So when Spring almost collapsed again, he calmed her gently.

"Wait for the others, I'll continue ahead," he told her anxiously, untying his spear and taking off before the trail totally faded.

He knew he was closing in; he could feel something, maybe a horse ahead of him, and he ran for all he was worth. Fear for Nattilie twisting his gut and spurring him to an even faster pace, keeping him running long after he should have dropped from exhaustion.

He bounded through the trees and caught his first sight of the cabin. Just as he saw his first blurry sight of Devan, with a bloody knife in his hand, blood all down his front. But the image was blurry, and he had to rub his eyes. All the running must have screwed with his eyesight.

Seeing him all bloody terrified him. More so, as he quietly jogged around to where the man was and heard what he was telling Nattilie, he felt himself go cold inside. And he heaved his spear through the ice storm. Feeling furious yet relieved, Nattilie was still alive.

He was still some yards away from the blurry Devan, but his spear took him by surprise just as Derek saw the flame hovering over the man's hand. The spear sank deep in Devan's lower back, and the man turned, flicking his hand at Derek.

Flame flew at Derek, but like the icy hail, it split around Derek, leaving him surprised but untouched. Then he pulled his sword and charged. It took Devan by surprise, and he stumbled back as Derek charged, as if he had expected the flames to get Derek. Devan was met by Nattilie, who grabbed the spear jutting from his back and shoved it deeper. A look of surprise lit Devan's face, or was it a grin? Derek wasn't sure which, with as blurry as the man looked; what he was sure of was that his sword cut the man's head off his shoulders.

Nattilie collapsed to the ground, crying, making Derek's heart ache. He wiped the blood from his sword, sheathed it, then pulled out his spear and wiped it off as well before going to her.

"Nat? Are you okay?" Derek asked hopefully, bending down to touch her quivering shoulders, his chest lighting brightly as he sent healing magic into her.

She jumped at his touch, looking terrified, and looked up at him with red, tear-streaked silver eyes.

Her look broke his heart, and he knelt next to her, putting his arms gently around her. She turned to him, sobbing hard into his shoulder. And he was relieved when he felt she was not physically hurt. But Devan's taunt, cruel and malicious, still echoed in his ears, and his fear stayed lodged in his gut.

"Oh, Nat, I came as soon as I could. As fast as I could. I'm so sorry," he whispered, holding her tightly.

"Vex?" she cried in a hurt voice. "I can't feel him."

"He's fine," Derek assured her gently. "He will be here soon with all the others."

Derek then sought Spring's mind, relaying to her the death of Devan and that Nattilie was safe. "Vex is with Spring, reach for him, and you'll find him," he told her comfortingly.

Only she was not comforted by it. She sobbed all the harder, clenching him tightly. "I can't," she sobbed in a panicked voice. "I've tried. He did something to me. I can't feel or hear Vex."

Her voice and hurt tone did something painful inside of Derek. "What did he do?" he asked, holding her closer.

She just began crying again. "I thought I'd never see you or Vex again," she sobbed. "When I saw you there behind him… Oh, Derek, I was so frightened. Thank you! Thank you so much for coming to rescue me," she told him, looking up into his eyes.

Then she shocked him by reaching up and kissing him lightly on his lips.

He was so shocked and worried for her that he pulled back from her. "It's okay, you're safe now," he told her softly.

When she just started crying again, he sat holding her, not sure what to do, and felt so confused. He could still feel her soft lips on his, in his mind, and he wondered if he was supposed to kiss her because when he pulled away, she had started crying again.

So it was a relief to him when he felt Spring descending to him through the storm. He heard a roar, then others. First came Spring's, followed quickly by Vex's, Charger's, and then by an even deeper roar that trembled the air.

Derek gathered Nattilie into his arms, and she clung to his neck in surprise as he easily picked her up and walked her outside into the hailstorm, his protective shield keeping them both free of the pelting ice. Once out of the barn, he kicked Devan's bloody head out of his way and was met by the dragons.

Vex was the first to land with a roar right in front of Derek and Nattilie. He set Nattilie down, and touching her shoulder, he put a dome upon her like Spring's and his own. She nearly tackled the dark blue dragon as she hugged him in relief, so happy he was still alive. He grumbled loudly in pleasure at seeing her, his nose puffing smoke.

"I can't hear him!" Nattilie cried horribly as she buried her head against Vex's neck. "I can't!"

Derek looked over at Spring as she too landed and saw a new dragon land behind her. It was as grey as the frozen ash around them and very thickset with huge, long wings that were flecked with crystal spikes.

"Nat thinks Devan did something to her, so she could not talk to any of us. I healed her, and Devan is dead. Neither has it fixed the problem. Can it be fixed?" He asked her hopefully in her mind.

He watched as Spring studied Nattilie uncertainly and sent him a picture of himself healing her. Nattilie turned from Vex to look at him, her hurt and pain plain in her silver wounded eyes, and that look made the warmth in his mark grow.

"Can you fix it?" she asked him hopefully as she saw him begin to glow.

He frowned, not quite sure he could. He had no idea what Devan had done to her. He knew he had to try for her, though. He did not even want to think about what Devan may have done to her to put such a haunted and frightened look in her eyes.

He walked confidently to her, hiding his doubt, and she hugged him close again. "It will be okay," he assured her and reached for her mind with his own.

His mind could not find hers. It was like it was not even there. He could not feel her or sense her with his mind or senses. It was just as if he were searching for Devan. He could feel the warmth in him building with his feelings, and he looked into her silver, tear-stained eyes.

"Let me see your mark," he told her gently as she met his eyes.

She stepped back and lifted her dragon-marked hand to him. He reached out, and she gasped as his fingers touched her mark. He drew in a breath, amazed at the feel of warmth she gave off as he released his energy into her and again reached for her mind.

But this time he tried a different route. His mind followed his energy flowing away from her mark and through her veins. He was almost thrown from her body when he hit the shield blocking her mind. Undeterred and furious, he sent his mind back at it, hitting the shield harder, then again feeling his body heating, and when he hit the shield again, he felt it give way a little. He drew upon his mark, and this time, the shield just melted away.

"Nat?" he asked in his mind.

"You did it," she cried out in joyous relief, and he swooned as her lips touched his own again.

Being in her mind when she kissed him was a lot more intimate than he had ever been. He felt her thoughts, and to his growing horror, saw her memories of what had happened and her fear at almost being raped. All of her feelings of being violated by Devan came to him, as well as her shame at her body's betrayal of her, and her liking of Devan's touch. Then her fear of her own feelings for Derek and her vast relief as he held her and made her feel safe.

All of it flowed through him in that split second that her lips touched his own. His eyes opened, his stomach twisted in anger and sickness at what had been done to her. And angry at himself for not being stronger and faster, for bringing Devan into her life so she would not have had to go through what she had.

"It's okay now," he whispered against her trembling lips and lightly kissed her back.

She hugged him, looking at Vex. Then, with greater enthusiasm, she looked up at him. "Thank you," she told him, close to tears again.

He did not know what to say, and seeing her cry hurt him in a way he didn't know possible, so he just held her close and stroked her long hair, happy she was alive and relatively okay. Then he let her go so she could go to Vex again.

"He hurt her badly!" he growled to Spring in her mind, wishing Devan was in front of him so he could take out all his anger on him again.

Spring nudged him gently with her head and sent a picture of Nattilie, beautiful and fierce, big and strong, to him in a reassuring way.

He rubbed her head affectionately. "I know she is strong and resilient, but inside, she is hurt. I could feel it. Take her home; she needs Em's help. I can't help her, and she is scared of men now. I could feel it whenever I touched her. She trembles with fear at each touch."

Spring looked at him, and a feeling of affection came from her. Then she looked back at the new dragon and nudged him forward towards Derek with her tail, sending a picture of a fierce ice storm to Derek's mind, giving him the dragon's name.

Derek walked over to it, and it stood up tall at his approach, not like Vex had when he had first met it. There was a proud and strong feel about this baby dragon. There was also a feeling and look of aggression to him that the other dragons lacked. It was not directed towards him; it was just a general aggression, and Derek knew this dragon would be fierce and huge.

"I am Derek," he told Cyclon in introduction. "Spring has informed you of all our rules?" he asked sternly.

The dark grey dragon with strange, blue, stormy eyes studied Derek curiously before snapping its jaws in a gesture Derek took as an acceptance of the rules.

The dragon looked so serious and grim that Derek could not help but smile and rough its head playfully. It growled, swatting at him with its big claw, and missed.

Derek laughed. "Boy, you are a big one."

A sudden coldness entered his mind, showing him a picture of himself healing Cyclone while he was in his egg. And Derek was surprised, understanding why it was trying to be so serious. It wanted to thank him.

He smiled with a nod as he looked at the baby dragon. "You don't owe me thanks, Cyclone," he told it seriously as he gestured around to all the others. "All of us are a family now. We would be a sorry family if we did not help each other."

He turned to see Vex coming towards him, and a picture of Spring taking Nattilie and the others away, to leave him and Vex here, came from the dark blue dragon.

Derek shook his head. "No," he told Vex softly. "She needs you to be near her. I will be fine. I'll take the horse to the barn and meet up with the others. Stay near her, Vex, she is strong but..." he sighed, cutting off what he was saying as Nattilie walked towards them.

"Spring says she is going to take me back," Nattilie told him in an excited voice.

Derek smiled with a nod, happy to see she was no longer crying. He turned to Charger. "Go let the others know that we found her and she is okay."

Charger butted his head into Nattilie affectionately, giving her a happy grumble as she rubbed his spiky head. Then he was flying off through the ice storm, its winds buffeting him as he dove through them and out of sight.

"Will you ride back with me?" Nattilie asked him in a hopeful voice, pulling his eyes back to her.

He looked over at Spring. "The saddle is not big enough, and Spring is exhausted. I'll ride the horse back to the others in the barn. Spring should have you home quickly now that she knows where we are."

Nattilie touched his arm tentatively. "How did you do this?" she asked in wonder, motioning to the dome over each of them, keeping the hail and wind out.

Her touch again made him meet her silver eyes, and for some reason, he felt his heart begin to race as she looked at him, making him realize just how glad he was that he had found her and that she was okay.

He did not know how it happened or why, but suddenly she was in his arms again, and they were kissing. It wasn't the soft, tentative kiss she had given him before, though her lips were very soft. This time, they kissed passionately, and he was surprised when he felt her tongue push between his lips and into his mouth. He pulled her close, rubbing her back, and felt his heartbeat a lot harder when she pushed up against him. Feeling her mouth open beneath his and her tongue in his mouth made him kiss her back just as eagerly.

Only a growl, low and threatening, called a halt to their kiss, leaving them both breathing hard, and Nattilie blushed prettily as she pulled back, looking up at him with wide-eyed wonder and a small smile.

"Thank you," she told him again before moving to Spring.

Derek could feel Vex's jealous eyes upon him as he helped Nattilie into the saddle, showing her how to cinch each of the straps to hold her in place. Both of their hands were touching as he showed her, and she blushed when she looked at him.

He held her hand for a second, meeting her eyes. There was so much he wanted to tell her, but he had no idea how.

"I was so glad when I found you," he told her seriously.

She smiled, gripping his hand. "You never answered my question," she teased. "How did you do this?" she asked, motioning to the dome.

His hand holding hers traced over her dragon mark. "I thought of a shield, one that can block ice and wind. We now know it can block fire as well," he told her before letting her hand go. "If this one I put around you fades, just think of it when you use your dragon mark."

He watched as they all left, then with his spear in hand, he went to saddle the horse, kicking Devan's head one last time before leaving on the horse.

None of them felt the vicious male's violent eyes that watched them leave.

CHAPTER TWENTY-ONE

Day 42; Aug 11th

Location: *Arizona*

The hailstorm swept unexpectedly down upon Ken and Katty. Only luck seemed to be on their side because when it did come, turning the ash-covered desert into a blanket of black ice, they were all safely hiding within a sandstone cave, which Keen had found to shelter in.

All of them had felt the change in the weather, but none of them had expected what came. The hail had fallen on the desert with thunderous pounding, filling the desert with sound that echoed, making it even louder.

Within the protective structure of the wide cave, Ken could see it coming down like thick sheets of black ice that quickly began to mass upon the ground. Stalker watched with him for a second before pacing the large cave with curiosity, sniffing at cracks in the walls or investigating little holes with his sharp claws.

Katty, on the other hand, ignored it all, sitting against the back wall beside Keen, rubbing his dull scales and trying to keep the small, agitated dragon calm while he got ready to shed.

"If it keeps up at this rate, we are going to be iced in this cave," Ken grumbled a little unhappily.

His back was turned from Katty, so he did not see the smile she gave at his anxiousness to go into the city.

After weeks of surviving the desert in its horribly depleted condition, they were now only an hour or so on foot from the nearest city. And that was because Keen, lucky for them, had refused to go any further once he had found the large sand cave. He had been determined to defend it against Ken and Stalker until a lot of coaxing and petting on Katty's part had made the agitated dragon reluctantly agree to let them in as well.

His aggression had come as a surprise to Katty because she knew, and Keen knew, neither Ken nor Stalker would ever do anything to hurt Keen. Ken, though, had not been too surprised after having watched Stalker when he had shed himself. He had explained it to Katty so she understood that it was not that Keen did not trust them; it was just a part of his nature. Dragons were solitary creatures, and when they shed, they were at their weakest. Keen's mind might be telling him rationally that they were no threat to him, but his instincts were not to let anything near him while he was at his weakest. That was why they tried to hide.

So Katty sat stroking his neck, keeping him calm because, despite his instincts, he never once tried to snap at her or worry about her nearness to him. She gazed at him wonderingly. After all these weeks and all she had learned from Ken and the dragons, she still found it hard to believe. Her whole life had been torn violently from her. If Ken hadn't come and pulled her out of her gloom, she didn't think she would still be alive. The death of her father had made her almost comatose.

Her life before the Meteors had been great. Her mother had loved her and her father a lot, but when Kate was six, her mother had caught cancer and had died fighting it a year later. Her father had raised her by himself, teaching her all about his automotive mechanic and gasoline business. At thirteen, she had already graduated from high school with honors and a scholarship in mechanical technology. By the time she was sixteen, she had already achieved a master's degree in business, and by seventeen, her father was teaching her how to take over and expand their business, making her a full partner.

Tomorrow, August 12th, if she was correct, was her eighteenth birthday. Thinking about it made her a little sad. It would be her first one ever without her father, and that affected her tremendously. Every year, her father had outdone himself lavishly, trying to spoil her and encourage her to be even more. She had never thought much about it, but that encouragement had made her want to be the best she could be. She had wanted to show her father that she was... worth his love, she guessed as she thought about it.

Now, looking at Ken, watching him stare determinedly out of the cave, she wondered if she was not just doing the same thing for him. Something about Ken made her want to prove herself to him. He was always pushing her to her limits, always encouraging her to do better than her best, and she did not think he had ever, even once, gotten mad at her. Sometimes, she had to admit that was a little infuriating.

As soon as her thoughts turned to Ken, a little grumbling noise came from the dragon under her hand, and surprised her. She caught herself smiling at his passiveness and rubbed his scales so he would not be so aggravated.

Ken, hearing the low growl and feeling Katty's eyes upon him, turned from the cave in time to see her look away and soothe Keen. He smiled at the sight, knowing she had to be as anxious to reach the city as he was, if not more so. She had not grown up like he had, fighting for everything, every day. His life had only gotten better after he joined the army. And then, because of how he had grown up, it had been natural for him to seek the hardest, dirtiest jobs.

He was turning back towards Stalker when a huge mountain lion ran into the cave, followed by two little cubs.

He saw Stalker swirl aggressively, issuing a gigantic roar that shook the cave and left Ken's ears ringing. The mountain lion, already frantic and panicking to find shelter for her young from the huge hailstorm, skidded abruptly to a halt, its fur raising, and a scared warning growl of its own filled the cave.

Had the mountain lion been alone, Ken would have chopped it for game and made a nice meal of it by letting Stalker leap upon it. But seeing it with young cubs and knowing so much had already died in the storms, making it a miracle the mountain lion and its cubs had survived this long, Ken stopped the tensing, ready-to-leap dragon. All the while, hearing Katty yelling to calm Keen.

"Stop, Stalker," Ken said in a loud, commanding voice, barely even heard over the thunder of the hail and ringing in his own ears from Stalker's ear-popping roar. "Don't attack her. Keep her away from Keen and Katty. Stay between them, only kill her if she tries to attack us." He said in a crouch himself, his K-bar in his hand.

He was off to the side of the lioness and her cubs. His voice made her swirl toward him as Stalker, looking vicious, growled lowly and stood defensively in front of Katty and Keen. Somehow, Katty was managing to keep calm.

The mountain lion roared at him, not wanting to leave the cave. Its head was cocked towards Ken; it did not seem to want to attack, though. It backed its cubs up against the other side wall, away from Ken, its fur raised and growling as it swiveled its head back and forth between Ken and Stalker, making sure neither threatened her young.

Stalker continued to growl threateningly, imposing himself between the lioness and Katty. He hugged the ground much like a dog would, his teeth gleaming in a display of deadly warning.

Ken slowly moved towards Stalker, making sure the lioness did not perceive him as a threat. For the next couple of minutes, a very unusual standoff began, with both the cat and Stalker continuing to growl, neither moving a muscle. Stalker in front of Katty and the lioness in front of her cubs. Once by Stalker's side, he placed a calming hand upon his head, and after a second, he stopped growling and just eyed the cat hungrily.

Ken could feel Stalker's strange curiosity. This was the first time ever that Ken had stopped him from a kill, and the dragon itched to understand it. They had eaten plenty of mountain lions before, so why was this one different, especially when Keen was about to shed and was at his weakest?

The minutes passed with neither side moving. Only the cubs seemed undisturbed by the tension in the air. At first, they had sensed their mother's alarm, but as time passed, they began to get curious. It wasn't long before one of them yipped in pain as its ear got nipped hard as it tried to wander from behind its mother. That contented both to stay for a minute, and the mountain lion slowly stopped growling, but her fur remained on end as she studied them and sniffed the air, smelling the peculiar dragon smell. It was almost like a fiery smell.

Ken made Stalker lie down, then he slowly knelt next to him, ready if the cat should try to make a move towards them, but relaxing, trying to be unthreatening to the lioness and her cubs.

The cat, knowing it could not keep its cubs corralled for long, looked out of the cave, then back, and roared as if to scare them out of the cave.

Ken couldn't stop Stalker this time. The cat's roar said this was its territory, and that boiled his own blood. Stalker stood up, his bulky body coming to full height, and he let out a territorial roar that left no doubt this was his, Keen's, Ken's, and Katty's territory. And if the cat couldn't accept that, he would kill it.

The lioness hissed and bolted out of the cave with her cubs, screeching in fear at her heels.

Once they were gone, Ken let out his breath.

"That was interesting," Katty mused in an admiring way as she looked at Ken and scratched Keen's dull scales.

Day 43; Aug. 12th

When Ken woke up in the morning, the hail was still coming down just as viciously as it had started, with no letup in between. And while he was not cold, he could see the clouds of mist that his breath was leaving in the air, so he had no doubt at all that it was freezing.

Before he had gone to bed, he had blocked off the cave's entrance with a blanket to try to keep out the hail and any other creatures that might stumble upon the cave while they were sleeping. And now, with his eyes as good as they were, he could easily see in the darkness that the entire cave entrance was almost covered in ice.

He knew Katty was still asleep without even looking at her. And when he did, he saw her curled up near Keen. She did not look cold either. Keen's rest seemed disturbed; he kept twitching and arching as he got close to shedding. Both of the sleeping dragons' breaths were misting in the air, too. That was when it really dawned on him that it must be cold. He looked around in surprise. He had never thought about it before, but ever since his first few days with Katty, they had never needed a fire and only used one for cooking their meat. They did not even use the blankets, except as a curtain sometimes when Katty worked or changed.

Even knowing now that the temperature was low, he could not feel the cold unless he touched the wall, and even then, to his amazement, the cold was no more than a feeling that let him know it was cold to the touch.

A little intrigued by that line of thinking, he decided he needed to test it out. He walked to the entrance of the cave and pulled some of the blanket off the ice now blocking the entrance, and placed his hand upon the ice to see how long he could hold it there before he was forced to move his hand from it. He felt the freezing cold immediately. But as the minutes passed, his hand felt no different, and the freezing cold brought no pain at all. All that came was a weird stiffness to his fingers, and after that, to his surprise, a slight glow started around his hand as his dragon mark, glowing on his chest, started working to protect him.

Shocked, he pulled his hand back and looked at it. It was cold and stiff at first, but after a second, his hand regained its warmth. He put his hand over his dragon mark; it was warm, but it was no longer glowing, and now he was no longer quite sure he had actually seen it glow.

Or maybe, he thought, he just did not want to believe he had seen it glow. But it had lit up, and if it was the reason he no longer felt the cold in a negative way, the reason he was now so much stronger, faster, and everything else strange he had noticed about himself and Katty, then how was it doing so?

Katty and he had both discussed their changes before they had even tried to talk to their dragons about them. Doing so, though, had just confused the dragons. In the dragons' eyes, they could see no difference; Ken was Ken, and Katty was Katty. And if they grew stronger and faster, the dragons could not understand why such things should worry them. It should be natural that they improve upon those things. And while that's how Ken usually felt himself, it was Katty who insisted that they look deeper into the why and how once she, too, had begun to notice it.

Frowning thoughtfully, he was sure now that he knew the how of it. There was only one way to explain the sudden glow of his dragon mark: it must be magical.

His thoughts were interrupted as Keen stood shakily, then circled around, unable to see. Ken knew instantly Keen was ready to shed.

"Keen, come over here by me, this area is clear," Ken told the anxious dragon.

At his voice, Keen swirled fiercely to face him, but his aggression was lost when he understood who had talked to him. Keen then moved slowly towards him in a jerky, hesitant manner.

Both Katty and Stalker woke at the sound of Ken's voice, and Stalker backed away from the smaller dragon, letting him pass.

"Right there is a good spot," Katty told Keen in a soft reassurance.

Keen automatically stopped and began to circle around again to get comfortable, then he lay down, his scales all twitching.

Ken turned to Katty and watched as she moved to Keen and softly stroked his scales, reassuringly. He pushed her long black hair back from her face, and he could not help but see her beauty. The last two days staying so close to her in this cave were making him look at her in a whole different light. She was everything and more than he had ever envisioned a woman could be. Well, besides her trying every now and then to pick a fight with him about something. The last fight she had tried to start with him had done nothing but call to his attention just how beautiful she was. She had no idea he knew she was just trying to test him. She had come to his partition in the cave, her hair all wet and wild, wearing only a long shirt, and accused him of hiding her comb from her. Then, when she had caught him staring at her in shock, she had blushed red and run out. It had made him smile when her plan had backfired.

Today, he knew it was her birthday. She had not said anything about it, but he had read it from her mind weeks ago, before they had both agreed not to read each other's minds, like they did their dragons. Not that they had much to hide from each other; it was more of a respect thing. The first couple of times they had merged minds, they had learned a lot about each other. And it was from her mind that he had gotten the idea about what to give her. It had taken him a lot of sleepless nights to make, not that he slept anymore anyway. An hour here or there gave him boundless energy. Something in Stalker's poison had changed his body more than the dragon mark itself. More than an hour of sleep made him restless. So while she slept, he had watched over her and made his gift.

"Kat," he told her after watching her coax Keen to calmness. She turned to him with a smile, rubbing Keen's head.

"Stalker and I are going to hunt. Keen is going to need to eat a lot, and we do not have too much saved. If this storm keeps up, we will be out of food in a day or two," Ken told her seriously.

"No," she said with a concerned frown. "We have enough here for Keen to eat; we made sure of it. Then we can go-" she began.

He shook his head firmly. "Come here for a second," he said a little nervously.

"It's storming hard out there. We got enough food to wait for it to die down a little bit," she continued before studying him as if wondering why he would want her to go to him.

When she got up and reached him, he held his hand out for her.

"Happy birthday, Kat. I know it's not the real thing you lost, but hopefully, it will let you remember it and your mother," he told her lightly, holding out to her a crystal necklace.

He had carved it delicately from Stalker's shed teeth and claws. It was an almost perfect replica of a necklace Katty's mother had given her as a child. It was carved in stars and moons, and right in the center of it was a full moon. But where the one her mother had given her had an owl inside the moon, this one Ken made had a little replica of Keen's head in it.

Katty stared at it in awe and gave Ken a big smile before hugging him tightly, looking up into his face with a little moisture in her silver eyes.

"How did you know?" she asked him curiously, trying not to cry at the unexpected gift.

Ken smiled down at her, his hands automatically going around her waist as she hugged him.

"I saw it the first time we merged minds and saw how much it meant to you and how sad you were that you lost it. I also saw how hard you looked for it in the gas station. Truthfully, I tried to find it for you myself before we left. I know this is not the same-"

She shocked him by leaning up and kissing him with tears in her eyes before pulling back with a smile.

"It's more," she whispered breathlessly.

Then she stepped back and slugged him in the shoulder hard. "Don't you think this gift allows you to leave?" she told him seriously. "You just want to distract me and make me cry. It's too dangerous, too cold."

He winced and rubbed his shoulder. "If I didn't have to, I wouldn't," he assured her in a serious voice.

She ignored him and held out the necklace to him. It took him a second to realize she wanted him to put it on and was not trying to give it back to him, as his suddenly pounding heart feared she might be trying to do.

He took the necklace from her and watched as she turned around, moving her hair to one side of her neck so he could put it on her. As he did, he smelled her hair and was surprised to smell a berry smell. The smell was enticing, and he leaned closer to smell her neck, his smoothly shaved cheek touching her neck.

She shrugged her shoulders with a laugh. "What are you doing? That tickles."

Embarrassed, he snapped the necklace on her, and she turned around, looking at him shyly.

"How does it look?" she asked, her fingers running along its length, following it down to where the full moon rested between her breasts, drawing his look.

It took him a second to realize she was doing it on purpose, and he looked at her seriously. "Now who's trying to distract who?" he asked in a teasing voice.

She blushed beautifully and reached up, cupping his face between her palms, making him look her in the eyes—one of the few times he was not wearing his wrap-around sunglasses.

"Why? Tell me the truth," she asked seriously, staring into his liquid silver eyes.

One of his hands touched hers, his thumb finding and stroking over the warm, metallic feel of her dragon mark.

"There are a lot of reasons. The first is because I have felt a group of humans in that town ahead of us, and I want to study them before we go in. The second is for meat, and the third-" He grabbed her hand and pulled her to the entrance of the cave. "-Put your hand on the ice, leave it there as long as you can or until I tell you to take it off," he told her in his teaching tone she was used to by now, and bent, putting his own hand on the ice wall now blocking their cave.

Katty gave him a confused look, then followed his instructions, wondering just where he was going with this. Was it another one of his tactics? Doing so, she instantly realized just how cold it actually was within the cave. It was as if they were in a freezer. Yet she did not even feel the cold. It took her a minute to realize what Ken was trying to show her. The dragon mark on her hand began to glow until the glow surrounded her whole hand. It began to tingle, and she could feel a weird warmth almost vibrating from her dragon mark. With a gasp of curiosity, she pulled back. The glow faded from it instantly, and the weird warmth and tingling stopped.

Ken smiled at her incredible look. "I think we are using magic from the dragon marks to keep from feeling the cold. I want to go experiment with it a little bit and see what all we can actually do."

His hand on the ice was glowing brightly. He could feel the warmth running down his arm and knew it must be the magic he was feeling. He studied the feel of it with his mind and senses, and soon his whole body was glowing as he found a way to fill his body with the warmth from the mark. He heard Katty gasp in shock.

"You're glowing!" she exclaimed with amazement.

He followed the tingling warmth in him to his dragon mark and instantly felt danger to his mind, like a zapping static that made him pull his senses back before he fried himself. Before he did, though, he felt inside the mark was a flood of energy. It was like a battery, full of power. But how did he release it? And what could he do with it when he did release it?

He let the power fill him even more, then tried to push it or focus it into his hand. It left him in a thunderclap that shook the cave and spilled ice from the roof, irritated both of the dragons, and suddenly filled the entire cave in steam so thick he could barely see Katty standing next to him.

Turning, he saw the ice covering the entrance was all gone, and so was the blanket that had kept the ice and wind out. And looking outside? He was flabbergasted. All of the ice surrounding the cave for thirty feet was gone. Not even water remained, just the frozen ash-covered desert ground.

"Wow!" he exclaimed in shock.

"How did you do that?" Katty asked in bewilderment.

He turned to her with so much excitement – and she looked so beautiful – that he couldn't help but hug her.

"The dragon marks are like gigantic generators for magic. If you open yourself to the mark and pull its warmth into you, you will be able to use its magic. But don't enter it-"

Suddenly, Katty was glowing in his arms, following his suggestion, and Ken's whole body began to tingle, and not in an unpleasant way. Curious, he opened himself to his mark, filling his body with its warmth, and in his arms, Katty gasped, her eyes going wide as she felt the same tingling Ken had. Only now that feeling doubled inside Ken as if their magic was reacting to each other.

"I think he's about to kiss me," he heard Katty's mind think excitedly. "About time, what do I have-"

Her thoughts were interrupted by his kiss. And all thoughts went out of both of them as the sensation of their magic tingled their lips, sending both of their hearts beating faster.

A loud growl pulled them quickly away from each other. Both of them gazed at each other in surprise. Stalker was watching them curiously, but Keen? He stared murderously towards Ken, though with his cloudy, sightless eyes, he was looking in a slightly wrong direction. His growl, though, was to the point: Stay away from Katty.

Katty ignored her dragon with a moan and leaned up, kissing Ken one last quick kiss before going to Keen and began soothing the very agitated dragon with some very affectionate rubs. After a minute, she looked at Ken.

"Go then, but come back in one piece," she told him firmly.

Ken smiled. "I promise," he told her devoutly.

"Let's go, Stalker. Hopefully, we can catch something hiding in all this ice," he told him eagerly.

CHAPTER TWENTY-TWO

Day 43; Aug. 12th

Ken left the cave feeling lighthearted, at least until he started to get pelted by hard ice, something that quickly grew annoying. But not enough to distract him from his thoughts on Katty. It was like he was seeing her for the first time. He had never thought of her as desirable. Her beauty was self-evident and appealing, but all he had thought about was teaching her to survive. Only, the better she got, the more time he had each day to get to know her. He had been right when he had first met her; she definitely had iron in her.

He got thumped by about six huge balls of ice, and his thoughts went out the window. He looked down at Stalker in disgust and motioned to the storm around them, which the hard-scaled dragon did not even deem to notice.

"Can't you do something about this?" he asked in an exasperated tone.

Stalker chuffed, then spat fire into the storm, as if to say he could do nothing about it. Then he hurriedly flapped his wings as a huge gust of wind caught his tucked wings and tried to lift him up and carry him away, making Ken smile as the dragon no longer looked unaffected by the hailstorm.

Ken looked at the ground around him, where all the ice he had evaporated had left it bare. What if he could evaporate all of the hail before it even hit him? He touched his dragon mark, willing it to tingle. He felt its warmth instantly and pulled upon the magic, letting it fill his body. Then, shining bright enough that Stalker had to squint to look at him, he raised his hand. What he needed was something to stop the hail and maybe even the wind. Heat, he knew, could not do it. What he needed was some type of air shield that would allow air in but keep out hail and fierce wind, like a windscreen. With that thought, his energy left him in such a rush that he gasped in freezing cold and fell to his knees dizzily.

He heard Stalker roar in shock, and then he gasped as heat once again rushed into him in a wave of warmth as Stalker touched him, sending energy sizzling into him.

"Thanks," Ken told the dragon as his breath came back to him. "What happened?" he asked, a little shaken by what had happened.

He looked around and saw that it had worked perfectly; only his problem was that it was too big, , and it was stationary—it did not follow him wherever he went. It was a large dome that covered the cave and was twenty feet in diameter.

A little hesitant, he moved outside the dome and tried it again. This time, he made it his size and hooked it to him. When that worked perfectly and drained him of only a little of the energy Stalker had given him, he then hooked one to his dragon, too. Each of them extended about three feet around them at all times. No matter how they moved, they could not get hit by the hail.

Satisfied with what he had created, he set about sensing for life. He sensed the mountain lion and its cubs instantly. They were not too far away, hidden, he guessed, in another sandstone cave near their own, beyond them, though. There was nothing but buried things close, and none of them were big enough to try to hunt.

So, with Stalker scouting up ahead, they headed towards the town, trying not to slip or trip on the thick ice growing thick upon the ground. It was nice not being pelted with hail, though, and Stalker was flying carefully, unsure about using the wind or fighting against it. Still, Ken could feel how happy he was to be swooping through the storm, totally unaffected by its harsh winds or ice chunks. Because of that, they made killer time to the city, and while they did, Ken experimented with the magic of his mark, finding many things like creating fire were very easy, but beyond the shield, if he was not touching something, like he had the ice, then he could not destroy or set it on fire.

When the city came into sight through the ice-filled wind, both he and Stalker were moving a lot slower. Ken's clothes were stiff and frozen against his skin, and he had to pull the camo jacket from his pack to hide the glow of his dragon mark on his chest.

He could sense a gathering of people in the middle of the town, but in the pitch-black darkness, he could see no lights. Even with his great eyesight, he was having trouble making out one building from another. All of the houses and apartments around him were abandoned; doors were left open, and most of the windows were broken, as if the whole area had been looted.

It felt weird to be walking down a street and see it deserted when a couple of months ago it had been teeming with life. All of the roads under the ice were riddled with potholes that had been caused by, no doubt, the Meteors. Cars littered the ice-covered streets, and not a few bodies could be seen under the ice. He could feel the presence of predatory animals hiding from the fierce storm inside some of the houses. Some were, to his surprise, quite large, but now he was not interested in hunting.

"Stalker, stay close to me, but out of sight; whoever still lives here doesn't seem too friendly," he told his dragon as he caught sight of yet more bodies. These ones were hanging from light poles.

Seeing them made him wish he had more weapons than just his K-bar.

Getting closer to the center of town, he spotted a store, and feeling no one near it, he ducked into the broken display window to see if there was anything worth finding.

"I'm going to look for some food and supplies," he told Stalker quietly, knowing the dragon would hear him, though he thought it unlikely he would find anything useful, seeing as the store had been ransacked. "See if you can find anything interesting and let me know if anyone approaches."

He went inside, stepping over a tipped-over A.T.M., his boots crunching on the ice that had come into the store through the broken windows. To his vast surprise, though the store looked heavily ransacked, he still found stuff he could use: a couple of duffel bags, hidden for both him and Katty. He couldn't wait to see her face when he brought it to her. He even found some canned goods, a lot of vegetables, and some corned hash and spam. He only found one can of tuna, though.

He was filling the duffel bags with no little joy when suddenly he swooned in pain. It was as if a gigantic fireball had hit him in the face. Then he heard the roar of defiance and fury.

Stalker! He yelled in pain and confusion in his mind, bolting from the store half-blind in pain.

Instantly, he felt them – people near him. One swirled in his direction, and he only got a quick glance, seeing a man holding binoculars and a crossbow, before he dove to the side. His reflexes, better than ever, kept him from a point-blank shot with the crossbow. Coming up, he dove again to find Stalker unconscious with a crossbow bolt in his mouth.

There was nothing he could do for his dragon at that second. Men were running towards him through the storm. But where they had to struggle through it, he didn't, and as the man closest to him reloaded his crossbow, Ken was on him. His mind was a mass of pain and no little rage.

He ripped the crossbow from the man's trembling, cold hands and, pulling his knife, slammed the butt of it into his jaw, dropping him like a stone. He then turned, lifting the crossbow towards the closest man while pulling the sheath of bolts from the falling crossbowman's back.

All of the men stopped uncertainly; most had binoculars on their heads. Ken knew they would not work as well as they were meant to now, but obviously, it had helped them see in the darkness, at least a little.

"Come any closer, and I will kill this man," Ken told them solemnly as he moved closer to Stalker.

"Dough man, do you see what I do, or am I just tripping? The storm doesn't even touch him," a man exclaimed in a muffled voice.

Behind Ken, there came a brief snapping sound and a lessening of the pain in Ken's head as Stalker woke up, putting a claw to the bolt, pushing it to the ground for leverage to hold it in place, then yanked his head back, pulling the bolt out of the roof of his mouth violently enough to snap the bolt as it came out.

"Are you alright?" Ken asked Stalker in his mind, concerned for his dragon racing through his mind.

In answer, Stalker stood up shakily and let out a very enraged roar that shocked the pitch-black sky and all of the suddenly confused and scared crossbowmen.

"Hold a second," Ken told him firmly as the dragon prepared to launch an attack that he himself was readying for as all the crossbows pointed right at him, ready to fire.

He could feel each of their intentions as he opened his mind to theirs and knew he did not have a second to spare. Reacting instantly, he pulled upon the warmth of his mark and made both his and Stalker's shields even stronger, able to block bolts and bullets and any fast-flying object. None of the men saw the flare of light under Ken's shirt. They were too busy pulling their triggers, sending bolts flying through the air towards Ken.

With his mind in the men's, feeling weird to hear all their thoughts and sick desires, he almost regretted what he had to do. Almost. He felt like throwing up from the sick images and lusts he saw in their minds: torture, rape, killing of children and men, and the enslavement of women and young boys. He wanted to gag at their foul thoughts and turned, pointing the crossbow he held at their leader.

"Now!" Ken snapped angrily as he shot their leader. As his bolt flew, so did the very furious, pain-filled dragon. Connected as he was to Ken, he saw his every intent and felt his sickness and rage at these men. Along with his own, it launched Stalker into the stream of bolts that filled the air, intent on killing Ken. All of them deflected off Stalker's shield, and flames ripped from his jaws, searing the first man he flew past as he tackled the second, biting into his throat and viciously ripping it open as the man collapsed under the vengeful dragon's wrath and weight.

To Ken's surprise, all of the combat-trained men froze in shock and growing horror as Stalker launched into the air and all their bolts skipped harmlessly away from him. Fear filled their faces as their leader dropped with a crossbow bolt right in the center of his neck. They were still moving in slow motion as Stalker killed a man, and Ken reloaded and shot the man farthest away, who had lost his determination to fight and was about to flee. He never got the chance; Ken's bolt again struck the neck, just above the vest that might have stopped the bolt. That seemed to wake all of them up; they dropped their crossbows and ran, fleeing in terror.

Stalker was on them, though, ripping into one man's hamstring, causing him to scream and drop. Leaving that man, knowing he could only crawl now, Stalker flew after the next. Ken calmly trotted over and killed the man with his knife. There were only two left, and they were racing blindly through the hailstorm towards the center of the town, where Ken now knew there were five more combat-trained men in their group, watching over the women and boys.

From their minds, Ken had learned the men had spotted him as soon as he entered the city. One of their spotters had been on the lookout for anyone who might have survived their attack and was trying to flee the town. That man had spotted Ken and alerted his leader with a flashing mirror, who had come with these men to investigate and kill him because they did not need strays.

All of the men were wearing thick, warm army clothes and body armor, but it did little to protect them from Stalker and Ken, and within a minute, the last two were as dead as the rest. By then, Stalker had collapsed.

Ken ran to him in concern. He could feel Stalker's pain, though the dragon tried to hide it. He knelt, touching the silver-gold dragon.

"Truthfully, how bad are you?" Ken asked seriously as he turned the dragon's silver head towards him so he could look at the weary dragon, and saw blood covering the whole dragon's front.

Seeing it and feeling the pain himself made fear fill him, and instinctively, as if sensing his raw emotions, the dragon mark on his chest lit brilliantly through his jacket, and he felt its warmth. He pulled as hard as he could, fear for Stalker overriding all of his thoughts, because the trembling dragon beneath his hand was so weak he could not even answer Ken.

Heal, he commanded fiercely as so much warmth filled him, his body lit like the sun in a flash of light that flew into the dying dragon. He had never tried to use so much. And as he released it, his energy left him in a rush even more forcefully than when he had created the dome over the cave. Instantly, blackness took his sight, his body freezing in the air as he began to lose consciousness. He fought it with all of his might while slowly feeling the silver dragon's wound begin to heal. When it was done, both he and Stalker lay upon the ice, trembling in the freezing air.

The cold kept Ken awake, forcing him to gasp for breath as both he and Stalker began to get pelted by the chunks of hail thrown by the storm and sent racing faster by the chaotic wind. He was so weary that it took him a long time to even remember where he was. Stalker next to him was not even conscious. Beneath him, the ice was freezing him, and he knew he was going to die of the cold if he did not move. He gathered his feet up under him and rose, swaying in the wind. He hooked the crossbow to his waist, already wearing the sheath of bolts around his back. Then he bent and carefully picked up the heavy, almost seven-foot-long dragon as if it weighed nothing. *At least,* he thought sluggishly, *my strength hasn't left me, or this would not be possible.* Stalker was a very heavy dragon now. He had eaten a lot since he had shed, and he had filled out a lot.

He needed warmth and automatically set his feet towards the center of the town. He staggered over the thick, uneven ice. He knew where the last spotter was holed up and was very careful to keep out of his view. And while Stalker's weight was not a bother for him, being unconscious, the large dragon was hard to keep up with, making him break out in a sweat. The more he moved, though, the less he felt the cold. When he reached the last spotter's house and could sense the man's mind, all snug and warm in a fire-warmed room up above him, he was relieved.

Ken entered the building quietly, and the man never even had a chance. Ken opened the door stealthily, and even though the man was looking right at it, he did not see him. Ken could sense exactly where the man was, let alone he could hear all the man's depraved thoughts, and he did not hesitate to lift the crossbow and put a bolt in the man's neck above his protective clothing.

That the man actually saw. His eyes widened, then the bolt took him; he stood up in surprise, then dropped just as quickly, clenching his neck.

Entering the room, he felt its welcome warmth immediately. He put Stalker in front of the fireplace and shut the door before going to the man's hidden stash of food and a bottle of Everclear.

With the food, he made his starving body a nice meal and saved Stalker some of the meat that had not been cooked yet. The Everclear he decided to keep, as well as the man's heavy coat, putting his own jacket in his pack and the bottle of Everclear in the coat's inside pocket.

After he finished eating, he thought about what to do. Only four men were left in the town, and after everything he had learned, he realized they deserved to die. All the things he had read in the other men's minds confirmed it. They had taken this town by force; each one of them was military trained. They had scouted the town while it was in the throes of the black sickness and hit it hard, killing all of the men, raping most of the surviving women, then turning the women and boys into slaves. The men he had seen strung up on the light poles had been part of their unit but had tried to kill their commander for the atrocities he let the men commit. All of the rest had taken their time torturing them for the four men they had killed before hanging them.

This man, whom he had just killed, had raped three of the women and one little girl that he had held in a place only he knew about—a house not too far from here on the outskirts of the center of town.

"Stalker!" Ken called out, shaking the dragon wearily. "Wake up, you lazy dragon."

Stalker growled lightly, then snapped his silver eyes open, blinking them a couple of times to orient himself. Then, to Ken's relief, he felt the familiar coolness of the silver dragon's mind. A picture of Ken, big and dangerously powerful, filled Ken's mind.

Ken laughed weakly and rubbed Stalker's head affectionately. "Didn't I teach you to only eat certain things?" he teased the silver dragon. "You almost died on me! Are you okay?" he asked in concern.

Stalker stood up from in front of the cozy fire, looked around, and growled angrily before miming like he was ripping something apart viciously, gnashing his razor-sharp teeth and shaking his head.

"Good," Ken growled angrily. "We have some damsels to rescue and some more men to kill."

Stalker watched him both eagerly and curiously as Ken pulled out and tossed him some meat. Then he pounced upon it hungrily.

"Don't eat any arrows this time!" Ken commanded in a growl as Stalker wolfed down the meat.

"It looks like we will have to bear the hail and wind this time. I am too tired to put up a shield, and we both need to save our strength for the walk back," Ken told Stalker as the silver and gold dragon began to lick clean all of his bloody scales.

Stalker got up to move to Ken, but Ken stopped him sternly.

"I know you mean well, but keep your energy. I know I wasn't able to heal you all the way; I can still feel your pain. You need the energy you do have to finish healing, so don't even try to give me any," Ken commanded in a voice that brooked no rebuttal.

Stalker turned away, licking his scales as if that wasn't what he was going to do at all, then he began his weird chuckle.

Ken sighed and gathered his strength. "Alright, let's go rescue some women and children," Ken said as he checked his knife and reloaded the crossbow.

Then his eyes caught something he had not seen in the man's mind. Leaning on the side of a couch by the window, hidden by a curtain, was a gun, a rifle. At first, he was just going to ignore it, but out of habit, he picked it up to see what type it was because he didn't recognize it.

And he was jolted to see it was a CO_2 rifle, a tranquilizer gun. He searched for a case and found it with a good stash of darts and CO_2 cartridges.

Damn, he thought. It was good that he found this; without his shield up, he would have been just a sitting duck for any shooter and never would have realized he could be shot from farther away than a crossbow. Most likely, had he seen the gun pointed at him, he would have laughed, thinking it wouldn't fire. What a fool he would have been then.

CHAPTER TWENTY-THREE

He turned to Stalker, holding the gun out, "We have something else to be wary of. If you see a man with one of these, keep your mouth shut and guard your eyes. I don't think one of these could get through your scales or kill you, but there is poison in these darts, and they could kill you if they get inside you. Your eyes and mouth will be vulnerable to it."

Stalker came and sniffed the gun in disdain, then went to the door, anxious to get the killing over with.

Ken put the gun in its case, then checked his crossbow and the man's own. He loaded it to carry one in his hand and the other at his waist. He filled the sheath at his back with as many bolts as it would carry and slung the rifle case on his back as well. He then put on the black ski mask and leather gloves he had found in the coat before, slipping on his sunglasses, and hoped that if someone did see him this time, they would mistake him for one of their own.

They left and entered the hailstorm again. He was glad he didn't feel the cold, but he did feel the annoying sting of the big hail chunks. Hunched against the wind, he and Stalker went to the man's house, using the man's keys to open the door. They both entered as he searched for presences with his mind.

The house was warm, and he quickly shut the door. It was also well-kept and clean. He could feel four people below the house; upstairs, it was pure darkness.

"Stalker, I don't want to see you if we can avoid it. Stay up here; I'll leave this door cracked open, and when you hear me coming, leave the house and wait for me," Ken commanded, cracking the front door a little.

It took him a second to find the door leading downstairs. He unlocked it quietly and reached again with his mind to ascertain who was down there, just in case they were waiting in ambush.

Three of them were fast asleep, while one seemed to be waiting to warn them if anyone came. She was listening intently because she could have sworn she had heard someone talking quietly. Her name was Karen, and when he went down the stairs and reached the door she was resting against, he could smell her fear.

"Karen, my name is Ken," he told her softly through the door in a calming voice as he felt her startlement and alarm that someone had made it to her door without her hearing a thing, and that someone, somehow, knew her name, which none of the 'Lords' here knew. "I am here to let you know that Alan is dead. You are all free now, but don't leave the house yet. There are still some men who need to meet justice for what was done here. Give me some time to deliver that justice. I know I am asking a lot. Alan confessed to me everything he had done to you guys; what all of them have done, and I swear to you they will all pay. I'm going to unlock these doors, but listen to me, this is the only place of warmth right now. There is a major ice storm outside, and if any of you leave, you will freeze to death in minutes."

As he talked, he heard them all wake up and come to the door, listening. A couple of them dared to hope, and as he unlocked the door, it was pulled open by a little girl before the others could stop her. And all of them stared up at him, their traumatized faces full of fear and hope.

The little girl, Miley, looked to be badly beaten, her face swollen, her eyes black and purple, and the look of hope she gave him made him cry because he knew what she had been through.

He knelt in anger, and the girl stepped back fearfully. He reached out, touching her cheek gently, and before he could stop himself, he was pulling upon the warmth of the mark he felt filling him, his body lit with light, and he felt his energy drain from his already tired body, making him stagger back with a gasp as he released his healing magic, healing the girl's battered face and body perfectly.

The women all gasped in awe as he lit up in light, and he could feel their eyes upon him as he wiped his eyes under his dark glasses and sat back upon the stairs to catch his breath. His heart was beating erratically as if he had pushed himself past all of his limits.

"Are you alright?" a pretty but terrified young woman named Amy asked him, unsurely.

He held up a hand without looking up. He could feel the world spinning around him dizzily. Then he heard startled, fearful gasps from all of them. Thinking irrationally that he was being snuck up on, he turned in a launching motion, bringing the crossbow up to fire, only to see an amused-looking Stalker coming down the stairs.

"I thought I told you to hide," Ken growled irritably.

Stalker began to chuckle in amusement, and before Ken could stop him, the silver and gold dragon touched him with his nose, causing Ken to gasp as a torrent of energy arched into him, rejuvenating him instantly.

Ken growled angrily at the weary dragon, watching his wings wilt at his loss of energy. "You don't listen well, do you?" he asked in a mad voice. "Just for that, you have been nominated for guard duty," he teased, amazed at just how well he felt now.

"What is that?" Miley asked in a curious but scared voice as she looked at Stalker with awe, thinking he was a dinosaur, which made Ken smile. Stalker did look a little like one, he guessed. Ken turned back to her.

"This ugly thing?" he asked, pointing to himself. "I am Ken," he told her in introduction.

Miley gave him a timid smile. "No, silly, that," she said, pointing to the exhausted Stalker, who decided to lie on Ken's feet and get comfortable.

Ken looked down at Stalker with a frown. "That is not that," he replied with a smile to Miley. "He would be Stalker. And while I go distribute some much-needed justice, he will be your big, bad, ferocious protector. Won't you, Stalker?" Ken asked lightly, pushing the silver dragon off his feet. Stalker looked up at Ken curiously.

"Can I touch him? What is he? He looks like a dinosaur, and he is bigger than any lizard I have ever seen," Miley asked as she moved closer to Ken.

Ken put on a doubt-filled face. "I don't know; you'd better ask him. He's a very fierce dragon," Ken told her playfully as he felt the eyes of the three women watching him, not sure what to take from him. All three had decided in their own way that he was a god or a protective angel, and feeling their awe of him made Ken want to leave very quickly.

"A dragon?" Miley replied excitedly. "But he is so small; I thought dragons were as big as castles?"

Ken smiled at Stalker's incredulous look. "Well, yes," he told her in amusement. "But Stalker is young. All dragons are young at one time."

Miley moved carefully closer, putting her hand out as she studied the silver and gold scales upon the dragon. "Stalker? Can I touch you?" she asked nervously.

In Ken's mind, he felt Stalker felt exactly as he did, feeling the three women study him. Stalker backed up nervously, looking very uncomfortable and uncertain at Miley's approach.

Ken laughed at Stalker's reaction. He could chase down men with no fear, yet let a little curious girl approach him, and suddenly he wanted to tuck tail and run, or fly in Stalker's case.

"Hey," Ken told Stalker in a teasing tone. "I told you to hide. Well, now the cat's out of the bag, so go on, let her touch you. That is, unless you are scared. She does look hungry; maybe she will pounce and eat you," Ken taunted hilariously.

Miley laughed at Ken. "I won't eat him, silly."

At Ken's taunting words, Stalker froze and warily bent his head, sniffing her little hand, then let her rub his head.

"Ohh, he has a lot of horns. And he is so warm," Miley said excitedly, and to her delight and Ken's own shock, Stalker let out a loud, purring, contented rumble as Miley got closer, hugging him for his warmth.

"How did you do that?" Amy asked Ken in an awestruck voice. Hearing it gave Ken the shivers. He studied them. "You all heard what I said?" he asked, ignoring her question, and told Stalker in a no-nonsense tone in his mind to stay and protect them while he went to kill the other men.

All the women nodded.

"Stalker needs some meat so he can recover some of his strength. So if you can, feed him. I will return when I am done, and this town is safe for you," Ken told them.

Then he bent, creating a new shield around his silver dragon, and put one on himself. That done, he walked towards the door, his mind already working on how to do it.

He was shocked when, as he started to leave, Miley ran over and hugged his leg. "Don't leave!" she cried in a suddenly frightened voice, holding tightly to his leg.

He was grateful when Karen came and picked her up. He saw that the girl was ready to cry, and he reached over gently, wiping a tear from her eye. "Be strong, Miley. I won't be gone long, you'll see. And Stalker, he will be here to protect you, won't you, Stalker?" Ken said, drawing Miley's attention to the silver and gold dragon.

Stalker growled, standing tall, and mimed ripping and tearing something apart.

Then, before he could see her cry, he bounded up the stairs and let what had been done to the little girl feed his rage at the four men still alive. Worry gnawed at his gut, though. What were all of these women and children going to do once he rescued them? All of their men were dead, and every single one of them had been horribly and sickly abused, beaten, and tortured in some way. He fed all that worry into his rage, too.

He strode right through the hailstorm like an avenging angel, the woman believed he was, right towards the center of the town. His senses were extended, trying to feel the four men by their thoughts. He found the first almost right away, coming out of a huge house, an umbrella held in one hand and a pistol in the other. He was wearing the same binoculars as the others had.

He hid as soon as he sensed the man. The gun was another CO2; from the man's mind, he learned that it could not shoot far, but its darts would put a man down in seconds. The man had tested it a couple of times just to be sure. The darts even went through their own body armor, something he had tested on those who had turned against them, but only at very close range.

He let the man get closer, then he stepped out from behind an iced-over car. His bolt took the man right in the throat, and as he dropped, Ken ran to him, stripping him of the pistol, holster, and belt clip holding filled magazines of darts and extra CO2 cartridges. The men, he had learned from this man; only had three guns. All of which had been taken from an animal control center: two rifles and one pistol. Their commander had the other rifle, but Ken had not seen it when he had killed him.

The house the man had just left was filled with women and children. He had been there to feed them. Ken knew they were safe for now, so he took the man's keys and belted the holster to his own belt before reloading his crossbow and heading towards the main headquarters for all the men, where he could feel all three of the others were.

He passed several houses with one or two people in them. All of them were women in various stages of fright and pain. He was so glad he had left Katty behind; she didn't need to see this, it would have torn at her heart.

He did not even bother to hide this time. Running in a rage to the building, it took him several minutes on foot to reach it, and before he did, he realized he had company: dogs. They were chasing after him. He had been wondering why the man had been holding the gun when he left the house. They had cleaned the town a while ago, so the man had not felt threatened that someone would kill him. It had been more of *something.*

Ken slowed, lifting the crossbow, not really wanting to kill the dogs, but they did not really seem too friendly. He entered their minds almost instinctively.

"Friend!" he told them in a commanding voice. "Stop!"

All three dogs stopped with a whimper, and two tucked their tails and ran off, yipping as they fled. The third was a huge dog, a bullmastiff, one of the biggest Ken had ever seen. It lay down on the ice and wagged its tail. Ken could tell it was still a young dog, but it seemed to be well-trained.

"Stay!" Ken commanded before continuing towards the huge mansion where the three remaining men were.

The dog whined as he left it and stayed for a second before slinking after him through the storm, staying back from him but following all the same. He wondered if he should kill it, but he shied from that thought; it didn't seem intent on killing him, and he was relatively sure he could get it to follow any command he gave it with his mind. So he ignored it and walked up to the mansion's driveway.

Inside the house, he felt twelve people, and outside, there was one, right in front of him.

"Creig, is that you?" the lookout man asked as Ken approached him confidently.

Ken did not bother to answer. He just lifted the crossbow and shot it.

Surprised, the man jerked back, and the bolt only struck the side of his neck.

"Shit!" the man growled, lifting his own crossbow and firing.

Ken dodged instinctively, but his shield reflected it, sending the bolt flying away. Even though Ken saw the man had horrible aim and would have missed from so close to him.

Ken took two steps forward and slammed the crossbow hard across the bleeding man's face. The crossbow broke, and the man fell unconscious on the driveway. Ken calmly pulled his knife and bent, slicing the man's throat before picking up that man's crossbow and reloading it.

The other rifle he saw was here, resting on a chair upon the porch by the door. He had learned from the man's mind that the commander had given it to him in case the prisoners tried to escape while he was gone. He hid the rifle in an ice tree by the door and was about to enter the house when he heard a whimper coming from the driveway.

Surprised the dog had gotten so close to him, Ken watched it as it belly-crawled across the ice towards him, as if hungry and begging for food. When it saw him turn and look at it, the big dog whimpered, its tail wagging wildly.

"Shh," Ken whispered with a groan and patted his pack on his back, finding some jerky he had found in the store. He opened three of the long sticks and tossed them to the dog. The dog sniffed them, then, gingerly holding one between its big icy paws, it began to gnaw on it with relish.

Seeing it occupied, ignoring both Ken and the ice pelting it, Ken unlocked the door using the keys this man had. Then, with the reloaded crossbow leading the way, he entered the hot house. The light was so bright in the house he almost thought he had been flared. He walked in squinting and was instantly spotted by two women, who both looked at him fearfully and were about to yell.

"Don't cry out. I am here to free you. Where are the other two men?" Ken told them forcefully in their minds.

One woman just passed right out. The other began to tremble in fear, a look of awe and hope springing suddenly upon her pretty face. She stepped forward hesitantly as Ken shut the door behind him quietly.

"Are you real?" she whispered in disbelief.

"Yes, Mary. Where are the men?" he asked patiently.

"You know my name!" she squealed in surprise.

Ken groaned. "Shh," he told her fiercely, holding a finger to his lips under the ski mask. "The men, hurry."

"One is in the kitchen, the other upstairs," she whispered, her mind full of confusion and shock.

"The kitchen is?" he asked, unable to feel where the men were with so many people and so much emotion in the house. It was hard for him to even read this girl's mind. All he heard was fear, delight, and hope. It confused his mind.

She pointed to the back hallway.

Ken nodded and motioned for her to stay as he moved cautiously towards the hallway and a door leading to the kitchen. His training picked up instantly. He would have felt better with a real gun, but so far, the crossbow had not let him down.

He heard a commanding voice from beyond the door, then a cry that thudded. The sound of it sent his blood boiling, and his anger rose even more. With it, he felt the warmth of his dragon mark wanting to be used, but he pushed it down. He felt more confident in things he knew how to use.

Feeling where everyone was in the kitchen, he opened the door and entered.

The man with the commanding voice was standing over a young, battered-looking boy. Behind them were two women trembling in fear, trying to ignore the man as they washed dishes. Like the others, he knew this man was combat-trained, and he had to make the shot perfect or the bolt would take one of the two women behind him.

As he expected, the man looked up to see who had entered, and his eyes went wide when he saw the crossbow. He began to react as he saw it. Only he was much too slow. Seeing that the man was only wearing a shirt, Ken shot him right in the heart. The man clenched at the bolt and fell back on the startled women, both of whom gave off little screams as the man fell upon their backs, blood coming from his mouth.

"Shh," Ken warned them quickly. As they stared at him, as if he would kill them too. "I am here to put an end to this madness. Don't panic, I'll be back." That said, Ken left, trying to find a way upstairs to the last man.

Once he found them, all he had to do was follow the chilling cries.

"Ow, ow, oh, stop, please stop, it hurts," he heard a young girl crying.

"Hurts, does it?" a man replied, emphasizing each word with the slap of skin on skin and drawing a cry with each one.

Furious, Ken kicked open the locked door to see a big man, naked, on top of a young girl who was tied to the bed with her arms and legs spread. The man was thrusting into her with all he was worth, making her arch with each thrust, her head hitting the headboard, and her firm breasts trembling each time he pushed deep into her.

"Ow, ow, ow, oh stop," she cried in a terrified voice.

The man was so entranced by screwing the girl that he did not even hear the door get kicked open; he just thrust harder and harder into her.

Sickened in rage, Ken dropped the crossbow and ran forward, snatching the man by the hair and yanking him bodily from the terrified, bloody girl.

That was when Ken really noticed how much he had grown. Before the storm, the man would have been an inch or so taller than his own six feet. Now he topped the man by a good three inches.

Ken threw the man so hard that he fell back and hit the door Ken had entered. He staggered, holding his side as the doorknob hit his side, and Ken laid into him with a jab and a hook that set the man up on his toes. Then, disgusted and in a rage, Ken pulled his knife in a smooth move and sliced down and across. The knife hit and sliced off the man's manhood, and he screamed as blood exploded everywhere. After that, the man lost the will to fight, and Ken reversed the knife, flipping it in his hand and stabbing him between his ribs, right into his heart.

The man dropped dead at his feet, and Ken stumbled in sickness, lifting his ski mask. He puked all over the dead man, gasping for breath. He could feel tears running down his cheeks and heard the girl trying to move on the bed. He wiped his mouth, pulling down his mask again, and walked to the bed, slicing the ropes holding the girl so awkwardly upon it.

Once he freed her, he felt eyes upon him and looked up to see a woman holding a crossbow at him, the one he had dropped.

"You killed my husband!" she screamed, pulling the trigger.

The bolt was aimed true and, catching him by surprise, would have hit his face — but it was deflected by his shield and lodged in the roof. Before he could move, there was a loud Bong! and the woman with the crossbow collapsed as if dead. Behind her stood a group of women, one of them the pretty one from downstairs, holding a frying pan.

Ken sighed and sank onto the bed, feeling sick, realizing he had killed all the men but would have been killed by a woman. He pulled off his ski mask, keeping his eyes closed until his sunglasses were back on.

There was a terrified squeak from the naked and beaten girl as he sat on the bed, and he looked to see her curled up fearfully by the headboard.

"Are they all dead?" the woman holding the frying pan asked hopefully, the only woman who dared to speak, drawing Ken's attention to her.

Ken nodded after a second, thinking he might be sick again. Then, wiping his eyes, he tossed her the keys.

"Free all the others. All of them are dead," he told her as he forced himself to stand up so he wouldn't terrify the scared girl anymore. All he wanted to do now was leave and go back to Kat. This place and all that had happened here made him sick.

"Why do you wear sunglasses when it's so dark? And how did you stop that arrow from hitting you?" Mary asked him as she handed the keys to someone else, who took off to free all the others.

Ken ignored her, turning to the naked and bloody girl. "How bad are you hurt?" he asked her in a soft voice, averting his eyes.

She stiffened when he talked to her, and he covered her gently with a blanket from the bed when she wouldn't grab it from him. He could see from her mind how traumatized she was and left her alone, turning to the other women now watching him as if wishing they could remember his every word and gesture.

"Will one of you make sure she's alright?" he asked. "I need to go find and release everyone who is locked up in this town."

"What's your name?" Mary asked, still holding the frying pan, but it was no longer cocked to strike someone.

"I am Ken."

"Are you from the government?" another asked in a frightened voice.

"I am a Green Beret, but I don't believe there is a government anymore," he told them truthfully, bending down and retrieving the crossbow. "One of you should see to her before she wakes, and if you believe she will be trouble, maybe keep her separated." He suggested, motioning to the knocked-out lady as he left, before he got sick again.

"Wait! Where are you going?" another woman asked. Ken ignored her. He didn't want to be rude, but to stay was to throw up, and he didn't want that. He ignored them all and left the mansion, stopping only to retrieve the rifle from where he had hidden it. He would have to search the commander's living quarters later for the other CO2 cartridges and darts.

He used his senses to find all the houses and buildings with women and children, then released them, talking only when he had to. He found clothes to bundle them all up in and ignored the dog, who had taken to following him after the first house. He sent everyone he rescued to the mansion.

By the time he reached the house he had left Stalker in, he had counted thirty-eight people, all of whom had been subjected to brutal and horrible abuse. Two were so sick that he could not help but heal them. When he finally felt Stalker not too far away, he was weary, tired, and just wanted to rest. It had been hard to convince the women to leave him once they found out he was rescuing them. All of them were frightened and worried, wanting to stay around him so they would feel protected, but doubting his word, the men were all dead.

When he heard Stalker's greeting, relief flooded through him. The sight of the silver dragon rushing out of the house with a welcoming roar heartened him.

"I missed you, too," he told the dragon wearily while scratching his head, drawing a loud purring growl from him.

He felt a coolness in his head, and a picture of Katty with a bigger Keen entered his mind. Surprised to know that, he jerked up to see Katty angrily glaring at him from the doorway of the house.

"Why didn't you warn me?" Ken demanded grumpily. Stalker just chuckled with his weird amusement.

As Ken was walking to the house, Miley came pushing past Katty, her hair blowing wildly in the ice storm.

"You're back!" she exclaimed happily. "Come see, come see, she has a dragon too!"

"Kat?" Ken asked as he walked through the storm, untouched by its howling wind and frozen pellets of ice.

"Just scout!" she snapped furiously. "That's all! You promised!" Then, rushing past Miley, she was pounding on his chest, and with his hands full, he couldn't stop her. "Do you know what it felt like when you almost died? Do you?" she cried angrily, tears filling her silver eyes, taking off his glasses to make him look at her.

"I couldn't..." he started to explain, then sighed. Leaning forward, he kissed her forehead. "I'm sorry, Kat. When I arrived and saw what was going on here? It was government men, Kat! Army! I'm so furious. The things they did?" he exclaimed with a sick shudder.

Katty held him close. "I know," she whispered softly. "They've told me. When I felt... We came here as soon as we could. I feared we would be too late. It was Keen who found Stalker here. Come, let's get out of the cold before this little one catches a cold." Katty said, resting her hand on Miley's shaking shoulders, pushing the freezing, but excited girl back into the house, followed by Ken and Stalker.

"I saw it!" Miley exclaimed in awe. "The ice and wind don't touch you!"

Ken entered after letting Stalker through and shut the door, putting both the crossbow and rifle by the door, feeling all the eyes in the house upon him.

"Did you kill all the bad men?" Miley asked curiously.

"They are all gone," Ken assured her.

Miley smiled joyfully. "He told me you would, showed me a picture of you all shiny and powerful," she said, petting Stalker's spiky back, making him purr and arch into her touch.

"He did, did he?" Ken asked curiously, cocking an eyebrow at Stalker, who steadfastly ignored him, rubbing his head over Miley's chest, making her giggle and scratch his neck.

"My lord?" one of the women asked meekly, drawing Ken's eyes.

"I am no lord. I am Ken, and this is Katty," he told her softly.

"I'm sorry, it's just that's what they made us call them, and it's just a habit," she tried to explain quickly, fearing he would get mad at her. "Are you human? I saw you heal Miley with a touch, and your eyes are silver..." She stopped, too embarrassed to continue.

"Of course he's human," Katty replied softly, looking at the woman with her own silver eyes. "Our eyes are only silver because of our dragons. Ken is a Green Beret. He saved my life as much as he has yours."

"I did not mean... I just wanted..." the woman named Wilma began, only to stop when she got flustered.

"What she was trying to say is that we all owe you so much for what you have done for us, Ken," Amy told him with raw sincerity, touching his arm.

He saw Katty's eyes flash and heard a light growl that, to his shock, did not come from Stalker, who was being overwhelmed with affection by Miley. Instead, it had come from Keen, drawing Ken's eyes to the much bigger dragon.

The dragon was now more gold than sun yellow, and the light blue of his under-scales now seemed to have light patches of white in places. His horns were a little bigger, all crystal, and he was just a tad smaller than Stalker was now—a good six feet and some inches long.

Ken turned back to Amy, feeling her hand still on his shoulder. "I have gathered everyone in or around the mansion that the men were using as their headquarters. Including you guys here, there are forty-eight women and children. This storm may last a long time—hell, we might be beginning an ice age again. It will be best if you stay together for warmth and your own protection. Gather all the supplies you can and keep them in a safe place so you can get a system going to ration them out. You will need it all in the weeks, if not months, to come," he told her seriously.

Wilma and Karen looked like they were both about to panic.

"You're going to leave us?" Karen asked in shock, about to cry.

"No, we will stay and help where we can," Katty told her firmly, unable to ignore Ken's shocked look, and turned to him. "Do you believe they could survive by themselves?" Katty asked him lightly, lifting a demanding eyebrow. "I've seen in your mind and in theirs what happened here. They won't last a week without strong guidance. And you know more about survival and what it will take to help them stay alive than most likely anyone still living." She explained it to him with a confidence in him that, he had to admit, made him feel better.

Before he could speak, his leg was captured. "Please don't leave!" Miley pleaded, fear filling her when she heard their conversation. "You said all the bad men are gone."

Ken looked at Stalker, who was watching him intently, then sighed, touching Miley's head. "I'm not promising to stay long," he grumbled uncertainly, feeling trapped by Katty's grasp on the situation ahead of this town. "Just long enough to teach you guys to survive," he conceded.

Miley beamed up at him, and he heard all four of the women around him sigh in relief.

Amy, again drawing a growl—this time from both Stalker and Keen—as she unexpectedly gave him a joy-filled hug. And Katty, Ken saw, looked both angry and thoughtful.

CHAPTER TWENTY-FOUR

Day 44; Aug 13th

His name was Chris Horte, and when he woke up, it was to the pounding, freezing hail and a huge headache that made him think his swollen jaw was broken. He also had frostbite in a few places of exposed skin, which he tried to fix as he fled along the road from the town that had turned into a death camp yesterday.

He had served three tours of duty in the Middle East and had seen and been involved in some carnage. But he had never faced a single man who could wipe out an entire unit. The man had been fast for someone his size. Chris still did not understand, as he fled along the road that night, how he had missed a point-blank kill shot, something he had never done before, or how the man could put him out with a single blow to his now throbbing jaw.

After that, he had awakened on the street, freezing cold, with no idea how much time had passed. He was just thankful he'd had all of his protective gear on, or he would have died instead of just receiving minor frostbite. Getting up, he had seen all of his partners and his leader lying dead upon the street.

That had surprised, if not frightened, him a little. He had carefully gathered a couple of their crossbows and bolts. Then, set on a little revenge, he made his way towards the center of the town. He noticed quickly that things were not right, and he was close to Alan's when he stopped in shock. Right outside of Alan's was the weird silver creature he had shot earlier. Only now, it was fine and wrestling around in the storm with a second one, which was gold in color.

He was surprised to see the silver one still alive. He had shot it through the mouth into its brain. Thinking it was the creature, Bradock had tried to convince them that it had eaten his dog. Only the one Bradock claimed to have seen swallow his dog had been a lot bigger and whiter.

By Alan's house stood a woman in camo. She was entering the house like she owned it, and her movements reminded him of the man who had attacked him. He had no doubt she was combat-trained; just looking at her made him wary. He knew combat training, and she had it in the confident way she moved. He watched as she called out, and the two creatures came to her, jumping into the air and flying to and through the door into the house.

It was then that he knew the town had been taken. He pulled back from the car he had been watching from and put a good distance between himself and the house. Freezing, he found a house far away that had a direct view of Alan's through the hailstorm, and from there he began a stakeout. Hoping to see and take Amy before he left.

He had almost fallen asleep when he saw the big man coming towards Alen's house through the hail storm. He was shocked when he saw something weird and incredible. The ice and wind did not even touch the man; the man's coat was not even ruffled by the storm. Out of the door came the silver creature, and it met the man with a roar that honestly would have scared the shit out of him. The man was not even bothered by it.

He watched it all from the safety of the house and felt his heart sinking. All the men were dead, the town was lost, and his whole unit was destroyed by this man. He knew it for sure when the man and lady both left with their creatures, taking the slaves, now free, towards the center of the town, taking Amy with them.

He was furious, but he didn't know what to do, so he swore in anger. To his astonishment, he heard a sound, and with dread saw one of the strange creatures cock its head and start toward him. He felt a big relief when the lady called it back to her.

After that, he gave no more thought to staying to get revenge or get Amy. The creatures disturbed him. He knew he had to leave, or they would find him, and he had to do it quickly before they killed him, too. Only now was he scared. Bradock must not have been lying. And if he hadn't been, then that meant there was an even larger white creature near the town somewhere. Unless maybe Bradock had mistaken it for the silver one? But that was doubtful since Bradock had claimed it had been over ten feet tall. He shivered. He was not laughing now like he had been when Bradock had told them about it. They had all thought it was bullshit until all the dogs began to disappear. Then they had just thought maybe there was a survivor hiding in the town, eating dogs to stay alive.

Now, he wasn't so sure. And that meant if he left, he might still have to face one of these creatures. But it was that or certain death here. So he gathered some quick supplies and headed down the ice-covered street into the storm of pellets, towards the military compound Darius controlled. That man would know what to do, and he definitely would want to know about these creatures and how Walker, Chris's own leader, had been killed.

He slept in a car on the side of the road, freezing and wishing like hell he had a way to warm up. And that made him think of Amy and all the things he had done to her to keep himself warm. Whether she had enjoyed it or not, she was a minx in bed. He had been surprised by her looks and her age to find out she was a virgin. Before the storm, he might have married her, but since then, it really did not matter. The world was changing, and only the strong would survive.

He smiled, having done a lot that first day, and every day since then to put a child in her belly. She had been the one woman he had not let anyone in the unit touch; they all had at least one, but the others were all fair game. Remembering Amy made him feel nice and warm. He loved it when they fought him, and she had never ceased.

She had been in the first house he had hit upon entering the town. A killer knockdown gorgeous body, still looking a little sick but beautiful nonetheless. She had run when he had kicked down her door, but it wasn't to hide as he had first thought. It was to fetch a huge meat cleaver. He had interrupted her trying to feed her sick dad and brother, both of whom hardly twitched as he kicked down the door and barged in...

He was broken from his thoughts, hearing a weird noise over that of the hail slamming into the car. It sounded at first like a growl, and fearing the white creature, he scrambled around, looking out all the windows, trying to see if he could see anything moving out there. He could see nothing, so he guessed it had just been thunder, but he was sure the car had moved too. Breathing hard and seeing nothing but hail, he forced himself to relax so he could warm up again...

Amy had imposed herself right in front of her sick father and brothers, thinking she could keep them safe. And he smiled at her naivety, seeing her hand holding the cleaver shaking.

"Put down the knife, and I promise I will be nice to you," he taunted her excitedly, gesturing with his crossbow, seeing her every movement in the dark house with his binoculars on.

"Get out of my house!" Amy had demanded angrily, gesturing with her cleaver.

He smiled sweetly. "Whoa, calm down, sweet thing. I don't want to harm you, but you will put down that knife, or you're going to get hurt," he assured her confidently, lifting the crossbow towards her.

He had given her time to do so, and when she continued to be stubborn, he pointed the crossbow a little past her, aiming for her father, and fired before she even knew what he was going to do.

As he had known she would, she gasped in shock and turned to see her father dying. The crossbow bolt went through his head. He saw her horror at the sight...

Again, the car suddenly jerked as if it had been hit. He bolted off the seat and looked out the window, his crossbow held at the ready. But again, there was nothing out there, making him think it must have been a gust of wind. All he could see was sheets of hail falling from the dark night sky...

At Amy's look, he had lunged forward and slammed the butt of his crossbow into her hand holding the meat cleaver. The cleaver went flying as Amy cried out in pain and shock. And seeing that her brother had barely even moved since he came in, he put his whole attention on Amy. He dropped his crossbow and, grabbing her by the throat, slammed her down onto her back, taking her wind from her. Then he was on top of her, a hand gripping her throat tightly, getting her attention as her face went red from the lack of air and blood to her brain.

"Don't struggle, and it won't hurt so bad," he had told her in an excited voice as both of her hands tried to move his from her neck.

His other hand snaked between their bodies and unbuttoned her jeans. She tried to toss him off her with her hips, and her eyes went wide with fear as she felt her jeans come undone. She instantly tried to scratch his face and gauge his eyes, but both of his hands caught her own, and she gasped as one of his hands gathered and easily pulled her arms over her head as he pushed up against her. Watching her panic wildly under him had excited him even more...

This time, something slammed into the door next to him, and he flew from the seat in fright, startling him from his memories and bringing a flash of anger to him. He again looked around and saw nothing to worry him. He wanted to go investigate, but then he would lose all of his warmth. Not to mention the white creature might be out there somewhere, just waiting for him. He shivered at that thought. No, he was safer and warmer in here. He watched for a while before relaxing again...

Amy had fought him fiercely as his free hand had pulled up her shirt so he could rest it upon her soft, trembling stomach. He stroked her hot belly with one hand, holding hers firmly in place above her head, and his hips held hers down. He was able to slide his hand down her soft skin, forcing his way under her jeans and panties. Her hips jerked, and as his fingers slid lower over her soft, trimmed bush, she tried to jerk her hips away from him and close her legs. But his own kept her legs wide, and her jerking back, her hips slid his hand easily under her panties until his fingers were grazing the hot warmth of her cleft.

She had screamed furiously and tried to bite him as his fingers delicately traced the plump, trembling flesh of her mound and slid along her pussy lips. The feel of her so hot beneath his fingers had made him hot and hard, and he eagerly plunged his middle finger into the velvet tightness of her mound, finding her hot wetness and spreading it as his finger pushed deeper and retreated, pushing in and out of her. He could not believe just how wet she felt around his finger, but she was tight, crying out as he forced his finger deep inside her trembling body. It was then that he felt her innocence. Her hymen had never been broken, and that made him all the more eager to have her.

"Boom."

The noise and shaking of something smashing hard into the car scared the shit right out of him. The car rocked as if it had been hit by a giant sledgehammer.

"Shit!" he exclaimed in fear, his heart pounding in his chest as he scrambled to look around. At this moment, he felt an undeniable urge to make a run for it. Something weird was going on, and he was getting tired of being scared. He could not see anything that could have hit and shaken the car like that, and he had a weird feeling that the white creature had found him and was trying to lure him out of the car. He shivered at that thought and from the cold. He didn't think he had been so scared in his life. He sat keeping watch for an hour, and twice he could have sworn he saw something huge moving through the icy sheets of hail. But finally, when he caught nothing clear, he lay back to warm up again...

He had been so elated to find her innocence, he almost missed seeing her brother crawling towards him with a bloody bolt in his hand. He quickly lashed back with his foot, kicking him in the head. The first knocked the sick man out. The second and third were to make sure he stayed down.

While he did, he felt Amy trying to scramble away, a very sensuous feeling with his finger still in her velvet flesh. She was yelling and screaming hysterically in fear. He had to catch her hips as she tried to get away and yanked her back onto the ground, her back flat against him. She tried to pull away again, and all she succeeded in doing, to his excitement, was pull down her jeans and panties. She freaked out trying to turn around so she could hit or scratch him, but seeing her bare bottom and trimmed mound made him catch her hips again and pull her back to him. One of his hands circled her bare stomach, holding her tight, while his other undid his pants.

She screamed, clawing and thrashing at his arm, and he yanked her onto her stomach, his knees going between her legs to keep hers spread as he got right on top of her naked backside, which was hot against his bare stomach as he pinned her chest to the floor with his chest on her back. He wiggled his legs, spreading hers wider as his hands forced her hips flat on the floor.

She struggled, screaming and crying in fear, trying to force him off of her or spin out from under him. He easily kept control of her, and she froze as the freed solid hot tip of his manhood moved between her legs to graze the soft skin of her inner thighs until he could feel her hot virgin mound against his tip. Holding her hips, he jerked her back to him and felt her tight, resisting, silken mound slide smoothly over and around his invading tip. Lifting her hips, he jerked forward over her hips, drawing a piercing cry as his hardness began to penetrate her tight virgin flesh. He gasped as he felt her stretch tightly over his throbbing hardness, caressing him in her trembling, silken mound. His hips lowered onto her, piercing and invading, breaking and taking her innocence, and sliding deep and hard between her legs. Then he took her hard, pulling her hips to him, sliding nice and deep into her wet velvet flesh, drawing cries with each powerful thrust until she just lay limply crying as he pushed deep and hard into her, while yanking her hips up onto and off of his conquering flesh, over and over until he collapsed onto her back and came deeply within her.

Again, the car shook, startling him, keeping him awake just when he had been about to sleep. All night long it happened, making him lie in fear, and when the time came for him to leave, he was shaking with the cold, weariness, and not a little fear.

When he had screwed up enough courage to finally leave the car, though, nothing happened. He was ready for it, too. It was the white creature that had tormented him all last night; he would kill it, just like he had almost killed the silver one. They weren't invulnerable, and others needed to know it.

So he had set off down the road towards the military base. And as he passed another car, he never saw what hit him; he couldn't; it swallowed him whole.

CHAPTER TWENTY-FIVE

Day 44; Aug. 13th

Location: Arizona

When Ken awoke the next day, he found that the women and children were already busy cleaning the town of its dead bodies. He spent the day helping them, organizing everyone still alive. Stalker stayed near him the whole time, and he could feel the looks of awe everyone gave him and his dragon. He had to force himself not to listen to their thoughts; they just made him feel weird, and certain of the women really made him uncomfortable with their thoughts.

He stayed away from those, especially after one woman had tried to corner him with thoughts of trying to steal some kisses from him in repayment for saving her from a beast.

That had been a woman named Amy, a pretty China doll-looking woman with fierce determination. But he had too much on his mind to be distracted. He ducked out of that without hurting her more than she already had been, only to find Katty's eyes upon him. He couldn't tell, but thought she looked jealous. But when he had started towards her, she had just left without a word, and before he could chase her down, something else had come up needing his immediate attention.

Luckily, among all the women there, he had found an R.N. She was a small woman named Tamra, and she knew her way around the little hospital in the town. With her help, they began helping those who were sick or had been really abused. He told her, while she studied him like an insect she wished she could study, to only come to him for his kind of help if it was something she could not deal with. While he was there, he posted a thirteen-year-old boy named Darby as her assistant so he could learn everything she could teach him.

Behind his back, the women had all unanimously appointed him their leader. When he had found out, he had politely declined the position, telling them firmly he was a soldier. He would gladly see to their protection, but not ask him to deal in politics. Then he had left without seeing who they had chosen as their leader.

There were only a few boys left alive in the town, a total of seven. Three of them were two years or younger. The rest were all different ages, the oldest being fourteen. He set out training them and the twelve women volunteers, led by Amy, almost immediately, showing them how to defend the town and themselves. They had more than enough crossbows for everyone in the city, but few of them were even strong enough to set the strings to load them.

By the time night fell, he was exhausted, but he still had a lot of stuff to do. He left the town with Stalker before someone else could stop him, carrying two Duffel bags and strolling through the hailstorm as he made his way towards the cave and all the stuff they had left there. Mainly, he wanted Keen's shedding and what remained of Stalker's.

He wasn't too far from the city when he felt something stalking him. Stalker instantly growled in warning, but when he turned, all he saw and felt was the dog coming towards him. Sighing, he waited for it. He had been sure he had felt something behind the dog, intent on killing it, but his senses were up, and he felt nothing out there at all.

"Come on, pooch," Ken called to it as it slunk to the ground when it saw him looking at it while getting pelted by the hail, thrown by a fierce gale that Ken was a little surprised had not let up. He was just thankful the ice was not piling up as badly as he had believed it would. In places, the ice was mounting, but in others, there were only a couple of feet of crunching ice. He was also a little surprised the big dog had left its shelter, wherever that was.

Unnoticed to them, a pair of big white eyes watched the dog go to him with jealousy and regret. Hungry, the eyes disappeared to find food elsewhere.

Stalker continued to growl and only quieted at Ken's stern look.

"Come on, boy," Ken urged again, and the dog slowly made its way towards Ken. He held out his ungloved hand and stroked the big dog's frozen fur. The dog came up past his waist, and it seemed relieved to have Ken pet it. It was shivering slightly with the cold as it entered his personal shield and looked up at him almost affectionately.

"Stay close to my side, and the storm won't bother you too much," he told the dog companionably as he again started towards the cave.

It was close to morning again when he returned to the town and entered a house, letting the shivering dog in with him and Stalker.

"You are a filthy beast, but strong and loyal. Go warm yourself up by the fire," Ken told the dog affectionately, rubbing its melted ice fur.

Hearing him, Stalker's head drooped down.

"Oh, don't you be acting so surely and jealous now, I've had enough of that today from you know-"

Ken began to scold Stalker, then felt eyes upon him and turned to see Katty watching him with sparkling silver eyes. His heart sped up in his chest instantly. The sight of her was breathtaking; she was jaw-droppingly beautiful.

He was used to seeing her as a fellow soldier in all camo. He had trained her for such, and he trusted her to have his six more than anyone he had ever met before. But this? He had never seen her like this. She looked every inch a delicate, beautiful lady. Her hair was pulled back and done up, curly and shiny black. She had on just the right touch of makeup, and the perfume she wore to enhance it was more than a little enticing. She had bathed and dressed up in a thin black nightgown, and her silver eyes looked mischievous when she saw his reaction. Then she gasped as, looking at her, he opened his mind to her, letting her feel how he felt about her and his reaction to the sight of her.

Ken hid his surprise and made himself look back at Stalker as if nothing had happened. Only Stalker was watching him all too closely, having felt Ken's reaction.

"Don't look at me like that," Ken told Stalker in his mind. Stalker began to chuckle as if he was really amused by what had just happened.

"Oh, go follow the dog," Ken snapped at him miserably. Showing his amusement, Stalker left to follow the dog, who was surprisingly lying next to Keen by the fire. To Ken, Keen looked to be sleeping, but he could swear he could see a crack of glittering silver showing under his slitted eyelids, watching Ken ignore or try to ignore Katty.

Ken put down the duffle bags and froze at the feeling of tingling excitement that shot through him as Katty touched his shoulder, sending a small healing spell into him that he had taught her how to do earlier when he had been organizing the hospital for those who needed it. Katty had learned it quickly, but unlike Ken, she was not able to heal people fast, and it took her a lot of energy to heal even minor things that took Ken a second and little energy to do himself.

They had experimented with some other things as well. Like fire, Ken could light things with a touch, whereas Katty could point at things and set them ablaze. For her, fire came easily. She still wasn't as powerful with it as Ken, but she could do a lot with it, whereas Ken could not. It was like that with a lot of things. Ken had to touch stuff to get his magic to work, while Katty didn't.

"I almost fell asleep waiting for you," Katty told him in a soft voice, rubbing his tense shoulders.

Unable to stop himself, he rested his hand on top of hers and looked back at her.

"You should have gotten some sleep. You need it a lot more than I do. You know, I hardly sleep anymore—" he began.

"You don't sleep enough as it is. All day today, you were busy. And now almost all night?" she complained, leaning up against his back, laying her head upon his shoulder.

"Besides," she sighed. "It's time that we talk."

"Talk?" Ken asked, suddenly nervous. "We talk all the time, I know I'm always busy-"

She laughed nervously. "Talk. Talk about us," she told him seriously in a soft whisper, her voice trembling a little as if she was suddenly a little scared.

His heart racing, he turned towards her, his hand now holding hers.

"Kat," he told her, looking into her silver eyes. "It has taken me a long time to realize how I feel about you. You are by far the best thing that has ever come into my life. And now, I don't know what I would ever do without you. What happened here proves it," he told her seriously before frowning. "But you know that I am a rough man. I'm not used to feeling such things as you make me feel."

She looked at him, smiling, her eyes warm and tearful, then reached up with her arms around his neck and kissed him.

"That," she told him happily, hugging him closer, "is all I wanted to hear. My whole life, I have focused on myself, wanting to excel in everything I do. My focus has been so exclusive that I never even gave thought to others. Then you came into my life like a true life white knight.

I had given up all of my hope in despair, and you came giving me reasons to hope again. I never believed in white knights until I met you. Here, after seeing all you have done to help these people, I realized I was not here just trying to gain your approval. I love everything about who you are and what you believe in. And when I felt I might lose you the other night, I realized I love you. Everything you are," she whispered to him fervently.

Ken looked down into her sparkling eyes, his heart pounding hard in his chest as he bent, giving her a light kiss.

"Kat, if I am your white knight, you are my queen. You are the only reason I stayed. You showed me a standard worth living by. I wanted to leave, but you had the strength to stay that I myself lacked. That is when I realized just how much you have come to mean to me. I love you, Kat."

That said, he gently pushed her back and pulled something out of his pocket, his real reason for going to the cave with Stalker.

"Kate Fox," he said seriously, going down on one knee before her. "Will you be my wife from now to eternity?" he asked her softly, a smile on his face as he handed her a crystal ring that had been carved intrinsically to show two dragons entwined tails.

The ring shone bright in the firelight, showing all the power both he and Stalker had imbued into it. Another reason they had both gone to the cave was that they had used all the magic they could without exhausting themselves to power the ring. It had a permanent shield spell that would block wind, ice, fire, and fast objects.

Seeing it, Katty gasped, her eyes filling with tears as she looked from Ken to the bright, glowing ring and back again, speechless.

"When? How?" she asked excitedly, her heart pounding much like Ken's was, as she reached for the glowing ring, wondering just when he had the time to make such a beautiful thing.

Instead of grabbing it, though, she blushed under Ken's look and held out her hand.

"Yes," she whispered breathlessly. "Always."

Smiling up at her, Ken slipped the ring onto her finger. He was startled when there came a flash of light that sent a tingling through them both. At first, Katty's, then his own dragon mark, lit up brightly.

And suddenly there was a second ring like the one he had made, only this one was bigger, so it would fit his finger like the one around Katty's.

The rings both flared brilliantly for a second before their light began to fade. As it did, Ken realized his sense of where Katty was nearly intensified three times. Then a wave of exhaustion hit them both. It hit Katty unexpectedly from what she had done, and she fell into his trembling arms, as only his fast thinking had kept her from unknowingly killing herself by using too much power.

Ken looked around the mansion, unsure of where to take her. He had let Katty pick where they would stay and had just followed his sense to wherever she was. He had only been in the mansion once before to make sure it was safe and defensible, which of course it had been. He had trained Katty extremely well. She listened to him phenomenally; she just chose not to listen at times.

Right now, she was unconscious in his arms, and had he not been touching her when she tried it, she would have died. He was just amazed that he himself was still conscious. She had used her magic, thinking to duplicate the ring. She'd had no idea the amount of power both Stalker and he had put into it. The result had drained her so fast that he had instantly protected her with his own and was barely conscious.

He stood on one knee, trembling, trying to get a coherent thought into his mind beyond not dropping Katty. He was still like that when Keen and Stalker came running into the room.

He felt a cool presence in his mind and recognized Keen as the gold and blue dragon, and showed him a picture of his dragon mark. But Ken's mind was so confused, he just held out his hand.

Keen touched his hand unhesitantly with his snout.

Ken felt an explosion rip up his arm and into his head, which was followed by a loud ringing. This time, he couldn't stop the collapse that came; he made sure Katty fell upon him as he fought consciousness, wondering why Keen would hurt him.

The last thing he remembered was seeing Stalker doing the same thing to Katty, only he made sure he touched her dragon mark to give her energy, whereas Keen had just touched his hand, unable to get to Ken's dragon mark on his chest.

* * *

He woke up in a fever, feeling like he had when Stalker had punctured him with his poisonous spikes. He was a little surprised to see that he was in a bed with soft sheets and a sweet smell that was enticing to him. It could not distract him from the fire and ice that seemed to flow through his veins, raging fiercely inside of him, making him grateful when he faded off to sleep again.

August 17th

When he awoke this time, he found himself curled around Katty, and he felt great, wide awake as if he had slept for eons. The room was bright even though there were no candles lit, and he could sense the moon was high above them by the magnetic pull he could feel inside him.

That enticing smell he remembered was Katty's hair, and intrigued, he leaned forward, pressing his nose into her delicate neck and drew in a deep breath.

"Mmm..." Katty moaned sleepily.

He watched, looking down on her as her eyes fluttered open, and he gave her a smile. Her eyes were a liquid, warm silver, and the look she gave him, with the feeling of relief and love that came from her mind upon seeing him okay and awake, sent a shiver of desire and excitement through him.

He leaned over, kissing her cheek, then her lips in a soft, tender kiss as she rolled over to look at him.

"I had it all planned out. A night such as you'd never forget," he whispered apologetically between small kisses. "Instead, I ended up having to be nursed back to health."

Whatever he expected, it wasn't what happened. Katty hugged him tightly and began crying.

"Oh, Ken. I am so sorry. I ruined everything and almost killed us both. Then Keen had to make a mistake and touch you without using your mark. You have been asleep for days. I'm so-"

Ken smiled reassuringly, putting a finger to her lips. "You have ruined nothing, Kat," he told her sincerely and leaned in, kissing her soft lips harder, a little more forceful and passionate this time.

Over and over, he kissed her lips, and as they swelled up, he ran his tongue over them, causing Katty to pull him closer and kiss him back, her mouth parting for his tongue as he pushed it into her mouth. He felt her heartbeat pick up to match his own, and he deepened the kiss, his head holding her cheek as his other hand dropped over her waist, slowly rubbing up and down her back, then down lower, feeling the curve of her hip and down and around to lightly take possession of her soft backside, rubbing it as they kissed and his tongue pushed inside her mouth, learning her lips, teeth, and tongue.

She gasped as he squeezed her backside, sending a tingling through her body as he pulled her more fully up against him so she was touching him everywhere. Her hands traced his thick shoulder down to his chest, exploring his hard pecs.

With a smile, he rolled her over onto her back, his hands pulling her wrists up above her head as he moved over her. She watched, her breath catching in excitement at his look as he gazed down at her lying below him.

The sight of her was breathtaking, her hair all tousled, a flush to her beautiful face, and her body, all soft and inviting to his gaze. Her black nightgown was molded to all of her curves: her perfect breasts, firm stomach, the little dimple of her belly button, and accentuating the V between her legs.

He leaned over her, pushing one of his thighs between her own, and kissed her lips again, nice and soft at first, then a little harder as he used his hands on her wrists to keep most of his weight off of her, but pressing on her enough to feel her breasts upon his chest as he deepened the kiss.

When she felt his thigh shift between her own, that tingling inside her grew, and she moaned in shock as his thigh slid higher between her legs and grazed her mound, a soft touch that ignited a fire in her lower body that flared inside her as she felt his thigh rub against her mound, sending a lightning of sensation through her body unlike any she had felt before. Moaning and breathing harder, she kissed him, thrusting her tongue in his mouth, opening her legs hesitantly as his thigh again rubbed her mound a little harder.

The feel of her soft, accepting body beneath his unraveled his composure, and as her legs opened wider for him, he moved more fully on top of her, both of his thighs spreading her soft ones a little wider, and leaning up, he watched as he lowered his hips and let her feel the fire she ignited in him. He saw her eyes widen, and her head went back in pleasure as his hard strength pushed up between her legs and pressed upon her mound. Kissing her, he felt her ragged breath as his hips bunched, rubbing him against her soft, inviting body, and fire shot through her body as her hips arched to push against him harder.

Still holding her hands, he moved his hips, soft and serious against her own, pushing and straining against her soft mound. Her back arched, and her legs widened beneath him, her hips tilting up, allowing the hardness of him to rub against her softness right where it felt best. He pressed again, and her eyes closed with a gasp of pleasure, allowing his mouth to kiss down her lips, chin, soft, sweet-smelling neck, and up to her ear.

"Are you ready for me, my little wild Kat?" he asked her teasingly, licking her earlobe while sinuously moving his hard strength against her soft mound.

"Oh, Ken, yes," she whispered as the tingling fire between her legs begged for something more.

Then, in a hesitant voice, as if a little scared, "I want to please you, but I've never done anything like this before."

Ken let go of her wrists and sucked her neck lightly as he pushed his hardness against her mound again, causing her to moan and arch her back. His hands slid down her arm, trailing lightly over her soft skin until they slid down over her gown to feel her soft breasts and hard nipples with his palms, then his fingertips.

When his hands moved over her gown to caress her breasts, she felt the sensation right between her legs, where she could feel him rubbing against her. She moaned and arched, trying to deepen his light touch, and felt her hips jerk when his fingers teased her sensitive nipples.

"You please me more than you know, Kat. You are everything I ever envisioned my woman would be like, but you're so much more," he whispered in her ear as his hands slowly and softly cupped the fullness of her perfect breasts. Just rubbing them, he could feel she wore nothing under the gown; her skin was hot beneath his palms, and she drew another pleasure-filled moan as he caressed both of them while, at the same time, pushing his hardness against the softness of her mound.

"Oh, Ken," she cried out as the tingling fire between her legs suddenly flared higher.

Both of them were breathing hard by the time he kissed back up to her swollen lips, and they kissed deeply, their tongues meeting and teasing each other.

Her hands began tugging off his shirt, and he sat up between her legs, pulling it off for her, while her hands moved to his sweatpants, pulling them off, causing him to gasp as her hands found his hard length beneath his boxers and lightly traced the length of it with curiosity on her face.

He smiled down at her, breathing hard. "And you fear you don't know how to please me?" he teased. "You're perfect, Kat."

She looked up at him and lay back with an inviting gaze, her knees drawn up, with him kneeling between them, her hands still stroking the hard length of him.

"I don't know if it's possible to please you as you have me," she told him breathlessly. "I ache, Ken," she moaned as his hands rubbed the top of her thighs through her thin gown.

Ken looked down, feeling excitement run through him as he smoothed his palms down her thighs, then back up and down again. Each pass, slowly pulling up her gown and revealing more and more of her smooth legs and thighs to his sight.

"Then let me take that ache away," he whispered, feeling the same frantic need to touch her skin as she felt in her.

He pushed her black gown up and over her white-toned, smooth thighs until finally, with an indrawn breath, he caught sight of her virgin mound, covered in a thick black bush.

The sight of her and the feel of Katty's hands pulling down his boxers made him long and hard as steel.

When his hardness was revealed, Katty's eyes widened as the sight did something between her legs that made her open them wider as the fire made her insides tremble with need. She ran a finger over his soft but steel-hard flesh, causing pleasure to jolt through him, making his hardness jump up against his stomach.

"You look ready," Katty whispered, suddenly nervous. Ken looked down at her adoringly. "Are you?" he asked in a husky voice.

His hands slid down over her smooth thighs, spreading them slightly as he lightly grazed up her inner thighs. He saw Katty's hips jerk up with a gasp of pleasure as, moving his hands up between her legs, he lightly touched her swollen mound with his thumbs, lightly running them up and down her very hot and wet virgin entrance, feeling her wetness against his thumbs. He used one of his thumbs to slide up higher upon her mound and pushed lightly but firmly upon the top, finding her clit and rubbing it in a soft circle.

"Ohh, Ken," Katty gasped in astonishment as pleasure shot through her.

He did it again, causing her to arch up, and she felt herself heat and moisten even more right where he was touching her so gently.

Ken pushed up her nightgown, up over her hips, over her trembling stomach, then over her well-formed breasts. And she gasped, grabbing his hardness hard as his hands glided softly to her breasts before caressing them gently and teasing her hard little nipples with the soft palms of his hands.

"Ken," she moaned breathlessly, arching up to his pleasurable touch and drawing another gasp from him as her hands moved over his length, feeling and testing his hardness, teasing his soft, swollen tip.

Breathing hard and aching to feel her naked against him, he pulled off her nightgown and moved over her, kissing her lips hungrily, their tongues catching and teasing. Then he was kissing down her neck to her chest, and her hands shot to his head in shock, a moan escaping her throat as pleasure clenched her hard in the sensitive part of her mound, causing her to tighten on his ribs, as his liquid soft mouth closed gently over first one then the other breast, his tongue licking and mouth sucking lightly on each nipple, drawing moan after moan from her. Then, as she was writhing in pleasure beneath him, he sucked her breast deep into his mouth, licking her taut nipple, causing her hips to rise up in question until, to his pleasure, he felt the soft hairs of her mound rub right against his tip.

The brush of her pubic mound against his tip sent an almost uncontrollable fire sweeping through him.

And her. "Now," she demanded frantically, needing to feel his scorching flesh on her and in her. Her hands went to his waist, pulling him down against her.

He looked down at her firm, curvy body and knew he couldn't wait any longer. He carefully lowered his hips, spreading her up and raising his knees wider, and watched as he moved his hard, sensitive tip down between her soft thighs until it pressed hotly against the wet, hot, swollen flesh of her virgin mound. The feel made him want to push hard and deep. Instead, he carefully rubbed his tip against her, getting wet and finding her virgin entrance. He slowly pushed against her, feeling her wet, tightness open slightly for his hardness.

When Katty felt his scorching flesh touch her sensitive pussy, she hid her fear and lifted her hips. Instantly, she felt his hardness press in upon her resisting flesh, stretching wide around him, and she clenched him tight.

"Oh, Ken, oh," she moaned, her head going back as she felt him slide even deeper inside her tight body.

He felt her hands clench hard as his hardness began to push inside her velvet tightness, and knew he was stretching her to the point of burning. He pulled up upon her hips and pushed his penetrating hardness deeper into her virgin flesh. Her wet tightness opened beneath him, sliding wonderfully around him as he slid deeper until her maidenhead resisted his further penetration. He pulled back, watching her as he rubbed his tip over her wet mound, coating his hardness in her wetness, before he pushed back inside her tight virgin pussy again.

"Ow," she cried out as she felt his hardness spear into her, sliding inside her virgin body until he met her maidenhead again.

When he felt tight flesh surround his tip and again began to resist his entrance into her hot body, he again pulled her hips up to him and pushed harder.

"Oh, Ken, oh ow ow," she moaned as she felt his wide hardness stretch her wide and slide deeper into her, penetrating the last of her youthful innocence and sliding wetly deep up inside her body until she felt he would reach her heart.

Pulling upon her hips, he felt her resistance snap, and her tight velvet flesh closed wonderfully around his hardness as he stretched her tightly around his entire throbbing length. He slid into her trembling body as far as he could, then, looking down and seeing her wide-eyed look, he bent, kissing her lips lightly and gently over and over until she slowly began to kiss him back, and slowly, he felt her trembling body begin to relax around his throbbing length. Her nails were dug into his back, but they slowly lost their hard grip on him as he gently kissed away the last of her pain and fears while her body snuggled around him, slowly adjusting to him being so far within her.

"Relax, my wild Kat," he whispered against her lips, teasingly. "And I will take that ache away."

He slid out of her tight, hot mound and pushed deliberately up inside of her again, filling her until their hips brushed firmly together, causing her back to arch up at the feel of him sliding deeply within her and making her gasp as the pain of his stretching her left for that hot tingling feeling she had felt so badly earlier.

With a smile, she kissed him hungrily, feeling that strange tingling between her legs alight anew, this time a lot more powerfully. The feel of him inside her was unimaginable, something she had never envisioned before this or could feel like this. He touched a place inside her she had not even known existed, and it felt like heaven. That feeling grew deeper as his thrusting pushed him into her a little faster, and his hands once again caught her breasts, gently caressing them and playing with her nipples.

"Oh, oh, oh, Ken," she heard herself moaning as even harder thrusts of his hardness pushed deep between her legs, turned that tingling into a giant bonfire. "Oh, oh, oh, oh god," she moaned, clenching his back as her hips met his, tilting just right to slide him deeper and farther into her trembling, fire-filled body.

"Stay with me," he urged her as he began to thrust into her a little faster.

Her hips met his faster, tilting so he could slide his hardness against her wet, silky mound in just the right way to turn the bonfire into an explosion that tensed her whole body hard, making her caress the entire hard length of him in her tight body. She cried out as a feeling so pleasurable shook her body and left her breathless.

Ken felt her have her first orgasm, tightening hard upon his penetrating length. The feel was so exquisite, he lost control and thrust harder into her body, using his hands to spread her knees wider as he pushed deeper, making her body arch up into his, her head going back at the feel of him pushing hard and deep over and over.

"Oh, oh, oh, yes, yes, oh yes," she moaned, and to her amazement, the fire came back just as hot, but even harder than before, and with a hard, deep thrust that pushed his hardness as far in her as he could, she felt his body tense, and his hardness jerked hard inside of her. It was a feeling unlike any she had ever felt before, causing her fire to roar out of control, and as she felt a torrent of fire shoot from him deep inside of her, she came again, clenching him tight.

"Ohhhh," she cried loudly, holding his twitching flesh deeply inside her.

Out of breath, Ken smiled, kissing her hungrily. "I love you, Kate. Always and forever," he told her fervently.

She kissed him passionately. "Always and forever," she promised.

CHAPTER TWENTY-SIX

Day 48; Aug 17th

After four days in bed, while Ken felt absolutely wonderful holding the sleeping Katy in his arms, he was now starving and thirsty. So, as he felt the sun coming up, he carefully extracted himself from Katty, covering her naked, beautiful body with a blanket. Then he found some camos just waiting for him on top of a dresser, but as he tried to put them on, he was surprised to see they no longer fit him.

He turned, finding a mirror, and just stared in dumbfounded amazement. The dragon mark shone upon his huge chest as if it were metal, and it looked smaller because his chest—everything on him—had grown again. He no longer had an ounce of fat on his body, yet he was thicker, and his muscles rippled. It looked like his bones had all thickened along with his muscles. Measuring himself, he saw he was now two inches taller than he had been before he slept. He was so shocked, he just stared in the mirror in disbelief.

The ring on his finger, it seems, grew with him because it fit him perfectly still. He looked at it curiously; it looked exactly like the one he had so painstakingly carved for Katty. It was so identical it would have fooled him, only it was a lot bigger, and he could feel the magic within it.

Unable to fit into any of his clothes, he went to the closet and went through it until he found a big, dark blue robe to throw on. As he did, he heard Katty moan and turned to see that she had kicked off the blankets and was stretching out seductively upon the bed with her eyes closed. The sight of her naked beauty excited him instantly, sending a burning through him, and he smiled as she opened her eyes and looked up at him. She, too, looked to have thickened and grown, not as much as he had, and definitely a lot more beautifully than he had. Her hair was long and shone with luster. She was so beautiful, he had to turn away, or he'd jump upon her in his excitement.

"I seem to have grown out of my clothes," Ken told her with amusement as he looked at the now too-small clothes, folded and back on the dresser.

"I noticed that last night. How big you were," she teased with a blush as she looked him over. "I was scared you'd rip me in two."

He laughed and walked to her. "And did I?" he queried in a seductive tone, while his hands found and traced her ankles as she propped herself up on the bed with her elbows to look at him, staring at him, seeing him hard and thick beneath the robe. The sight started a familiar tingle in her lower stomach.

Ken was totally enthralled by the sight of her and bent, kissing her ankle as his stomach growled with his body's hunger. He smoothed a hand over her smooth leg up to her inner thigh before pulling back with a smile.

"I'm so hungry. I could eat you," he teased, kissing her ankle up to her thighs.

Katty blushed deeper and pulled away, getting off the bed.

"While you get yourself something to eat, I'll go find you some larger clothes," she said and looked down at his feet. "I'll find you some boots and new glasses too."

"How much did you grow?" Ken asked curiously, studying her body as she moved to get dressed.

"Two whole sizes this time," she told him after a second, feeling his eyes linger upon her as she put on her bra and panties. "How? How is this possible?" she asked in a worried voice.

Ken watched her with a small smile of appreciation, as she was not too shy or embarrassed to let him watch her dress.

"It has happened to me a couple of times before. Only the first time was this drastic. I think Stalker and Keen mixed their magics inside of us, and this was one of the results of it. I also feel more powerful than ever—" Ken began.

Katty smiled appreciatively. "You look more powerful than ever. You're almost seven feet tall now!" she exclaimed with heat in her voice that sent a shiver of excitement through Ken as he watched her dress in her camos.

Ken laughed. "Get out of here before I ravish you all over," he teased, taking a step towards her.

Katty blushed but shook her finger in a negative sign. "You can ravish me later, after you have eaten. It's been a long time since I was able to get you to even drink any water or broth. I'm just glad you're okay now," she said worriedly as she went and hugged him tightly, surprising them both when she was easily able to lift his heavy body. "I was so worried you wouldn't get better and so mad at Keen and Stalker. I was only sick for a day, so when you didn't get better after, I did..."

He interrupted her with a loving kiss. "I'm fine now, go find me some clothes, Kat, unless you want me naked all the time; then you'll just have to wait a little while. If I have been asleep for four days, I need to check and see how everything is progressing."

He looked towards the window but couldn't see out of it because the curtains were drawn over it. "I take it the storm is wreaking havoc?" he asked.

Katty leaned her head against his broad chest for a second before pulling back. "A lot of the hail has stopped falling, but it's still coming down, and the wind is just as fierce, and to everyone else, it is still dark as night out there," she replied, leaning up to kiss him long and deep, smiling against his mouth as she felt him grow hard against her stomach. "I'll go find some clothes and have Keen go scout the city."

He watched her leave and went down the stairs to the kitchen. He felt Stalker's eyes upon him with a feeling of worry, something he had never felt from the dragon. He couldn't see the silver dragon but knew he was nearby.

"Go with Keen and ensure the city is secure still," he told Stalker irritably.

He heard a grumbled reply, then felt Stalker's cool mind brush in his concern. A picture of him, huge and powerful, entered his mind with a questioning feel to it.

"I'm fine. I just need to eat; we will talk about this later," he promised in a dismissive tone.

He set about cooking a large meal, finding everything he needed in the kitchen cabinets. Then he got a fire going in the large stone fireplace in the front room, where there was already wood and a pot rack waiting to be used. When he touched the wood, it was instantly engulfed in powerful flames as energy leapt from his fingertip to it. Smoke quickly filled the room, making him open the chimney to let the smoke out. The wind instantly began to whistle inside the chimney, but he ignored it as he began cooking himself some chili and beans. He was putting some in a big bowl, starving to eat it, when he felt Katty returning to the mansion. Only now she was not alone. With her came other women, all hurrying to get out of the freezing cold.

Surprised Katty had brought guests, knowing he was wearing only a robe and knowing the mansion was preternaturally cold, he stood up, looking around with a worried frown, and searched for the warmth of his dragon mark and tried to make the house warmer. He had tried to do a similar thing in the cave, but it hadn't worked because he needed to touch something to conduct magic into it. Only this time, the house heated pleasantly, and he didn't lose any energy doing it, at least not enough that it was noticeable. He knew instantly Keen's touch had changed and expanded his abilities even more, just as it had his body.

He then finished bowling up the chili and reached out to Katty, still far away from the mansion. "Should I set some places at the table?" He asked her in her mind instantly, feeling her shocked surprise that he knew she was coming with others when she was still so far away. Then came a wave of overwhelming love and affection for him.

"You don't worry about that; go upstairs, and I'll bring you some clothes," Katty told him as she led the others quickly through the streets. He caught from her mind all of them were bundled, holding umbrellas, but Katty herself wasn't touched by the storm in any way. "Oh, don't get grumpy. If you're that hungry, take your chili upstairs with you," she teased in an amused tone as she heard his thoughts.

"I love you, too," he replied with a smile as he broke the connection and ate his chili before filling the bowl again and going upstairs as he felt them enter the driveway.

When Katty entered their bedroom, carrying two duffel bags in her arms, Ken swept her into his arms, kissing her long and passionately, pulling her close. She met him with enthusiasm, kissing him back eagerly until both of them were breathing hard with excitement. His hands moved from her waist down to feel and rub her backside, pulling her even closer to him so she could feel his eagerness for her up against her stomach.

She moaned in his mouth, dropping the duffel bags, and as he caressed her soft backside and pulled her hips higher, she used her hands around his neck to pull up and wrap her legs around his back. Both of them paused in pleasure as he pressed his hardness right between her legs, where she wanted to feel him, where she was now burning with the need to feel him hot inside her. Her tongue battled his as her hands ran through his hair.

He kissed her lips, her neck, and her ear. "You're lucky you brought company, or I would have you screaming my name right now," he teased her, nibbling her earlobe softly.

She smiled at him, sliding sensually down his body, rubbing his hardness up her body, before pulling back with a mischievous look. "I brought you some clothes," she told him breathlessly, surprised he had excited her so quickly. She didn't want him to stop; just the sight of him had her body throbbing with excitement, and she could feel the same feeling coming from him.

She picked up the bags and took them to the bed, turning her back to him. She could feel his eyes following her every move carefully, and she could not stop herself from teasing him a little, adding a little twitch to her hips as she walked and bending over the bed to open a bag.

She was pleasantly surprised when she felt him come up behind her, pressing against her.

"You keep that, and I will take you right here, guests in our house or not," she heard him whisper in her ear, sending a shocking thrill of excitement through her. That left her burning, even more so when she pushed back against him. The feel of his hardness against her sent a tingle of anticipation throughout her body. His reminding her that they had guests in the house was the only thing that kept her from telling him to ravish her as he had promised earlier. It brought her back to reality, but she was so hot now that she almost didn't care.

I'm tempted to let you, she thought to herself, loving the feel of his hard body against her. She could not believe that in all her life she had never thought of sex, but then she was glad she hadn't. No one could have made her feel like Ken did.

"I think we're both so hot it won't take us long. They wouldn't know," Ken whispered to her temptingly, and she gasped as his big hands cupped and caressed her breasts, teasing her suddenly hard, tingling nipples.

"We can't," she moaned with longing.

Instead of answering, his hands slid down her stomach, and her heart thumped as she felt excitement course through her as he undid her camos.

"Ken!" she said in shock.

He kissed her neck. "I want you right here, right now."

She trembled slightly at the powerful ache hearing him gave her, and her hands fluttered in uncertainty as he grabbed the waist of her pants and pulled them down to her knees. And seeing he was actually going to do it, she felt fire burn right between her legs. She turned her head, kissing him enthusiastically, and felt his hands slide over her waist. Then, with a thrill, she felt his fingers move over her stomach and around to press against her soft mound through her panties, drawing a moan from her.

He moved his fingers against her hairy mound, feeling how soft and warm she was beneath her panties, and yes, she was ready. He bent her over the bed and slid her panties down.

She gasped as he spread her legs wider, and she felt the tip of his hardness nudge up between her thighs until it was pressing firmly upon her wet, silky pussy. She jerked in surprise, fire shooting through her belly to her mound as she felt the soft, smooth tip of his hardness firmly push up into her, splitting her wide around him as he held onto her hips and thrust into her from behind, sinking and sliding deep into her slick, trembling flesh. The force of his hardness spearing inside of her made her arch and jerk forward against the bed. Her tightness gripped him hot and hard as he slid wonderfully deep inside her swollen pussy, pulling back and feeling her silken flesh pulse around him, making him thrust again. She bit her hand to hold back a cry of pleasure as he thrust hard and deep between her legs until her bottom smacked into his hips.

Then he pulled out and thrust harder, again, and again, causing her to arch, moan, and whimper as the intense pleasure built within her at each filling thrust of him. Holding her hips, he pulled her back onto him with each thrust until the only sound was of them slapping softly together, bringing them both closer to the edge. She could feel him rubbing and sliding inside her in such a way that she knew she was seconds away from orgasming and screaming his name. Luckily, he pushed her flat on her stomach, lying on her back, and sealed her mouth with his as he thrust harder and faster inside her body. She arched with each powerful thrust and bit his lower lip to keep from crying out loud as she came trembling around his hard, penetrating flesh, and with a hard thrust that sent him deep within her womb, he felt her clench him tight and came deeply inside her himself.

He pulled out, both of them out of breath, and smacked her soft bottom playfully. "You'd better get dressed; your guests are awfully curious about what's taking you so long," he teased.

"You're the one who needs to get dressed. They are here to see you, not me," she replied with a contented look as she pulled up her panties and camos.

He groaned. "Now what?" he asked.

Kissing him, she just smiled and, looking very pleased, left the room, her hair slightly messed up.

Okay, he thought, *two can play that. Let her explain herself when they see her looking as if she had been very thoroughly kissed.*

He went to the duffle bag, opening it to find all the clothes he could need: boots, camos, boxers, sunglasses, jacket, shirts, gloves, a larger ski mask-all of them were the right sizes. He had to give it to Katty; she knew his sizes even when he didn't.

Once he was dressed with his knife on his belt, he went downstairs. The second he entered the kitchen, he felt all their eyes upon him.

"Ladies," he said, acknowledging them as Katty motioned him to a place at the table.

The women all looked at him with sly smiles and open smirks; only Amy wasn't looking happy.

"Let us be first to congratulate you both on your… shall we say marriage…" Amy said with masked jealousy while looking amused. "Katty tells us you made her ring yourself?"

Ken tried not to read their minds, but the looks he was getting made him too curious. And he almost groaned when he did. They all knew what they had been doing upstairs, and Amy, though she kept it hidden easily, was extremely jealous of Kate and was bound and determined to pull Ken from her. Not because she disliked the much younger woman—actually, everyone there held Kate in awe, deferring to her in everything, no matter that she was so young. Amy was determined because she was in even more awe of Ken. She was also the only one who realized Ken was now bigger and thicker, and it excited her sexually. So much so, Ken pulled from her mind in embarrassment as Amy had a vision of Ken doing to her what that pig, Chris, had. Only Amy knew she would enjoy it if Ken bent her over and filled her with his strength. To her, he was a god.

That, though it made him groan, was not why he wanted to groan. And he turned to look at his wife, lifting an eyebrow questioningly. She had roped him to this town snugly, and he could not see a way of denying it.

Katty, of course, ignored his look, turning to Marsha and continuing the conversation they had been having before he had come down, showing off her crystal diamond hard ring.

"Thank you," Ken told Amy firmly. "As soon as we find a priest, we will say our vows before him. But for now, we will have to settle for the interesting ceremony we had."

A woman he had not met before smiled at him with amusement. "It must have been some ceremony. Your lady has kept you all to herself for four days and nights. We were beginning to think she was keeping you captive," she teased, making Katty go bright red.

The woman held her hand out to Ken, and he moved his chair next to Katty to take her hand.

"My name is Merrel, and it is a pleasure to finally meet this honorable man so many have been telling me about," she said in introduction.

Ken shook her hand carefully and kissed Katty's forehead before taking his seat.

"I see what you have done, my sweet wife," he told Katty in her mind. "I will have to find a way to punish you now," he teased her and sent a picture to her mind of him bending her over his lap and spanking her bottom.

She went red and squirmed in her chair.

Hiding his smile, he turned to Amy, the leader of these women here who only answered to his wife, who he learned to his surprise was now the town's governess—a town they were now calling "Miracle."

"My wife informs me you have something to ask me?" He asked Amy, getting right to the point, trying to think of a way to tell them no. The only problem was that he knew his wife was right. Only he could do it for right now.

Amy looked at Katty nervously. She had hoped to dance around the issue until they had eaten, and she could hear an unhappy tone in his voice that made her wonder if Katty had told Ken, despite her promise not to. *But what did it really matter?* She thought. *If she had someone like Ken, she'd tell him everything, too.*

"No," Ken reassured Amy quietly. "My wife did not tell me what you want. But you want me to leave her, leave all of you unprotected, to go chase after something that might not even be—"

Amy frowned, interrupting him, wondering not for the first time if he could read her mind. The thought made her blush. "How you know that is beyond me; we have kept this very secret. Only we here in this room know it. In fact, the fewer who know, the better. I don't want to cause more hysterics and the loss of hope you have created within our town. And I know you just got married to your wife and don't want to leave her. But for four days, you have been secluded with her. I don't mean to be mean; I waited as long as I possibly could to come and ask you. But you must agree, the welfare of all of us is paramount to any single want any of us has."

Ken frowned thoughtfully and opened himself again to their thoughts. He'd had no intention of telling them he had been sick for the last four days, but with all of them wanting to believe he was some kind of god, he had to break that image before it caused problems for both him and Katty.

"I am not saying I won't do this. But I won't do it for at least a week or so. I have been secluded for the last couple of days, not because of what you think, but because I have been extremely sick and exhausted. I don't even remember anything from those days. And now that I have woken up, there is much that I need to do which should have already been done," Ken told them all seriously.

He saw them all frown worriedly.

"Sick?" Amy said in surprise. "Are you better? You don't look sick."

"I am much better now, but my dragon took a serious wound during the fighting, and it almost killed us both," he told them truthfully, using that as an excuse they might actually believe.

All the women gasped in shocked worry.

"Is he better? None of us has seen him since the day after," a woman named Lara said in a disturbed voice.

"He is fine now, checking to make certain the town is still secure and safe," he assured them. "But it is because of my dragon that I must stay. Soon he will be growing, and he will need a safe place when he does. Until then, I will not leave."

Amy nodded thoughtfully. "Then there is one more piece of business we still must conduct."

Katty nodded. "But it can wait until after we have all eaten," she told Amy firmly, and all the women nodded in agreement.

The food was gone too soon for Ken's liking. Hoping to stall what they wanted to do, he ate slowly but ravenously. As he ate, he felt both Stalker and Keen getting close. He waited until he finished his last bite, then his chest lit up brightly through his shirt as he waved a hand experimentally towards the door, testing to see if he could actually open it from so far away.

All the women, even Katty this time, were surprised as the door opened, then the wind caught it, slamming it wide until it bit the wall. A second later, both Stalker and Keen walked into the house.

"Shut the door," Ken told Stalker and watched from where he sat as the silver dragon reached with its claw, catching the door, then used its head to shut it against the wind.

"Thank you," he told the grumbling dragon as Keen chuckled at him. "Is everything clear?" Ken asked.

Stalker growled, and a coolness entered Ken's mind. Pictures of wolves around the city filled his mind, then one of Stalker and Keen taking down a couple of owls to eat, then a picture of the city with nothing wrong with it.

"Good, I was worried it took you so long," Ken told the now grumpy dragon.

It was his first sight of Stalker in days, and he could easily see the beginning of Stalker's shed. He studied the dull silver of Stalker's scales and wondered if what Stalker had shown him was true. The silver dragon was almost seven now, but Stalker claimed the next time he shed, he'd be large enough to carry Ken upon his back. So, Ken had taken Stalker's old shed and used it to make a saddle. The scales would rest upon Stalker's own, so they wouldn't bite into Ken as he sat upon them. They had been sewn with leather, so Ken could sit comfortably on the saddle. He was already thinking of ways in which he could improve his design for Kate's saddle.

Grumbling, with smoke rising irritably from his nose, Stalker came to sit beside Ken in between him and Katty.

While Keen, not far off, stared jealously at Ken, Ken just ignored him and roughed Stalker's irritated head companionably, drawing a rough grumble from Stalker.

The women all sat watching him with awe and curiosity until finally Amy spoke up. "As governess, it falls on you to ask him," Amy told Katty.

Katty nodded and turned to look at Ken seriously. "I know how you feel about politics and where you see yourself in relation to them. But we both know that without you, there would be no town for us to look after. We both now must think of the welfare of our town. There is no one who can meet the needs of this post, none who is as situated as you are to fill this post. By a unanimous vote, we have nominated you to be our general. As such, all decisions pertaining to the defenses and welfare of our town or the defense of our civil rights."

Ken grimaced and interrupted her, "Why not just name me a deputy or sheriff?" he asked in a troubled voice.

Katty smiled, "Because until we know what remains of our government, you will have to take the greater burden. Be thankful I got them to settle on naming you only as our general; others—" she looked ruefully at Lana, "wanted to name you our prince or lord." She then looked at Amy. "Still others wanted to name you our president or, at the very least, our governor."

She sighed as she saw his face. "I assured them you would never go for any of those. But until such a time comes when we can determine if anything is left of our government, we must appoint you as the defender of our town and whatever government we can restore ourselves to. That is, if you will accept such a nomination."

Stalker growled loudly at all the things Ken was feeling, and every lady turned to look at the dull silver metal dragon, his gold scales looking more like copper as he stood grumpily by Ken's side. Only a hand rubbing his head, from Katty, calmed him down.

"So be it," Ken said seriously but in a reluctant tone. "But I have conditions, and they will be followed — or you will find yourself another 'General,'" he said, his tone making it clear to every woman present that he was dead serious. He looked at them each in turn. Only his wife was left from his all-seeing gaze. "If I give you, or any of you, an order, it will be followed. I have no doubt there are other men like those who took this town, still out there looking to do the same thing as these other men did. They will outnumber this town easily; they will want everything we have, and they will do anything to get it. If I give an order, I expect it to be followed immediately. You can get mad and complain, just do so as you're doing it or after the order is followed."

He then frowned, "While I was sick, I had a dream. I am still trying to make sense of it, but this much of it I am certain of: the worst has not yet begun. But there is hope for us. I can feel it even now. It is pulling me north to move north. There may be no choice but for all of us to leave the safety of this town, and if I say that the time has come for us to do so, you can get mad and complain. But you will listen, and you will leave this place when I say it. I will not let some stubborn person die because they feel this is their home, nor will I allow a stubborn person to put the whole town in jeopardy because they don't want to go. So, if you want me as your general, listen to me now, prepare to leave. This place is not defensible against large numbers, and to the north, there is a beacon of flame and hope. In that, I must ask you to trust me. I myself don't know what it is, but I believe this person you want me to be - you will find him or her there. If you can accept those terms, then I will step up and become our people's general," he told them seriously.

All the ladies began talking at once, and while they did, Katty turned to Ken, looking at him in surprise.

"You feel it too? It's not just me and Keen," Katty asked curiously.

Ken held her hand, tracing her hot, dragon-marked hand. "Stalker has been feeling it since he hatched. I thought he was imagining things, but really, that was how I found you. Stalker was being pulled north, and though I didn't understand it, so was I, so north we went until we found you. And now, after what happened," he said, looking around to see all the ladies talking, "I can feel the pull too."

Katty nodded. "Keen has felt it since his hatching, too, only he is not really sure what it is," Katty agreed.

Ken looked at Keen, who stared back almost challengingly. The sight for some reason made Ken's blood boil, and feeling it, Stalker growled deadly and grumpily at Keen.

The sound drew everyone's attention, and before Ken could stop the irritated dragon, Stalker pounced, tackling the smaller dragon hard.

Keen roared defiantly, then yipped in pain and surprise as Stalker easily dominated him, holding him down, his teeth around Keen's neck.

"Okay," Ken sighed, "let him up."

And just as suddenly as his blood had heated, he went calm. Keen, in a way of apology, walked over to Ken. And Ken rubbed his head affectionately until the pride-hurt dragon began to smoke and purr.

"You stop getting jealous of me, Keen. We are family," Ken told the gold dragon softly.

Ken had only a small warning from his instincts to react as he tensed beneath his hands, Keen tackled him out of the chair. All the ladies gasped in fear. Ken knew he was just playing, testing him as he did with Stalker, but he should have waited until they didn't have company. Because Keen didn't, Ken was a little rough with him.

As suddenly as Keen attacked, he was yipping over and over in submission, pinned beneath Ken, who had rolled with the dragon, snatching him out of the air, slamming the golden dragon upon the wood-tiled floor with one of Ken's big arms around the back of Keen's spiky neck, his other forearm locked under Keen's chin, forcing the dragon's head and neck back. A feeling of raw power and excitement filled Ken at Keen's submission, and unable to stop himself, he threw back his head and roared victoriously.

The deep, fearful sound shocked him. It sounded nothing like a human roar. It was deep, loud, and a little terrifying. Hearing it, Stalker roared victoriously himself, and to all of them, they were surprised to hear Stalker's roar sound small in comparison to Ken's.

The ladies, including Katty, all seemed shocked. Though some were scared, Katty, Amy, and Welma were all excited. Katty appeared both angry and flustered, as if she, too, felt what Ken did but was upset about how easily her dragon had been made to submit.

Katty smiled, though; hadn't she submitted herself to Ken? That thought made her blush, and she turned to the ladies, not wanting to read their thoughts, especially Amy's; she looked excited enough to make Katty angry.

"You must excuse my husband's behavior," she told the shocked, excited, and admiring ladies. All of them had lost their slightly scared feelings and were watching Ken with renewed interest as he released her dragon and stood up lightly, brushing off his camos. "I swear he's a big kid at times."

All the ladies laughed softly.

"Oh, there is no need to apologize; this is your house," Amy began, her face flushed.

Ken took a seat, interrupting her. "Sorry about that. Certain kids lack discipline and don't understand yet that there are times to be serious," he told them while his scolding look took in both Keen and Stalker.

Keen wilted beneath his look. But Stalker stood tall by his side again, grumbling as if to say that Ken couldn't be talking about him.

Ken smiled at his dragon. "Yes, you too. Can't you both see we have guests? You both frightened the ladies. So go apologize to them," Ken commanded them both.

The ladies all watched in amazement as both dragons walked to each of them. Before now, none of them had been allowed or even dared to get so close to either of the dragons. Only the girl, Miley, had that honor, petting and playing with them. So, each of them used this rare opportunity to touch them, and Amy got Stalker to purr so loudly that the sound shook the cups on the table.

"They really do understand everything you tell them," Amy stated in amazement, running her hands all over the silver and gold dragon.

Katty smiled. "I think at times they are smarter than we are."

"How do they communicate with you two?" Lana asked curiously.

Katty looked at Ken; she didn't want to say the wrong thing, so she just let him answer.

Holding Katty's hand, Ken turned it, sticking the dragon mark with his fingers, drawing everyone's attention to it before he looked up at them to see all of their curious faces watching him intently.

"These marks bind us to our dragons, letting us feel what they feel and letting them feel what we feel," Ken explained.

Amy studied him with a mischievous smile, "We have all seen and touched Katty's mark, where is yours at?" she asked curiously.

"It's on my chest," Ken replied.

"Can we see it?" Amy asked, her smile widening, and instantly Ken felt Katty's annoyance and jealousy.

Looking at her, though, she kept it off of her face and watched as Ken unbuttoned his camo shirt, then pulled up his tight white T-shirt to show them his chest. He regretted it instantly as he felt all of their eyes caressing his rippling stomach and chest.

Her eyes gleaming, Amy leaned forward. "May I?" she asked, touching his mark. "Is there a reason why yours is so much bigger than Katty's?" she asked curiously as her fingers lightly trailed over the mark covering his left pec, making Ken shiver.

He could feel Katty's fast-rising anger and barely in check emotions. And Keen was beginning to smoke, studying Amy intently as if she had just become a sudden threat to Katty.

Amy, who missed very little for being as petite as she was, sat back with a smug little smile, her fingers tingling, as well as other places in her body. She quickly changed the subject as Ken put his T-shirt down and buttoned up his camo. *One day,* she swore to herself, *he would be hers.*

"We agree," Amy said. "To your terms, of course. Every one of us trusts you with our lives; we won't leave this place lightly. Most of us have lived here all of our lives. But our lives are worth more than some houses. So, if you believe it becomes imperative that we must leave, then we will follow you wherever you take us," she assured him, pointedly not looking at Katty.

By the time they had left, Katty was fuming. "They're like cats in heat around you!" she snapped angrily.

He smiled and pulled her roughly into his arms, feeling her stiffen angrily as he did. "They may be cats in heat, but they are not my little wild cat," he whispered in her ear as he snuggled her neck, making her heart beat pick up and lean against him. "Now to eternity," he told her fiercely, kissing her neck.

CHAPTER TWENTY-SEVEN

Day 48; Aug 17th

After leaving Ken's Mansion, Amy felt restless and just walked out into the hailstorm, ignoring the others wanting to be alone. She didn't know how to feel. She had missed her period, and she just knew now that she was pregnant with that beast's baby. Worse, she felt miserable because she did not want it. She could not even stand the thought of that sick bastard's taint being inside her body. It made her violently ill, just as men made her sick—or at least they had.

Then she had met Ken. He was a god among men. Just looking at him made her want and feel something she had never wanted or felt before. As irrational as that was, the funny part of it was that he now lived in her house. And Amy wasn't going to say anything. She never wanted to live there again, and no one else was going to tell them.

She sighed with frustration and regret. What was she thinking? She was no competition to Kate. She was small and petite, only five-four, while Kate was a goddess in her own right, tall and supermodel-shaped. Though Kate could be so big and still so shapely, it baffled her. The woman was a huge, pale Amazon.

Lost in her thoughts, she ignored the hail pelting her umbrella and the howling wind trying to blow her away. She walked through the town, letting the cold, freezing air numb her pain at being pregnant. She was so furious when she thought of it. She wanted to kill Chris. She had looked for his body, wanting to spit upon him and stomp his face until she felt better for all he had subjected her to—killing her father and brother, then raping her over and over.

Furious, she screamed her rage out into the storm, not realizing she was crying from the thoughts of losing her father and brother. They had been her life.

She had been raised in the town. Her father was a politician and had spent the last two years as the town's Mayor. Her brother had already been making his platform to follow their dad as Mayor. She herself had been beloved by everyone. She knew politics like the back of her hand, schooled at the knee of her father. At twenty-four, she was an accomplished woman, with two years left on an eight-year scholarship, her head set on becoming a judge. She had been totally focused, with no boyfriend since she had almost been raped when she was fourteen. She'd had a couple of close girlfriends, but nothing anyone had ever suspected, lest she hinder her father's image. Then the storm had come, and with it, the vile monster calling himself Chris.

She had been so mad later that night when she found out Lana had stayed up and burned the men's bodies all night long. Not that she could actually blame her. Lana was a tough woman, but she'd had to watch with a noose around her neck as her twelve-year-old daughter had been tied up and raped over and over in front of her, before the men had slit the girl's throat. She had just been furious and wanted to rid herself of her pain by striking out at the dead monster. And she had not even gotten that chance.

She suddenly felt unclean. Just thinking about Chris made her feel dirty and violated. Not even thinking, she started stripping off her bundle of clothes, knowing she was out of the town, just out of sight of anyone in a deep, snow-like ice pile. One she quickly learned was surprisingly softer than most of the ice around.

Having stripped totally naked and still crying, she furiously began to scrub herself with handfuls of the small ice pellets. She shivered in the intense cold, but used it to numb the anger and fear she felt. Giving the freezing cold little thought, just wanting to feel whole again, clean. She collapsed to her knees, crying. How was that possible when she had that bastard's evil taint inside her?

She screamed furiously again, cleaning herself roughly. Why? Why couldn't she have met someone like Ken sooner? If she had, someone like Chris would have never dared to touch her. Let alone that scum Brad, who had given her X when she was fourteen, took her out back, felt her up, dry humped her, then tried to pull up her dress and rip down her panties while she fought him off in a daze, feeling him spread her legs and try to take her virginity. A close thing, because she had felt him push up against her mound and begin to nudge up inside her, stretching her around him. Only a rock to his head had kept him from pushing up inside her deep enough to take her virginity. She scrubbed herself harder. Why had she not learned to defend herself earlier? Just the little bit Ken had shown her so far made her know she could easily kill someone like Chris with her bare hands. The things Ken had taught her were so simple she couldn't believe she had never thought about doing them before. No one would ever take advantage of her again.

No, now she was in control of her life…?

She stopped scrubbing, ice falling from both of her hands as she froze in place. Her blue eyes were wide in astonishment. Right in front of her, just inches away, was an amazingly beautiful dragon. So huge compared to her. She had no idea how it had gotten so close to her. It blended into the ice perfectly. So perfectly, it looked like an ice sculpture. Only its pale white, silver-pupiled eyes made it stand out from the rest of the ice in her vision.

Only looking into its hypnotizing eyes, she did not feel a bit of fear—just awe. She had thought the silver, gold, and gold-blue dragons had been a symbol of power and beauty. But this dragon in front of her made them look like a cherry blossom compared to a crystal white rose in full bloom. They were nothing compared to her... Her? She was magnificent. Without even thinking, her heart pounding with excitement, she reached forward towards its head, so close to her. And to her amazement, it moved forward, its nose gently nuzzling into her breast, over her heart.

A cold shard of freezing cold pierced her body, sending a burning pain into her left breast. It was so cold that the feeling numbed her whole body, just as she had wished the cold would.

Her small hands lovingly stroked the dragon's head, feeling neither hot nor cold beneath her palms as she ignored the pain and rubbed her huge head. A feeling came from the dragon under her palms that shook her bones in a pleasant vibration, but there was no sound. Even though she knew the dragon was purring, much like Stalker had to her gentle touch.

She felt a coolness enter her head, then some flashes came in her mind. The first was a picture of Chris, terrified behind the glass window of a car—he was trapped. The next picture was quick of the dragon, swallowing Chris whole.

Then a feeling of cleanness hit her, and a picture of Amy herself came to her with the feeling that she was strong and clean of his vile evil. She knew instantly she was no longer pregnant, and her relief and joy were so abundant she cried out, hugging the big, glorious dragon in genuine thanks. This brought about a greater vibration of contentment into the air from the dragon. So deep were the vibrations that they shook and cracked solid ice around them.

Then the dragon stepped back, and Amy noticed in shock that covering her entire left breast was a huge white dragon-head mark outlined in crystal. It looked and felt like metal. Touching it, she felt a cool feeling course throughout her body. The mark felt cold beneath her palm, but suddenly, she no longer felt cold—she felt perfect.

She looked up at her dragon with awe. She could feel the dragon's hunger to hunt, eat, and enjoy the kill. Her dragon looked ferocious—almost twenty-four feet long, with six horns upon her head. Two small ones over her nose, two more small ones over her eyes, and two large ones on the top of her head. All of her horns, teeth, and claws were pale white dragon ivory. She had a row of ivory spikes down the back of her head, neck, back, and down her tail. Her tail was long and thick, ending in a huge white ivory ball. Her claws were large, but unlike Stalker's and Keen's, hers were serrated with spikes down the bottom of each. And unlike the two other dragons she had seen, hers had four wings—two regular ones and two more that were attached to her front legs and sides. Each wing was edged sporadically with spikes. Her scales were a metallic ice white and absolutely perfect.

Envy, Amy knew instantly. Because every dragon would want to be her or want her.

Envy was looking at Amy impatiently, wanting to go hunt, and feeling it, Amy quickly dressed.

"Lead on, Envy," Amy told her, knowing her dragon wanted her to come.

Envy looked at Amy dubiously. A picture of Amy appeared in her mind, with a feeling that Amy was too slow. Too... new.

Then came a picture of a fierce-looking man holding a glowing spear, riding upon the back of a smaller red and gold dragon. It filled Amy's mind hesitantly. And Amy had the feeling Envy wanted her to climb onto Envy.

Amy smiled excitedly. She went to the big dragon, who lifted a huge front leg for her to climb onto, and when Amy did, Envy lifted her, helping her climb onto her wide back.

As soon as Amy was on, she instantly hugged Envy's neck tightly. And like a freaky ghost wind, Envy flowed over the ice, half running, half gliding over the desert. It was so fast, the world just flashed quickly around her. The power of it left her feeling breathless. How could her dragon move so fast without flying? Even flying would have seemed much slower than this.

Then, out of nowhere, Envy was tackling a wolf. Amy held her neck tight and gasped in pain as a paw kicked her arm, almost making her let go. But almost instantly, the pain was gone as a rush of coolness numbed her nerves. There was still a bloody scrape upon her arm, but it didn't bother her, and she saw it was already starting to heal.

In fact, nothing bothered or worried her anymore, well, besides Katty having Ken. Just thinking about him made her warm. And surprisingly, she felt a similar feeling coming from Envy, but Envy felt that way about Stalker.

Amy stayed with Envy all night, both of them thinking about Ken and Stalker, while Envy began to teach Amy about the cold that was now her life and how to use it to hunt.

CHAPTER TWENTY-EIGHT

The next few days passed swiftly for Ken. He was busy nonstop, setting defenses and teaching them how to defend themselves. Especially Amy; to his astonishment, she began to excel above all the others. But beyond that, if he noticed any difference in her, it wasn't obvious.

Besides, her not being so obnoxious with her thoughts of them mating. In fact, he felt relief when he felt nothing coming from her but determination as he taught her weapons and hand-to-hand combat. He was too busy helping everyone to even notice he could not feel her thoughts if he tried. Where she came, all that could be felt was coolness. But he had learned not to read her mind, so he never even tried.

He had gone house to house, business to business, and store to store, finding everything they could use. Altogether, they found six BB guns, all of them rifles, two swords, a katana, and a military saber. The women were working on finding the keys so they could check the police's evidence room. They had tried to break in, but it had been useless until they found the keys.

With a map, he had gone over all the closest towns, cities, and the military base, trying to decide which route would be the best to find survivors. The military base worried him; it wasn't far away, and if the men there were any like the unit here, they could be in trouble. He did not want to believe they would be, but after seeing what happened to this town, he was not going to take any chances.

The storm did not let up; it had begun hailing again fiercely, then would slow only to pick up again. And the sky did not seem to be getting any lighter. It didn't matter to Ken's sight, but he was starting to worry about the women. If the storm continued, he was sure people were going to have no choice but to start braving it to find the things they needed to survive, and sooner or later, one, two, or a group was going to stumble upon their city. If it were a group, the women's eyesight needed to be sharp so they would not get caught by surprise.

He had done what he could to make the town defensible and keep the lookouts from being spotted by any scouts. Now all he could do was wait and keep training them.

As Stalker got ready to shed, Ken led the blind, dull silver dragon back to the cave. The saddle he had made for Stalker had been done by the best estimation he could make; he had not finished it yet; the straps would have to wait until he saw just how big Stalker would be. As he left the town, he took it with him, as well as one of the swords. The military saber he was familiar with, he had strapped it across his back with a sheath of bolts because at his waist was the holster of the CO2 pistol and his Kbar knife on one side, and a strung crossbow hung from the other side.

The dog, as always, was by his side, staying close to him, so the hail didn't pelt it. When they reached the cave, they weren't even there a minute when Stalker strolled back out of the cave and began the violent twitching that started his shed.

Ken watched him, keeping the dog in the cave. None of them was even aware; they were being watched by Envy and Amy. But then, the ice dragon ruled the ice; on it, nothing was as powerful as she, and Amy was quickly becoming just as competent. To Amy's surprise, her hair was changing the same color as her dragon's scales, and her eyes were now exactly the same as her dragon's. No one knew, though, because she was careful to always wear her blue contacts. She had taken to hiding her hair under a wig, and while that was noticeable to people who knew her, she told them it was so her hair wouldn't freeze. But mainly, she stayed away from everyone, telling them she needed time to herself because she was no longer 5'4", and she spent most of every day and night with Envy. She returned to the town only to train when Ken taught; she was very careful to keep away from Katty when she taught. If anyone noticed her change, it would be her. Katty was a force to reckon with, and Amy did not want to fight her; she just wanted Ken.

Ken stood in the mouth of the cave, a little surprised; his shield over the cave was still holding firm. There was not a bit of ice upon the ground in or around the cave, causing the ash to crunch frozenly under his boots as he paced next to Stalker. Around the shield, the ice was almost five feet high.

This storm was making it even harder to hunt for fresh meat, and if it continued the way it was, it would be the death of them all. Fewer and fewer animals were surviving the freezing cold. The last couple of days, he had spent using the dragons to herd some horses Stalker had found. He had brought them into town and had the ladies taking care of them the best they could. The task had taken up much of his and the dragon's time, time he had wanted to spend with Katty before he was forced to go scout these towns and the military base for survivors.

Not to mention, scout north and try to see why he and Stalker were being pulled that way. So, while he had been herding horses and a few animals for meat, Katty had been training the ladies and boys.

None of them but Amy had a knack for soldering. The freezing temperatures made them shake when they needed to be firm. Yet they all felt fierce determination, and not one of them quit. They would get frostbite before admitting the cold was getting to them. He had to give it to them for that. They were bound and determined to prove themselves to him and Katty. They even took to calling themselves "The Dragon Squad," something to which, to his surprise, Amy was not behind. In fact, Amy seemed to just disappear at times, and once, a woman named Kelly had come to him worried about where Amy was. Kelly was Amy's best friend and was worried. Ken had tried to sense Amy, but he could not sense her at all. Yet not five minutes later, Amy walked into town like she had just gone for a walk.

The recruits were just too raw, he thought now as he watched Stalker; he just hoped he had a lot more time to train them before someone stumbled into their town. He had no doubt it would happen, if not soon. And when they came, they would snatch anything they could get their hands on, including the ladies and kids filling this town.

* * *

Amy was standing next to Envy when Envy suddenly swirled in alarm. Both Amy and her dragon had been so focused on Ken and Stalker that they never felt the wolves coming, packs of them.

Envy caught the biggest, swallowing it with a quick snap of her jaws, then they were past the big dragon, heading towards Amy.

Amy felt her dragon's alarm and saw Envy go into a frenzy of slashing and tail-smashing that sent wolves flying. Seeing it, Amy felt coolness fill her body, and she drew upon it hard, letting it fill her body just as three wolves leapt upon her.

She didn't have time to reach for her belt knife or crossbow. *I need claws like Envy*, she thought, and was thrilled when her hands froze with coldness, changing into huge serrated talons like Envy's own. She slashed out instinctively, catching the first wolf in the chest and throat, and her talons cut and sliced deeply, so much so that the wolf's head fell from its body. She was too busy to notice as a wave of exhaustion hit her, and she almost stumbled into the second and third wolf.

But they were both snatched out of the air by Envy's hard tail. Then, as Envy ate her fill, the wolves were past them.

* * *

Growling in deep thought, Ken almost didn't catch the flicker of a shadow in the storm outside his shield. Instantly, he sent his senses out, and his mind reeled in shock.

"Silent, to me," he swore, calling the big dog out of the cave, loading his crossbow, though he knew it would do little good.

"Stalker, you need to hurry, now!" he growled urgently.

His silver dragon had just popped its head off and was slowly shedding its scales. Ken didn't know if his dragon heard him because at that time, the wolves came rushing out of the storm, fighting each other as they caught sight of them.

Ten, twenty, almost thirty wolves, all thin and gaunt, some bleeding, their fur matted with ice and blood, came snarling at them, trying to be the first to reach them.

It was the first time in a long time that Ken had actually felt fear. His crossbow bolt took the first to leap into the shield. Silent eagerly took the second, towering over the smaller wolves as he issued a challenging growl that took the wolves by surprise. Now in front of Stalker, Ken pulled his sword and heard Stalker issue a defiant roar as Ken slashed into the wolves as they jumped from the ice, trying to protect both Silent and Stalker as well as himself as his sword swung furiously, cutting the leaping wolves down.

* * *

Not far away, Amy gasped as energy ran through her suddenly exhausted body. She lit briefly as Envy touched her with her snout, sending freezing ice into Amy's veins.

Invigorated, Amy turned to attack the wolves who were now attacking Ken. But a firm, huge claw curled protectively around Amy's belly, and a picture came to Amy's mind of Stalker, big, furious, and protective.

True enough, a second later came Stalker's roar, and Amy, afraid for Ken, was forced to watch.

* * *

The wolves howled and growled, then yipped and died from Ken's sword. And somewhere in between, Ken felt the rush of magic swarm hotly through his body, and he pulled upon it, letting it come.

His sword began to glow, becoming sharper, longer, and faster in his hand until it was a white-hot blaze in the darkness that set the wolves screaming in pain and panic as it touched them.

Then he cried out as a wolf caught the back of his leg, trying to hamstring him and bring him down. He fell, swinging his sword and taking its head off, just as he was blinded by a fierce wave of hot, blue-white fire that filled the air.

The roar that followed was so loud and deep, it took Ken a second to realize it had come from Stalker. The furious dragon's fire scorched the air, sending the sound of cries and searing flesh throughout the darkness.

Then the wolves, all yipping and crying, fled in fear and panic. He got onto his feet again as they fled and caught sight of Stalker for the first time. The dragon was furious, and it followed, pouncing upon the wolves and searing the surrounding air, burning and killing them as it used its long crystal claws to slash into and knock over others that were on Silent, trying to kill the big dog who had his jaws wrapped around a wolf's throat.

Ken blinked his eyes until he could see again, then he stared at Stalker in amazement. The shiny silver dragon was huge, and his appetite matched it as he gulped down fried wolf after fried wolf. Ken watched him eat and chase the others until all that was left were the bodies of thirteen dead wolves. Stalker had to be over fifteen feet; his scales seemed to glow in the darkness, lit by the fire he was spewing at the terror-filled, fleeing wolves.

Ken rushed to Silent, who was trying to struggle up onto his feet. Blood was matting the big dog's fur. An ear was missing, and the big dog's face and sides trembled from the large gashes left by the wolves' teeth. Even the dog's tail was broken. He was amazed to find the dog still alive and quickly knelt by its side, feeling a twinge in his own hurt leg as he did. Silent whimpered and licked his hand as he knelt, touching the dog's heaving sides.

"It's okay, boy, they're gone now," Ken told him affectionately.

He felt his mark and pulled upon it, sending some healing magic into the dog. As he did, he thought about making the dog stronger and impervious, like he himself was to the cold. A wave of exhaustion hit him, and to his vast amazement, a small dragon mark, almost like his own, suddenly branded the big dog's shoulder where he had touched it. Silent's dragon mark was that of a crystal dragon talon.

The big dog jumped up and licked his face, and Ken smiled before standing again and looking wearily at his sword in his hand. It was still glowing softly; a dragon mark, silver and gold, was now etched upon the glowing blade. It was definitely longer and sharper than before, and now it was a perfect fit in his hand, as if the hilt had molded to his grip.

A gigantic victorious roar shocked the air, and Ken looked up to see Stalker ripping into a smoking wolf, crunching it, bones and all. All around them, the ashy ground smoked, with wolf carcasses strewn all around them.

Stalker turned to look at Ken, and he felt Stalker's cool mind touch his own, showing him a picture of himself, big and powerful, with a questioning tone to it.

Ken smiled, sheathing his sword in the small sheath, knowing he was going to have to find another sheath for his sword now.

"I'm alright, just a little tired," Ken told Stalker, reassuring him as the silver dragon studied him intently. "My god, you have gotten big. Took you long enough," Ken chided. "Damn things almost killed us," he said in disgust, kicking one of the dead wolves.

Stalker swallowed the rest of the wolf he was eating, licking his chops before walking to Ken. Ken reached up, rubbing Stalker's itchy scales, and was rewarded with a large appreciative rumble that seemed to vibrate through Ken.

Then he gasped as Stalker's snout touched him, sending energy bursting through him like a dam bursting. He had to hold tight to the dragon to keep his injured leg from collapsing. This time, knowing he'd get bigger, he wasn't mad at Stalker. The wave of pure energy made him dizzy and feel better; he began to really scratch Stalker's scales, where he could feel the dragon was itching unbearably.

Stalker tumbled over, scattering ash and spooking Silent, who backed off uncertainly as if unsure what to make of the suddenly bigger Stalker, while Ken scratched the rumbling dragon's scales.

When he finished, Stalker pounced upon a dead wolf Ken had sliced open and began to eat to his content. While he did, Ken looked himself over. Stalker had tried to heal him, but it had not worked, so he tried himself, seeing he had a huge gash in the back of his leg. He really didn't know how he was still standing upon it, but it didn't hurt, and it had stopped bleeding, so he ignored it when he saw he couldn't heal it and looked the rest of himself over. He had some teeth marks on one of his forearms, but they were slowly healing. He went into the cave to fix himself up and clean his cuts the best he could before he dressed in some less bloody camos.

* * *

Amy and Envy chased after the fleeing wolves. Envy was on an eating mission, and with her new claws, Amy helped her kill the wolves, fighting them fiercely for hurting Ken. She had wanted so badly to go help him, but Envy was right. Both of them were strong, and Envy needed to eat; she had given Amy a lot of her energy, and she needed to replenish it.

While Envy ate, Amy experimented with her claws. She could make them appear or disappear at will now, and doing it didn't drain her energy at all. All she had to do was get angry, and they appeared, or hungry, as she learned watching Envy eat and got hungry herself. Envy tried to get her to eat with her, but the sight of bloody meat just was not appetizing to Amy, even though she had to admit she had a certain animalistic urge to try it.

Instead, she just watched as Envy ate all of the wolves they had killed. It had been so easy to kill them. The wolves could not match her new strength or speed, and with the ice all around her, she was learning all the tricks Envy took the time to teach her. The skating mist run was her favorite. She could run so fast upon the ice that nothing but Envy could outrun her, and she was just learning. Another trick was ice armor; she had learned that instinctively fighting a fast wolf. She had just frozen solid, causing the wolf to bounce right off of her. Its claws and jaws were ineffective against her solid ice flesh until Envy had snatched up the wolf and chuckled silently at Amy's trick, sending a wave of admiration to Amy as she ate the wolf.

Yes, the ice was now Amy's domain, and the more she learned, the more she loved it and Envy.

* * *

By the time Ken had left the cave to measure Stalker for his saddle, all the wolves in front of the iceless cave were gone. Nothing could be seen of their recent battle. Stalker was lying, noticeably farther, right in the middle of the shielded area, his eyes closed and licking his chops, contentedly.

Ken smiled when he saw the big dragon had turned from a fierce fighting machine into a fat and lazy beast in just a couple of minutes.

"Next time, give me some warning," Ken grumbled. "Your fire was so damn bright it nearly blinded me."

Stalker lazily opened one of his big eyes and began to chuckle, a loud, deep sound that reverberated in the dark sky.

"I'm glad you're amused," Ken muttered as he began taking his measurements for the saddle straps. "Good god, how many of those nasty beasts did you eat?" he asked, incredibly as he stroked a hand over Stalker's hot, distended belly.

A picture of wolf after wolf filled his mind.

Ken laughed. "That is just way too many to count," he teased, measuring Stalker's neck.

Stalker nosed him affectionately.

"Oh man, what's that smell?" Ken teased, pushing Stalker's huge head away from him. As he did, he noticed how soft Stalker's scales still were and pushed a little softer. "No!" Ken said firmly. "Keep your mouth away from me, you smell like you've been eating mangy mutts for weeks without brushing," he teased and looked over at Silent. "No offense to you," he told the big dog as Stalker again tried to rub his huge head affectionately against Ken's chest. "Yeah, we are definitely finding you some mint to chew."

Stalker grumbled and hit Ken with his hard tail.

"Ow, big guy, learn to take a joke," Ken said, rubbing his lower back.

Then he stood back, studying the big dragon. He touched Stalker's head gently. "I'll wait to saddle you until you've hardened up a bit. That will give you the night to burn off all that extra weight you're now carrying."

Ken then paused as Stalker's head suddenly came up, and he turned to look out towards the town.

"Uhoh," Ken told Stalker softly as he felt both Keen and Katty coming towards them at a rush. "I think we might be in trouble."

Stalker growled lightly in what Ken thought was agreement before the big dragon lay his head back down and closed his eyes.

Ken smiled, rubbing his silver and gold scales, and waited for his wife to arrive. It didn't take long for Keen to come swooping down. He flew around them, making sure they were okay, before his eyes caught sight of dead wolf carcasses just outside the shield and swooped down upon one and happily began to eat.

A minute later, Katty walked into the shield, walking to Ken, looking around worriedly.

"What happened?" she asked in concern as she studied Ken worriedly before looking at the sleeping Stalker.

"Some wolves tried to make a meal out of us," Ken told her as Silent happily jumped up upon her, licking her face.

"Ohh," Katty gasped in amazement as she saw the miniature dragon mark upon the big dog's shoulder. "Did Stalker touch him?" she asked curiously.

"No, it happened when I healed him," Ken told her as he walked to her, his measurements in his hand.

Katty studied him carefully. "Are you hurt? I felt something through my ring. I almost thought my finger had been sliced. Then, Stalker had called out to Keen to come eat, and we came as soon as we could get here. I tried to make Keen fly to you guys, but he wouldn't leave my side; he's too stubborn," she complained as she bent to take a look at his wounded leg, but couldn't see anything through his new camos.

Ken pulled her up. "At least Keen was smart; they were close to fifty wolves in that pack," he told her worriedly as he hugged her close, nuzzling her neck.

She pushed him back. "That can wait," she told him seriously as she smiled. "How bad is your leg? I think I should look at it. And don't tell me it's not hurt; I can see you trying to hide a limp. Why haven't you or Stalker healed it?" she asked in concern.

"Stalker and I both tried. I don't think Stalker can heal; just give me energy and strength. And I don't think I can heal myself more than my body automatically does," he explained as he let her lead him back to the cave.

Ken stopped as he realized Stalker was gone, and he caught the huge dragon stalking silently, creeping up upon the unsuspecting Keen.

Katty turned just as Keen let out a startled roar, his mouth full of a wolf he was intent on swallowing.

Ken saw Katty's eyes widen and felt her heartbeat frantically through her hand in his, and he quickly reassured her.

"Don't worry, Stalker won't hurt him," he told her calmly as Stalker easily pinned the smaller dragon and mimed swallowing the startled dragon whole. Then he ripped the wolf from Keen's mouth and swallowed that whole before plumping down right on top of the indignant dragon, right in the middle of the hailstorm, looking full and content as he lay his head down and went back to sleep.

They both watched as Keen, firmly pinned under Stalker, slowly and angrily extracted himself from beneath the heavy, bigger Stalker, huffing indignantly, smoke puffing out from his nose and mouth with the effort it was taking him to get out from beneath Stalker. Then, ignoring Stalker, he went to eat another wolf.

After a second, they both entered the cave with smiles upon their faces.

"I can't believe how big he got!" Katty exclaimed in surprise as she motioned for Ken to drop his pants so she could see how bad the wound on his leg was.

Ken nodded. "I knew he would get big this time, but even I am amazed at his actual size. I almost didn't make the saddle harnesses big enough to fit him," Ken told her as he began to undo his camos.

Feeling her concerned eyes upon him as she saw the big blood bandage around his leg, he smiled calmly at her.

"It's not as bad as it looks," he tried to assure her, but her frown deepened as she undid the bandage and finally saw the true extent of his wound.

"How do I?" she asked him worriedly.

A little surprised, Ken could still walk. The whole back of his leg was a bloody, mangled mess of shredded skin and muscle.

"The same way as you did the ring," he told her through a wince as she examined the wound with trembling fingers. "Use the dragon mark the way I showed you, and try to tell it what you want. Think about it," he paused as her hand began to glow.

"Ahh," he gasped as warmth flowed into him. He knew instantly, just like when she had done the ring, that she wasn't strong enough to heal him, and not wanting to go through that again, he grabbed her hand as she began to tremble with the effort.

"Stop," he told her softly, then again more gruffly when she just continued to try.

Katty did not listen, though she knew she had to heal him. There were too many chances for him to get infected from the wound or the ash. Since they had come to this town and saved the women and children, they had all regaled her with stories of people dying from the black death caused by infections, the ash caused. Even small scratches had caused death when they got the Ash infection. So, she gritted her teeth and forced even more magic from her mark.

When Katty didn't stop, and he knew from her mind that she wouldn't, he sighed and, touching her, he sent his own strength into her to help her heal him. Thanks to Stalker, he now had plenty of energy, but by the time they had finished, they were both gasping for breath.

Ken then pulled her into his arms, feeling her trembling with exhaustion.

"Next time I tell you to stop, stop!" he growled in concern as he held her lovingly close. "It wasn't that bad; I was already healing and would have recovered fine."

Katty hit his shoulder hard, the sound of the thud echoing in the cave. "Recovered!" she said incredulously. "Half of your leg was gone. You had bled out and were acting as if nothing was wrong," she said, starting to cry with the thought of almost losing him.

"Shh," Ken told her comfortingly, holding her tightly and stroking her hair. "It's okay now."

"You can't leave me alone," she whispered against his broad chest. "I'm not strong like you are."

Ken lifted her chin and looked into her liquid silver eyes with a small smile. "How are you not strong?" he asked, incredulously. "You're my little wild cat," he said appreciatively, kissing her lips tenderly. "You're stronger than any one of those women out there... And Amy..." He pulled from her mind her insecurity, "It's nothing compared to you. They all look to you because every one of them knows it. Yet, Amy's lived here her entire life, and it's you she even looks to. Every one of them had given up before you took charge and gave all of them, even Amy, hope. I won't be gone long; remember, sweetheart, you roped me into this. I do it for you. And you were right, I can do no less. You gave me the strength to see that without you, my little Kat, I would be out there somewhere all alone."

Katty stopped crying and lightly and lovingly kissed him back.

"I won't be going alone," Ken assured her after a second. "But you were right, if these women all heard it right, then that military base is full of survivors and what is left of our government. I need to see for myself if it is true and make sure they are not like the men who took over here. While I am gone, continue what we have been doing. Teach them all how to defend themselves and this town, and look out for those wolves."

Before he could continue, Katty reached up, kissing him. "You're not leaving, yet," she told him suddenly, breathless, pulling him to their old makeshift bed.

CHAPTER TWENTY-NINE

Aug 16th

Location: *Wyoming border.*

It took him a long time to make it back to the shelter. The wound in his neck kept breaking open and leaking pus. Thankfully, though, it seemed to finally be healing. It still worried him as he scrambled over the hills and forests of ice created by the hail and rushing winds.

His fury and his desires for revenge and Nattilie made him continue on at a fast pace. He ran almost all the way back to the shelter, resting only when he found a place to hole up to get some sleep. He knew he had to reach the shelter before Jean and Mark did; he wanted a surprise waiting for them when they arrived. He would destroy the dragons, their riders, and make Nattilie his forever.

Just the thought of her frustrated him; why he had wasted time when he could have conquered her, he just didn't know. Something about her hating him and herself for wanting him had made it worth it. Then Derek had shown up just as he was spreading her luscious legs and about to take her. He had gotten to her a lot quicker than he had thought, even possible with all the precautions he had taken.

Hell, he had been lucky he had taken the precautions he did. But then it wasn't the first time he had almost been caught taking a girl's virginity. Nattilie was the only one to remain alive after he caught them, though. And this one by far had been the most daring and dangerous.

His precautions had not gone perfectly, though. His plan had been to fake his death, then come out in surprise and kill his killer while their overconfidence was up. Who would suspect a just-killed person to strike out and kill them when their back was turned? And it would have worked perfectly, too.

First off, he had not planned on getting a knife stuck in his neck; that had been a bitch to take out and staunch the blood so he could continue to work his newfound magic without being caught. Then there was the fact that his fireball, thrown with all the rest of his strength, had just dissolved around Derek like it had been nothing but illusion itself. When he had seen that, the shock of it, not to mention the exhaustion it brought him, dissolved all of his plans.

It had taken everything he had left to keep his illusion from falling. He had felt relief when he tied the illusion and watched Derek chop the horse's head off. The illusion, at least, had worked better than he had thought. Too bad the rest of his plan fell through. He had been supposed to leap out from behind the overconfident boy and kill him, but the leaking of his neck had weakened him so much that all he could do was lie shivering and hide until Derek had left, taking the other horse.

That had made him furious. To watch Nattilie get away when he had her dead to rights. At least now they all believed he was dead. And the next time he caught Nattilie, no one would even know he was involved, and she would be his trophy forever.

But first, he needed to turn the shelter against Derek and his dragons.

He stumbled into the shelter, to the shocked looks of all the men he knew. But not one of them recognized him. All they saw was a young sixteen-year-old boy with strapping good looks and blood all over the front of him, leaking from a makeshift cloth bandage around his throat.

As soon as he entered the shelter, he collapsed. Men came gathering around him instantly, asking him questions, and he played his part perfectly. A young man from Wyoming who had witnessed the vilest massacre ever. His whole town had been set upon by a man with silver eyes, with a black beast from hell that rained fire and ate everyone in the town who had survived. He had barely escaped with his life, and now he, too, would die of the vile beast's poison in him.

The men in the shelter listened to his tale avidly with shocked and fearful expressions. They had heard of such people and beasts, they assured the young boy; the beasts were called dragons, and the man with the silver eyes must have been marked by a dragon.

They hustled him to the infirmary, where he was then waited upon by Sherry and her daughter Hannah, neither of whom recognized him. But he did Hannah. He'd fantasized about her before.

Hannah obviously liked his looks and blushed prettily when he looked at her, sending his blood racing. They both listened to his story with horror, and Hannah gripped his hand at the horror of it all as her mom disinfected, cleaned, and stitched his neck before leaving to get new bandages.

"What's your name?" Hannah asked him as her mom left, and she put away the things they used.

"George," Devan told her in a soft voice. "You look young to be a nurse. Have you been doing it long?" He asked, although he already knew the answer.

"I'm almost 18. My mom is teaching me to become a doctor like her." Hannah told him importantly, blushing when he gave her an impressed look.

She came over to take his temperature, and he reached up, touching her wrist, and looked into her eyes.

"You find me attractive, don't you?" he asked lightly, opening himself to his magic.

Her eyes widened, and she looked shyly around. "I do," she whispered in a scared voice.

"Then come to me tonight. I find you attractive and find myself in need of you. Don't be scared. Do whatever I want, and my touch will bring you more pleasure than you dreamed possible." He commanded.

The feeling of exhaustion hit him, but it was nowhere near as bad as when he had used the same compulsion on Nattilie.

Hannah licked her lips nervously, staring at his hand touching her arm, sending tingles of pleasure throughout her body.

"Tonight?" she asked hesitantly.

He smiled and put his hand on her thigh, under her uniform. She gasped, her eyes wide, going wider as his fingers moved lightly up her inner thigh, and she grasped the bed in pleasure as his fingers lightly moved up between her legs under her uniform to run lightly over her panties. He instantly felt them dampen as he rubbed along her virgin cleft.

"Tonight?" he asked, lifting an eyebrow.

She looked at him, stunned, even more so when his fingers crawled up her panties to the waistband and pulled them down, so his fingers could slide down her soft flesh until he felt her hairy mound, then her slick, velvety pussy. Her breathing picked up, her legs widening as his fingertip ran over her slick, wet pussy before pushing inside her tight, hot young body.

"Tonight!" she gasped as his finger pushed inside her soft mound, feeling how hot and tight she was.

Her hips jerked as his finger pulled out and pushed back in, then faster and faster. Until suddenly he heard her mom coming and pulled his hand from beneath her uniform. And with an excited look, she hurried away, not knowing or understanding that he had spelled her to look exactly like Nattilie in his eyes.

That night, he stayed in the infirmary to fight off a fake high fever, and he waited with excitement. If he couldn't have Nattilie yet, he'd have the next best thing, someone who looked exactly like her. All the frustration inside of him about not getting to take Nattilie's innocence was about to be released.

When he saw Nattilie walk in nervously, all of his anger and lust for her rose to the surface.

"Is everyone asleep?" he asked hopefully.

She nodded.

"And no one will come?"

She shook her head, "No one is in the infirmary to need checking on."

"Then shut and lock the door."

He watched her with growing excitement as she did, then motioned for her to come to him as he stood up. And he gazed upon her, seeing Nattilie's goddess-like beauty as she came to stand nervously in front of him; she was still wearing her nurse's uniform.

"Do you want me?" he asked.

Her eyes were wide, but she nodded.

"Have you ever done anything like this before?"

"No, I'm a virgin still," she said with a gasp as his hands reached out and lightly caressed her soft breasts through her uniform.

She then moaned as his hands grabbed her breasts roughly, and he moved forward, kissing her lightly. She stood trembling slightly in his hands, her lips unsure and tight against his own. But as his touch made her tingle and sent pleasure coursing through her inexperienced body, her lips loosened, kissing him back just as lightly.

Hungry to feel more of her/Nattilie's beautiful body, he moved his hands from her firm breasts down lightly and smoothly over her ribs, stomach, hips, and then down and around to feel her soft, luscious bottom, making her moan in his mouth as he pulled her closer, letting her feel for the first time his excitement and hardness as he pushed against her stomach.

Her eyes widened at the intense feel of it, and he knew by her heavy breathing that she had felt the pleasure of it right between her legs.

Her mouth tentatively opened beneath his own as his questing tongue licked her lips before plundering her mouth. Her arms went around his back as he thrust his tongue in her, and remembering what it had been like to teach Nattilie how to kiss, he slowly taught Hannah the same way.

His hands moved around her hips, over her uniform to slide over her lower stomach until his fingers were pressing softly upon her virgin mound, causing her to gasp hotly in his mouth and spread her legs wider, so his hand could slide between her thighs and lightly graze and tease her tender mound with his fingertips through her uniform.

She kissed him more enthusiastically as her breathing picked up, her tongue tentatively touching his own and pushing into his mouth as his hand pulled up the skirt of her uniform until his fingers were again grazing her mound, but this time with only her panties between them. The feel of her hot wetness beneath his fingers made him groan with need as she clenched him tight, moaning as her finger felt her soft, plump mound.

After a second, breathing hard himself, he stepped back, taking in her looks and seeing Nattilie standing red-faced before him.

"Show me how much you want me," Devan told her as his gaze took her in appreciatively.

She gave him a nervous, confused look before she slowly and shyly began to undress. But as he watched her, she became firmer and started to tease him as she unbuttoned her uniform and began pulling it down over her shoulders, revealing Nattilie's creamy soft skin and nice, perfect breasts encased in a white bra. Then she pushed her uniform lower, over her ribs and taut stomach, wide, gorgeous hips, and revealing a pair of pink panties with a rose over her plum-looking mound. They fell lower past her long, beautiful legs until it was off.

The sight made him want to ravish her. The power of the dragon mark had made this a much more exciting game. Instead of wanting to see their dread, he now only wanted to see their uncontrollable need to please him, something he had never cared for before. But with Hannah now looking exactly like Nattilie… he wanted to make her love him. An irrational thought that made him growl at himself for his own stupidity as he studied her beautiful body. He could still glimpse Hannah beneath the illusion if he tried, and she was very pretty in her own innocent way. But Nattilie was just breathtaking in her innocence.

"You have seen the movies, 'seduce me,' make me want you as much as you want me," he told her, sitting on the bed, wondering what she would do in her innocence to try to entice him.

He saw Hannah take a deep breath, then she moved to an IV stand and, holding it, began to move against it like it was a strip pole and she was a stripper, her hips swaying and gyrating, moving sensuously, while her legs spread, putting on an amateur but very arousing show for him that stirred his excitement for Nattilie even more.

She then turned her back to him, holding the IV stand, and bent over, showing off her backside and her plump mound through her pink panties. Her hands touched her ankles and slid slowly up the inside of her legs up to her thighs, then up higher to run her fingers over her mound, then around her hips to caress and rub her backside before looking at him lustfully, excited by his looks. She then began to torque, shaking her innocent bottom at him until he groaned and moved up behind her.

She didn't stop and gasped as he pushed up against her, bent a little so when she pushed back against him, his hardness pushed against her mound, and the motion of it almost made him come.

His hands moved around her waist, pulling her against him as she rubbed and gyrated against his hardness. Then he slid his hands up over her sides and ribs up to caress her breasts through her bra as he pulled her up against him.

Then they were kissing passionately, while his hands left her breathless as they cupped and caressed her firm breasts. They were smaller than nattalie's, but they felt great and soft in his palms as he unsnapped her bra and made her cry out with pleasure. His rough hands held her hot breasts lightly, feeling her hard nipples rub against his palms as her hips kept pushing back and rubbing against him.

He pinched her nipples lightly, then harder, making her cry out and kiss him harder. Then his hands were sliding over her stomach, under her panties, making her head go back as his fingers slid lower over her hairy mound down to find her virgin softness. His finger easily penetrated her slick, tight pussy, pushing deep and drawing an excited moan from her as his touch sent a burning fire through her that made her legs tremble.

Kissing her neck, he looked down her body to see nattalie's perfect breasts and his finger moving in and out of her swollen mound. It was kind of exciting being able to see him doing it to two women at once. He moved his finger in and out of her velvety sheath faster and faster until she was panting, and he felt her hands searching and finding his hardness.

Unable to wait any longer, he moved her back to the bed, and she watched him nervously as he released her, turning her to face him, and undid his pants, freeing his hardness. Then, his hands on her hips, he pulled down her pink panties, making her cry out and land back on the bed as he kissed her mound between her legs.

He looked down, enjoying the sight of Nattilie totally naked and lustful before him. She lay back hesitantly, her wide eyes upon his raging hardness, and he moved to her, spreading her legs and pulling her hips to the side of the bed, his eyes roving her long beautiful legs to her lovely swollen mound covered with her thick bush and above all her charming virgin pussy.

With a look of rampant lust, he fell upon his virgin victim, clasping her in his arms as he lay upon her soft, glowing body. He covered her lips with passionate kisses, and Hannah met him with a little cry of ecstasy as his touch sent pleasure jolting between her widespread legs, making her hips lift to him as her legs crushed his hips, already feeling the soft, broad tip of his hardness pressing scorchingly upon her wet, velvety, virgin pussy.

Looking down and seeing Nattilie below him, feeling the hot contact of Hannah's pink pussy, he began to push up against her until his tip was covered in her wetness, causing her head to go back and her hands to grip the sheets below her hard as her soft tight pussy spread and stretched wide around his tip, letting him feel more fully her hot velvety flesh.

With a faint squeak of anguish, Hannah cried out as she felt him stretch her around his penetrating hardness, his hard length sinking into her virgin mound. Seeing the beautiful thing, his hardness had stung; he gloated over his victim being impaled with his hardness.

"Oh, Oh, Oh," she cried as his conquering flesh invaded her soft, young body and lay skinned inside her trembling heat before pushing up inside her even deeper until he met the resistance which her youth had opposed to his entry into her.

"Oh, stop! It won't go in," she suddenly begged, arching in pain and trying to pull away as his hands spread her legs wider so he could push further into her tight, resisting mound.

"Oooh, Oh, oh please," she gasped, her head back and tears in her eyes.

Looking down, he could see where his hardness had made a bridgehead inside of her, just his broad tip surrounded by her bush-covered mound. Feeling her wet slickness slide over his tip, he pulled out and pushed it back in, toying with her until she was gasping with the feel of his tip popping in and out of her. Then he began to edge into her, causing her to pant and jerk with a series of little shrieks as his hardness slid a little farther into her. Placing his hand under her hip, he pulled her hips up towards him and thrust into her again.

"Oh, Oh, oooh, you're hurting me!" It seems it will burst me open. It stretches me so!" She cried, scratching his back in pain as her pussy opened wide to receive his hardness.

He pulled out and slid back in, feeling her virgin flesh open a little wider around him.

"Oh, oh dear! Oh! Ohh! Wait a minute! Oh, oh, oh! Not so hard! Oh, oh, don't push any further, it hurts, oh, oh, please stop. I shall die. You are tearing me open! You are indeed, oh, oh, oooh!" she pleaded tearfully.

He folded her closer and altogether ignored her cries. He pushed and slid deeper inside her virgin mound, proceeding to divest her of her maidenhead. Wanting and wishing she were Nattilie, he knew she would not have pleaded for him to stop. She had wanted it no matter the pain. He felt Hannah's virgin resistance yield beneath his persistent invasion, and her pussy, throbbing tightly around him, slid silkily around his length. Lifting her hips and using a hand to spread her legs obscenely wide, he thrust into her young body hard, piercing through her virgin mound and breaking through that opposing flesh of her hymen. Instantly, he felt himself sink wonderfully deep inside her.

He then began to thrust hard and deep into her, drawing louder and louder cries and moans as her pain slowly left, and the pleasure of his skin inside her left her trembling with each powerful thrust into her tight, hot body. Seeing Nattilie writhing in the throes of passion beneath him made him pull out of her and roll her over so he could see her beautiful backside.

Hannah tried to get away, scared by his look, but he pinned her on her stomach, using his legs to spread her own, bent over the side of the bed, presenting him with a lovely view of her behind and swollen pink pussy.

When she tried to scream, he pushed her head down into the mattress, and keeping her thrashing legs spread, he pushed his hardness into her, thrusting hard up between her legs, making her scream again and jerk forward under the impact as he sank deep into her swollen mound.

Thinking about Nattilie made him all the madder, and remembering her jerking on his nuts infuriated him. He thrust into Hannah's young body harder and harder, deeper and deeper, feeling her jerk and throb around him as she tried to get away. He placed his other hand on the small of her back to hold her in place as he pulled out and thrust deeper and harder into her.

He didn't even notice when she stopped moving. As he thrust hard and deep in her unresponsive, tight body, coming deep inside her, he realized she was dead. He could use that to his advantage, though.

He dressed her in his own clothes, then cast the illusion of the young man over her prone body, faking his own death, and then left the shelter without anyone seeing him.

He couldn't stay there anyway, just in case Jean and Mark brought Derek with them. Here, he had already done his best to discredit the dragons and their bonded humans. The death of the young man would instill an even greater fear in the shelter.

Now, he had to go ignite the fear in other places.

EPILOGUE

Aug 31st

Location: Central America

Despite the freezing hail, Marques was sweating and swearing up a storm as he forced his men to follow him through the ice-covered trees and dangerous ice-covered trail, leading up the mountain. He was trying to make them be as quiet as he could. But with a group of fifty freezing men, carrying and sliding a huge, heavy dragon bone cage up the mountain with Glare's help, it was like trying to ask a chainsaw to be quiet.

Ahead of them, flying low between ice-covered trees, he could see Glare's twelve-foot green frame drop to the ice-covered rocky ground and look back at him impatiently. He knew none of the men behind him, who could barely see ahead of themselves in the darkness of the storm, could see what he was seeing. He was surprised he could see so well. It would not have been possible had he not been using his new helm. It didn't quite match his new golden dragon scale armor, but it looked fearsome. In fact, he looked fearsome.

After finding the dead dragon, he had scavenged everything he could from it. The dragon scales had been nearly impossible to cut through; not even diamond blades could notch the scales. It wasn't until one of

407

his men got the idea to use one of the dragons' claws to cut through it that they made any progress. And even then, he had to force the very reluctant Glare to free one of the claws.

That done, he had to rig up a sawing system so his men could use the claw to cut off all the dragon's scales, skinning it for all its valuable parts.

While he had watched them, he came up with the idea for the dragon bone cage and a couple of other things. The cage was just the thing he needed to capture the big black dragon. He used many of the bones to create two intrinsic cages, and then he sent Glare to find out where the black dragon was.

He had used most of the other bones to create far more powerful weapons, such as wing bones, which were flexible yet stronger than any metal. He used to make crossbows, using tendons and muscles for the string. With those, though, he had to use metal bolts. The power of the string snapped anything else. He had used the bigger red scales to make another armored suit heavier than this gold one he was wearing, and used Glare's shedded silver scales to make a couple of pairs of gauntlets which fit his hands perfectly.

When his men were cutting the dragon's rib bones for the bigger cage, he had learned the secret of the dragon's skull. One of his men had stood inside the giant skull and looked up into the sky out of its half-empty eye. The man had been shocked to see the sky clear and bright as day, like the ash wasn't even there.

He had been summoned to test it out himself; the sight had amazed him, so he had tried Glare's shedded skull, and it had allowed him to see a lot better, not as powerful as the gigantic red skull, but enough to want to wear it all the time. He had instantly had his men make it into a helm for him.

When his men looked at him, he could see their fear. He looked like a dragon wearing a green dragon helm with two crystal horns over his black eyes, golden dragon scale armor that nothing could pierce, a red dragon scale cape, silver scale gloves, a tranquilizer rifle, a dragon bone crossbow with bone bolts upon his back, and a machete and tranquilizer pistol at his waist. He knew he looked deadly and intimidating.

He already had his men making more weapons and armor. He had found two of the black dragon's sheddings inside the dragon's stomach and had used the smallest of the red dragons' slender teeth to be shaped into crystalline swords, having found just the perfect man to do it, too. He didn't know much about sword fighting, but they would look good on his back and cut through anything.

He had been hoping to find more dragon eggs, but besides three empty ones inside the red dragon's stomach, he had been unable to find any more. He had taken to sending Glare out each day to try to find other dragons, but besides the black one, Glare hadn't been able to find any other.

According to the green dragon, the black one was living in a cave high up in the mountain they were now climbing. Better yet, though, it was close to shedding again. He knew from watching Glare shed twice that the black dragon would be at its weakest right before and after it shed, and that it would be starving afterward.

He had fashioned the smaller of the two cages with that in mind. He just hoped the cage would hold the dragon. He could not use anything to tie the bones together; he had tested it on Glare, even using the red dragon's muscles and tendons to tie it together. Glare had been able to eventually get out. Instead, he had to whittle the bones to snap into each other without release. The only release was on the front of the cage, which was impossible for a dragon to open. Glare couldn't, but he was much smaller than this black one and would be even more so when it shedded again. Glare was almost small enough to fit through the bones, but he couldn't break or loosen them. Now he just had to wait and see if he had made the smaller cage big enough. Based on Glare's shedding, the green had almost doubled in size each time. The black dragon was much bigger than Glare's twelve feet, so he had made the smaller cage forty feet around. He just had to get the dragon into it.

He found Glare waiting for him right where he had told the green to stay, not too close to the cave but close enough to see it through the hail and ash. He motioned for his men to stop and start setting up the trap, then motioned for Glare to get closer to the cave and watch for the dragon.

Every noise his men made as they set up the cage made him want to flinch. He knew the dragon was blind by now, but its fire could still kill them, if not him. He was counting on his armor to save him if he got flamed. He just did not want it to come to that.

Glare sighed in relief, and when he mimed, the black was twitching but asleep.

"Bring the sheep," he said quietly.

Moving behind the cage, he watched as his men hurried the sheep into it, tying all four halters to the back of the cage, causing them to start "BAA"ing loudly. At the sound, he motioned his men to run.

He then mimed to Glare to shut the cage when it was time. Then he ran up on the sheep, smelling like a dragon in his dragon scale armor and helm.

The sheep instantly panicked, "BAA" ing loudly again as their halters kept them from fleeing the cage.

The noise they made did not take long to wake the furious blind dragon. She came stalking heavily from her cave with a vicious roar at whoever had encroached upon her territory. The sound made two sheep drop-dead in fright, while the other two bleated in fear, a sound a hungry dragon could not refuse.

She lumbered out of the cave and down the mountainside in a blind rush, roaring again, and followed the sheep's sound, right into the cage where she tore viciously into them.

She never even noticed the cage snap shut behind her.

The End of Book 1

ABOUT THE AUTHOR

Robert Austin was born in 1980 in Orange County, California. From an early age, he developed a deep love for storytelling, adventure, and the worlds that books can create. That passion eventually led him to begin writing his own stories, where imagination and perseverance helped bring entirely new worlds to life.

Meteor is his debut novel and the first story set in the Dragon Mark universe—a sweeping adventure of survival, loyalty, and the powerful bond between humans and dragons. Inspired by themes of resilience, courage, and hope in the face of overwhelming odds, Robert's writing explores how strength can be found even in the harshest storms.

Today, Robert continues expanding the Dragon Mark series while working to bring new stories and characters to readers who love epic fantasy and unforgettable adventures.

FOLLOW THE AUTHOR

Thank you for reading Meteor, the first book in the Dragon Mark series.

If you enjoyed this story and would like to follow Robert Austin's future books, updates, and new adventures in the Dragon Mark universe, visit:

www.robertaustinauthor.com

There you can:

- Learn more about the Dragon Mark series

- See new artwork and scenes from upcoming books

- Get updates on future releases

- Follow Robert Austin's journey as an author

Your support means everything. Thank you for being part of the adventure.

Publish with Us

619-565-8281
https://www.seerendippublishing.com/